# PRINCESS AND QUEEN
# OF ENGLAND

*Portrait of Mary II.*
*from an engraving in the Archives at The Hague.*

# PRINCESS AND QUEEN
# OF ENGLAND

## Life of Mary II

BY

### MARY F. SANDARS

AUTHOR OF

"Honoré de Balzac: his Life and Writings"
"Lauzun, Courtier and Adventurer"
"Louis XVIII"

WITH PHOTOGRAVURE PLATE AND 26 OTHER ILLUSTRATIONS
IN HALF TONE

LONDON

## STANLEY PAUL & CO

31 ESSEX STREET, STRAND, W.C.

*First published in 1913*

DEDICATED

TO

MY MOTHER

# PREFACE

No biography of Queen Mary II. has appeared since Miss Strickland devoted a volume to her in the "Lives of the Queens of England." This volume is written with Miss Strickland's usual picturesqueness and literary skill; but her political prejudices have prevented her from according the slightest sympathy to either William or Mary—in fact, in her bitterness against them, she has occasionally distorted, or at least rearranged, historical facts. Besides, since she wrote, much fresh matter has become available. Dr. Doebner and Countess Bentinck have published some of Mary's letters, and, what is more important, portions of her Memoirs, which were intended for no eye but her own.

Therefore, whatever excuses may be needed for the quality of this biography, no excuse is, I think, needed for attempting it, and I can at least say that all possible care has been taken to verify the statements it contains, and to conceal or distort nothing.

In the letters written by Mary when Princess of Orange to her friend Lady Bathurst, I have had access to completely fresh material, and the fact that James made a determined attempt to separate his daughter from her husband has never, I think, been recorded in any English history or biography. However, Dutch contemporary sources seem to prove the existence of an intrigue with this object, which,

though carefully hushed up in England, was in
Holland a matter of common report. The affair
is a curious page in history.

I must thank Earl Bathurst and his brother
Colonel the Hon. Benjamin Bathurst, M.P., most
warmly for allowing me to make use of copies of
the letters written by Princess Mary to their ancestress; and Earl Bathurst for permitting the
reproduction for this book of two of the portraits
in his possession.

My gratitude is also due to the Duke of Portland
and to Mr. Richard Goulding for the loan of copies
of the letters of William III. which are at Welbeck
Abbey; to Dr. Krämer, Keeper of The Hague
Archives, and author of a life in Dutch of Queen
Mary, for much valuable information, and for permission to reproduce two fine engravings of William
and Mary; to the Earl of Orkney for allowing his
portraits of Elizabeth Villiers to be photographed;
and to Mr. A. M. Broadley for selecting many
valuable prints in his collection for the adornment
of this book, and especially for giving me access to
the unique album of William and Mary views,
broadsheets, and other matters collected by the
late Sir W. Fraser and now in Mr. Broadley's
library. I must also thank Admiral Sir Nathaniel
Bowden Smith for his kindness in looking through
some of my proofs.

MARY F. SANDARS.

# CONTENTS

## CHAPTER I

## CHAPTER II

## CHAPTER III

# CHAPTER IV

# CHAPTER V

# CHAPTER VI

# CHAPTER VII

# CHAPTER VIII

## CHAPTER IX

## CHAPTER X

## CHAPTER XI

## CHAPTER XII

## CHAPTER XIII

## CHAPTER XIV

## CHAPTER XV

## CHAPTER XVI

## CHAPTER XVII

# CONTENTS

## CHAPTER XVIII

## CHAPTER XIX

# LIST OF ILLUSTRATIONS

# AUTHORITIES CONSULTED

" History of England," Macaulay.
" Life of Mary II.," Agnes Strickland.
" History of My Own Times," Gilbert Burnet.
" Memoirs of Great Britain and Ireland," Sir John Dalrymple.
" Diary," Samuel Pepys.
" Diary," John Evelyn.
" Memoirs," Sir William Temple.
" Mémoires de Jacques II."
Dr. Hooper's Narrative in Appendix of " Life of William III.,"
    Duncannon.
" Lady Russell's Letters."
" Life of Mary II.," 1795.
" Account of the Conduct of the Duchess of Marlborough."
" The Other Side of the Question," Ralph.
" Diary," Dr. Edward Lake, " Camden Miscellany," Vol. I.
" Apology," Colley Cibber.
" Memoirs," Sir John Reresby.
" History of England," Echard.
" History of England," Rapin, and Tindal's Notes.
" Mémoires de la Révolution Anglaise," Lamberty.
" Life of Tillotson," Birch.
" Historical Letters," Sir Henry Ellis.
" Shrewsbury Correspondence."
Birch, Additional MSS., British Museum.
Harleian Collection, British Museum.
Verney MSS., British Museum.
" Révolution de 1688," Mazure.
" History of the Stuarts," Oldmixon.
" Fall des Hauses Stuart," Klopp.
" Court of England," Jesse.
" Lexington Papers."
" Original Papers," Macpherson.
" Lettres de la Duchesse d'Orléans."
" Clarendon-Rochester Correspondence."
" Mémoires," Gramont.
" Fairfax Correspondence."
" Memoirs relating to Lord Torrington."
" Lord Torrington," Admiral Colomb, " United Service
    Magazine," May, 1899.
" Leven and Melville Papers."
" Whiston's Memoirs."
" The Coronation Book," Canon Perkins.
" Balcarres Memoirs."

" Life of Mrs. Godolphin," Evelyn.
" Calisto, or the Chaste Nymphe," John Crone.
" State Letters of Henry Earl of Clarendon."
" Life of Edward Earl of Clarendon."
" Life and Letters of Sir Henry Sidney."
" Négociations de M. le Comte d'Avaux en Hollande."
" Relation of State Affairs," Narcissus Luttrell.
" Life of James II.," Foxe.
" Relation Véritable du Voyage de son Altesse le Prince d'Orange, etc."
Stopford Sackville Letters, British Museum.
" Letters of Lady Mary Forester."
King William's Chest, Record Office.
State Papers, Record Office.
" La Vie et la Mort de Marie Stuart," 1695.
" Royal Diary and Character of Queen Mary," 1705.
Additional MSS., Birch Papers, British Museum.
" Hyde Correspondence," Singer.
Burnet's MS. History, British Museum.
" Mémoires de Monsieur de B.," British Museum.
" Overblyffsels van Geheuchgenis," Conrad—Notes by Dr. Fruin.
" Life of Thomas Ken," Dean Plumptre.
" An Account of the Ceremonial at the Coronation of King William and Queen Mary."
" Burnet's Sermon at the Coronation," 1689.
" The Manner of the Proclaiming of King William and Queen Mary, Feb. 13, 1689."
" Tenison's Sermon in Westminster Abbey, March 5, 1695."
" Form of Proceeding at the Funeral of Queen Mary."
" Mort de Marie Stuart," Monsieur de M.
Nottingham's MS. Letters to Hatton, British Museum.
" An Account of the Duke of Gloucester," Jenkins Lewis.
" Memoirs of Queen Mary," edited by Dr. Doebner.
" Lettres et Mémoires de Marie Reine d'Angleterre," edited by Countess Bentinck.
Archives at The Hague.
Letters at Welbeck Abbey in the possession of the Duke of Portland.
Queen Mary's Letters in the possession of Earl Bathurst.
" The Court of William III.," Edwin and Marion Grew.
Nottingham's MS. Letters, British Museum.
" Original Letters," 1st Series, Ellis.
" Hampton Court Palace," Law.
" Kensington Palace," Law.

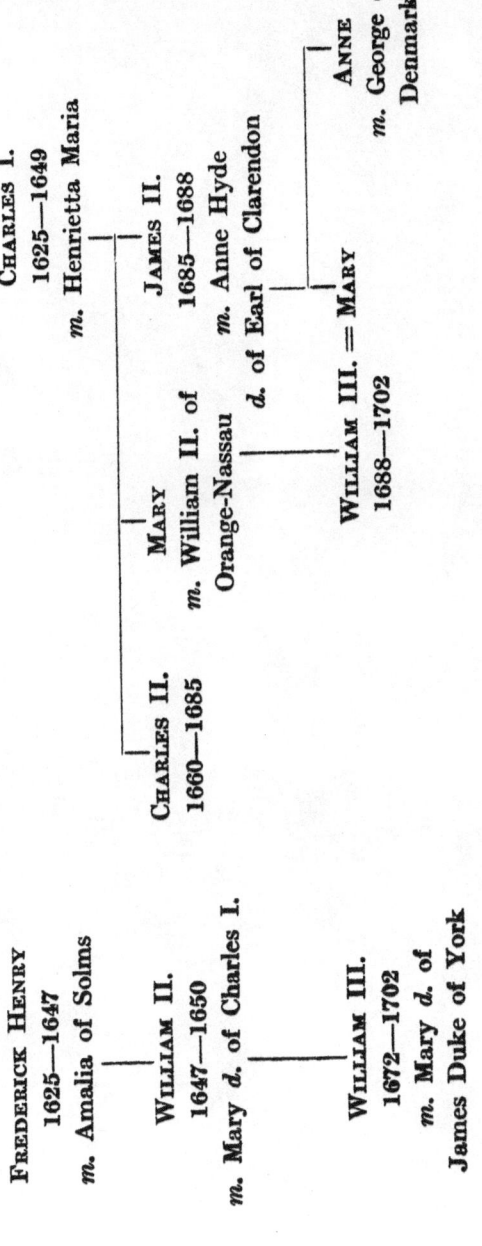

# HOUSE OF STUART

**CHARLES I.**
1625—1649
*m.* Henrietta Maria

**CHARLES II.**
1660—1685

**MARY**
*m.* William II. of
Orange-Nassau

**JAMES II.**
1685—1688
*m.* Anne Hyde
*d.* of Earl of Clarendon

**WILLIAM III. = MARY**
1688—1702

**ANNE**
*m.* George of
Denmark

# HOUSE OF ORANGE-NASSAU

**FREDERICK HENRY**
1625—1647
*m.* Amalia of Solms

**WILLIAM II.**
1647—1650
*m.* Mary *d.* of Charles I.

**WILLIAM III.**
1672—1702
*m.* Mary *d.* of
James Duke of York

xix

# MARY II

## CHAPTER I

IN the latter part of the year 1660, the year of the Restoration of Charles II. to the throne of his fathers, much excitement and gossip were caused by the question of the relations between James Duke of York—afterwards James II.—and Anne Hyde, only daughter of Edward Earl of Clarendon, Lord Chancellor of England.

They were attached to each other—of that there was no doubt; and talk waxed loud when it was discovered that Anne Hyde was about to become a mother. Was she already married to the Duke of York? Would he marry her? There were rumours and counter-rumours. Pepys reports them day by day in his "Diary." The Duke of York had promised Anne Hyde marriage, had signed the document with his blood, and then had stolen it out of her cabinet![1] The Duke of York repented having dishonoured her, said one; he had done the same to others abroad, remarked another, more cynically minded. So tongues wagged.

Meanwhile one sagacious onlooker—who had, indeed, more opportunity than the vulgar for observation—had settled the matter to his own satisfaction:

[1] Pepys's "Diary," October 7, 1660.

" Soon after the Restoration, the Earl of Southampton and Sir Anthony Ashley Cooper, having dined together at the Chancellor's, as they were returning home, Sir Anthony said to my Lord Southampton, ' Yonder Mrs. Anne Hyde is certainly married to one of the brothers ' (Charles II. or the Duke of York) ; and when his companion asked him how so wild a fancy could have entered his head, ' Assure yourself,' replied he, ' it is so. A concealed respect (however suppressed) showed itself so plainly in the looks, voice, and manner wherewith her mother carved to her, or offered her of every dish, that it must be so.' " [1]

Sir Anthony Ashley Cooper was right; Anne Hyde was indeed married to the Duke of York.

In spite of the dislike felt by Henrietta Maria for Lord Clarendon, the Princess of Orange, sister to Charles II. and the Duke of York, showed her goodwill to the Hyde family by assigning them a house at Breda when they were in exile during the Protectorate ; and a vacancy occurring among her maids of honour, she was anxious that the place should be filled by Anne Hyde, the Chancellor's only daughter.

According to Clarendon's account, he at first refused this honour, not wishing his daughter to lead a Court life, and only yielded at last at Charles's intervention. In a letter written by Clarendon to Lady Stanhope, proof certainly exists that he did his best to prevent Anne Hyde from accompanying the Princess of Orange when she went to see her mother, Henrietta Maria, at Paris.

Clarendon on this occasion wrote to Lady Stanhope [2] that the Queen had treated the Princess of Orange with coldness since Anne had been in her service, and had shown her dislike for his daughter so plainly, that he thought it would be

---

[1] Locke's "Memoirs of Lord Shaftesbury."
[2] "Clarendon State Papers," Cologne, July 16, 1659.

well for her to remain in Breda with friends while
the visit was made. Had his advice been followed,
the course of history and of Anne's fate would
most probably have been altered, for it was on this
visit to Paris that she met the Duke of York, and
that he fell violently in love with her.

Anne Hyde was not beautiful; indeed, according
to Pepys, she was " a plain woman, and like her
mother, my lady Chancellor." [1] The pencil entries
she made in a pocket-book bound in ass's skin
when she was between fifteen and sixteen years of
age still exist,[2] and show that in her youth she was
like her daughter Mary, of a very sentimental
nature. The entries begin :

" I was born the 12th day of March O.S. in the
year of our Lord 1637, at Cranborne Lodge, near
Windsor, in Berkshire, and lived in my own country
till I was twelve years old, having in that time
seen the ruin both of Church and State and the
murthering of my King."

After detailing her different changes of residence
and noting her dear Aunt Bab's death at the age of
twenty-four, she states that " God is an eternal,
infinite, inimitable, almighty, infinitely wise, and
infinitely good Spirit "—an axiom which appears to
have been copied from one of her lesson-books.
Then she descends to more personal matters, and
we read :

" Je m'en vay mourier d'amour, mais ce n'est
pas pour un infidel comme vous.

"ANNE HYDE."

" Adieu pour jamais, mais n'oubliez pas la plus
miserable personne du monde.

"ANNE HYDE."

---

[1] Pepys's " Diary," May 1, 1662.　　　[2] British Museum.

Perhaps, however, the object of adoration was of
the writer's own sex, as in the effusions penned by
Anne's daughter Mary, which we shall read later
on, for the last entry is :

" Barbara Aylesbury, je l'aime plus que moy
meme mille fois.
                              "ANNE HYDE."

The terseness of these self-revelations and a
certain intensity about them seem to distinguish
them somewhat from ordinary girlish outpourings,
and Anne, when exposed to the advances of the
Duke of York, showed considerable acumen and
discretion.

In James's own words,

" She [Anne Hyde] showed as much judgment
as virtue in the conduct of this affair, which she
managed so adroitly that the Duke, carried away
by passion, made her, some time before the Restoration, a promise of marriage." [1]

Certainly the passion must have long been a
thing of the past when the Duke penned this calm
appraisal of Anne's qualities ; but at the time he
chronicles, it was ardent ; and on November 24,
1659, after the return of the Princess of Orange to
Holland, James and Anne Hyde were contracted
to each other at Breda in Brabant, and thence-
forward lived together secretly as man and wife.

After the Restoration they were married at
night, which was then the fashionable time for
weddings, at Worcester House, on September 3,
1660. Dr. Crowther, the Duke's chaplain, performed the ceremony. Lord Ossory gave Anne
Hyde away, and Ellen Stroude, one of her servants,
was also present. Six weeks later their eldest son
was born.

The greatest consternation and fury prevailed

in the royal family when it was rumoured that the Duke of York had taken his sister's maid of honour to wife. The Princess of Orange was horrified at the disgrace brought on it by the marriage of her brother with a person who was as, she expressed it, "one of her servants"; and Henrietta Maria wrote a "very sharp letter to the Duke, full of indignation, that he should have so low thoughts as to marry such a woman." She announced to Charles that "she was on her way to England, to prevent, with her authority, so great a stain and dishonour to the Crown."[1]

She came, and disappointed Pepys, who went to see the newly arrived royalties dine, and notes in his "Diary" of November 22, 1660: "The queen a very little plaine old woman, and nothing more in her presence in any respect nor garbe than any ordinary woman." Apparently the "little plaine old woman" was full of activity. Possibly at her instigation, certainly with her connivance, a plot more suited for a melodrama than for the pages of history, was set on foot to destroy Anne Hyde's reputation, by accusing her of misconduct with Sir Charles Berkeley, a young courtier of dissolute life, who was induced to come forward and promise to marry her.[2]

At first the plot seemed likely to answer its purpose, for the Duke of York was either in reality convinced by it, or considered it expedient to bow before the storm of his mother's anger. He therefore "resolved to deny that he was married, and never to see the woman again who had been so false to him."

Meanwhile the time for Anne's delivery drew near, and the King, who seems to have remained neutral during the whole affair, sent the Bishop of Winchester, the Duchess of Ormond, Lady Sunder-

---

[1] "Life of Edward Earl of Clarendon," vol. i. p. 384.
[2] *Ibid.*, vol. i. p. 389.

land, and other ladies to be present when the child
was born. The Bishop did not spare Anne, asking
her " in the interval of her greatest pangs, and sometimes when they were upon her," " whose the child
was of which she was in labour." [1] She asseverated
constantly that it was the Duke's, and that she
had been married to him in the presence of witnesses,
who would, she was sure, come forward in due time
and avow the fact.

The ladies present were convinced of her innocence, and when the Duchess of Ormond expressed
their conviction to the Duke of York, she perceived in
him " a kind of tenderness," which at least showed
that his affection for Anne was not extinct.

Nevertheless, though most people, knowing
Berkeley's character, refused to give credence to
the calumny, and the King showed plainly that
he did not believe it, Henrietta Maria continued
to assail the Duke's ears with it. James was
in consequence most miserable, and refused to go
into society, or to take part in any of his usual
amusements. At last Sir Charles Berkeley's conscience pricked him, and he confessed that in
order to prevent the " inconvenience and mischief " [2]
such a marriage must cause to the Duke, he had
slandered the unfortunate Duchess. The Princess
of Orange, who had been attacked with small-pox,
admitted on her deathbed her complicity in the
detestable plot. Thereupon the Duke, who had
become " melancholie and dispirited, and cared
not for company, nor those divertisements in
which he formerly delighted," appeared " with
another countenance," and wrote to Anne that
" he would speedily visit her," and that he begged
her " to have a care of his son." To satisfy
public opinion the Duke, Anne, and the two
witnesses, Lord Ossory and Ellen Stroude, made

[1] " Life of Edward Earl of Clarendon," vol. i. p. 389.
[2] *Ibid.*, vol. i. p. 392.

depositions on oath to the effect that the marriage service had been performed on the date named, according to the rites of the Church of England.

Anne was now acknowledged as Duchess of York, to the delight of her family, whose arrogance at their alliance with royalty did not endear them to the world at large. Henrietta Maria, forced to bow to necessity, took the wise course of receiving her daughter-in-law with as much cordiality as though she had approved of the affair from the beginning, and said she had resolved to show her in the future the affection of a mother.

The royal family, however, never became reconciled to Anne Hyde's elevation. Some one remonstrated with the Duke of Gloucester, the King's younger brother, on his lack of civility to his sister-in-law, as likely to prove prejudicial to him if Charles were to die without issue, and James and Anne or their children ascended the English throne. The Prince replied that he believed it was not prudent, but that the Duchess " smelt so strongly of her father's green bag that he could not get the better of himself, whenever he had the misfortune to be in her presence." [1]

The marriage of the presumptive heir to the throne with a lawyer's daughter was indeed most unpopular in the country ; and when on April 30, 1662, the subject of this memoir came into the world, Pepys notes in his "Diary" that "The Duchess of York is brought to bed of a girl, at which I find nobody pleased." The infant was born at St. James's Palace, and was baptized in the chapel there according to the rites of the English Church. She was named Mary, after her ancestress, Mary Queen of Scots, her godparents being Prince Rupert and the Duchesses of Buckingham and of Ormond. [2]

[1] Dartmouth's note to Burnet's "History of My Own Times," vol. i. p. 299.
[2] "Life of Mary II.," 1695.

The nurseries were established in Lord Clarendon's house at Twickenham, and there, and afterwards at Richmond Palace, the royal children spent a part of each year. They were often, however, with their parents at St. James's Palace or at Hampton Court, and Pepys notes, on September 12, 1664, that, on visiting the Duke of York there, he "saw him with great pleasure play with his little gîrle, like an ordinary private father of a child."

Fifteen months after Mary's birth a boy, who was given, like his uncle, now dead, the title of Duke of Gloucester, came into a world in which, like his brothers, he was not destined to linger very long, and on February 6, 1664, James's second daughter, Anne, was born; Mary, at three years old, being one of her sponsors.

The married life of the Duchess of York was full of trouble, for out of the four sons born to her and James, three died during her lifetime, and she also lost her third daughter. Lord Clarendon's demeanour during the illness of two of these children filled the naïve Pepys with admiration. He writes in his "Diary" of May 14, 1667, that he went to the Lord Chancellor's house on business, and continues :

"Here I understand how the two Dukes, both the only sons of the Duke of York, are sick even to danger ; and that on Sunday last they were both so ill, as that the poor Duchesse was in doubt which would die : the Duke of Cambridge, of some general disease, or the other little Duke, whose title I know not, of the convulsion fits, of which he had four this morning. Fear that either of them might be dead, did make us think that it was the occasion that the Duke of York, and others were not come to the meeting of the Commission which was designed, and my Lord Chancellor did expect. And it was pretty to observe how, when my Lord sent down to St. James's to see why the Duke of York came not, and Mr. Povy, who went, returned, my Lord did ask (not how the Princes or the Dukes do, or other people do, but), 'How do the Children?'" [Pepys, in his veneration for royalty, cannot forbear a capital letter]—"which methought was mighty great, and like a great man and grandfather. I find everybody mightily concerned for these children, as a matter wherein the State is much concerned that they should live."

The Duke of York's children had of late become of great importance to the nation, as there seemed no prospect that Charles II., who had married shortly after his brother, would have children by Catherine of Braganza, and James was next in succession to the throne.

The Duchess of York appears to have been a strong-minded woman. Pepys hears that she " do come now like Queene Elizabeth, and sits with the Duke of York's Council, and sees what they do; and she crosses out this man's wages and prices as she sees fit for saving money: but yet . . . she reserves £500 a year for her own spending; and my Lady Peterborough by and by tells me that the Duchesse do lay up mightily jewels." [1]

This, it must be said, was repeated to Pepys by one of the Duchess's enemies. Burnet takes a more indulgent and possibly a truer view of the character of a woman who from her sudden elevation in station must have had a difficult part to play, when he says:

" The Duchess of York was a very extraordinary woman. She had great knowledge, and a lively sense of things. She soon understood what belonged to a Princess, and took state on her rather too much. She writ well; and had begun the duke's life, of which he shewed me a volume; it was all drawn from his journal; and he intended to have employed me in carrying it on." [2]

[1] Pepys's "Diary," January 28, 1668.
[2] Burnet's " History of My Own Times," vol. i. p. 298.

Before her death she grew extremely stout, being,
according to Hamilton, " one of the highest feeders
in England."[1]  Pepys, after kissing her hand,
comments on its fatness and whiteness; and in
the " Life of James II." written in 1702, we are
told that " it was her misfortune rather than any
crime, that she had an extraordinary stomach."
Both daughters inherited their mother's inclination
to embonpoint, but Mary at any rate did not share
her mother's love for the pleasures of the table,
for her tastes were so simple that she is reported
to have said she would willingly live in a dairy, and
have no other sustenance than milk.

The Duchess of York appears to have been an
affectionate mother. When she was in Dover
in May, 1670, a correspondent writes to her:
" The parks look very thin, the King and Duke
not being there and the Queen's chapel strange
when she is praying at Dover.  I hope your Sweet
Highness will soon return to the little children "[2]—
a wish which sounds as though the children counted
for more in the Duchess's life than they did in
the lives of many of her royal contemporaries.

The Duke of York was considered to be led
entirely by his wife; but on one point she was
powerless—she could not make him a faithful
husband.  Pepys reports on May 15, 1663, with
evident sympathy for James, that " the Duke's
Lady, I am told, is very troublesome to him by her
jealousy."  She did not apparently scruple to
follow his example, for we are told by Burnet[3]
that she changed her religion to conciliate her
husband, as he had thrown off all restraint in
his love-affairs, when he discovered that she had
been unfaithful to him with the handsome, fasci-

---

[1] " Grammont Memoirs," 1846 edition, p. 274.
[2] Teague Power to Duchess of York, Record Office.
[3] Burnet's " History of My Own Times," Oxford edition, vol. i.
p. 394.

nating Henry Sidney. Sidney was in consequence
banished from Court. It must be said in defence
of the Duchess of York that, in the eyes of the
scandalous Court of Charles II., the fact that
Sidney was, or pretended to be, in love with the
Duchess would certainly imply her guilt. On the
other hand, a passage in a letter written many
years later by Montagu in England to Sidney at
The Hague, refers to "the relation you had to
the late Duchess." [1]

Lord Clarendon was horrified when he heard
of his daughter's intention to leave the English
Church, and wrote to her very sternly on the
subject; while he told the Duke of York that
the Duchess's change of religion would bring "irre-
parable dishonour on her husband and father, and
ruin on her children." [2] As James was secretly
a Roman Catholic himself, he very naturally did
not sympathise with this view of the matter, and
Clarendon's remonstrances were of no effect, though
the Duchess's change of religion was not publicly
announced.

In the year 1665, when the Lady Mary, as she
was called, was three years old, the Great Plague
devastated London, and the King and Court
moved to Hampton Court to escape danger of
infection. As the sickness increased and spread
over the country, Hampton Court was considered
too near the metropolis for safety, and it was
therefore decided that the Court should move
to Salisbury. However, just before the start,
another change was made, it being judged best, in
the disturbed state of the country, for the King
and his brother to separate, so that in case of disturbance there might be two centres for the troops.
The Duke of York therefore took up his abode

---

[1] "Henry Sidney's Diary and Correspondence," February 20,
1680—Montagu to Sidney.
[2] Clarendon's Letter, December, 1670, Record Office.

in York, where he lived in great magnificence, and
was entertained by the surrounding gentry. Possibly this was the happiest time of his life, for,
though his marriage had not pleased the people,
he was at this time very popular. His brother-
in-law, Lord Cornbury, writes: "The Duke and
Duchess are highly feasted and entertained in the
North, and are so pleased that they care not for
removing." [1]

It must have been pleasant to be absent from
Charles's Court for a time, for the Queen's indignation at the position of Lady Castlemaine reacted
on the King's temper, and the Merry Monarch had
become morose and disagreeable. Before the end
of September, however, the Duke of York was
obliged to follow the King to Oxford, for Parliament was to assemble there in October, and
matters of great moment would be under discussion.

Meanwhile the Princess Mary grew and flourished.
Pepys mentions seeing her, " a little child in hanging
sleeves, dance most finely so as almost to ravish
me, her ears were so good." Her education—except
her spelling, as we shall see later—seems to have
been carefully conducted, and even making due
allowance for the eulogistic spirit of the old bio-
graphers, who represent her as a paragon of talents
as well as virtues, she appears, unlike her sister
Anne, to have been quick and intelligent. Her
governor was the Bishop of London, Dr. Henry
Compton, the man most instrumental in insisting
that the royal children should be educated in the
religion of the Church of England. He seems to
have exerted considerable power in the Duke of
York's household, and to have used his influence
to guard his charges from the least fear of Papistry,
as it was then called. In fact, as James com-

---

[1] Lord Cornbury to Mr. Evelyn, September, 1665, "Fairfax
Correspondence," vol. iv. p. 324.

plained at the time of his daughter's marriage with
the Prince of Orange, his children were the children
of the State, and he had no power over them.
Great credit is certainly due to the Bishop, for
early impressions are powerful, and Mary's religious principles, and her devotion to her own
Church, were her most salient characteristics, were
in fact the mainspring of all her actions.

Dr. Edward Lake, Archdeacon and Prebendary
of Exeter, was chaplain to the two Princesses,
and the Lady Frances Villiers held the post of
governess. She may have been chosen for this
much coveted situation solely on the score of
suitability, but we cannot help suspecting that
the fact that her husband was uncle to Charles's
mistress, Barbara Villiers, the notorious Lady
Castlemaine, had something to do with the appointment.

Peter de Laine was the Lady Mary's instructor
in French, and he speaks with admiration of her
absolute knowledge of the language, while for
dancing, in which all her life she excelled, she had
several masters.

At six years old the Lady Anne was sent to Paris
to the care of her grandmother, Queen Henrietta
Maria, to be cured of a bad affection of the eyes.
She returned in July, 1670, Colonel Villiers taking
his wife to Dieppe to fetch her back. This visit
to Paris was kept absolutely secret, and the child
was supposed to have spent her time at the sea-
side, because of the intense dread of France and
of Popery among the English.

Mary's eyesight gave her continual trouble in
mature life, but she does not seem to have
suffered in childhood as did her sister ; at any
rate she received the whole of her education in
England.

When the Princess was nine years old, she lost
her mother, who had been failing in health for

some time, and died at St. James's Palace on
March 31, 1671.

On her deathbed Anne Hyde received the sacrament according to the rites of the Romish Church.
She had attained her highest ambition, but in
doing so she had roused unappeasable jealousies,
and her end was not happy. It was necessary to
deceive every one till the last, but it was noticed
that for fourteen months before her death she had
never received the sacrament, always excusing
herself for her omission by the plea of ill-health
or of business. She told no one, however, of her
change of religion. She had promised Morley,
Bishop of Winchester, who had been her father-
confessor since she was twelve years old, to let
him know if she ever felt doubts or scruples about
her faith, but she did not dare to confide even in
him, though she stayed with him at Farnham after
she had become a Roman Catholic.

When she was dying, Blandford Bishop of
Worcester was sent for, but found Catherine of
Braganza, wife of Charles II., sitting beside the
dying woman.

" Blandford was so modest and humble, that he
had not Presence of Mind enough to begin Prayers,
which probably wou'd have driven the Queen out
of the Room : But that not being done, she pretended Kindness, and woud not leave her, He
happen'd to say, I hope you continue still in the
Truth : Upon which she ask'd What is Truth ?
And then, her Agony encreasing, she repeated the
Word Truth, Truth, Truth, often ! " [1]

One of her maids of honour, Margaret Blagge,
afterwards Mrs. Godolphin, who was evidently not
aware of her secret communion, says :

" She was full of unspeakable torture, and died
(poor creature) in doubt of her religion, without
the Sacrament or Divine by her, like a poore

[1] Oldmixon's "History of the Stuarts," vol. ii. p. 560.

wretch ; none remembered her after one weeke,
none sorry for her ; she was tost and flung about,
and everyone did what they would with the
stately carcase." [1]

We are told elsewhere that her last words to
her husband were : " Duke, Duke, death is terrible,
death is very terrible." [2] The change of creed was
an awful step in those days, for to seventeenth-
century minds it might mean eternal damnation ;
and if Anne had become a Roman Catholic from
other motives than conviction, she might well be
haunted by fears when the time came for her
to die.

Mary, we are told, felt her mother's death very
much. In addition to the maternal care shown to
them both, Mary and Anne may have owed much
to the fact that, though surrounded by the tempta-
tions of the corrupt Court of Charles II., Anne
Hyde may have gone astray herself, she trans-
mitted to them some of the attributes of her ancestors, those quiet country ladies and gentlemen
who lived contentedly on their estates, the men
only occasionally journeying to London on important business, and their wives never leaving
their homes, but finding ample occupation in
their children, their neighbours, and their house-
keeping.

The Hyde parentage on one side explains, I think,
much in the personalities of both Mary and Anne
which would otherwise be quite incomprehensible.
Mary, indeed, was removed at the age of fifteen
from the English Court, and lived in absolute subjection to a man who would have tolerated nothing savouring in the slightest degree of flightiness,
but even this does not account for the absolute
purity, not only in deed but in mind, which were
her attributes.

[1] Evelyn's " Life of Mrs. Godolphin," p. 13.
[2] Dr. Denton to Sir R. Verney, Verney MSS.

Anne, however, married to a stupid man, for
whom she could have felt little affection, had no
such safeguard ; but though she carried her
friendships with her own sex to a height which
was foolish, and most undignified for one in her
position, the breath of scandal never touched her.
She did not inherit the more attractive qualities of
the Stuarts, and seems indeed to have taken her
attributes from some clodhopping squire, or good
but stupid housewife, among her mother's for-
bears.

Mary, on the other hand, possessed in a large
degree the Stuart charm, but united with a strictness of principle which was certainly very alien
to the spirit of the race.

In 1673 James made a second unpopular marriage. After trying in vain to induce an English
lady to become a Roman Catholic in order to
marry him, he sent the Earl of Peterborough to
choose him a wife among four princesses, all of
whom seemed more or less suitable. Lord Peterborough selected the Princess of Modena. She
had not yet completed her fifteenth year, and
wept bitterly and protested her intention to become a nun when told she was to marry a
man so much her senior, and to spend her life in
a country of which she had never before heard.
" Who is the Duke of York ? " she asked her
mother. James, however, was in high spirits, and
on receiving the news that his marriage by proxy
to the Princess had been accomplished, he sent for
the Lady Mary to tell her that he had " provided
a playfellow for her." Indeed there were hardly
four years between the stepmother and stepdaughter, and, till separated by the tragic circumstances of their lives, they seem to have been
on terms of intimacy and affection.

The English nation objected strongly to this
match ; " the lady being a papist of the strictest

PORTRAITS OF THE DUKE AND DUCHESS OF YORK AND THE PRINCESSES MARY AND ANNE.

From a picture by Sir Peter Lely. In the collection of Viscount Dillon.

16]

class, and the whole affair managed by the French interest ; " [1] says a contemporary writer.

An anecdote of Mary's girlhood which remains to us, illustrates Anne's character more vividly than that of her sister. The two Princesses were walking in Richmond Park, and saw an object in the distance, which according to the elder Princess was a man, according to the younger a tree. They began to dispute about the matter, but when they came so near to it that it was obvious that Mary was in the right, and she cried triumphantly, "Now, Anne, you *must* be certain what it is !" Anne would not look, but turned away, repeating obstinately, "No, sister, I still think it a tree !"

The only other information we possess about the Lady Mary's childhood is given us by letters found lately in Cirencester House, a few of which were published by Colonel Bathurst in the " Quarterly Review " of January, 1911. They are written, some before and some after the Princess's marriage, and her correspondent is Miss Apsley, the daughter of Sir Allen Apsley, a personal friend of the Duke of York. Mary's orthography is far from perfect, and in this respect she compares very unfavourably with her mother, whose girlish effusions are at least well spelt. It was the fashion in those days to have very sentimental friendships, and the Princess cherished for Frances Apsley the romantic attachment often felt by a girl for a friend some years older than herself.

Apparently, Frances Apsley at one time lived at St. James's Palace, and learnt with the Princess. Later, she returned home for her education, as the Princess, writing to her from Holland, says:

" But your leaving St. Jamese hous began this parting." However, as she remarks in another letter that, " you know it has allways bin my

---

[1] "Memoirs of Sir John Reresby," 1831 edition, p. 177; Coxe MSS., vol. xlv. folios 90–2.

choise to ritt to you when I coud have seen you," [1]
it is probable that some of these loverlike effusions
may have been stealthily delivered between lessons
in the Palace itself.

Mary addresses her friend in these letters as
her " husban," and signs herself " Clorinne." The
first of them was written, Colonel Bathurst thinks,
when the writer was nine or ten years old.

One of the series runs thus, and the breathless
reader longs in vain for an occasional stop :

" tow leters you have had today dear Aurelia
from me I hope you will read the third tho you I
supose are tired with them now I hope my pardon
is sealed by you dear dear dear dear dear dear
Aurelia I may if I can tel you how much I love
you but I hope that is not douted I have given
you proves anuf if not I will die to satisfie you
dear dear husban if al my hares were lives I woud
lose them al twenty times over to sarve or satisfie
you in any doute of my love think but if you were
married to Mr. sute who is as I gese the man in
the world you love best how much you wold love
him nay so nay a thousand times more longer
better should I—nay I do love you. I love you
with a heart intire I am for you al one desire I
love you with a flame more lasting then the vestals
fire thou art my life my soul my al that heaven
can give deaths life with you without you death
to live what can I say more to perswade you
that I love with more zeal then any lover can I
love you with a love that ner was known by man
I have for you excese of frandship more of love
then any woman can for woman and more love
then ever the constanest love had for his Mrs
you are loved more then can be exprest by your
ever obediant wife vere afectionate frand humbel
sarvant to kis the ground where you go, to be

---

[1] Bathurst Collection: Letter from Holland, March 3, 1678.

your dog in a string your fish in a net your bird in a cage your humbel trout—MARY CLORINNE.

"Saterday three a cloke in the afternoon." [1]

Childlike, the Princess Anne copied her sister in her adoration for Frances Apsley, whom she termed "Semandra," while she adopted the pseudonym of "Ziphares." Both these names were borrowed from a tragedy by Nathaniel Lee entitled *Mithridate*, in which Princess Anne acted, being coached for her part by Mrs. Betterton, who must, one would think, have found her task difficult.

Mary affected to be extremely jealous of her dearest " husban's " affection for her sister, as will be seen from the continuation of her letter :

" after my prayers to almighty god I come dear husband to make peace with you for it is a strang thing for man and wife to quarel but I find to my great sorrow that this has bin long contriving in you head for you have bin always with my sister, grudge one minut stay with me but now at last you have found a hapy acation thoug a very unhapy one for me to quarel with me but I am sure I take it very il of you for so slit an acation I told you al along that if I shoud dy I could not have told it and you may be sure that if I wold have told it to any body it hade bin to you my dear crual unkind Aurelia. not but that I think my sister dos desarve your love better a great deal than I and so doutles she dos and has according to her desart but since you have forsaken me quite I have still the marks that you loved me once and now I do not dout but my hapy sister has the cornelian ring unhapy I should have had she wil wright to you unkind Aurelia when you are at the house but still I hope you wil not go tow sone for then I shoud be robed of seeing you unkind husband as wel as of your love but she

[1] Bathurst Collection: "Quarterly Review," January, 1911.

that has it wil have your heart tow and you letters
tow oh thrice hapy she, she is hapyer then ever I
was for she has tryoumpht over a rival that wonce
was hapy in your love til she with her aluring
charmes" [it is difficult to imagine the stolid little
Anne with these attributes !] "removed unhapy
Clorine from your heart, pray Aurelia I canot leave
that loved neam yet dear Aurelia for this is the
last time I shall cal you so answare this letter
that I may have own letter of your dear hand
wrighting to look upon and say this gold ring
this pice of cornelian ring and this letter came
from the crual fair that loved me once. now some
time a good fancy comes in to my head that this
unkindnes of your proceeds frome excesse of love
but oh that good faincy is crost when I consider
with what eger hast you cald my hapy rival
when I dinied to tel you and with what coldness
she fain'd to come but at last how you wispred
then lauft, as if you had said, now we are rid of
her, let us be hapy, while pore unhapy I sate
reading of a play my heart was ready to brake for
I was read where Massanisa come first to sophonisba
and thought that saene so like my misary it
made me ready to cry but before my hapy rival
I would now show my wekness but now with
Sophonisaba I may cry out she thinks me fals
though I have bin most true and thinking so
what may her furie doe if I have said any non-
sence pray forgive it for I think I am almost mad
but with this prayer I leave you that in your new
choise you may be hapy that she may love you
as well as I for beter I am sure she canot so with
my prayers I leave you think of your unfortunate
"MARY CLORINE." [1]

Another fragment of a letter is interesting but
puzzling. It evidently refers to a scandal in which

[1] Bathurst Collection.

the Duke of Monmouth was involved, and it proves that Lady Frances Villiers's young charges were not guarded with much strictness from Court gossip, or even from intercourse with the maids of their maids of honour.

" . . . came thare but they both beged very hartely that they wold no tel the Duke of Monmouth that wold and not tel his wife and Mrs Nedam [?] that they wold tel nobody of it but espetialy Mrs Jenings" [so early does the future Duchess of Marlborough take her place in the annals of Court gossip] " so thay all promising her thay wold not tel but Mrs Trevors maid sad the divil take her if she did not tel Mrs Jenings the first time she see her for Mrs Jenings her self did lay with my lady Hambelton in the town but her servants lay at Eton. thay all ware as good as there word a whole fortnight and then Mrs Worsley told the Duches so Mrs Jenings cam hom and Mrs Trevors maid was as good as her word then the duches hering of it was mighty angry at it and now mrs Needam is gone away and says nobody shal never here of her more this is all that I can tel of this news but the Duches of Monmouth they say do take it mightily to harte, and since it has been known has never bin abrode nor never has sen the Duke of Monmouth since, for that very day it was known Lord Craven sent for him to London before it was known. There is no more to say than that I al your obedient wife
" Mary Clorinne."[1]

· Occasionally the pathos in the letters may seem to us a trifle overdone, as in the following passage : " your crying when you wright wil essely be belived from me I did so too in my last letter but did not tel you so becaus I thought you wold not belive me."

[1] Bathurst Collection.

The Duke and Duchess of Monmouth loom large on Mary's horizon, and her stepmother, the Duchess of York, figures occasionally as " the Duches." Sarah Jennings has even in these childish days begun to make a stir—she quarrels, she acts as intermediary, in short she comes prominently before her little world. Anne also makes her appearance, but mostly, as we might expect, in a passive relation. Mary and Anne play cards or take their dancing-lesson together. Sometimes, however, as we have already seen, the younger sister tries to appropriate one of Mary's friends, and there is a little real, and a great deal of simulated, romantic jealousy in consequence. In these early letters the Duke of York is not once mentioned, nor is the King; those important luminaries evidently revolving in larger orbits than the one traversed by the young Princess.

A letter, dated " Sunday too a cloke," is particularly interesting, as in it Mary condescends to step down a little from the heights of sentiment, and to tell us about the commonplace details of her daily life. We learn from this source that the Lady Mary was permitted to see her " dearest Aurelia " on Sundays and holy-days, so that the friendship was, so to speak, authorised. A Miss, or, in the phraseology of the time, Mrs., Barkley, was not, however, equally pleasing to those in authority. Therefore it was necessary for Mary, and also for Anne, who was evidently her sister's faithful plagiarist in everything, to carry on a clandestine correspondence with her. So, while Mary had her dancing-lesson with Mr. Gorey, Anne retired to her closet to indite her precious letter, but on this occasion she had not time to seal it before being summoned to dance, so she left it in her sister's charge. Mary put it into her pocket, and began to write her own, intending to seal them both at the same time. Sarah Jennings, evidently

already the confidential friend and go-between,
came in to fetch the letters, and Mary, who was in
a hurry, called to her begging her to seal Anne's
letter.[1]

Unfortunately, the closet door was open, and
some one, who is only referred to as " Lady," but
who was evidently Lady Frances Villiers, was heard
approaching. Mary jumped up, " as red as fire,"
and, to distract her governess's attention from
what she was doing, asked how she liked the new
" manto " she was wearing. This query she
managed to make with her back turned to the
intruder, which sounds an awkward proceeding,
and Lady Frances, evidently suspecting that
something forbidden was in progress, inquired
what the Princess was doing in the closet.

Mary, with much presence of mind, but con-
tempt of veracity, said that she had called Mrs.
Jennings into her closet to show her the new
portrait of the Duchess of York, and that Mrs.
Jennings had then taught her a new way of sealing
the letter she had just written to Mrs. Apsley.
Fortunately, the governess, after remarking dryly
that Mrs. Jennings was very ingenious, withdrew
without making further awkward inquiries, and
the letters were carried away in safety by the
enterprising Sarah.

Mary was evidently afraid that her correspondent would find this narrative rather commonplace,
for she finishes with a postscript written in the
orthodox style :

" Oh stay, dear Aurelia, I'l sware I had forgot
ye chife part of my letter that is to tel you I love
you better then I can exprese dear dear dearest
husban if you woud you shal know it agin yt I
am your most dutyfull loveing wif.

"M. C."

---

[1] Bathurst Collection: " Quarterly Review," January, 1911.

The friends also exchanged letters by the agency of a Mr. Gipson (Gibson), the Princess's drawing-master, who seems to have been a most obliging postman. He was a dwarf who had belonged to Henrietta Maria, and he married a dwarf and had nine full-sized children. He accompanied the Princess Mary to Holland, and is often mentioned in these early letters.

On one occasion the Princess fears her " dear Aurelia " intends " to breck quite with her," as she has not " wright " to her by Mr. Gibson.

" I had wright a letter [she says] and put it in my pocet but when he came I was a singing so he staid a great while for me and when I did come to him I was not there a minet but in came Mother Wise and called me out to a daughter of my Lord Windsors who came at yt unsesonable hour to make a visit so in the mene time Mr. Gipson went away that I could not give him the letter this sad misfortune made me wright this letter and send both by a foot man contrary to your comand to know the reson of your unkindness to me you faithful wife.

" M. CLORINE." [1]

Another letter is provoking. It begins with a promise to be full of " seecrits," and commences auspiciously with, " I was one day in a very weare humore and so was Mrs V.[2] and T.[3] and my Mam,[4] and as we wear a talking of mad pranks we——" However, after wandering to other subjects, and only incidentally telling us the " good nuse " that the " Cort " is coming to London on the August 2, and that the writer hopes that she will come

[1] Bathurst Collection.
[2] Evidently one of the Villierses, Lady Frances Villiers daughters, who were educated with the Princesses.
[3] Possibly Miss Trelawny, who was educated with her.
[4] Her nurse, Mrs. Hemlock.

too, she decides that the secret is of such great importance that she "durst not trust pen and ink with it," and we hear no more.

The sentimentalities expressed in these letters are at first rather astonishing to the reader, but it must be remembered that to perform in masques and comedies, in which words of the most passionate nature were used, formed part of the education of the two Princesses. In Evelyn's "Diary" for December 15, 1674, he says :

"Saw a comedie at night at Court, acted by the ladies only, amongst them Lady Mary and Ann, his Royal Highnesses two daughters. . . . They were all covered with jewels."

The "comedie" was a masque called *Calisto, or the Chaste Nymphe.* A repetition of the performance was given on December 22, and on this occasion Miss Blagge, who afterwards married the statesman Godolphin, and who took the principal rôle, that of Diana, wore about £20,000 worth of jewels, and lost a jewel which she had borrowed from the Countess of Suffolk. The stage was carefully swept, but it could not be found. "The press was so great that 'tis a wonder she lost no more," Evelyn remarks. However, the Duke of York paid for the lost trinket. The young performers were trained for their parts by Mrs. Betterton. Henrietta Wentworth, who became later the Duke of Monmouth's mistress, took part in the performance, as did the ubiquitous Sarah Jennings.

The masque was written by John Crone, to whom the task was entrusted through the influence of the Earl of Rochester, while Dryden, to whom belonged by right the privilege of composing any plays in which royalty was to act, only wrote an epilogue for it, and this was not made use of. The story of *Calisto* was taken from the second book of Ovid's "Metamorphoses," and in our day would not have been considered quite suitable for performance by girls of fifteen and thirteen—the ages of the two Princesses. Miss Blagge, who is praised by her contemporaries as a miracle of virtue in a dissolute age, objected to being obliged to act in it, but, having only lately given up her position as maid of honour to Catherine of Braganza, was unable to refuse. She writes to Evelyn :

" I am extreamly heavy for I would be free from that place " [the Court] " and have nothing to do in itt att all : but it will not be for the play goes on mightyly, which I hoped would never have proceeded farther. . . . Would you believe itt, there are some that envy me the honour (as they esteeme it) of acting in this play, and turn malitious jests upon me." [1]

The appearance of the young ladies of the Court—not to speak of the Princesses—as amateur actresses, was certainly somewhat daring, for women did not act even on the public stage till the Restoration, and then so few of them were available that the female parts were often taken by men. Kynaston, one of the actors, made up as such a handsome girl that, as theatrical performances then took place at four o'clock, fashionable ladies were proud of taking him in their coaches in his make-up for a drive round Hyde Park after the play. Charles II. too was mollified and amused when appearing sooner than he was expected at a tragedy, and, asking why he was kept waiting, he was told by the manager that the Queen had not yet shaved.[2]

The novelty of women on the stage accounts for the fact that Margaret Blagge, evidently considering that her acting was a terrible sin which could only be expiated by prayer, retired between the scenes to her devotions.

The Princess Mary, however, to whom Crone dedicated the masque, does not appear to have

---

[1] Evelyn's " Life of Mrs. Godolphin," p. 96.
[2] Colley Cibber's " Apology," chap. v.

felt the same scruples, but the writer's difficulties
were, as he tells us, great, and he describes them
pathetically, though with evident pride in the skill
shown in surmounting them. There were to be
seven ladies in the play, and only two of these
might be in " men's habits." [1]   After having chosen
Calisto as his heroine because she was the " exact
and perfect character of chastity, and therefore
a very proper character for Princess Mary to
represent," he was confronted with the difficulty
of writing " a clean, decent, and inoffensive play
on the story of a rape "—a difficulty which would
to most persons appear insurmountable.

However, eventually everything was arranged
in a manner satisfactory to those concerned.
The Duke of Monmouth and several other gentlemen
danced in the prologue, in which appeared also
two of the King's mistresses.   In the play itself
the Lady Mary took the part of Calisto, " a chaste
and favourite nymph of Diana, beloved by Jupiter ";
the Lady Anne represented Nymphe, also " a
chaste young nymph "; while Lady Henrietta Wentworth, for whose connection with Monmouth the
play of *Calisto* may have been in part responsible,
took the rôle of Jupiter.   The Countess of Sussex
appeared as Juno, and Lady Mary Mordant per-
sonated Psecas, the villain of the piece, who was
envious of Calisto and beloved by Mercury, otherwise Sarah Jennings.

" Autres temps, autres mœurs."   Any one who
reads *Calisto* now will most probably wonder that
James should have allowed his young daughters to
act in it, or that the virtuous Evelyn should say that
" it was exactly modest and suited to the persons." [2]

The next event in the Princess's life which is
recorded seems a foretaste of much which followed.
She reached the proper age for confirmation, and

---

[1] Crone to the Reader.
[2] Evelyn's " Life of Mrs. Godolphin," p. 99.

the Bishop of London went to the Duke of York to ask for permission to prepare her for the rite. The Duke replied that his conscience did not allow him to participate in the ceremonies of the Anglican Church, or to allow his daughters to do so, and that he only consented to their being educated in the faith of the English Church because he knew that otherwise they would be taken from him.

The next day James met the Bishop—who must have been in an awkward position—and asked him whether he had spoken to the King on the subject ; to which the Bishop replied that he had been about to ask his Royal Highness's permission to do so. Of course the King ordered the preparation for the Princess's confirmation to continue, and James's conscience was satisfied. He had not proceeded to extremities, yet had testified that his daughter's religious training was being conducted against his will ; and he says himself that he wished that " the thing should happen in this way." [1]

Those who blame Mary bitterly for want of filial respect and affection in 1689 should, I think, remember that, from her earliest years, circumstances had compelled James to renounce all authority over her. He himself called her " a child of the State," and she was taught to look on her father's religion as false and superstitious, and to owe obedience to the King, and not to him.

[1] " Mémoires de Jacques II.," vol. ii. p 193.

# CHAPTER II

MEANWHILE political events were shaping Mary's
destiny. A great European struggle was in progress—a struggle against the encroachments of
Louis XIV., who, thirsting for universal domination,
used the power given him by his command of the
vast resources of a country which he left at his
death exhausted and bankrupt, to enlarge the
territories of France at the expense of the nations
surrounding her. United with the great question
whether Protestantism should be allowed to hold
its own unmolested, or should be ruthlessly stamped
out as a hateful heresy, this struggle was in reality
the ruling factor in European politics of the seventeenth century. The fact, however, was sometimes
obscured, and the issue complicated by alliances
between France and states naturally her enemies,
who, with the guile engendered by weakness hoped
to avoid destruction by conciliating the tyrant.

England was of little support to any other
Power, for its attitude during Charles II.'s reign
was impossible to count on from week to week, or
even to understand at the moment, so complicated
were affairs, so deep was the King's dissimulation,
in which he was imitated by most of his statesmen,

29

and so various were the influences at work. "There
is nothing but fluctuation in the statesmanship
of England,"[1] said de Witt. To one thing at
least Charles was constant—he detested the Dutch
and was, like his brother James, strongly French
in his predilections and sympathies. On the
other hand, in England the passion for political
freedom was strong, and with it was allied an
intense dread and hatred of France with its absolute government, and the Popish religion which,
to English minds, was inseparably connected
with it.

Charles was astute enough to realise this fact in
all its bearings ; and on one point, among much that
was variable, he was determined—at any cost he
would die King of England. "Brother, you may
travel if you will, I am resolved to make myself
easy for the rest of my life,"[2] were his words to the
Duke of York. He foresaw plainly the calamitous
result of his brother's policy, and told the Prince
of Orange that "when the Duke should come to
reign, he would be so restless and violent, that he
would not be able to hold the kingdom four years
to an end."[3]

On the other hand, Charles could not maintain
his kingly dignity as he conceived proper without
the help of France, for without her aid in raising
money, it would be necessary to convoke Parliaments continually, and to submit to their outspoken criticisms and restrictions of his liberty of
action. Charles did not wish, he told the Earl of
Essex,

"to be like a grand signior, with some mutes
about him and bags of bowstrings to strangle men
as he had a mind to it ; but he did not think he
was a king as long as a company of fellows were

---

[1] "Memoirs of Sir W. Temple," vol. ii. p. 67.
[2] Oldmixon's "History of the Stuarts," p. 690.
[3] Burnet's "History of My Own Times," vol. ii. p. 415.

looking into all his actions, and examining his
ministers, as well as his accounts ! " [1]

The jealous fear felt by the House of Commons
for Charles, especially after it was suspected that
he, like his brother, had become a Roman Catholic,
showed itself in intense parsimony. Even if he
had submitted to its domination, it is doubtful
whether sufficient money would have been doled
out to defray the necessary expenses of government; and Charles would certainly not have received enough from his "faithful Commons" to
satisfy the costly caprices of the frail ladies with
whom he surrounded himself.

Therefore recourse to France was indispensable ;
and treaties were drawn up so secret and so absolutely contrary in effect to the policy ostensibly
prevailing, that they could not be divulged to the
most confidential Ministers, and it was, on one
occasion at any rate, necessary for Charles to
write out the whole of the agreement himself. In
spite of the utmost care, however, inconvenient
facts showing England's absolute dependence on
France would sometimes leak out, and the uncom-
promising attitude of the Duke of York on religious
questions was of the utmost embarrassment to the
King. If Charles wished to satisfy the nation, and
so to prevent any possibility of having to "start
on his travels again," as he phrased it, it was absolutely necessary that the turbulent English should
be sure that the Duke of York's descendants would
always belong to the Church of England. No
better way of accomplishing this could be desired
than by marrying James's eldest daughter to her
cousin, William Prince of Orange, who was the
principal representative of Protestantism in Europe.

William of Orange was the posthumous child
of William II. and of Mary, eldest daughter of
Charles I. He was born on November 4, 1650, a

[1] Burnet's "History of My Own Times," vol. ii. p. 1.

week after the death of his father. His education
was entrusted to an Englishwoman, Catherine Lady
Stanhope, who had been governess to his mother ;
and he was brought up in the Palace in the Wood,
just outside The Hague, and doubtless often played
with his mother's lively maid of honour Anne
Hyde. When he was nine years old, the Princess
of Orange died in England, and he was left in the
charge of his grandmother Amelia, the widow of
Henry Frederick of Orange. This beautiful and
clever lady had not at all agreed with the policy
of her son William II. Her disapproval seems to
have been well founded ; for by his imprudent
attempts at high-handedness William II. had so
alarmed the States, that the Orange family were
looked on with suspicious jealousy by the Commonwealth of Holland. Therefore during William's youth
an edict was enacted by which members of the
family were perpetually debarred from holding the
Stadtholdership, or position of Chief Magistrate.

Jointures to William's mother and grandmother
and a large sum lent to help Charles I. of England
had served to impoverish the heads of the Orange
family ; and the future King of England came into
the world at a time when the fortunes of his house
were at a low ebb. Many anecdotes are told of his
infancy and childhood. We hear of his being born
in a room hung with black, of three circles of light
being seen over his head, these symbolising the
three crowns he was afterwards to wear, of his
discreet behaviour at two years old at a Dutch
supper-party, and, a little later, of his noisy games
with his cousin, Elizabeth Charlotte, who afterwards became second wife of Philippe Duke of
Orleans.

The principal fact, however, which is important
to our consideration of him as future husband of
Princess Mary is that he was from infancy delicate ; and that during his youth he was surrounded

PORTRAIT OF PRINCESS MARY.

From a portrait by Sir Peter Lely. In the Collection of Earl Bathurst.

by little which could call forth his affections, and
much which would make him suspicious, cautious,
and reserved. He was essentially a child of the
State. While one party considered that it was
necessary to the glories of Holland that the House
of Orange should recover its ancient prestige, and
should, by the pomp and magnificence of its trap-
pings, bear testimony to the wealth and importance
of the United Provinces, the faction in ascendancy,
with de Witt at its head, was most anxious to limit
the power of the young Prince and to prevent him
from following in his father's footsteps, and en-
croaching in the smallest degree on the liberties
of the people. De Witt, however, not realising the
small part family ties played in the policy of
Charles II. in comparison with the all-important
question of pecuniary help from France, hoped to
conciliate William's Stuart uncles in England, and
to obtain at least their benevolent neutrality for
Holland, by following their behests, and arranging
that the young Prince should, with due limitations,
take his proper position in the country.

We are told by Temple, who was English Minister
at The Hague in 1668, that de Witt announced to
him that he " never failed to see the Prince once
or twice a week, grew to have a particular affection
for him, and would tell me plainly, that the States
designed the Captain-Generalship of all the forces
for him as soon as by his age he grew capable of
it." [1] It is probable that de Witt's affection was
not returned. William, however, was extremely
cautious and reserved, and, living from his early
youth in an atmosphere of State affairs, no doubt
realised the imprudence of showing his mind
to one whose interests were necessarily opposed
to his own, so that his guardian doubtless did not
realise the force of the feelings enlisted against
him.

[1] "Memoirs of Sir W. Temple," vol. i. p. 315.

Mingled with that patriotism which was from
the time of his childhood William's ruling passion,
was an intense desire for the return of the House of
Orange to the dignities forfeited by his father's
imprudence. William has been called cold ; but
no one who reads his private letters to Bentinck
can endorse that accusation. Reserved he certainly was, cautious, suspicious, and dry in manner ;
but where he loved, he loved deeply, faithfully, and
with passionate devotion. After the death of his
mother, the only relation with whom William had
to do was his paternal grandmother, who, according to Sir William Temple, was "a woman of the
most wit and good sense, in general, that I have
known!"[1] She had a strong distrust for England. When the Duke of Buckingham, whose
marital infidelities were notorious, assured her of
the fondness the English felt for the Dutch, and
said that "they did not use Holland like a mistress,
but loved her like a wife," she retorted, "Truly,
I believe you love us as you love your own wife."
She, no doubt, imbued William strongly with
her own sentiments ; and possibly in very early
youth the foundation was laid of a feeling of
antipathy to the English, which prevented William
understanding the nation over whom he was to
reign in the future, and made him an unsym-
pathetic, and therefore an unpopular ruler.

Certainly, Charles in those early days gave his
nephew good cause for distrust. The union of
France and England for the destruction of Holland,
united with the announcement that Charles had
become a Roman Catholic, formed the basis of the
secret Treaty of Dover, about which Henrietta of
Orleans was Louis XIV.'s Ambassador to Charles.
This treaty was under consideration in January,
1668 ; though on the 23rd of that month the
Triple Alliance, which Charles tells his sister was

[1] "Memoirs of Sir W. Temple," vol. ii. p. 317.

made contrary to his inclinations, was formed at The Hague between England, Sweden, and Holland, against the encroachments of France. It was difficult for some time to persuade Charles to assent to the conditions of the Treaty of Dover; and much delay was caused by a discussion as to whether the public announcement of the King's change of religion should precede or follow the declaration of war with Holland. The treaty was signed in May, 1670, and one with slightly altered conditions in June, 1671, but (though the terms of the treaty were kept absolutely secret) the change its policy engendered was apparent almost as soon as the Triple Alliance was concluded.

Charles's intense dislike of the Dutch is expressed very strongly in some of his letters to the Duchess of Orleans. In one he remarks that the Dutch have treated him and the French King " scurvily," that he will " never be satisfied till he has had his revenge, and is very willing to enter into an agreement upon that matter whenever Louis wishes for it." [1]

In 1670, while the arrangements for the Alliance which was intended to ruin his country were in progress, William came to England to pay a visit to his uncles. Charles, with that knowledge of character which was one of his principal talents, was not afraid to entrust his nephew with the great secret of his change of religion. He told him that the Protestants were a factious body, divided among themselves since they had separated from the main body, and that he wished he " would take more pains and look into these things better, and not be led by his Dutch blockheads." [2] This confidence apparently astonished William of Orange extremely, and he did not forget it, though he

---

[1] Sir John Dalrymple's " Memoirs of Great Britain and Ireland," vol. i. p. 66—Letter, February 27, 1679.

[2] Burnet's " History of My Own Times," vol. i. p. 495.

mentioned it to no one, except Zulestein, till after the death of Charles.

Charles was evidently piqued by the seriousness of the young Prince's demeanour, and at a supper-party at the Duke of Buckingham's he managed to make him tipsy ; when, among other manifestations of his condition, he delighted the frivolous company on his return to Whitehall by breaking the windows of the rooms occupied by the maids of honour, who had to be rescued in a hurry.[1]

William's objects in this visit were to ask for his uncle's intervention in the question of the Stadtholdership, and to insist on the payment of the money owing to him. It is rumoured that he also intended to moot the project of a possible marriage with his cousin the Lady Mary, then a child of eight years of age ; a proposition to which Charles was at the time inimical, and of which the Duke of York must have heard with the utmost horror. William undertook nothing without much consideration, and there was doubt for some time as to the advisability of this visit, and many debates on the question of whether he would be likely to succeed in his aims, and therefore whether his report to the States on his mission would advance him in public estimation.[2] This was specially important just now, as a few months earlier he had for the first time been allowed a voice in public affairs, being given a seat on the Council of State, with the same privileges as had been enjoyed by his ancestors.

William seems to have won favourable opinions in England. Evelyn says that he has " a manly, courageous, wise countenance," [3] while, according to Lord Arlington, who would in the future fall under the Prince's dire displeasure, but whom he

---

[1] "Memoirs of Sir John Reresby," 1670.
[2] Instructions to Dr. Rompf, Record Office.
[3] Evelyn's "Diary," November 4, 1670.

now considered a friend, he was a " young man of the most extraordinary Understanding and Parts." [1] The only adverse criticism is indirectly a compliment. Charles had hoped to induce the Prince to join in the downthrow of Holland in consideration of being made head of a principality under the protection of France ; but Colbert writes to Louis XIV. that the King " finds him so passionate a Dutchman and protestant that even although your Majesty had not disapproved of his being trusted with any part of the secret, these two reasons would have hindered him." [2] William would never separate his interests from his country and acquiesce in her overthrow. He was entertained by the Lord Mayor and the Aldermen at dinner at Drapers' Hall on December 6, and then went to Oxford, where he was received by the Heads of the Colleges, and stayed to see the " Christmas Splendours " [3] of London.

Outwardly there was friendship between the Prince of Orange and his uncles, but in 1672 the whole aspect of affairs was changed, and William's fierce indignation roused, by the united English and French declaration of war against Holland.

The French promise of subsidies to Charles had been extensive, and included twenty-five millions of livres, in exchange for the hand of the Princess Mary. [4]

Holland was absolutely unprepared for war ; and, horrified and alarmed at the danger which they considered had been brought about by the disregard of the Commonwealth for William of Orange, the people murdered the de Witts, who had been for so long their rulers, made William Stadtholder, Captain-General, and Admiral of their

[1] Arlington's " Letters," November 21, 1670.

[2] Sir John Dalrymple's "Memoirs of Great Britain and Ireland," vol. i. p. 47.

[3] " Life of Queen Mary," 1695.

[4] Oldmixon's " History of the Stuarts." vol. ii. p. 599.

forces, and rose against their enemies. In William they found a leader who would fight to the death. " I shall die in the last ditch," [1] he said when told he would most probably live to see his country undone; and his actions matched his words. Later, in gratitude for William's determined stand against the French, the Stadtholdership of Holland, and of West Friesland, was settled on him for life, and on his heirs male after him.

Charles began to look upon his nephew with more respect than formerly, and made many attempts to separate him from his Spanish allies; but the war was to rage for some years longer.

In February, 1673, peace was declared between Holland and England, but the States and their Spanish allies now started an offensive war against France. Charles was anxious at any cost to secure a general amnesty. He despatched Lord Arlington and Lord Ossory to William, to try to detach him from his Spanish allies, and to offer him the hand of the Princess Mary. William, however, was obdurate, he refused to desert the Spaniards, though he admitted to Sir William Temple, the English Envoy, that he found them most troublesome and undependable as allies.

William was furious with Arlington, who treated him, he said, like a child. Certainly Arlington does not appear to have been a very tactful envoy, as he wrote to William reminding him that " there are wounds among you, which will bleed afresh if they be but touched." [2] The Prince was furious at this expression, which he looked on as a threat, and said he knew what it meant, for Lord Arlington had told some one that Charles could get the Prince of Orange served in the same way as de Witt had been, if he liked to set about it. William was

---

[1] Sir John Dalrymple's " Memoirs of Great Britain and Ireland," vol. i. p. 53.
[2] " Memoirs of Sir W. Temple," vol. ii. p. 301.

more angry than Temple had ever seen him, and
Arlington's words must have been specially galling
if the allegations of William's enemies had any
grain of truth in them, and he had really had a
hand in bringing about de Witt's murder.

To Lord Ossory was confided the delicate matter
of offering William the Princess's hand. Charles
was now most anxious for the marriage, as he considered that it would not only make William man-
ageable on the question of peace, but would also
be most advantageous to the Duke of York, who,
as a Roman Catholic, was hated by the English.
In fact, in a letter to his father, the Duke of
Ormond, Lord Ossory says :

" The King told me his nephew and his niece's
marriage was the only thing capable of helping the
Duke, and that for that, as well as other reasons, he
had spoken to the Duke of it, who consented that,
upon the Prince of Orange's desiring it, I should
undertake the proposition would be accepted." [1]

It is impossible to gather the exact course of
events from the conflicting accounts. In one of
them we are told that, to the suggestion of the
marriage, William replied coldly that his " fortunes
were not in a condition for him to think of a wife," [2]
and that James was furious because his beautiful
daughter had been put in a position to be rejected
by her cousin. He said that he " had liked not
the thing from the first," and blamed Lord Ossory,
who had, he declared, been too hasty. Lord Ossory
defended himself rather feebly, declaring that
James was quite mistaken in thinking that the
Prince had intended to refuse his cousin's hand.
On the other hand, Sir John Dalrymple [3] says that,
from many of the despatches, it appears that the

---

[1] Carte's " Life of Ormond," vol. i. p. 264.
[2] " Memoirs of Sir W. Temple," vol. ii. p. 294.
[3] Sir John Dalrymple's " Memoirs of Great Britain and Ireland,"
vol. i. p. 148.

proposed marriage between the Prince and his
cousin was prevented by the French Court ; and
that the King and Duke of York then expressed
strongly their dislike of William of Orange, and
their hope of marrying Mary to the Dauphin.
James always showed a distaste for the Dutch
marriage, a distaste which evidently sprang from
affection for his daughter, and which, from his point
of view, was amply justified. It seems, however,
extraordinary that he who considered his eternal
salvation would be imperilled if he were to become a
member of the English Church, and who was willing
to sacrifice even his kingdom for his principles, should
for any consideration have eventually allowed, not
only Mary, but Anne, to marry Protestants.

Shortly after the unconscious Mary had been
refused by her future husband, an event happened
which was destined to have considerable influence
on the happiness of her married life. Amid
universal consternation William fell ill of smallpox.
The demeanour of the nation showed plainly that
he had become its mainspring ; nothing could be
attempted, everything was in suspense, till it was
seen whether the Prince would fall a victim to a
malady which had often proved fatal in his family.
During his illness his faithful servant Bentinck
nursed him with a devotion which was truly admirable. For sixteen days, when the illness was
at its worst, William never asked for anything by
night or by day, but Bentinck answered him as
though he never slept. Everything William ate he
took from Bentinck's hand, and it was only when
he was convalescent that Bentinck begged leave
to go home as he could bear up no longer. It was
well he did so, for he was already ill with smallpox
and very nearly died of it. William and Bentinck
had been friends from early youth, but it is certain
that gratitude for Bentinck's heroic devotion laid
the foundation of that passionate affection which

breathes through all William's letters to him, and there can be little doubt to any one who has read these letters, with their constant reiteration of love for Bentinck, desire for his company, and intense interest in his wife, family, and whatever concerns him, that Mary's married life would have been happier without the existence of so powerful a rival in William's affections.

On William's recovery he still held firm to his compact with his allies, and Charles, who was most anxious to act as mediator between France and Holland, a post which would, he hoped, allow him to intrigue secretly with both, found him quite impracticable. However, difficulties beset the Prince, for a strong party in Holland were now most anxious for peace, and a Congress to treat for this began to sit at Nimeguen; but it lasted for two years, while the war continued without intermission, and William still refused to make a separate truce with France. Even his trusted friend, the Pensioner Fagel, was now anxious for peace, and said that he did not know of a single man in Holland who was not of his mind. "Yes," said the Prince, "I am sure I know one! and that is myself; and I will hinder it as long as I can; but if anything should happen to me, I know it would be done in two days' time." [1] William then used a simile which seems curiously illustrative of his character.

"He had seen [he said] that morning a poor old man tugging alone in a little boat with his oars, against the eddy of a sluice, upon a canal; that, when, with the last endeavours, he was just got up to the place intended, the force of the eddy carried him quite back again; but he turned his boat as soon as he could, and fell to his oars again; and thus three or four times while the Prince saw him; and concluded,

[1] "Memoirs of Sir W. Temple," vol. ii. p. 377.

this old man's business and his were too like
one another, and that he ought, however, to do
just as the old man did, without knowing what
would succeed, any more than what did in the
poor man's case."

The Prince required all the moral support he
could obtain from his convictions, for the position
of affairs seemed almost desperate. Only his will
prevented the signing of a separate peace between
Holland and France, and as a consequence the
reduction of Holland to the position of a province
under French protection. Even the Spaniards,
in whose interest he was struggling, failed to
support him, for they considered the preservation
of Flanders so important both to England and to
Holland that they might safely leave the care of
it to them. Charles, on the other hand, was again
secretly intriguing with France, and sent William
propositions which were, the latter declared, dictated by Louis XIV., who would not have dared,
without Charles's intervention, to offer the allies
such one-sided terms. William cried passionately
that he was treated like a child ; and could distinguish his hated Lord Arlington's hand in what
he contemptuously termed the " whipped cream " [1]
of some of the sentences. Sir W. Temple read the
despatches from England to him, and saw his face
change as he listened to some of the provisions,
though he only said the matter had better be
discussed after dinner. However, on his way out
of the room, he could contain himself no longer ;
and as he passed Temple he said under his breath
that he " must rather die than make such a peace."
The news, with its implied intimation that it was
hopeless to expect help from his slippery uncle,
spoilt his dinner. On receiving further communications from Charles couched in the same style,
he said wearily that, being in, he must go on,

[1] "Memoirs of Sir W. Temple," vol. ii. p. 395.

and expressed the necessity of endurance by the significant words that "when one is at High Mass, one is at it,"[1] meaning, as Sir William Temple remarked sagaciously, that when there is a great crowd, it is impossible to get out.

Nevertheless, his acute and cautious mind was still working at expedients, and he had seen for a long time the advantages that would accrue to him from marrying his cousin Princess Mary, if only the moment for this event were chosen judiciously. If an English Princess were the wife of the Dutch Stadtholder, it seemed to him that Charles would not be able to leave Holland to her fate; and so the alliance might save his country from ruin.

Other considerations were no doubt present with him, considerations which we cannot in fairness refer wholly to ambition. William was constitutionally cautious and cunning; the Jesuitical maxim that the end justifies the means was certainly one of his principles, and he felt no scruples about lulling his victim with fair words till the moment came to strike. Diplomacy often seems outside ordinary laws of morality. William with his few pawns found a board covered with powerful pieces arrayed against him, and doubtless his conscience did not reproach him when he resorted to spoken or acted diplomatic falsehoods. They did not stand in the way of his being a sincere and religious Calvinist, who believed thoroughly in the doctrine of predestination, and considered himself chosen to be the champion of the Protestant cause, then greatly outnumbered and oppressed by the mighty of the earth. Charles II. had no children, the Duke of York's sons had all died in their infancy, and though the Duchess of York was enceinte, the baby to be born to her might be a girl, or might follow the fate of the other children and never live

[1] "Memoirs of Sir W. Temple," vol. ii. p. 396.

to attain manhood. At any rate Mary was at present presumptive heiress to the crown of England, and England was struggling for the conservation of her liberties and religion under a King who was secretly a Roman Catholic, and with all his tact and cleverness could not hide the fact that he longed to be despotic; while the next heir had not his brother's charm or talents, and was hated for his leanings to absolutism and his bigoted Papistry. A fair vista may well have opened to William of the knitting together of the two Protestant countries of Europe as a bulwark against the Antichrist of Papacy; the only shade in this beauteous vision being cast by the fact that his wife, not he, would occupy the throne of England.

At all events, while the preliminaries for the Congress of Nimeguen were still in progress, Sir William Temple, the English Envoy and William's trusted friend, who was despatched to Holland whenever a treaty was to be made between that country and England, and was disliked by Charles as being in the Dutch interest, was sent for suddenly by William.

When Temple arrived at the Palace of Hounslaerdyck, William suggested that they should walk in the garden. There he told the Envoy that he had often been pressed to marry by his friends, that the deputies of the States every day urged him to do it, and that, though he did not wish to follow their advice till the end of the war, he had promised to think seriously of the matter, and so he had; and had determined to marry. He did not care, however, for the proposals made to him from Germany and from France. Indeed (though he did not tell Temple this), the proposal from France, which was to the effect that he should marry Louis XIV.'s beautiful natural daughter by Louise de la Vallière, had excited his utmost indignation; and he had sent back an answer which the French

King never forgave, to the effect that the Princes
of Orange did not wed with Kings' bastards.

Continuing, the Prince said that the most satisfactory proposal came from England, but that he
refused to consult Temple about this, unless he
would promise to answer, not as the English
Ambassador, but as a friend, or at any rate a private
person. Friends of his in England, he said, who
wished him and the States to head the discontents
there about the French war, which were very strong
and might lead the King to lose his crown, advised
him not to make the marriage, as it would identify
him with the Court, and thus do away with his
influence with the English people. If the Court
policy were not very radically altered, William
remarked significantly, there would soon be a great
disturbance in England. Another matter occupied
his attention, a matter it would seem extraordinary
to the world that he should show concern for. He
was determined that he would not marry unless he
liked the qualities of his future wife, particularly
her humour and disposition. He might perhaps,
he said,

"not be very easy for a wife to live with—he
was sure he should not to such wives as were generally in the Courts of this age ; that if he should
meet with one to give him trouble at home, 'twas
what he should not be able to bear, who was
like to have enough abroad in the course of his
life : and that after the manner he was resolved
to live with a wife, which should be the best he
could, he would have one that he thought likely
to live well with him, which he thought chiefly
depended on her disposition and education ; and
if I knew anything particular of the Lady Mary in
these points, he desired me to tell him freely." [1]

To this address Temple replied diplomatically
that he was very glad to hear of the Prince's resolu-

---

[1] "Memoirs of Sir W. Temple," vol. ii. p. 335.

tion, and considered that he could only do himself
good by marrying in England, while he deprecated
the idea that Charles II. could possibly be in danger
of an uprising among his subjects. As to the
Princess's disposition he could himself say nothing
about it, but he had heard both his wife and sister,
who were friends of Mary's governess, speak of it
as all that could be desired.

The Prince and Temple discussed the subject for
about two hours, and it was in the end decided that
William should write to both Charles II. and the
Duke of York on the subject, and that the despatches should be entrusted to the charming Lady
Temple, formerly Dorothy Osborne, who should be
charged with the office of endeavouring to find out
as much as possible about the young Princess.

Charles's double dealing did not alter William's
resolution ; and after Bentinck had been despatched
on a confidential mission to England, and had
arranged matters with Lord Danby, William suddenly abandoned an attempt to besiege Charleroi,
and shortly afterwards started for England. This
raising of the siege of Charleroi gave opportunity
for a bitter jest from Lord Mulgrave when William
was in England and did not leave his seat when the
Englishman paid his respects to him. " I suppose,"
said the wit, " that he can rise before nothing
less than a town ! " [1]  Diplomatic matters were
William's object as much as matrimonial, but perhaps his precipitancy, and the unusual abruptness
of his actions, showed that Lady Temple's account
of the Lady Mary had been alluring, and that for
once William remembered that he was a man, and
dreamt of love and of future snatches of domestic
happiness, sandwiched between wars, hunting,
and diplomacy.

[1] Dartmouth's note to Burnet's " History of My Own Times,"
vol. ii. p. 120.

# CHAPTER III

To understand why Charles, who hated the Dutch, and was even at this time engaged in arranging a secret treaty with France, seriously contemplated a marriage between William of Orange and his niece, we must realise the state of the English nation at the time.

Speaking of the King and his brother, Courtin, the French Envoy to England, remarked in one of his despatches to Louis XIV :

" I can answer for it to your Majesty, that there are none of your own subjects who wish you better success in all your undertakings than these two Princes do. But it is also true, that you cannot count upon any except these two friends in all England." [1]

The whole English nation hated the Dutch war and the alliance with France, and Danby, the Lord Treasurer, who had been the agent in many of Charles's shady transactions with France, and whose share in these matters had leaked out, felt that his only chance of escaping from ruin was to take some decisive action which would show his and his master's complete detachment from French interests. He was therefore doing his utmost to influence Charles in favour of the Dutch matrimonial

[1] Sir John Dalrymple's " Memoirs of Great Britain and Ireland," vol. i. p. 154.

alliance, and Charles, harassed by an unruly House
of Commons, who objected strongly to the war, and
did not seem to be suitably impressed when he
sent indignant messages, declaring that the making
of peace or of war was his own prerogative, with
which it had no right to meddle, at last yielded to
dire necessity. He did indeed dismiss the " Parliament men," as he called them, but he recognised
that the temper of the English nation was dangerous,
and to show his Protestant sympathies he summoned his nephew to England.

The Court was at Newmarket, where Charles led
a life of amusement thoroughly congenial to him,
when the Prince, according to Sir William Temple,
"like a hasty lover, came post from Harwich to
Newmarket." [1] The brilliant Court, amusing itself
with gay trifles, must have seemed a strange contrast to William's life at home, with its large and
serious interests, and its constant pressure of
anxiety. Not that Charles II. can have led a life
free from care ; but the gay temperament of the
Merry Monarch enabled him to rejoice in the
pleasure of the passing moment. While William
struggled against almost overwhelming odds for
the political existence of his country, Charles was no
patriot, and could console himself in the possession
of a dexterity which would enable him to die King of
England, whatever might happen after his decease.

Meanwhile Lord Danby strained every nerve.
His fate was quivering in the balance, and no
time was to be lost. On William's way down
the staircase to his first interview with the King,
he met the anxious statesman, conducted by Sir
William Temple, coming to visit him. Surrounded
by a dense crowd, the Prince had only opportunity
to whisper that he hoped often to meet Lord
Danby in the future, and to have much business
and conversation with him. Lord Arlington, who

---

[1] "Memoirs of Sir W. Temple," vol. ii. p. 419.

PORTRAIT OF WILLIAM III.

Reproduced by the kind permission of Dr. Krämer, Keeper of the Archives at The Hague.

had formerly considered himself the Prince's principal
friend, was intensely disgusted at being completely
ousted ; but, as Temple remarks, this " could not
be wondered at by such as knew what had passed
of late between the Prince and him ! " [1]

Meanwhile the Duke of York was furious with
Lord Danby. He sent for him as soon as he heard
that William had arrived, and told him in a passion
that he

" understood the intrigue and knew that he was
the chief manager of it, but they should be all
disappointed, for the King had promised never
to dispose of his daughters without his consent,
and that this was a match he would never agree
to. Lord Danby immediately acquainted the
King, who said it was true he had given his brother
such a promise, but, God's fish " [his usual oath],
" he *must* consent." [2]

Many difficulties were in the way, for the King
and the Duke of York were most anxious to have
a peace drawn up according to their, or rather to
French, views, and while the Duke of York, as we
have seen, loathed all idea of the proposed marriage, the King wished to hold the question in
abeyance, to be used as a bait wherewith to pur-
chase William's political docility. William, on the
other hand, always well posted in English news and
fully aware of Charles's difficulties, was conscious
of the strength of his own position. He therefore
determined to be an accepted suitor before the
political questions were discussed, that he might
not be hampered afterwards in making the best
terms he could for Holland and for his allies.

With this object in view he evaded the attempts
made by his uncles to draw him into political dis-

---

[1] "Memoirs of Sir W. Temple," vol. ii. p. 420.
[2] Dartmouth's note to Burnet's "History of My Own Times,"
vol. ii. p. 120.

cussion, and said that he wished first to see the young Princess.   The King, affecting blindness to the diplomatic bearing of the move, laughed at the Prince's wish as an instance of a lover's impatience. He consented, however, to leave Newmarket a few days earlier than he had intended, that William might the sooner make the acquaintance of the Lady Mary, who was in London. History is silent as to the occasion on which William saw his bride for the first time, but it is certain that no hint of the character of suitor in which he presented himself was whispered to her, and she evidently received him with her natural vivacity, and with a gaiety which he would not see again for some time.

Mary was then fifteen years old, and was a woman who matured very slowly ; so that she was unusually young for her age.  She was essentially a Stuart in physique, having the oval face characteristic of her race, almond-shaped eyes with rather drooping eyelids, a characteristic which she shared with her husband, a well-shaped nose, a prettily rounded chin, and a delicate complexion. Later, she wore her hair raised on a cushion, a style which does not suit her face so well as do the curls on each side of the face and on her forehead, with which she is represented in her early portraits.  She was extremely graceful and was a beautiful dancer.   Under the discipline of William's often expressed displeasure, she developed much prudence and discretion, but, in striking contrast to her husband, she was always a great talker, and we can gather, from hints given by different chroniclers, that she was at this time a rather naïve person, who said what occurred to her, and made no effort to conceal her feelings.

Brought up in an atmosphere of trifles, with her childish sentimental friendships, her delight in dancing and in gaiety, and her absolute ignorance of the world, she was the antipodes to her serious, taciturn suitor, whose mind was so occupied with great aims that he despised the little amenities which soften and adorn life; while his bad health and overburdened condition had the effect of making him moody, ungenial, and dry in manner. However, even in this interview the acute observer could discern in her that sweetness of disposition which he considered the chief requisite in a wife, and we are told that he was " so pleased with her person, and all those signs of such a humour as had been described to him upon former inquiries, that he immediately made his suit to the King and the Duke ! " [1]

Charles and the Duke of York, however, being no doubt quite aware of the impression the beautiful Lady Mary had made on her cousin, thought she would be a valuable lever to bend William to their will, and kept firmly to the point that discussion of the marriage must be preceded by a settlement of the terms of peace. William was equally determined in declaring that the marriage question must be settled first, and independently of the other, for if he were to submit to his uncles, the Allies, who would at the best have to be contented with a bad bargain, would consider that he had made this match at their cost. He " would never," he said, " sell his honour for a wife." [1] As the King still refused to give in, Lord Danby felt in despair about bringing the negotiations to a happy termination; and it was in vain that the Prince paid a special visit to the Duke of York to speak of his desire of marrying his daughter, for the Duke kept firmly to his position, and said the peace must be arranged before the marriage !

The negotiations seemed at an end, for both parties were obstinate; but the same day an unexpected ultimatum on William's part made a sudden change in the situation. Sir William

[1] " Memoirs of Sir W. Temple," vol. ii. p. 420.

Temple visited him after supper, and found him in the worst possible humour. He wished, he said, that he had never come to England, and would like to remind Charles that he had in the past received appeals from many of his discontented subjects, and to warn him that if he were allowed to go unsatisfied now, he would become the King's bitterest enemy.

This menace, which seemed a counterblast to the words which had roused William's bitter anger when used by Arlington to him, he requested Temple to convey at once to Charles. In the meantime Danby had been busily at work, and had collected—or pretended to collect, as he knew well the King would never trouble to read them —a number of letters written, he said, by the King's best friends in England counselling the marriage. He reinforced the production of a large bundle of them by all the arguments for the marriage he could muster.

"'The Prince,' objected the King, 'has not so much as proposed it.'

"The Lord Danby reply'd : ' He has spoke of it only to me, because he apprehended he shou'd not succeed in it.'

"' My Brother,' replyed His Majesty, ' will never consent to it.'

"'Maybe not,' says Lord Danby, 'unless you take upon you to command it, and I think it is the Duke's Interest to have it done more than Your Majesty's. All people are now possess'd of his being a Papist, and are very apprehensive of it, but if they see his Daughter given to one who is at the head of the Protestant Party it will very much soften those Apprehensions, when it appears that his Religion is only a personal Thing, not to be deriv'd to his Children after him.'"[1]

These arguments no doubt helped to prepare the King for Temple's final attack. In the vicissitudes

[1] Oldmixon's "History of the Stuarts," vol. ii. p. 605.

of a money-getting career Charles had become inured to insults, and he wisely considered that, in the disturbed state of England, William of Orange in a state of open hostility would be a source of the utmost danger to his crown. When therefore he received the Prince's message, possibly softened in its passage by the diplomatic Temple, instead of expressing indignation at its insolence, he remarked blandly that he had never yet been deceived in judging a man's honesty by his look, and that if he were not deceived in the Prince's face, he was "the honestest man in the world." "I will trust him," he went on, "and he shall have his wife, and you shall go immediately and tell my brother so, and that it is a thing I am resolved on." [1]

The Duke, who was in reality furious at this change in Charles's plans, and considered with justice that he should have been the first person to be informed of it, mastered his feelings sufficiently to show nothing more than surprise at this most unwelcome intimation. Having recovered himself, he improved the occasion by saying:

"The King shall be obeyed, and I would be glad all his subjects would learn of me to obey him: I do tell him my opinion very freely on anything; but when that is done, and I know his pleasure upon it, I obey him."

Charles then sent for the Prince, and at the same time ordered a Council to be called, so that the matter should be clinched before the French party should have time to interfere. "Nephew," he said, "it is not good for man to be alone, I will give you a helpmeet for you." The Duke of York was obliged to feign cordiality, and the King gave a little hint to the Prince in the words, "Remember that love and war do not agree very well together." [2]

---

[1] "Memoirs of Sir W. Temple," vol. ii. p. 421.
[2] Oldmixon's "History of the Stuarts," vol. ii. p. 605.

It must have been with a heavy heart that the Duke of York prepared himself to break to his daughter the news of the marriage arranged for her. On October 21 he dined at Whitehall; and after dinner went to St. James's Palace and took the Princess into her private room. Nothing is known of what passed at the interview, so it is impossible to tell whether the Duke had enough self-control and affection for his daughter to put the best face on the matter and to paint her future in glowing terms, or whether he gave vent to the disgust and indignation which filled his heart. At any rate, she was in the depths of despair at the announcement, and wept all that afternoon and the following day. She was only a child, and she had evidently not taken a fancy to her cousin; indeed, the serious, sickly looking young man was hardly likely to be attractive to a gay, lively girl of fifteen. Then, too, he belonged to the hated Dutch nation with whom the English were generally at war, and on whom the King had doubtless often expended his wit, and her father poured the diatribes of his wrath in her hearing—that dull, snivelling nation of psalm-singers, the very antipodes of all that was gay, amusing, and to her taste. The poor child wept too at having to leave England and all her friends, among them the "dear husban" and the darling sister from whom she had hardly ever been separated. Colonel Bathurst considers that the following letter was most probably written at this time, but as, like all the other effusions to the "dear husban" it is undated, this cannot be proved.

"For Mrs. Apsley

"If you do not come to me some time dear husban that I may have my bely full of discourse with you I shall take it very ill. If you can before you go to dinner when you come from Mr. Lily for

I have a great deal to say to you concerning I do
not know how now to set in the letter.  If you can
you will mightyly oblige your faithful wife,

"MARY CLORIN.

"I have wright it in such a heand that I believe you
canot read it, pray burn it and send word whether
you can or no by the berer."[1]

Meanwhile intrigues were already on foot to
stop the marriage ;  and Danby was obliged to
exert all his energy to prevent this catastrophe.
Barillon, the French Ambassador, was horrified and
amazed at the news, and claimed the help of the
Duchess of Portsmouth, who as Mlle. de la Querouaille,
had been left in England by the Duchess of Orleans
at the time of the Treaty of Dover, to influence
Charles in the French interest.

Danby, however, at once called together the
Council at which the news of the marriage was
to be announced, and at this the Duke of York
declared that he hoped he had now given sufficient
proof of the honesty of his intentions for the public
good, and " that people would no longer say that
he wished to change the government of the Church
or State ! "[2] We are told elsewhere that he
promised that he would " never hinder but that
his children should be educated in the religion of
the Church of England "[3]; but it is noticeable that
James, who was doubtless rather ashamed of this
pledge, does not mention it in his memoirs.  After
the sitting of the Council the Prince was presented
as her husband to the Lady Mary—who must still
have had red eyes, from her day spent in tears.
Therefore, though Louis XIV., who received the
news, " as he would have done the loss of an

---

[1] Bathurst Collection: "Quarterly Review," January, 1911.
[2] "Mémoires de Jacques II.," vol. ii. p. 203.
[3] "Camden Miscellany," vol. i.—"Dr. Lake's Diary."

army,"[1] stopped his allowance to Charles II. and
entered into intrigues to rouse the popular party
in England against him, though James wrote an
apologetic letter to Louis XIV.'s confessor, saying
that the marriage had been made against his will,
and Lord Arlington sulked because he had not been
called in to assist at the affair, nothing could now
be done to stop the marriage.

On October 22 the Council came in a body to
congratulate the Princess, and the Lord Chancellor
Finch—the future Lord Nottingham—made her
a congratulatory speech. The Lord Mayor and
the Aldermen followed their example. Then came
deputations from the Judges, the members of
Doctors' Commons, and the African Company.
In fact, till her marriage on November 4, 1677, the
Princess lived in an atmosphere of deputations,
addresses, and festivities, which had at least the
merciful effect of preventing her from thinking of
the dreaded future.

The festivities in the City were curtailed owing
to the indignation felt by the good London burghers
at the fact that the trousseau was provided in
Paris. Nevertheless, bonfires were lit, and bells
were rung in celebration of the expected happy
event, which relieved the minds of the English from
the dread of Popery.

On October 29 the Lord Mayor sent " a Solemn
invitation to the Prince and the whole Court."[2]
To celebrate the occasion "the Mayor, Sheriff,
Aldermen, and City Companies went in Barges
covered with green and blue, and adorned with
banners bearing the arms of their different Companies, to Westminster Hall. Then, with the Ar-
tillery, and the Marshal of the town," they proceeded
to the Guildhall, where a free dinner was given,
at which the King, the Duke of York, the Prince

---

[1] Burnet's " History of My Own Times," vol. ii. p. 124.
[2] Echard's " History of England," vol. iii. p. 433.

of Orange, and the Ladies Mary and Anne were present. A Frenchman who was at the feast expresses amazement at English plenty and profusion, and remarks enthusiastically: "If I were to describe to you the number of the dishes, and how they were raised one above the other in pyramids, as also the amount of venison and of pies, it would seem incredible to you." [1] The wealth and magnificence of the City magnates—who, after all, were only "bourgeois"—specially astonished the Frenchman. He relates with a touch of awe that the King of England had three "bourgeois"—we wonder how the sturdy and independent burgesses would have approved of being described as chattels of the Sovereign—who surpassed in their households all the other bourgeois of the earth. These were the Lord Mayor, and the two Sheriffs of London, "at whose tables there are generally four venison pies, a great piece of roast beef, and twenty or thirty other dishes filled with exquisite meats." This inventory, he adds, does not include the dessert.

The formality of receiving the approbation of the States-General to the alliance had to be waited for; but as soon as this arrived, there was nothing else to cause delay, and the marriage was performed in the Princess's own rooms at nine o'clock at night on Sunday, November 4. The Archbishop of Canterbury was very ill at the time, so the ceremony was performed by Mary's governor, the Bishop of London. Lady Frances Villiers was suffering from smallpox and was in a dangerous condition, and several of the spectators of the wedding must have been feeling ill, a fact which cannot have added to their liveliness. The Princess Anne was sickening for smallpox, and her miserable physical feelings must have added to her grief at the prospect

[1] "Relation Véritable du Voyage de son Altesse le Prince d'Orange en Angleterre," p. 48.

of losing her sister. The Duchess of York was confined two days afterwards, and in her condition must have felt it difficult to hide her grief at the departure of the stepdaughter, to whom she had always been a playfellow; while to James the marriage performed against his will was gall and wormwood.

Charles II., with that kindly tact which was one of his good qualities, felt it necessary to exert himself to cheer the weeping bride and to lighten the general gloom, and we are told that he was " very pleasant all the while ! " [1] Jocose interruptions to the marriage ceremony were evidently quite allowable, at any rate in a King, as our informant, the Princess's chaplain, did not apparently see anything irreverent in them. When Charles gave his niece away, he remarked with a sly hit at the bridegroom that he hoped the Bishop of London would make haste, lest the Duchess of York should be delivered of a son, and the marriage never come off ; and on the Prince endowing his bride with all his worldly goods, he told her to put the money in her pocket as it was all clear gain. When the young pair retired to bed at eleven o'clock and Charles drew the curtains round them, he did not leave them without a jest.

On the morning of the next day Bentinck was sent by the Prince with a present for the Princess of jewels to the value of £40,000. To feel that the marriage was safely accomplished and he free to turn his mind to political matters, must have given the bridegroom deep satisfaction. Three days later, however, an event took place which certainly marred his pleasure, though to the Duke of York it no doubt gave extreme joy and relief. At nine o'clock in the evening of November 7 the Duchess of York was safely delivered of a son, and Mary was no longer presumptive heiress to the

[1] "Camden Miscellany," vol. i.—" Dr. Lake's Diary."

English crown. "The child is little, but sprightly and likely to live," says Dr. Lake. The next day William was obliged to be joint sponsor with the King to the unwelcome arrival, Lady Frances Villiers taking the part of godmother as proxy for the Lady Isabella, the infant's eldest sister, who was still a baby herself.

The marriage once over, grave consultations took place between the English royal brothers and William of Orange, on the conditions of the peace. Danby and Temple were also present, and the latter has left in his memoirs an account of the proceedings. The matter was of extreme difficulty, the aims of the two parties seeming absolutely incompatible. William insisted on the importance of a strong frontier being made round Flanders to bar the encroachments of Louis XIV., who, once master of Flanders, would have Holland at his mercy. He refused to move from this position, though Charles tried to conciliate him by promising that his own lands should be as safe under France as under Spain. In the end Charles gave in, or pretended to give in, to William's terms, and sent Lord Duras, in place of Temple, who had at first been mentioned, as Ambassador to Paris, to persuade Louis XIV. to accept them.

Meanwhile the Prince was proving himself but an indifferent lover, and the Princess was extremely unhappy. A dispute had taken place between them in which William seems to have been in the right, though he evidently expressed his views without gentleness or consideration. The Princess, however, yet unbroken by the mixture of love and fear which was in the future to make her absolutely in subjection to her husband, did not scruple to refuse obedience to him. Her sister Anne, to whom at this period of her life she was extremely devoted, was seriously ill with smallpox at St. James's Palace, and William, who had, as we know, had sinister experience of the malady, was very anxious that Mary should move to Whitehall to avoid infection. Mary, however, like a wayward and miserable child who clings to home heedless of all other considerations, and to whom this move seemed no doubt the beginning of the end, refused to leave St. James's Palace.

Dr. Lake, Archdeacon of Exeter and rector of two City parishes, who had been for several years chaplain to both Princesses, tells us this, and does not scruple to add that he used his farewell interview with the Princess in the endeavour to persuade her to grant him preferment.

"I appeal'd to her highnesse to this purpose" [says the worthy Chaplain], "that I had the honour frequently to retire with her into her closet, but did call God to witnesse that I never said there or elsewhere anything contrary to the holy Scriptures, or the doctrine or discipline of the Church of England, and I did hope the things I had instructed her in might still remain with her; that I had been with her seven years, and no person who hath lived so long at Court but did make a far greater advantage of his time than I have don, having gotten but £100 a year, wherefore I did humbly request her highnesse, that at her departure she would recommend me to the king, duke, and the Bishop of London."

If the Princess did this, Dr. Lake would "endeavour to requite the favour by being very carefull of the right principling and instruction of her sister the Lady Anne, of whom I had already all possible assurances that she would bee very good!"[1] a promise which implies a condition hardly redounding to the credit of the worthy chaplain, and we cannot feel very sorry that he never obtained preferment.

In her answer the unfortunate Princess thanked

[1] "Camden Miscellany," vol. i.—"Dr. Lake's Diary."

Dr. Lake for all his kindness to her and promised to do all she could for him, " but was able to say no more for weeping, so turned her back and went into her closet." Doubtless her continual sorrow at the idea of leaving England, combined with her disregard of his wishes, irritated the Prince; possibly he visited on her the anger with which the slippery dealing of Charles over the negotiations must have filled an acute and well-informed observer such as he. However that may be, it is certain that at a time when common humanity would have dictated a little kindliness towards the helpless girl, who was about to leave home and friends, to be completely under his power, the Prince behaved with an unkindness which almost amounted to brutality.

It was settled that the Prince and Princess should sail for Holland on November 16. The 15th was Catherine of Braganza's birthday; and a ball was held to celebrate the occasion, at which the Princess appeared in all her jewels. It had been specially arranged that this should finish early, so that she should not be overtired for her journey next day. Not once did the Prince of Orange speak to the Princess at the ball, he paid no attention to her when they went to the play together, nor had he visited her at St. James's Palace on what was supposed to be her last day in England. The Court began to whisper about his " sullenness or clownishness." [1] At eight o'clock the ball was over, and the royal family bade farewell to Mary, as her start was to take place early next morning. However, the weather was so unfavourable, that the King persuaded his nephew to put off the journey. This the Prince did with the utmost reluctance, and he announced that he would go on Monday the 19th, even if it were only just possible for the boat to keep on its way! So

[1] " Camden Miscellany," vol. i.—" Dr. Lake's Diary."

anxious was he to return to Holland ; or at any rate to quit the uncongenial atmosphere of the English Court.

There were certainly, as Dr. Lake remarks,[1] "many unlucky circumstances which did seem to retard and to embitter the departure." The Princess Anne was still seriously ill, and it was impossible for the sisters to meet; while the death of Lady Frances Villiers, Mary's trusted friend and governess, seemed of terrible omen for Anne's recovery. Who could tell whether Mary would ever see her beloved sister again ? Several of the girls in her suite must have been as sorrowful as she. The Villiers sisters had lost their mother only a few days earlier, and were leaving their father behind ; Anne Trelawny's father and uncle were both seriously ill; the father of Mary's nurse, Mrs. Hemlock, was just dead ; while Mr. White, a gentleman who was to have been in attendance on her, was left behind seriously ill.

However, William must be obeyed. On Monday the 19th the wind had changed to the west ; and at nine o'clock the Prince and Princess, accompanied by the King, the Duke of York, and the Duke of Monmouth, took barges at Whitehall and went down the river. The Princess wept bitterly all the morning. She left two letters to be given to the Princess Anne on her recovery ; and begged the Duchess of Monmouth, to whom she was much attached, to think of her often, and to accompany her sister to chapel when she was sufficiently recovered to be able to go for the first time. When she took leave of Catherine of Braganza, the Queen tried to console her by saying she was at least better off than herself, who, when she came to England, had never seen even the King. Mary, however, who no doubt did not consider her present knowledge of her husband a reassuring experience, was

[1] "Camden Miscellany," vol. i.—"Dr. Lake's Diary."

prompt with her answer. " But, Madam," she answered, " you came into England, but I am going out of England " ! and the Queen could think of no rejoinder.

The royal party dined at Erith, where the Prince and Princess, accompanied by the King and Duke of York, went on board the yacht *Mary*, which was to convey them to Holland. Mary's father and uncle accompanied her till they were in sight of Gravesend and returned to Erith so late that it was only just possible to reach London that night.

The Duke of York no doubt said farewell to his daughter with gloomy prognostications, as, in addition to his dislike of the marriage for political and religious reasons, he must have felt grave misgivings as to the likelihood of her finding happiness in her married life.

The Prince and Princess had not even now left England finally, for before their departure an incident occurred of which much political capital on either side has been made, and which has been related in various ways according to the bias of the writers. It seems, however, easy to account for the occurrence without blaming either the King for turning his nephew and niece out of the kingdom hurriedly, and in a penniless condition, or charging the Prince of Orange with the sinister design of ingratiating himself with the English people to the detriment of his uncles.

Apparently, when the yacht arrived at Sheerness, the weather was so bad that all the ladies except the Princess were ill, and the King sent to beg the Prince to return to London. Though William was determined not to do this, and was most anxious to proceed on his journey, the English captain strongly dissuaded him against attempting to cross while the wind was contrary. On November 22 the Prince and Princess therefore landed at Sheerness, and, having spent the night at the house of

Colonel Dorrel, the Governor, they went on to Canterbury next day, the Princess being accompanied by Lady Inchiquin, and one of her dressers, and the Prince by Bentinck, Odyck, and Horn.

Not having calculated on the delay in their journey, the royal party had not enough money to supply their necessities, and Bentinck was sent to see whether he could borrow plate and money from the Corporation for their use. This body was, for some mysterious reason, afraid to lend anything, and the travellers would have fared badly had not Dr. Tillotson, then Dean of Canterbury, collected all his own plate, and borrowed money, which he presented to them.

They stayed in Canterbury from Friday, November 23, till Monday the 26th, all the gentlemen in the country round flocking into the city to pay their respects to the Prince, and to offer provisions for his table. On Sunday he—and we will suppose the Princess, though she does not seem worthy of mention in the account from which we cite— attended a service and a sermon at the Cathedral, and on Monday morning the royal party embarked at Margate on the *Montagu*, commanded by Sir John Holmes. Two days later the yacht set sail, and on Thursday, November 29, landed her passengers at Teyheyde, on the coast of Holland, two hours' drive from Scheveling.

JAMES II.

From a portrait by Kneller.   By permission of the Trustees of the National
Portrait Gallery.

# CHAPTER IV

THE Prince and Princess made a quick voyage,
but it was impossible for them to go up the Maes
because of the quantity of ice encumbering the
river, and they therefore landed at Terheyde, a
village on the Dutch coast, and drove from there in
about two hours to the Hounslaerdyke Palace.
The States sent the Hoffmaester to Hounslaerdyke
to compliment the Prince and Princess on their
arrival, and the royal party went incognito to
see The Hague.

On December 14, 1667, the State entrance to
the capital was made, and the whole road from
there to Hounslaerdyke was crowded with people
waiting to see the procession. It was suitably
magnificent, for though William was obliged by the
condition of his finances to be generally extremely
economical, he was fully aware of the necessity
of keeping up the prestige of the Orange family as
representative of the wealth and importance of
Holland.

The Princess entered The Hague seated in a
coach drawn by eight skewbald horses, with Lady
Inchiquin, the eldest of the Villiers sisters, seated
beside her. Lady Inchiquin, it may be noted,
held the post of head of the Princess's maids of

honour, and to her was confided the duty of paying the salaries of the other ladies.

The bridge at The Hague was decorated with green garlands, and with words which our informant translates thus :

> "Live Sacred Worthy, blest in that rich Bed,
> At once thy Mary and thy Belgia wed,
> And long, long live thy fair Brittanick Bride,
> Her Orange and her Country's equal Pride." [1]

Twelve companies of burghers with their ensigns were drawn up at the bridge to welcome the happy pair, and through the town twenty-four young girls walked on either side of Mary's coach, singing and strewing herbs. At the town-hall the carriages passed through a triumphal arch, made of foliage surmounted by grotesques, and bearing the arms of their Highnesses, and at Hoogstraat another triumphal arch had been erected. In the evening elaborate fireworks were shown in the town, and excited much admiration among the people.

There were three palaces at The Hague—the one known as The Hague, which looked out on the Vivier, or fish-preserve, a piece of water in the middle of the city; the dower-house called the Old Court, which was a little way out of The Hague, and the palace known as "The House in the Wood," which was the Princess's chief residence during her life in Holland.

This palace, in which William of Orange had spent his childhood, is about a mile from The Hague, and was built by Amalia, William's grandmother, in 1647, in memory of her husband, the Prince Stadtholder Frederick Henry. It was in the midst of a forest of oak-trees, and was surrounded by beautiful gardens. A wing had been added on either side by William to make it large enough for the accommodation of the Princess and her suite.

[1] "Life of Mary II.," 1695.

In the time of William and Mary the house faced down a long avenue, with an open space in front, in which a statue of Frederick Henry was the most prominent object.

The principal and most noteworthy room in the palace is the domed ball-room, which is covered with paintings. In the very top of the dome, and thus surmounting the whole erection, is a portrait of Amalia von Solms by Vandyck, and all round are pictures representing her life, and that of her husband. The birth of Frederick Henry is depicted, with his father, William the Silent, looking on, and the precocious baby trying to seize his father's spear. Frederick Henry's marriage to Amalia fills another panel, where, clad in full panoply of armour and seated on a big white Flemish horse, he raises his bride, who kneels meekly on the ground, but nevertheless does not forget her claims to consideration, for Cupids bear behind her the many coats of arms which prove her high lineage. A huge fresco by Jourdaens, occupying the whole of one side of the ball-room, represents what his widow evidently considered the crowning achievement in Frederick Henry's life—the taking of 's Hertogenberg. The conqueror is here represented in a magnificent triumphal car, drawn by four prancing white steeds, and surrounded by a crowd of figures emblematic of victory. His son, William II., rides beside his chariot, and a statue of William the Silent looks down upon the restless scene.

A picture hard by of Charles I., who is evidently drawn from imagination and is represented as trampling on anarchy, has not the merit of historical accuracy any more than that of correct portraiture. The room must have given Mary a sense of home, for above her head was the delineation of the marriage of an English Princess—another Mary, her aunt—to William's father, with the nine

provinces as unclad children dancing in joy at the
union; while in a much smaller panel close at hand
the marriage of William II.'s sister to the Great
Elector of Brandenburg is depicted. In a later
scene Amalia and her four daughters weep beside
Frederick Henry's tomb, it being noteworthy
that her son William II., with whom she had
quarrelled, was not considered worthy of a share
in his mother's and sisters' sorrow.

Amalia had died not very long before William
and Mary's wedding, and we may fancy that the
wise old grandmother might have been of some
help and comfort to the young wife in her early
married troubles.

Several of the Princess's maids of honour were
destined to cause her distress and anxiety. Of the
Villiers sisters, one of whom poisoned the whole of
Mary's married life, we shall often hear. Jane Wroth,
daughter of Sir Henry Wroth of Durrants, Enfield,
would also give her trouble; while many tears
were caused her when, indirectly owing to Elizabeth
Villiers, she was forced to part with Anne Trelawney, who had certainly been indiscreet, though
her indiscretion may have proceeded from affection for her mistress. Anne, who had been
brought up with the Princess, was daughter of Sir
Jonathan Trelawney, and sister to the Trelawney
famous as one of the Seven Bishops imprisoned
by James II.

Mary seems from the first to have endeared herself to the Dutch people by her kindly politeness
to the burgomasters' wives who came to see her,[1]
while every one was struck by her gentleness, sweetness, and obedience to her husband. She for her
part soon loved her adopted country. She admired
the simplicity of the Dutch people, and their
frugality, which caused them, according to Sir

---

[1] "Life of Mary II.," 1695.

William Temple, to think it as much a disgrace to
live up to their incomes as people in other countries
would consider it to live in "vicious or prodigal
extravagance." [1] She was also much struck by
their extreme cleanliness, which is impressed upon
us with so much reiteration by contemporary
writers that it gives an unpleasant idea of the
extreme dirtiness of the English at that time.
Certainly if William wished to be popular, he
could not have chosen a wife more adapted to
assist him in his design.

At first the Princess's time was fully occupied
with receptions, formalities, and festivities ; but
she managed, three days after her arrival, to write
the following letter to show Miss Apsley she was
not forgotten :

> "HAGUE,
> "*December the* 17.

"I am very much ashamed that my dearest husban should ritt to me first for tho there coud not
be a greater plesure in the world to me yett it was
my dutty as wife to have ritt first and I hope you
will be so kind to me to belive it was for want of
time for you may imagin that not being well
setled and haveing a great deal of company perpetually so taks up my time that I was fain to
rise this morning before day to ritt some few letters
of which yours was the first that was ritt I have
but one thing to troble you with to remember me
to your sister Apsley and lett my lady Wentworth
know I would have ritt to her my self to have
thankt her for her news book but that I have not
time so desire you to do it for me. I am willing
to ritt a littell to as many of my friends as I can
therefore you will excuse me if I do not say much
to you whome I love like my own life and do not

---

[1] "Memoirs of Sir W. Temple," vol. i. p. 158.

think my love is so wake that crosing the sea will put it out be but just to me and love me with all your heart and I shall ever be your kind loving wife.

" MARY CLORIN.

" you se tho I 'have another husban I keep the name of my first." [1]

Under the circumstances there is something pathetic in the cry of the lonely girl to her " first husban " to be " just to me and to love me with all your heart," for it is very evident that she was not receiving either justice or love from William of Orange.

His behaviour to his young wife in England is perhaps explicable by the fact that he visited on her his wrath at her father's and uncle's delinquencies, but his continued disregard and even unkindness in Holland can only be traced to the fact that he had fallen under influence which caused him to consider his girl-wife insipid and uninteresting.

The Villiers sisters were rather older than Mary, and were evidently years more advanced than she in worldly knowledge, and Elizabeth was at once marked out by the Prince of Orange for special attention. Elizabeth was not good-looking—in fact an uncomplimentary witness, after speaking with enthusiasm of the Princess's beautiful white complexion, well-proportioned nose, white teeth, red lips, fine neck and figure, and gentle, dignified movements, remarks that it is difficult to see what there was to inspire love in Elizabeth Villiers's " squinting eyes, crooked body, and indifferent complexion." A tolerably good figure—which it

[1] Bathurst Collection: "Quarterly Review," January, 1911— "Letters of Queen Mary II."

is puzzling to reconcile with the " crooked body "
he has just mentioned, and a white and well-shaped
neck, are the only beauties this critic will allow
her. In his eyes William's infatuation for her is
a striking example of the truth of the proverb
that " Love is blind," but evidently the state of
affairs is explained by the last sentence in his
description, where he remarks in a perfunctory
manner, " Her mind was tolerably quick and
subtle." [1] Elizabeth was evidently extremely
clever, and a good talker, and William loved to
discuss political matters with her.

Swift, who says that she " squinted like a dra-
goon," [2] was, in her old age, very fond of her society,
and talks of sitting with her alone from two till
eleven at night. Elsewhere he says : " She is the
wisest woman I ever saw ; and lord-treasurer
made great use of her advice in the late change of
affairs." [3] What chance had the poor Princess,
who evidently developed slowly, and was very
childish at the time of her marriage, against an
exceptionally clever, lively girl ?

Mary, too, was very sensitive and timid, and was
handicapped by fear of her husband, a fear which
did not leave her even when she had become passionately attached to him. When he chid her, she
wept, and his chidings were frequent. She was
in a minority, for there were generally three Villiers
sisters at her Court, and when Anne Villiers, who
was also on terms of great intimacy with William,
married Bentinck, William's greatest friend, the
Princess must have felt absolutely alone.

Anne Villiers appears to have been very different
from her sister Elizabeth, for a contemporary, who
had good opportunity for judging, calls her a

---

[1] "Mémoires de Monsieur de B.," " cornette " to Bentinck, who
is identified with Daniel de Bourdon.

[2] Journal to Stella, October 28, 1712.

[3] *Ibid.*, September 15, 1712.

"woman of virtue and merit," and on a later
occasion she and her husband dared to espouse the
Princess's cause against William, and in consequence
were for a time in disgrace.[1]

However, in these early days of the Princess's
married life, though she suffered much from
William's neglect, it seems unlikely that she had
any certain information of his infidelity. The
fact that later James almost succeeded in bringing
about a separation between her and her husband
by informing her of it, certainly favours this
supposition, and while it was to the interest of
most of those who surrounded her to keep the
matter secret, it was certainly to no one's advantage to rouse William's wrath by revealing it.

William's affection for Bentinck and unhappiness
when parted from him find constant expression in
his letters. After Bentinck had married Anne
Villiers, who seems to have suffered from extremely
bad health all her married life, William's solicitude
was intense, and appears extraordinary in one
who often seemed so much taken up with the
ambitions and cares of life that he had little opportunity for its affections.

"I write to you with a tear of joy because I
find by your letter that your wife is better."[2]
"It is impossible to express to you with what grief
I quitted you this morning. I cannot live without
you. If ever I have felt that I loved you, it is
to-day. I conjure you to return as soon as your
wife is out of danger."[3]

Such remarks occur continually in the letters of
William to Bentinck, and the combination of
mistress, friend, and friend's wife was too much for
Mary. She was hopelessly outnumbered, cast into
the shade, and neglected. During her troubles

---

[1] "Mémoires de Monsieur de B."
[2] Letter, Welbeck Library, August 5, 1679,
[3] Ibid., September 6, 1679,

her intellect developed quickly, though she was too timid to reveal her mind at this time to William, and he did not realise till much later that he had married a woman who, owing to his want of sympathy, had never shown him the best that was in her.

The Princess had many admirers and sympathisers among the men and women forming her little Court, though from the circumstances of the case they were powerless to help her, and she was most probably unaware of their indignation when she was treated harshly or neglected by William. Sir Gabriel Sylvius, William's chamberlain, was among those who were indignant at his treatment of his wife. Sir Gabriel had married a Miss Howard, many years younger than himself, a friend of the virtuous Mrs. Godolphin, whose early death caused much grief to her friends. Evelyn, who was one of the most devoted among them, had joined with her in helping Sir Gabriel with his love-affairs, "out of pity for the languishing knight"; and the differences with the young lady's mother, "old Mrs. Howard," being at last arranged through the joint agency of Evelyn and Mrs. Godolphin, the marriage was successfully brought about.

Sir Gabriel, who had latinised his former surname of Wood [1] in the interests of diplomatic dignity, blamed the Prince bitterly for his marital deficiencies. William in fact does not seem to have possessed the knack of inspiring affection in those immediately surrounding him, and most of the English at The Hague appear to have disliked him extremely. It is therefore curious to note that the one person who grew fond of him was his neglected wife. His domination over her was absolute, and though he ruled to a great extent by fear, Mary became so much attached to him

[1] Plumptre's "Life of Ken," vol. i. note to p. 137,

that the whole world counted for nothing in her
eyes beside the slightest manifestation of his will.
Occasionally, her affection seems servile, but, though
childish at this time, she was never stupid ; and
she soon understood her husband as most of her
compatriots never did. There is something admirable in the sweetness of a nature which could
look beyond slights, unkindness, and just causes
for offence, and love William—as she undoubtedly
did—for what he was, for his high aims, his knowledge of men, and his unflinching determination
to act on them, in spite of physical infirmities
which must have made his life a martyrdom.

The glimpses we have of the Princess during her
early married life do not show us the husband and
wife as sharing in the least in the same pursuits.
On the pretext that the State officers often came
to eat at William's table, and that it was not
suitable for her to receive them, the Princess did
not even have her meals with her husband. In
fact, Mary seldom apparently, saw William, except
when chidden by him, and spent her time playing
hide-and-seek with her ladies in the woods round
"The House in the Wood," working, or playing
at cards.

"There is, perhaps, no example on earth of a
Princess of her age who passes her life in a life so
narrow, so innocent, and so deprived of worldly
pleasures." [1] Nevertheless, the Princess, when
seated on the throne, often looked back with regret
on the simple amusements at The Hague. Though
she was nearly always shut up with her attendants,
and was not allowed to receive even The Hague
ladies without William's special permission, she
had many occupations, for she read aloud, painted
miniatures, an art in which we are told that she
excelled, and played on different instruments.

She had too a good deal of fun with her maids

---

[1] Lamberty's "English Revolution," vol. i. p. 207.

of honour, " having mad times," she calls it, though
she was particular to exclude unsuitable jokes,
as her chaplain records with approval. She, who
showed later in her life that she was capable of
great affairs, developed slowly ; besides, she was
treated like a child, and kept completely out of the
serious matters which made up her husband's life.
Possibly he may have discussed certain aspects of
these with Elizabeth Villiers—at any rate, he only
visited his wife's apartments at supper-time, and
then he was tired and expected her to entertain
him. Her other amusements seem to have been
gardening, and taking long walks, though, according
to d'Avaux, the French Ambassador, for about two
years, when William was afraid that James would
obtain influence over her, she was practically a
prisoner. At other times, however, we hear of
her making expeditions to Amsterdam for shop-
ping, where she was generally disappointed at the
want of opportunities for laying out her money
to advantage compared with those in London.
Her correspondence with her " dearest dearest
dearest Aurelia "—it is impossible to count the
" dearests "—continued, and among the sentimental
verbiage in which it abounds, occur passionate expressions in which what the French call the *cri de
cœur* makes itself heard. These prove, I think, that
Mary's affections were not satisfied, and that she
felt her husband's neglect deeply, though she was
too proud and reserved to show her feelings even
to her most intimate friends. Later, when Miss
Apsley married Sir Benjamin Bathurst, the tone of
the letters changes, the sentimentalities disappear,
and the Princess appears as a very cordial correspondent, who entrusts many commissions to her
friend in England.

This change did not take place, however, till
some years after the time we are considering, when
a letter to her " dear husban " addressed from

Goest Dyck, contains a rather pathetic passage in which Mary apologises for not having answered a letter from her correspondent's mother sooner, " but then I was so sleepy and now am just going to catch rabits. My whole time heer has been taken up since I am come with such sort of devertions for this place affords no other." [1] Occasionally the Princess played cards on Sunday, at the news of which delinquency her late chaplain, Dr. Lake, was much shocked—not, apparently, because he considered it wrong to do this, but because the Dutch were strict, and Sabbath-breaking " would doubtless give offence to that people." [2]

A few weeks later Dr. Lake, was even more troubled by the news that the Princess, who " was grown somewhat fat and very beautiful withal," was sometimes going, by the connivance of Dr. Lloyd—whom he detested as his supplanter—to worship with the English congregation at The Hague.

" This church is served by a nonconformist Minister out of England, and maintained by the States to draw people thither for the increase of their trade. Nor would Dr. Brown suffer the late princesse royale to be drawn thither, though in the worst of times, when there was hardly any trace of a church of England."

Of this unorthodox Dr. Lloyd it is related that, when in 1658 he held the post of private tutor at Oxford, he persuaded a London merchant to personate a patriarch named Jeremias, who was supposed to have come from some far-off Eastern Church to confer with Oxford theologians on the reform of his Church. Great was the sensation at the University; and the grave stranger with long hair and beard was received with the utmost

[1] Bathurst Collection: " Quarterly Review," January, 1911— "Letters of Queen Mary II."
[2] " Camden Miscellany," vol. i—" Dr. Lake's Diary."

veneration. "Divers Royalists craved his blessing on their knees." [1] When the truth transpired
—owing to the laughter of the patriarch in the
midst of a Greek oration—Lloyd was obliged to fly
before the wrath of his superiors. This incident
did not, however, spoil his career, as, after acting as
the Princess's chaplain, he became in succession
Bishop of St. Asaph, of Lichfield, and of Worcester.

The question of the Princess's place of worship
was rendered very difficult by the fact that she
had no regular chapel in which to hold services ;
but when Ken's friend, Dr. Hooper, who succeeded
Dr. Lloyd after a few months, came to The Hague,
he persuaded the Princess to allow her dining-
room to be fitted up as a chapel. This she readily
assented to, and after that always had her meals
in a small dark parlour. Nothing could of course
be done without William's permission, and when
the chapel was nearly finished, he ordered Dr.
Hooper to be in attendance on a certain day, and
he would inspect it.

"As there was a step or two at the communion
Table, and another for the chair where the Princess
was to sit, he kicked at them with his foot, asking
what they were for ? which being told in a proper
manner, he answered with a hum." [2]

The Prince, Dr. Hooper complained, only went
to the chapel on Sunday evenings. The Princess,
however, attended the service twice daily, and
begged Dr. Hooper, if she were ever late, to show
himself in her apartments, and she would come
at once, so that the congregation should not be
kept waiting.

William lived in a state of constant warfare against
his wife's chaplains, who were almost as much
afraid of the influence of a Calvinist husband

[1] Plumptre's " Life of Ken," vol. i. p. 66.
[2] Trevor's " Life of William III.," appendix to vol. ii.—
" Hooper's Memoirs."

as of a Roman Catholic father; while William, though not daring to tamper with Mary's membership of the English Church, never scrupled to show his impatience at its ceremonial. A continual duel went on. Evidently at William's instigation, Mary, who was a great reader, was provided with books calculated to give her a favourable view of the Dissenters. To counteract these the chaplain provided the Princess with Eusebius's "Church History" and Hooker's "Ecclesiastical Polity," which would, he hoped, duly magnify the Church of England in her eyes. William came in one day while she was reading one of these books, and at once showed his displeasure, exclaiming with much eagerness : " What ! I suppose Dr. Hooper persuades you to read these books ? " [1]

In Holland universal tolerance was the law, and when Dr. Hooper—rather tactlessly, it must be allowed—spoke against indulgence being shown to the Roman Catholics and the Dissenters, the Prince said bitterly, " Well, Dr. Hooper, *you* will never be a Bishop," and remarked to some one in his confidence that if " he ever had anything to do with England, Dr. Hooper should be Dr. Hooper still." After this it is interesting to note that during one of William's absences from England after the Revolution, Queen Mary conferred on Hooper the Deanery of Canterbury, and that on the King's return he showed much displeasure at his wife's action. This appears rather unreasonable on William's part, as we are told that Hooper's was one of the names he had given her to choose from. Some years after Bishop Ken had been deprived of the See of Bath and Wells, Hooper succeeded to it.

The Prince tried to disgust the chaplains of the Church of England by underpayment and discour-

[1] Trevor's " Life of William III.," appendix to vol. ii.— " Hooper's Memoirs."

tesy, and Dr. Hooper's newly married wife, whom her husband had persuaded to come out of England at the Princess's urgent request, was never even presented to him, though he talked continually of this being done. When Mrs. Hooper was enceinte, she insisted on returning to England, in spite of the Princess's entreaties ; and Dr. Hooper was very naturally delighted to find an excuse for leaving Holland.

Before Hooper's departure the Prince apparently felt a little shame at his treatment of the chaplain, who had received no payment for his services for a year and a half, and after his marriage had not even been fed at Court, but had kept himself and his wife. Before Hooper embarked—bearing with him letters from the Princess to Miss Apsley and to her mother, who had been ill— [1] one of Bentinck's servants was sent to offer him £70 in Dutch money for his year and a half's service. He refused this, giving a crown of it to the servant, and saying that,

" as he had discharged all his debts and owed nothing to Holland, and was provided for his passage, he did not know what to do with it, and therefore desired him to carry it back again to his master, who, if he pleased, might order him to be paid in England ; if not, it was no matter." [2]

However, the money was promptly paid when Dr. Hooper returned to England.

Owing to Charles's omission to pay her dowry, the Princess was very poor ; and she apologised when, in saying good-bye to Mrs. Hooper, she presented her with a cup, cover, and salver, with her own and the Prince's arms engraved on it, which was of the weight of gold, but was in reality only gilt.

According to the articles of Mary's marriage settlement, which was drawn up on November 13,

[1] Bathurst Collection : Letter, January 16, 1680.
[2] Trevor's " Life of William III.," appendix to vol. ii.—" Hooper's Memoirs."

1677, the Princess was to receive a sum of £40,000 from England.

The first instalment of this was considered due six months after the wedding, and the whole was to be paid in the course of the next two years. Besides this, £10,000 a year, to be paid every three months, was to be settled on the Princess by her husband, and she was to have two residences, one at The Hague, and the other on jointure lands. Trustees were to be appointed by the King of England to ensure that William's part of the bargain at least was faithfully performed. The Princess was also to be allowed by her husband £2,000 a year for her privy purse.[1] This, it was carefully explained, was not to include what was spent on her food, clothing, carriages, or servants' wages—in fact it was to be what we now call pin-money. She was to have English attendants, who were to be chosen for her by Charles II.; and it will be remarked that, thanks no doubt to Charles's mistress, Barbara Villiers, the Villiers family were in this way amply provided with lucrative posts.

Church of England services were to be provided for the Princess's benefit, and if William were to die leaving her childless, she might return to England if she chose to do so, and might take with her all her personal possessions, including her jewellery. If she had children, it was specially premised, in view of their possible inheritance of the English throne, that they were not to be married without the consent of the King of England.[2]

The precious papers containing this agreement were deposited in two boxes—one of them gilt—for which £16 was paid ; but a certain excuse for William's stinginess towards Mary's English servants may be found in the fact that there was the

[1] Copy of William and Mary's marriage contract in Welbeck. Library.

[2] Letter, December 4, 1677, King William's Chest, Record Office.

PORTRAIT OF ELIZABETH VILLIERS.

From a portrait by Kneller.    In the collection of the Earl of Orkney.

greatest difficulty in obtaining the money from
England. Danby writes, in reply to remonstrances
from William, that the Prince must not think him
negligent, for he is doing his best to send £20,000 ;
but would like to know to whom it ought to be
paid.[1] This was in 1678, and it appears from
letters written about the same time, to Laurence
Hyde, by Sir William Temple, and by the Prince of
Orange, that even towards the end of the year the
long-promised dowry had not been produced,[2] and
that the £20,000 which should have been paid in
1677 had never been received by the Prince. The
English Parliaments of those times did not evidently
think the keeping of their promises obligatory.

Once the monotony of the Princess's life was
broken by a journey she took all over Holland with
her ladies. They travelled in a barge and worked
and played at cards as they went. No particulars
of the journey can be gathered, but doubtless it
was undertaken for political reasons—that the
Princess's kindliness and charm of manner might
increase the popularity of the House of Orange.
Mary was at this time only sixteen years old, but
if William had ever condescended to turn his
acute eyes intelligently upon her, he would have
realised that she was by no means a person to be
despised. Dr. Hooper, her chaplain, said that during
the year and a half that he was in attendance on
her he never saw her do, or heard her say, a thing
that he could wish she had omitted.

With all her sweetness she was no nonentity,
and had such authority over her ladies that if she
merely looked serious, and so showed disapproval
of anything they said, there was at once silence
among them. She had, too, a great sense of the

---

[1] Danby to William, September 30, 1678, King William's Chest,
Record Office.

[2] " Clarendon Correspondence "—Letters from William of Orange
July 5 and October 6, 1678.

6

fitness of things, insisted on being served properly, and only received a message or petition from the person whose office it was to present it.

Even in quite early days she had a deep affection and admiration for her surly, unloving husband. When she had been married about six months, the Prince, after hunting all the morning, received letters, on his way back to The Hague for dinner, telling him of the investment of Namur by Louis XIV., and was obliged to leave at once for the seat of war. His wife was certainly not treated with much consideration, for the first intimation she received of this sudden resolution, which many of his well-wishers considered mistaken, was the arrival of one of his officers, who was to start two hours earlier than he, and who came to take leave of her. However, she was allowed to accompany him on his journey as far as Rotterdam, where "there was a very tender parting on both sides."[1]

The Princess's feelings at this juncture may be gathered from a letter to her : " dearest dearest dearest dear husban " in England, in which, while assuring her correspondent of her undying affection, for when once she loves anything or anybody, nothing will change her mind, she says :

" I suppose you know the prince is gone to the Army but I am sure you can guese at the troble I am in I am sure I coud never have thought it half so much I thought coming out of my own country parting with my friends and relations the greatest that ever coud as long as I lived hapen to me but I am to be mistaken that now I find till this time I never knew sorow for what can be more cruall in the world than parting with what on loves and nott ondly comon parting but parting so as may be never to meet again to

[1] " Clarendon Correspondence "—Laurence Hyde to Lord Clarendon, February 22, 1667.

be perpetually in fear for God knows when I may
see him or wethere he is nott now at this instant
in a batell I recon him now never in safety ever in
danger oh miserable live that I lead now I do
what I can to be merry when I am in company
but when I am alone thin tis that I remember all
my grifes I do nott now wish to see any friands
for I shoud but be a troble to them dear Aurelia
do nott take it ill with you I coud be because to
you I shoud dare to spake which to angells I dare
nott. Forgive me that troble you with this but
take it as a mark of my love for I dare ritt this
to you which I hardly dare think before anothere
now I am in my closet I give my selfe up to my
griefe and mellancolly thoughts and you may
belive tis a great comfort that I have a friand
in the world to ritt them to I hope it won't be
long now before I shall go to Breda where I shall
se the prince for that is so neer the Army he can
live in the town and go to it any time at a quarter
of an hour warning when I am there if I don't
ritt dont wonder for may be I shant have time
or twenty things may hapen however be asured
of this that if I will you shall still heer all my misfortunes as a marke how I love you.

" Marie Clorinne." [1]

In a postscript to this she begs her friend : " well
dont say anything of all I have ritt to you for I
am ashamed of it pray dont."

Mary was beginning to learn the lesson of self-
control early, and it would have been well could
those who commented severely on the gaiety
which she assumed by William's orders, when,
after her father's fall, she appeared in England as
Queen, could have seen this letter, and realised
that at sixteen years of age the Princess was learn-

---

[1] Bathurst Collection: " Quarterly Review," January, 1911—
" Letters of Queen Mary II."

ing the hard lesson of stifling the appearance of every natural feeling.

It is interesting to compare this naïve expression of Mary's love for her husband with the only mention of her in William's letters to Bentinck before he left Holland for England. The letter in which this occurs was written some years later from The Hague, where William had just arrived, and had at once sent to inquire after Madame Bentinck; and among longings for Bentinck's society we read the words, written perhaps with complacency, perhaps, we may hope, with stirrings of remorse: " My wife came to Dieren on Saturday, and was very sorry that I was setting out on Sunday." [1]

It is possible that during the first months of his married life William visited on his unfortunate wife the indignation he felt at the vagaries of English tactics. The political results of the marriage were a bitter disappointment to the Prince. Charles quickly proved either his want of will or want of power to influence French diplomacy, and Duras' mission to Paris was of absolutely no use to the Allies; while Louis, always judicious in his choice of agents, was so well served in Holland by envoys who fomented disaffection towards William, that on August 11, 1678, the States-General accepted the French propositions without consulting the Prince. The battle in which Monmouth fought at the side of the Prince of Orange in a vain attempt to relieve Mons, took place the day after the peace was ratified, William being ignorant, or in his fury feigning ignorance, of the fact.

The Prince was absolutely disgusted with State affairs, and after his return he went to Dieren to hunt in the Veluwe, like, says Sir William Temple, " a person that had little else to do." He was

[1] Letters in Welbeck Abbey.

most indignant with the King of England, and said to Temple despairingly :

" Was ever anything so hot, and so cold, as this court of yours ?  Will the King, that is so often at sea, never learn a word that I shall never forget since my last passage, when, in a great storm, the captain was all night crying out to the man at the helm, Steady, steady, steady ? " [1]

[1] " Memoirs of Sir W. Temple," vol. ii. p. 462.

# CHAPTER V

MEANWHILE hopes, doomed unfortunately to disappointment, brightened Mary's life for a time. In the years 1678 and 1679 she expected to become a mother, and on one of these occasions she wrote in high spirits to her " dear husban " in England.

She had been ill, apparently with ague, and begins with many apologies for not having written since her recovery. She goes on, and, there being only one stop in the whole long letter, it is necessary to start in the middle of a sentence :

" but if anything in the world can make amend for such a faut I hope trusting you with a secrett will which though in it self tis not enough yett I tell you tis on yett I would hardly give me self leave to think on it nor no body leave to spake of it nott so much as to my self and that I have nott yett ritt the Duches word who has allways charged me to do it in all her leters it is what I am asham'd to say but seing it is to my husban I may tho I have reason to fear becaus the sea parts us you may belive it is a bastard but yett I think upon a time of need I may make you own it since tis you out of the four seas in the mean time if you have any care of your own reputation consequently you must have of your wifes so you ought to keep this a secrett since if it shud be known you might get a pair of horns and nothing els by the bargain but dearest Aurelia you may be very

well assured tho I have played the whore a litell
I love you of all things in the world. tho I have
spoke as you may thing in jest all this while yett
for god sake if you love me dont tell it becaus I
woud nott have it known yett for all the world
since it cannott be above 6 or 7 weeks att most
and when ever you heer of it by othere people
never say that I said anything of it to you in the
meantime I beg of you to say nothing as you hope
ever to be trusted anothe time." [1]

It is sad, after the evident delight expressed in
this letter, to see that on April 19, 1678, the Duke
of York wrote to the Prince of Orange :

" I was very sorry to find by the letters of this
day from Holland, that my daughter has miscarried ;
pray let her be carefuller of herself another time ;
I will write to her to the same purpose."

The Duke of York and Prince of Orange were at
this time maintaining an ostensibly friendly correspondence on the subject of a sudden change in
English, or at least in Court, policy. Louis XIV.'s
indignation at the Dutch marriage had caused
him to coquet with the popular party in England ;
and both Charles and James were now lamenting
the Peace of Nimeguen, and were apparently contemplating a war with France, in which William
of Orange proposed that James should come over
to Holland, as commander-in-chief of the united
Dutch and English forces.

However, all these preparations came to nothing ;
as Charles was engaged almost at the same time
in a secret treaty with France, by which, in consideration of receiving a large sum of money, he
assented to the Peace of Nimeguen. By keeping
this treaty secret and pretending that he was
forced by the Dutch to make peace, he hoped to
obtain money from Parliament for disbanding his

[1] Bathurst Collection: " Quarterly Review," January, 1911—
" Letters of Queen Mary II."

troops.[1] Meanwhile James continued his friendly and apparently confidential correspondence with his son-in-law, and, while carefully concealing the fact of Charles's treaty with France, he urged him for his own sake to make peace.

All this time, knowing nothing of political intrigues, Mary lived her lonely life. Though we may sometimes smile at the transports of love expressed to the "dear husban," the "dearest dearest Aurelia," there is something pathetic about these outpourings, when we think of the forlorn girl who, separated from her friends and relations, essayed a task which seemed beyond her powers—that of winning by submission and sweetness a husband whose heart seemed irrevocably closed to her.

That the Princess kept up her interest in acting is shown by the following letter to her from Lord Ossory about a play of which he was the author:

"My daughter Juligium writ to me lately, that it was yr High^ses pleasure, to see a play of myne, called Herod the Great. I therefore most humbly lay it, at yr High^ses feet." "I writt this play," Ossory continues later in the letter, "some years since haveinge observed that every nation, had bin acted on the English Theatres, except the Jewish who's storys afforde as great Argument for the Stage, as any. This is the last that I have writt, or ever intend in write, haveinge consecrated my mind to more serious subjects."[2]

Probably among the "more serious subjects" was included the charge of the English regiments at The Hague. These were commanded by Lord Ossory till his death on July 30, 1680, when the post was conferred on Sidney.

One pleasure at least the Princess had about this time, for in October, 1678, while the English

---

[1] Sir John Dalrymple's "Memoirs of Great Britain and Ireland" —Barillon to Louis XIV., May 27, 1678.
[2] Royal Archives at The Hague.

Court was making its usual sojourn at Newmarket, the Duchess of York and the Princess Anne came over to Holland strictly incognito to pay a visit to the Princess of Orange. In telling the Prince of Orange of their intended visit, the Duke of York mentions the second time the Princess had hopes of becoming a mother.

"I was very glad" [he writes on September 27, 1678] "to see by the last letters, that my daughter continued so well, and hope now she will go out her full time. I have written to her to be very careful of herself, and that she would do well not to stand too long, for that is very ill for a young woman in her state."

"The incognito ladies," as James called them, wished to be "very incognito!" Lord Ossory was to be their escort, and they sent a Mr. White to The Hague before their arrival to find a lodging for them near the House in the Wood. Sir William Temple, to whom, as British Resident, the Duke of York had written about the matter, said that it would be very difficult to observe the Duchess's wish of being unknown; especially as the Prince was absent, and could not be consulted, and the Pensioner was horrified at the idea that due honour should not be shown to the royal party on their arrival. They were established in the Princess-Dowager's house, which had evidently up till now been the abode of the British Embassy, and which the luxurious Sir William Temple had not found very comfortable. In a letter to Laurence Hyde he says :

"Her highness's coming removed both your family and mine at a very short warning, and I got into the next house I could find, which was Monsieur Armanvilliers', which I find the only warm house I ever yet met with in Holland, and so return no more to the wide old Court." [1]

1 "Clarendon Correspondence"—Temple to Hyde, October 25, 1678.

To move out of the British Embassy, and to find other quarters for themselves at short notice, was the utmost required of the English: for the Prince's servants were so anxious to do honour to the royal guests, that they insisted on making all the preparations themselves.

We know no particulars about this visit, except that the Princess received her sister with extreme delight, and that the three ladies were on the terms of the greatest intimacy. The Duchess of York's pet name for her stepdaughter was " Lemon," because she had married an Orange, and all her letters to her about this time are addressed to " My dear Lemon." The Prince of Orange evidently exerted himself to do honour to his guests, and the visit was a success, for James writes to him on October 18, after the return of the royal guests to England, that the Duchess was

" so satisfied with her journey and with you as I never saw anybody ; and I must give you a thousand thanks from her and from myself for her kind usage by you. I should say more on this subject, but I am very ill at compliments, and you care not for them."

The Princess of Orange found the damp and relaxing climate of The Hague extremely unhealthy, and suffered much from ague during the winter of 1678. We hear in one of her letters to her " dear dear husban " that after suffering from this trying illness for five days, she had gone to Dieren to get rid of it. She remarks that Dieren is a long way from " the Hage," and that as she has only just arrived she can tell her correspondent nothing further about it.[1] According to the letters published by Colonel Bathurst, the principal occupation of her life appears to have been to sit for her portrait. She was portrayed by Wissing as well as by Lely ; and specially to please the " dear

[1] Letter in Bathurst Collection.

husban," who did not like either of these present-
ments of "Clorinne," she consented to be painted
also by her old friend Gibson, the dwarf. She was
evidently very tired of continual sittings, and said
that no one but her "dearest Aurelia" would be
able to induce her to have another portrait painted.

Before long, Mary received a second visit from
her family, for at the beginning of 1679 the
indignation against the Roman Catholic Duke and
Duchess of York became so strong, that the King
felt certain that before long he would have himself
to leave England unless his brother did so. He
naturally chose the latter alternative; and the Princess, writing to Miss Apsley, says:

"I will nott speke of the sad coming of the Duke
and Duches who are by this time I hope well att
Brussels.
"HAGE, *March 28th,* 1679."

On March 12 the Duke and Duchess of York
arrived at The Hague, and though they were
supposed by a polite fiction to have come incognito,
the Prince of Orange, accompanied by persons of
high quality, received them on landing with the
greatest honours. Three thousand Guards were
drawn up before the Duke, while William put himself at the head of the Gardes du Corps and saluted
his father-in-law sword in hand.[1] The States-
General wished to show James further honours,
but as he had come incognito he excused himself.

However, a little later we hear complaints that
the Prince did not treat his father-in-law with
sufficient respect, and that James was painfully
conscious of this.

The Duke and Duchess of York were not popular
at The Hague; indeed, though tolerance of different
forms of worship was the rule in Holland, their

[1] "Clarendon Correspondence."

religion was hardly likely to recommend them to
the Dutch. Eventually James left The Hague
abruptly, and evidently with some alarm as to his
own safety ; for we are told that when he suddenly
moved from there to Brussels " Everybody that
comes in are in a maze at the Duke's going. They
said, at the French ambassador's that he was
poisoned, for he complained of a great pain in
his belly." [1]

The Princess's health was still in an unsatisfactory condition. Her father writes from The
Hague on April 25 : " My daughter's ague continues still, and her eleventh fit is now upon her ;
but the cold fit was not so long as usual, so that
I hope it is a going off." [2]

Evidently he was right, for in a letter to William
he says : " I am exceedingly glad that my daughter
has missed her ague ; I hope she will have no more
now the warm weather is come." However, the
Princess again suffered from ague in June. Nevertheless, according to Sidney, she was looking so well
in August that he could not believe her to be
in need of remedies ; though she had decided
to go to the baths at Aix-la-Chapelle. She returned in time to receive her father, stepmother,
and two sisters towards the end of September.
This meeting with her dear sister Anne, who in
her letters still receives the pseudonym of " Prince
Ziphares," must have given the Princess great
pleasure. " She has always had for him "
(" Ziphares "), of whom, as a rival for the affections
of Aurelia, she pretends to be jealous, " a love to
great to increas and to naturell not to last allways." [3]

Mary was much charmed with her little step-
sister Isabella, not yet three years old, and destined, like the other children born to James and

[1] "Henry Sidney's Diary and Correspondence," vol. i. p. 50.
[2] Clarendon Correspondence.
[3] Letter in Bathurst Collection.

to Mary of Modena in these early days, only to
have a very short life ; for after the royal party
left The Hague she wrote to Lady Harriet Hyde
to tell her of the pleasure it gave her to receive
news of her sister Isabella

" that I may hear how she does, which will be
the grates joy that can be to me when I hear she
is well, and otherwise a very great affliction for
though she is so little as not to be sensible of the
love I have for her, yet I cannot help telling it to
you." [1]

While the Princess enjoyed intercourse with her
relations, James's residence at The Hague was
causing the Prince much embarrassment. When
he at last left, Sidney certainly voiced William's
sentiments in saying :

" We are in great hopes that the Duchesse, with
the two Princesses, will soon follow his Highness ;
though others are of a contrary sentiment, believing
the Duke will rather return hither, wherein I hope
they will be mistaken, and shall willingly pardon
their error." [2]

James had not been long in Brussels before
news of Charles's dangerous illness arrived from
England, and he travelled in disguise to Windsor,
and appeared there, to the surprise of all who
were not in the secret of those who had summoned
him. The King recovered, and the Duke was
obliged to return into exile, having persuaded
his brother to send the Duke of Monmouth
also beyond the seas. James was now anxious
to visit The Hague again. His ostensible object
was to see his daughter, and " to endeavour to
undeceive those who persuade her she is yet with
child," [3] but, as William and his advisers knew,

---

[1] " Fairfax Correspondence," vol. iv. p. 277.
[2] " Henry Sidney's Diary and Correspondence," vol. i. p. 126.
[3] Dartmouth's note to Burnet's "History of My Own Times,"
vol. ii. p. 198.

his real object was political, and his design was
probably to warn his son-in-law against the designs
of the Duke of Monmouth, who had also taken
refuge in Holland.

The news of James's projected visit filled the
Prince of Orange with annoyance. Though James
was not clever enough to circumvent his son-in-
law's policy, he quite understood that the latter,
like Monmouth, was an aspirant for the crown of
England, and he had an awkward habit of referring
to matters best left in obscurity. For instance, he
said one day in the course of conversation that he
could not be William's friend if the latter had
designs on the crown, but that in everything else
he would.[1] Such remarks were most difficult to
parry, for William was well aware that some of the
English wished to render James powerless during
his ostensible reign by installing William and Mary
as Protectors of the kingdom, and others, more
revolutionary, were bringing forward the Exclusion
Bill, which was intended to prevent James's accession to the throne altogether.

Knowing these facts William considered that he
would never enjoy the affection of the English
unless he were to separate himself completely from
his unpopular father-in-law, and James's visits
to The Hague were, under the circumstances, most
inconvenient. It was William's opinion that, owing
to James's folly in attempting to force his mistaken
religion on the English people, he would never
reign over England, which, unless William were to
exert himself strenuously, would become a Republic,
and so Mary would lose her inheritance.

Mary's succession to the throne would also be
imperilled should her father succeed in his designs,
and establish the ascendancy of the Roman
Catholic religion in England. Doubtless, William
was too well acquainted with his father-in-law's

---

[1] " Henry Sidney's Diary and Correspondence," vol. i. p. 156.

peculiar incapacity for diplomacy to consider this contingency probable, but as one of the most remarkable features of his statesmanship was his power of taking in every possible aspect of any affair in which he was engaged, this possibility had doubtless occurred to him.

Therefore, though the Prince of Orange was uncertain about the exact object of James's visit, he felt sure that it portended something disagreeable, and said that he would not be able to resist telling the Duke his mind, " which he was sure the Duke will not like." In fact William was " mightily out of humour," and with reason, for it must be remembered that though he would even at this time, according to Sidney, " be very willing to be put into a way of having the Crown himself," [1] the whole matter of winning it was extremely precarious and complicated ; and his chances might be ruined by a false step. That he fully realised this is seen by the extreme care he took to weigh the question of whether he should go to England, as he was advised by many Englishmen to do, or whether, if he were to do so, he might harm himself by becoming in the eyes of the popular party accessory to the unwelcome measures passed by the Court.

However, William received James with the utmost cordiality, invited him to hunt, and offered him the use of his house at The Hague. Hospitality was easy ; but when the Duke took the Prince aside and kept him in conversation for about an hour, Sidney perceived that the latter " was not much satisfied." [2]

It is to be hoped that the Princess enjoyed her father's visit, and it is certain that she at least had no conception of the complex web of intrigue by which she was surrounded. She met James at

---

[1] " Henry Sidney's Diary and Correspondence," vol. i. p. 130.
[2] *Ibid.*, vol. i. p. 41.

the Italian Opera, and she and William accompanied him on October 9, on his return journey, as far as Mayslandsluys. He had spent about a fortnight at The Hague, and now saw his daughter for the last time.

In July, 1679, William received a valuable accession to his Councils by the arrival at The Hague, as Envoy from Charles, of Henry Sidney, brother of Algernon Sidney, and of Dorothy, Dowager Countess of Sunderland, who had been celebrated by Waller as Sacharissa.

This charming gentleman, who, as we have seen, is supposed to have touched the heart of Mary's mother, the Duchess of York, was uncle to Lord Sunderland, one of the faithless and venial politicians who surrounded, first James, and then William. Contemporary gossip credits Lady Sunderland, about whom, at Lady Marlborough's instigation, Anne wrote with bitter dislike to her sister, with an attachment for her handsome uncle by marriage.

Like Bentinck and Temple, Sidney was soon admitted to William's intimacy, and was the intermediary between him and the malcontents in England. He dined continually with the Prince, and was occasionally expected to return the civility at an hour's notice, a want of ceremony which he found inconvenient. Sidney speaks of receiving the Prince and Princess and the Prince of Hanover at a ball at his own house. In spite of these occasional entertainments, life at The Hague was intensely dreary to a man who had delighted in the dissipations of Whitehall, and he remarks that the maids of honour, at whose liberty to invite foreign Ambassadors to dinner he is much astonished, are his only solace. "The Princess's maids are a great comfort to me, and on Sunday invited me to dinner,"[1] he says.

[1] "Henry Sidney's Diary and Correspondence," vol. i. p. 55.

PORTRAIT OF MARY II.

In the possession of A. M. Broadley, Esq.   From the Fraser Collection.

One of the facts which astonished Sidney most on his arrival at The Hague was the relation between William and the French Ambassador, who never paid the Prince the least civility, and announced that he was not sent as Ambassador to him, but to the States of Holland.[1]

Another arrival at The Hague this year (1679) exercised a more direct influence on the Princess's life than did the charming Sidney. This was Thomas Ken, afterwards Bishop of Bath and Wells. The post of chaplain to the presumptive heiress to the British crown was, under the circumstances, of peculiar importance, and Bishop Compton, on whom fell the burden of the choice of suitable persons, seems to have exercised his responsibilities wisely. The appointment was much coveted, as it generally led to preferment, though the Prince's peculiarities must have made it difficult to find any one of the character and standing required who could or would undertake its duties successfully. Ken followed his friend Hooper, and was no doubt fully aware of the disagreeable side of the position. His motives in undertaking it were high, and the spirit in which his life was led is shown by the text written in Latin on the flyleaf of two books which were his constant companions : " Seekest thou great things for thyself ? seek them not." [2]

Although Ken was horrified at the want of filial duty Mary, in his opinion, showed when she became Queen of England, he always felt a warm affection for her, and considered her more misguided than actually sinning. For the Prince his feeling was different, and indeed William gave Ken no cause to love him. Even the dissipated Charles felt a respect for the " little Ken who tells me of my faults." When he was about to visit Winchester, where Ken was prebendary, the latter

[1] " Henry Sidney's Diary and Correspondence," vol. i. p. 48.
[2] Plumptre's " Life of Ken," vol. i. p. 139.

firmly refused to give accommodation to Nell
Gwyn, who was to accompany his Majesty. "A
woman of ill repute ought not to be endured in the
house of a clergyman," he said indignantly.[1]
Later, the See of Bath and Wells fell vacant, and
Charles was besieged with applications for the
Bishopric. However, he settled the matter sum-
marily by saying: "Odd's fish! Who shall have
Bath and Wells but the little black fellow who
would not give poor Nelly a lodging!"

William of Orange looked on things differently,
and was furious when Ken persuaded his cousin
Zulestein, who had seduced Jane Wroth, one of
the Princess's maids of honour, to fulfil his promise
of marrying her. The wedding took place during
William's absence from The Hague, and William,
who thought the connection a mésalliance for one
whose father was his own father's illegitimate
brother, was, on his return, intensely indignant,
and threatened Ken with dismissal. Ken, with
the spirit which, in spite of his saintliness, was
characteristic of him, refused to receive his dismissal
from William, but at once tendered his resignation
to the Princess. However, William eventually
curbed his indignation, for Ken was already widely
known and honoured in England, where his abrupt
withdrawal from his post would have occasioned
much comment. Perhaps too, when he had cooled
down, he felt a certain respect for Ken's action, for
the latter notes in a letter to Compton written after
this occurrence: " I am at present in as much favour
with the prince, and am as obligingly treated by
Mr. Benting [Bentinck] and all here, as I can desire."

Zulestein did not regard the matter quite in
the same light, and evidently, at any rate at first,
felt regrets for the brilliant match he might have
made. Huyghens, William's private secretary, says
in his diary for October 8, 1680 :

[1] Plumptre's "Life of Ken," vol. i. p. 158.

" Sylvius (the Prince's Marshall) said to me again when I told him that Zulestein spoke ill of Dr. Ken, that this was because he had helped to oblige him to declare himself with regard to Mlle. Worth, with whom he had amused himself for a long time."[1]

Another of Ken's triumphs during his year at The Hague, and one extremely appreciated by both the Prince and the Princess—especially, we may surmise, by the latter—was the conversion of " Colonell Fitz-patrick " from the Popish religion, and his reception into the English Church. Sidney had, in the first instance, brought about a meeting between Ken and the Colonel, who had often spoken to him about becoming a Protestant. After six months' consideration the Colonel made up his mind to cross the rubicon, and to take the sacrament in the Princess's chapel, " to the unspeakable joy of her royall Highnesse, who on all occasions gives demonstrations of her great and zealous concerne for the Protestant Religion."[2]

The Princess testifies her pleasure in a letter she writes to Miss Apsley, in which she says :

" I may tell you the Good news of Colonell FitzPatrik being turned protestant and that he is to receive the sacrement next Sunday with me. I cant give you a more full account having not [heard] since then, but this that he has done it of his own accorde wch when he first spoke to the Prince of he imidiately sent Dr. Ken to him who is very wel satisfyed with his resons and will this post give a full account of it to the Bishop of London."[3]

The Prince, the Princess, Sidney, and Bentinck were all present when Fitzpatrick was formally received into the English Church, and the whole

[1] See Fruin's notes to " Droste Overblyffsels van Geheugchenis," p. 435.
[2] Plumptre's " Life of Ken," vol. i. p. 150.
[3] Bathurst Collection.

Court at The Hague were much delighted at the
conversion. The Prince was much interested in
the affair, and commanded Ken to send an account
of it to Compton Bishop of London. Sidney, however, informs us that the proselyte did not bear
a very high character, indeed, had been accused of
forgery.

A proposition made about this time by Compton
that a union should be attempted between the
English Church and the Dutch Dissenters did not
meet with Ken's approval. Dr. Lloyd, he said,
had already written to him on the subject, and he
considered it most unadvisable to attempt anything of the sort, as it would entail constant
controversy, from which his predecessor, Dr. Hooper,
had already suffered. The Dutch looked on the
members of the English Church as half Papists,
and would be sure to demand that " the princess
may come to their sacrament, which hitherto she
has never done, and if ever she does doe it, farewell to all Common prayer here for the future." [1]
In that case Ken would either have to leave the
English Church or to give up his post. Apparently, after this decided letter, the Bishop of
London allowed the matter to slumber, but his and
Ken's attitude at this time, foreshadows the line
they were each to take when the accession of
William and Mary to the English throne, confronted
them with the most serious problem of their lives.

Meanwhile life did not brighten for the Princess ;
in fact, contemporary accounts abound in comments on her unhappiness. In the early months of
the year 1680 she was terribly ill, and was not
expected to live. " Colonel Fitzpatrick," writes
Sidney on March 17, " staid with me great part of
the afternoon : we talked much of the Princess's
illness, and her not being likely to live." On the
next day he notes in his " Diary " : " They brought

[1] Plumptre's " Life of Ken," vol. i. p. 146.

me word that the Princess had had a very ill night, and was worse than she had been." Eventually she recovered; but the Englishmen about her began to be very indignant at the Prince's treatment of her. We are told, with what we may hope is exaggeration, that the Prince made her cry every day, and Dr. Ken in particular was furious at his unkindness, and said he would remonstrate with him, even if he were kicked downstairs for daring to interfere.[1] Sir William Temple, in spite of his fondness and admiration for William of Orange, was anxious about the condition of the neglected wife, and writes from Sheen on April 27 (1680) to say how glad he is to hear of her recovery; while Sir Gabriel Sylvius spoke most hotly about the matter, declaring he was sure that the Princess felt her husband's harshness, and that it contributed to her bad health. It is satisfactory to find that by August she was well enough to enjoy herself with the gaiety natural to her, as Sir Gabriel writes on the 20th of that month : " At night the Princess came from Cleves, much pleased with the entertainment she had had at Mr. Spaen's, two leagues from thence, where she lay all the while."

Other people besides his wife suffered from the Prince's surliness. The English maids of honour, except those specially honoured by his attention, had a very melancholy time, and we hear that one of them, Lady Betty Selbourne, " complains and wails horribly." [2]

In 1681 or 1682 Frances Apsley, Mary's " dear husban," married Sir Benjamin Bathurst; and Mary, in her letter congratulating her friend on her approaching marriage, wished her " nine months heance too boys for on is to comon a wish." [3]

---

[1] " Henry Sidney's Diary and Correspondence," vol. ii. p. 20.
[2] *Ibid.*, vol. i. p. 41.
[3] " Quarterly Review," January, 1911 — " Letters of Queen Mary II."

The character of the Princess's letters has now
altered, and in place of the sentimental effusions of
her early days she sends sundry and manifold
commissions to her friend. Throughout these transactions the Princess shows her delicate thoughtfulness for others as well as her generosity. She
will not introduce a certain fashion into Holland
because she does not consider the purses there
long enough to bear it, and later she begs her
correspondent to give £20 a year from her to
one of her goddaughters. The Princess Anne is
to settle whether the sum shall be paid quarterly
or yearly ; but Mary, mindful no doubt of her
sister's normally impecunious condition—a condition for which we must consider Lady Marlborough as in part responsible—asks Lady Bathurst
to be her almoner, promising that the money shall
be promptly refunded.

In another letter the Princess requires, " against
I come bake out of the contre a long laced scarfe
some English whitt gloves a black and whitt hood
and to suits of night cloths." She will pay " all
her detts at once." Later she wants what she
cannot obtain in Holland—the material for a
" blake razed satin " dress. " You must leve a
border round plain to be embroidered that I can
have done heer very well and the shapes of the
body. I am in great hast for it and therefore
desire you woud lose no time." On another
occasion the commissions were : " 2 cotten peticotes
a paire of sleeves such as may be worn now and a
rolle or what els you may call it I know not but I
mean such a thing as is worn upon the head with
a black gowne." [1]

In one of her letters to Lady Bathurst the Princess,
in her curiously involved style, makes a complaint
which will appeal to many of her readers. She says :

[1] This and the remaining extracts in this chapter are from
letters in Lord Bathurst's Collection.

" in both yours you complain for want of news and some time refer me to my sister who seldom write me a word but you are not alone of it, the humore, for all who ever write to me do the same thing but anothere time I desire you not to fear repeating what I have heard allready, for I had much rathere venture being told a thing twice then not to heare it at all."

Mary had evidently asked that some pincushions should be made for her by Lady Wentworth, Lady Bathurst's sister, who was much hurried over finishing them, and in expressing sorrow for this the Princess says :

" that was your faut who imployed her without letting me know time enough that no body els coud, pray remember me very kindly to her and give her many thanks for them."

The accounts between the Princess and her faithful friend must have been complicated, and we must hope that the latter eventually recovered all that was owing to her. Fortunately, the Princess appears to have been most businesslike.

" I like my Bibles mightelly " [she says on one occasion] "but I must tell you while I think of it that I dont remember to have seen in the bills I have paid last, eithere for the paper Book I had or the 5 gineys I did once allmost a year ago desire you to give Bridget Homes, I have thought of it often enough but never remember to write to you before."

The " paper book," by the way, was not easy to procure, owing to the want of exactitude shown by " Mr. Knox," who was, we may suppose, the bookbinder. Aurelia was obliged to write twice to the Princess on the subject, and the latter apologises to her friend for the " troble she has had about it." It dawns slowly upon the reader as he reads from time to time of this paper book that it is evidently destined to be the receptacle for that most precious document, the Princess's diary, for the discovery of parts of which we owe a debt of gratitude to both Dr. Doebner, and to Countess Bentinck. When we realise this, the details acquire fresh significance :

" and now I must desire you to make Mr. Knot " [Knot or Knox is evidently immaterial] " bind me a paper book as fine as he can but with blew tirky leathere and gilt leaves, the outside I leave to you because there may be some new way wch I have not yet seen of ordering it onely I desire once more it may be fine, as for the bignes I woud have it of the size of Salles introduction to a devout life the paper allso of that thicknes but not above a 120 leaves in it this I woud desire you dear Aurelia to send me as sone as possible and belive me ever the same till death.

" It may come by the post if you make a leathere case to keep it from harm."

What can this be but the diary ? And what would we not give to see it as it came into the Princess's possession, with shining gilt edges, blue morocco binding, and adorned with the most elegant and most fashionable designs which could be imagined by the united brains of the dear Aurelia, and the artistic, if inexact, Mr. Knox !

Lady Bathurst was often in an interesting condition, and there is something touching in the interest and sympathy which the Princess—with her intense longing for children—showed her friend. " I shoud be sory for my dear Aurelia's touth ake but that I beiive tis a sign of some thing wch you woud not be sory for," she says.

Lady Bathurst lost several children, one of them being Mary's godson. Condoling with her on the death of one of them the Princess says :

" childrene who dy before thay are capable of sining are I think very hapy beeing onely taken out of a troblesome world wch few who know it perfectly if thay had nothing thay loved in it woud be sory to leave and if one coud hinder one self seting ons heart to much upon those we love we shoud be the redyer to dy."

Nevertheless she sympathises heartily with her friend. " I am no good judge of such a losse," she says ; " yet I pitie you for it very much." In the same letter she congratulates Lady Bathurst on the advantageous marriage of a niece, but remarks characteristically :

" tho' in one respect I shoud think it very much the contrary since he is of anothere religion and I think that ought ever to be the chife, and therefore cant chuse but wonder at such a choise or how any can prefer worldly advantages to that."

The Princess refers several times to the " sore eys " which were her trouble all her life, and often completely prevented her from either reading or writing. Mary of Modena had sent over a " picture drawer " to paint the Princess, and she was so much afraid of making her eyes red during the progress of the portrait that she wrote only to the King, and Queen, and to her sister ; and apologises for being obliged to neglect all other correspondence.

One of her letters shows an indignation which is rare with her ; and thinking of their future relations, it is curious to realise that what called it forth was an imputation on the character of her sister Anne. To understand her letter we must know that Lord Mulgrave had caused great scandal by writing love-letters to the Princess Anne, and that to make matters worse she was supposed to favour his addresses. In consequence of this terrible affair it was considered necessary to find a husband for her as quickly as possible, and Prince George of Denmark was eventually selected to fill the post.

The letter is only dated The Hague, November 27, but was evidently written in 1682, Anne being married on July 28, 1683. Her sister writes :

" If I coud love you better than I did before your last letter would make me do so, to see the concern you are for my pore sister. I am sure all who are truly her friends must be so, for my part I never knew what it was to be so vext and trobled as I am at it, not but that I believe my sister very innocent, however, I am so nice upon the point of reputation that it makes me mad she shoud be expossed to sch reports, and now what will not this insolent man say being provokt, oh, my dear Aurelia tis not to be imagined in what concerne I am that I shoud ever live to see the onely sister I have in the world, the sister I love like my own life abussed and wronged. I coud write thus till tomorrow morning and not express half I have in my heart, but keep it to yourself, for tho tis a thing as publike grown yet I have not the heart to spake of it but to my best friends adieu, dear Aurelia I deserve some pittie as well as my pore sister for all her afflictions I recon as my own."

A letter in answer to one from Lady Bathurst, who was, it must be remembered, confidante to both sisters, and had written to the Princess of Orange the day before Anne's marriage, says :

" you may believe twas no small joy to me to heer she liked him " [Prince George of Denmark] " and I hope she will do so every day more and more for els I am sure cant love him and without that tis impossible to be hapy wch I wish her with all my heart as you may easely imagin knowing how much I love her."

In this letter Mary says she has entrusted Anne with some commissions, and these Anne, with her usual indolence, evidently passed on to Lady Bathurst. Mary remarks rather pathetically that she has asked her sister to do something for her ın the hope of being entrusted with some commission in return,

" for there is nothing pleases me more than to be employed, but I don't heer of any yet and indeed this place afords so little of anything but what one has much better in England that I fear I shall not get any at all."

However, Anne apparently did on one occasion pay her sister's adopted country the compliment of ordering some clothing from there, as elsewhere it is stated that she owed Mary £22 15s. for a bedgown she has sent for,

" out of wch you " [Lady Bathurst] " may pay yourself the 5 pound for Mr. Knox " [for binding a romance very finely] " and ye od money wch togethere is 6-1-6 so yt you will have 6-13-6 over wch my Mam " [her nurse or personal maid] " will direct you to who it is to be paid towards a bill for a stufe."

The Princess, it will be noticed, is most business-like, and kept careful accounts, and for Lady Bathurst's instruction a list of figures is appended to this letter.

# CHAPTER VI

ABOUT this time the health of Charles II. again
gave cause for much anxiety, and at Louis XIV.'s
request the Duke of York was recalled to England.
Though he was not allowed to remain there, but
was despatched with his family to Scotland, the
change was extremely welcome to him, as was the
fact that his rival Monmouth was kept in exile.
Monmouth, however, not being able to bear his
banishment any longer, escaped to Scotland, and
made an almost royal progress through the country,
being received everywhere with enormous enthusiasm.

Meanwhile William had roused his father-in-
law's indignation by inducing both the Dutch and
the Spanish to send over papers petitioning for the
exclusion of the Duke of York from the English
throne on the score of his religion; and James
was made intensely anxious by the fact that
during his enforced sojourn in Scotland the Prince
paid a visit to England. The ostensible reason for
this visit was to remove misunderstandings between himself and the King, but Charles felt well-
founded distrust of his nephew's motives, and considered that he intended to ally himself with the
popular party in England. When the Prince told
him that they were in the majority, Charles answered that William thought so because he spoke

with no one else ; and after the visit was over he remarked : " I wonder why the Prince of Orange and the Duke of Monmouth are so fond of each other when they both aim at the same mistress." [1]

Certainly William's attitude to the Duke of Monmouth was most friendly ; for when, as a consequence of Monmouth's assumption of royal rank, he was again exiled from England, and returned to The Hague, which was now the focus of all those who were discontented with Charles's government, William treated him, and allowed the Princess to treat him, with the utmost familiarity. Mary's complaisance indeed went so far that the French Ambassador complained [2] that—of course, at William's instigation—she showed special honour to Monmouth's mistress, Lady Henrietta Wentworth, whom it may be remembered she had known from her childhood. To the last Monmouth maintained that, as his marriage to the Duchess of Monmouth had taken place without his consent, his connection with Lady Henrietta Wentworth, who had reclaimed him from vice, was blameless in the sight of God.

Monmouth was much delighted with the attentions shown him, because he knew that the Duke of York, who had, as we know, been treated with scant courtesy by his son-in-law, would be much annoyed to hear of them.

" The Duke " [(of Monmouth) says Sidney] " writ to the King to let him know how kind the Prince had been to him ; he said it would so vex the Duke. I doubt he hath said so much that it will make the Prince cool in the alliance."

Monmouth was careful to show the Prince the utmost respect. It was remarked by Louis XIV.'s Ambassador, who watched the relations between

[1] Sir John Dalrymple's " Memoirs of Great Britain and Ireland," Part I. Book I. p. 14.

[2] " Négociations du Comte d'Avaux," vol. iv. p. 118.

the two with much jealousy, that when they were
both on horseback and William dropped his cane,
the Duke of Monmouth at once jumped from his
horse to pick it up, William meanwhile remaining
immovable.[1]  So might the heir to the English
throne treat a bastard closely allied to royalty.

There was the key to the situation. William
held the balance. Cool and wily, he would not
go a step further than he thought expedient, and
doubtless he fully understood the Duke of Monmouth's limitations ; and looked upon him in
the light rather of an ally against the Duke of
York, than as a possible rival in the contention
for the crown of England. Therefore, while willingly receiving marks of respect from him, he insisted that the troops should salute Monmouth as
they did their General. He went further, and in
his anxiety to identify himself with Monmouth in
the eyes of the popular party, he publicly rebuked
a Dutch mayor for having given up one of Monmouth's followers to Charles II. for punishment,
dismissed him with contumely from his presence, and
told him that he would never receive him again.[2]

According to Bentinck's constantly reiterated
public announcements, these attentions were paid
to Monmouth as Charles II.'s son and at his special
request. However, the Duke of York, who was
now back in England and was treated with so
much favour that it was said that the King wished
him to reign *before* his death, as he would never
reign *after*, certainly spared no pains to show that
he at least strongly disapproved of them, and
wrote to remonstrate with his son-in-law. William's reply, addressed to Bentinck, was to the
effect that Monmouth was the King's son, and
that William knew, that though Charles had removed him from his presence, " in the bottom of

---

[1] " Négociations du Comte d'Avaux," vol. iii. p. 104.
[2] *Ibid.*, vol. iv. p. 61.

his heart he has some friendship for him, and cannot be angry with him." [1]

James wrote the following letter to his daughter to comlpain of the Prince's conduct:

"WINDSOR,
"*June* 6, 1684.

" I had not your's of the 9th till Wednesday, by which I find you have received mine. I wrote to you upon the subject of Lord Brandon, and I easily believe, that you might have forgotten for what he might have been in the Tower, yet others could not be ignorant of it, nor have so short memories; and I must need tell you, it scandalises all loyal and monarchical people here, to know how well the Prince lives with, and how civil he is to the Duke of Monmouth and Lord Brandon; and it heartens exceedingly the factious party here, which are a sort of people one would think the Prince should not shew any countenance to; and in this affair methinks you might talk with the Prince (though you meddle in no others :) the Duke of Monmouth, Lord Brandon, and the rest of that party, being declaredly my mortal enemies. And let the Prince flatter himself as he pleases, the Duke of Monmouth will do his part, to have a push with him for the crown, if he, the Duke of Monmouth, outlive the King and me. Some posts since I wrote pretty freely to the Prince upon this subject in general, to which I have yet had no answer. However, it will become you very well to speak to him of it." [2]

On receiving this letter the Princess wept, but said she could do nothing, as the Prince was master

---

[1] Sir John Dalrymple's "Memoirs of Great Britain and Ireland," appendix to Part I. Book I. p. 124.
[2] *Ibid.*

and she was obliged to obey him. "She is much changed since then," remarks the caustic d'Avaux drily.[1]

Changed indeed did the Princess become during her married life ; and this transformation, which was to show itself in a startling manner later on, may be traced to the fact of her deep attachment to the taciturn, exacting husband, by whom, according to the views of the Englishmen surrounding her, she was disgracefully treated.

Mary was a woman of quick perceptions, as she showed when she held the reins of government in England ; and in spite of her sweetness and amiability, she was not easily deceived. We are told an anecdote which proves this on the subject of Sir William Temple. Wishing to ingratiate himself with one whose religion was the great preoccupation of her life, he sent a message to the Princess at the end of his and Sir Leoline Jenkins's Embassy at The Hague, asking that he might be allowed to receive the Communion in her chapel. The Princess sent orders to her chaplains that everything should be ready, "though I am persuaded," says she, " he does not intend it, and by tomorrow will bethink himself of some business or excuse, yet my Lord Ambassador Jenkins I doubt not will be there, though he has not sent formally to me." [2] The matter turned out exactly according to her conjectures ; so Sir William Temple's judgmatic move brought him after all no credit.

A woman of this keenness of judgment would not be long in discovering beneath a repellent exterior the heroic characteristics of the man to whom she was married. Casual observers might be offended by his " disgusting " dryness of manner, and his unfortunate neglect of the little courtesies of life. In spite, however, of the undoubted hard measure

---

[1] " Négociations du Comte d'Avaux," vol. iv. p. 57.
[2] Wynne's " Life of Sir Leoline Jenkins," vol. i. p. 305.

CONTEMPORARY PRINT OF QUEEN MARY'S LANDING IN ENGLAND.

In the possession of A. M. Broadley, Esq. From the Fraser Collection.

112]

meted out to her, Mary had sufficient sweetness of temper, perceptive ability, and knowledge to realise how many of William's unamiable qualities were caused by ill-health, and to understand that she had married a man of deep religious principles, whose aims were higher and wider than those of the generality of men. In the beginning she no doubt obeyed him from compulsion, but as time went on, her reliance and faith in him became the mainspring of her life, so that she referred everything to him, and saw everything through his eyes.

Meanwhile the Duke of York had now been allowed to return to England, owing to the intervention of Charles's mistress, the Duchess of Portsmouth, who hoped to obtain money from him.[1] James and his son-in-law were on very bad terms, and William complained bitterly of the insolence of the English Envoy, Chudleigh, who joined with d'Avaux in fomenting disturbances against him in Holland. The French Ambassador, too, had evidently been instructed to make himself as disagreeable as possible to the Prince and Princess, for he had positive orders from his master that, whenever the Princess sat in a great armchair he should do so too ; and that, if there was but one in the room, he should endeavour to take it from the Princess and sit in it himself.[2] James, on his side, had, as we know, many causes for complaint against the Prince. He writes on October 3, 1684 :

" I have had your's of the 2nd, and you may be sure that I shall do my part in what concerns you, but it is necessary you do your's to satisfy the King ; and pray consider, whether he has had reason to be satisfied with several things you have done for some time past. I could say more to you upon this subject, but am not encouraged to do it,

---

[1] Burnet's " History of My Own Times," vol. ii. p. 447.
[2] " Henry Sidney's Diary and Correspondence," vol. ii. p. 142.

since I have found that you have had so little consideration for things I have said to you, which I
thought of concern to our family, though you did
not." [1]

On the subject of the Duke of Monmouth, William
did not show the slightest inclination to submission.
In fact, in January, 1685, he specially invited Monmouth to The Hague. As the latter had just
fallen under the King's displeasure for his complicity in the Rye House plot, by which the King and
Duke of York were to be assassinated and the
Protestant Succession secured, James's indignation was natural. However, Monmouth declared,
and most probably with truth, that he was not
privy to any idea of murder.

William's policy at this juncture included so
much waiting on circumstance that it is difficult
to follow with understanding. There seems, however, to have been some truth in Charles's reproach
during his visit in England, when he said that the
Prince only consorted with malcontents, and therefore could not judge the real state of the country.
The Hague was the refuge of all those who were
indignant with Charles's policy and feared the
Roman Catholic proclivities of the Duke of York,
while all William's correspondents were of the same
way of thinking. In consequence, if he did not
overestimate the discontent in England, he at
least underestimated the intense conservatism
and respect for the order of things established,
which seems inherent in the British mind.

William appears to have considered that Charles
was tottering on a throne which James could never
inherit; and that his best chance of ingratiating
himself with the English lay in dissociating himself from the Court party, and identifying himself
with their beloved Monmouth. It is an easy

[1] Sir John Dalrymple's "Memoirs of Great Britain and Ireland,"
vol. i. p. 125.

mistake to impute small motives to great men,
and in justice to William it must be remembered
that not only the question of whether the crown
of England should rest on his or on his wife's head,
but that of the very existence of Holland as an
independent country, nay more, even the preservation of Protestantism in Europe, depended on
the downfall of the present government, or misgovernment, in England.

Therefore William embarked on a line of conduct which would in the course of the next few
months oblige him to humiliate himself in a way
which must have been intensely galling to his
proud nature, while it would give his father-in-law
a triumph which would be keen if short-lived.

Monmouth arrived at The Hague at eight o'clock
in the evening, and Bentinck was sent at once to
his lodgings, and conducted him to the Prince of
Orange, who received him with many demonstrations of joy.  Monmouth then went up to see the
Princess, but she could not receive him, being half
undressed,[1] as she was going to bed early, in preparation for receiving the Communion next morning.
Her despotic husband insisted, however, that she
should at once dress herself, come to his rooms,
and there receive the Duke.  William then begged
him to establish himself in Prince Maurice's palace,
and offered to provide him with all the servants
he would require.  The Duke was also granted the
privilege of entering the Prince's chamber at any
time—a privilege hitherto only enjoyed by Bentinck—and it was soon remarked that it was of no
use to pay court to William without paying court
to the Duke also, so that in consequence Monmouth
was feasted and made much of by the principal
people of Holland.

The English nation was to be assured of one
fact at least—the husband of the heiress to the

[1] "Négociations du Comte d'Avaux," vol. iv. p. 212.

throne was absolutely on the side of the Protestant
champion of their liberties.

Balls were given in honour of Monmouth, and
were attended by William, who hated such diver-
sions. At these entertainments Monmouth was
always given the post of honour as the Princess's
partner, and before going to dine with William he
first conducted her in to her private dinner. In
fact the French Ambassador remarked with spite-
fulness that " no one understood how the Prince
of Orange, who is the most jealous of men, could
put up with the airs of ' galanterie ' which everyone could see existed between the Princess of
Orange and M. de Monmouth." [1]

It must have been a pleasant change for the poor
Princess, who practically led the life of a prisoner,
to be encouraged to hold intercourse with this
charming young man. Monmouth came in the
afternoon to teach her special dances, while she
and he learnt to skate together, the Princess only
consenting to this, d'Avaux is obliged to admit,
through her desire to please her husband. However, as nothing Mary did could possibly be right
in the eyes of Louis XIV.'s Ambassador, he comments severely on her ridiculous appearance, " with
her skirts very short and half turned up, and iron
skates on her feet, while she learnt to slide
sometimes on one foot, and sometimes on the
other." [2]

To French views of royalty, hedged round with
due observance, it may well have seemed that these
lessons should have taken place in private ; but
in the pursuit of his policy William cared little for
minor considerations. Besides, the Dutch sense of
ridicule not being as keen as the French, the
difficulties of their adored Princess in learning a
new accomplishment very probably inspired them

[1] " Négociations du Comte d'Avaux," vol. iv. p. 226.
[2] *Ibid.*, vol. iv. p. 241.

with sympathy, instead of a Gallic desire to write
neat satirical couplets on the event.

On another occasion the Prince's commands must
have been intensely bitter to the unfortunate
Princess. The anniversary of Charles I.'s death
on the scaffold had always been observed as a day
of mourning among his descendants. Therefore,
on February 16, 1685, the Princess dressed herself
in deep mourning, and prepared to spend the day
in prayer and solitude. However, orders were sent
her by her husband to put on gay attire, and
instead of having her dinner in private and alone,
as was her custom, she was commanded to dine
in public with him. Dish after dish was handed
to her ; and, sitting in misery, she passed them
almost untouched. We may hope that the strength
of her feelings was hidden from William by her
sweet evenness of temper, and submission to his
will. However that may be, in the evening, with
what seemed a crowning outrage to her, he made
one of his rare visits to the theatre, and she was
forced to appear with him there.

Thus William's political purposes were answered,
and the heiress to the English throne showed her
complete dissociation from the policy which inspired
her two uncles, and had led her grandfather to the
scaffold. Viewed from a wide standpoint, what
were one woman's feelings—even if she were made
so unhappy that, young, beautiful, and naturally
endowed with gaiety, she often had no pleasure in
life—compared with the welfare of Europe and the
triumph of the true religion ?

The difficulties and complications of William's
policy were manifold. While in the sight of the
English people he wished to be absolutely dis-
sociated from his Stuart uncles, it was important
for his prestige and position with the States, that
in Holland he should accentuate his position as
husband to the presumptive heiress to the English

crown, and should be considered to be on good
terms with his Stuart uncles.  Therefore Bentinck
announced everywhere that, in treating Monmouth
as he did, William was acting with the knowledge
and consent of the English King, and William
insisted that, in spite of Charles's indignation at
Monmouth's vagaries, he was in reality extremely
fond of his son, and would be grateful to any one
who treated him with kindness.

These announcements possibly had the desired
effect on the Dutch people.  If, however, they ever
came to Charles II.'s ears, which they probably
did through the kind offices of the French Ambassadors at the different Courts, they must have
increased his already deep indignation against his
nephew.  Zitters, the Dutch Envoy, carried the
King apologetic letters from the Prince full of
sorrow for having lost his favour, and ascribing
this misfortune to evil done to him by enemies at
the English Court.  The King answered that the
Prince had no enemies at the Court, and that in
sending such messages he was making fun of him
as well as of M. Zitters, for he well knew that he
had himself alienated the King by " conducting
himself in a manner very opposite to what he ought
to have done, as well in regard to general affairs,
as in the case of the Duke of Monmouth, and the
other conspirators."

After listening to further excuses on the Prince's
behalf, the King laughed bitterly, and said that
the Prince of Orange was cleverer than any one
else, as he took such care of a man whose designs
would either establish a republic in England, or
support chimerical pretensions, which could only
succeed by the ruin of the Prince of Orange himself.[1]

The alliance between two men who " both wor-
shipped the same mistress," and should therefore,

[1] Fox's " Life of James II.," appendix, p. x.

by the nature of things, be rivals, was incomprehensible to Charles; but the Prince had taken his opponent's measure, and knew him to be but a man of straw.

However, on February 19, 1685, at seven o'clock in the evening, news came to The Hague of the death of Charles II., which had taken place three days earlier. When the tidings arrived, the Princess was giving audience to The Hague ladies. Therefore the Prince did not go up to her rooms, but sent to request her to come down to his, where, in the presence of the Duke of Monmouth, he broke the news to her. Mary was much distressed at the death of her uncle, from whom she had always received much kindness; while Monmouth, who seems to have been genuinely fond of his father, and who knew that his worst enemy had mounted the throne, received the information with the utmost anguish. He left the palace shortly afterwards, but returned at ten o'clock, when he and the Prince were shut up together for about two hours. During this interview the Prince gave Monmouth very good advice, exhorting him to do his best to gain the new King's favour, and to wait patiently till his friends, "among whom he might always count upon him, could do something for him."[1] Before daybreak Monmouth left The Hague secretly, being provided by the Prince of Orange with sufficient money for his journey.

[1] "Mémoires de Monsieur de B."

# CHAPTER VII

James II. ascends the throne—The English Envoy's insolence to the Prince and Princess of Orange—Chudleigh—Skelton—Monmouth leaves The Hague—Monmouth's expedition—Question of William's complicity in it—Monmouth's execution—Lady Mary Forester's letters to the Princess—Ball on William's birthday—"The Kermesse"—Mary's sweetness of disposition.

WILLIAM OF ORANGE had been at fault in his calculations, for James II. mounted the throne without any opposition on the part of his subjects. He was in fact acclaimed with a certain amount of enthusiasm, for in the speech to his Council with which he inaugurated the new administration, he made a solemn promise to maintain the established government, and to support and defend the Church of England. He wrote an affectionate letter to his daughter notifying her uncle's death; and William, in order to keep up the illusion of unity with the English King, read this to the States as though received by himself. James's letter to his son-in-law, on the other hand, was extremely cold. It ran thus:

"WHITEHALL,
"*February* 6, 1685.

" I have only time to tell you, that it has pleased God Almighty to take out of this world the King my brother. You will from others have an account of what distemper he died of ; and that all the usual ceremonies were performed this day in proclaiming me King in the city, and other parts. I must end, which I do, with assuring you, you shall find me as kind as you can expect." [1]

[1] Sir John Dalrymple's " Memoirs of Great Britain and Ireland," vol. ii. p. 11.

CONTEMPORARY PRINT OF MARY II.'S ARRIVAL AT WHITEHALL STAIRS.

In the possession of A. M. Broadley, Esq. From the Fraser Collection.

120]

James was happily confident in the strength of
his position, and he did not even object to the
idea of the Prince of Orange paying a visit to
England. "His Britannic Majesty finds a little
pleasure in seeing the Prince reduced to submission," [1] writes Barillon to Louis XIV. James
showed early that he intended to continue the
late King's relations with France. He was moved
to tears of joy when Louis XIV. unexpectedly
presented him with a handsome sum of money, and
he refused to receive the humble apologies sent
him by the Prince of Orange, unless the latter
would consent to attach himself to France. One
favour James granted the Prince—the recall of
Chudleigh, who had been, to William's intense
disgust, put in Sidney's place as Envoy from
England. It must, however, be admitted that, as
Sidney used all his powers to work for the Prince
of Orange, he could hardly be considered a satisfactory emissary from Charles's or James's point of
view. With Chudleigh, William was on the worst
possible terms. There were many causes for dispute between the two men, and Chudleigh had
shown his disregard of the Prince on all possible
occasions. Once he carried his insolence so far
that, meeting the Prince and Princess driving in
a sledge along the principal drive in The Hague, he
pretended that they were masked, and wished to
be incognito, so ordered his coachman not to give
way to them.[2]
On another occasion he gave orders to the
officers under Dutch command not to salute the
Duke of Monmouth, and did not communicate
these orders first to the Prince. In the interview
which took place after this, William lost his temper
with the impertinent Envoy, and advanced his cane
within an inch of his nose. Chudleigh complained

[1] Fox's "Life of James II.," appendix, p. xxxvi.
[2] Burnet's "History of My Own Times," vol. iii. p. 13.

to Charles, and was forbidden to visit William
again.[1]

Skelton, the next Envoy to Holland, was not, however, much more acceptable. He hated the Dutch,
and his appointment was considered a slight to
William, who had specially begged that he should
not be sent in Sidney's place when the withdrawal
of the latter had first been mooted.

The English regiments in the pay of Holland were
a constant cause of dispute between James and
William. James wished to put Roman Catholic
officers at the head of them, or to recall them to
England, and William refused his father-in-law's
demands. James then ordered the officers to throw
up their commissions, but only very few obeyed
him, Skelton's son being among the number. He
held an office in the Princess's household which he
was anxious to keep, but the Prince dismissed him
saying : "Those who will not serve the States, shall
not serve the Princess." [2]

At the announcement of James's accession,
William had at once realised that the continued
residence of Monmouth at The Hague would be
impossible. Hitherto, in spite of Charles's public
disapproval of his son, William had known that
any attention shown to him was in reality very
pleasing to his father, who had been delighted
with the cordial reception Monmouth received at
The Hague in 1683, had privately supplied him with
money, and had written to him with his own hand.[3]
Though, after the Rye House Plot, Charles was
really indignant with Monmouth and no longer
countenanced him secretly, there was always a soft
spot in his heart for his handsome son. James, on
the other hand, was a good hater ; and he detested

---

[1] Sir John Dalrymple's "Memoirs of Great Britain and Ireland,'
Book V. p. 10.
[2] *Ibid.*
[3] Echard's "History of England," vol. iii. p. 705.

the Duke of Monmouth.  Skelton, the new Envoy,
was ordered to have Monmouth despatched to
England that he might be in the King's power.
William, however, did his utmost for Monmouth.
He had already, as we have seen, advised him
wisely, and now he sent Bentinck to him with news
of the design, and with money, and advised him to
go into foreign lands.  The despair of the unfortunate Monmouth was intense ; and he is described
by the French Ambassador as being heard, after
his interview with Bentinck, " crying and making
lamentations " [1] in the little house where he lodged.

Before leaving The Hague, the Duke went to the
Princess—his friend and companion in many days
of pleasure—and begged her to intercede for him
with her father, and " to assure James that for
the future he would not have a more zealous subject, or one more attached to his service." [2]  Mary
complied with her cousin's request, and there is no
doubt that she felt very strongly for him.  James,
however, considered Monmouth's submission an
artifice ; while his humility, and the meekness of
the Prince of Orange, strengthened the English
King in the belief that his own position was im-
pregnable, and that he was safe in any breaches of
the law he might commit with the object of bringing England back to the Roman Catholic religion.

Monmouth fled first to the Spanish Netherlands.
He was expelled from there by the Marquis of
Grana at James's instigation,[3] and went in despera-
tion to Amsterdam, where he says that he fell in
with the wicked men who tempted him to the
design of invading England.  Fletcher, a Scotch
gentleman who accompanied Monmouth, said he
had " good ground to suspect that the Prince of

---

[1] " Négociations du Comte d'Avaux," vol. iv. p. 271.

[2] Fox's " Life of James II.," appendix, p. xxxvi.—Barillon to
Louis XIV.

[3] *Ibid.*

Orange had underhand encouraged the expedition, with the design of ruining Monmouth "; and Sir John Dalrymple says that this authority is high, because Fletcher was in a position to know, and was incapable of lying. On the other hand there is no doubt that William did his best by advice and money to put Monmouth beyond the arm of James's vengeance.[1] In support of William's innocence we have the evidence of his letter of April 30, 1685, to Lord Rochester, in which he says :

" I can assure you, on the word of a man of honour, that I have not known, nor know to this moment, whether the Duke of Monmouth is in Holland. It is true, that it has been said that he was wandering between Rotterdam and Amsterdam, and even that he had been at the Hague ; but although I have done what I could to be informed of the truth, I have not been able to ascertain it, and thus, much less to find means to have him told to leave Holland, which was certainly my intention, knowing that it was not right for him to be in a place so near to where I was, and if I can yet discover him, I will execute my first design." [2]

It may be said that this letter was written to James's brother-in-law, and that for political reasons William had been known on other occasions to asseverate with the utmost solemnity statements which were, to put the matter mildly, slightly misleading. The following extracts from letters to Bentinck, who was in England during Monmouth's expedition, and with whom it must be remembered William was absolutely confidential, seem, however, quite conclusive proofs of his innocence :

" I am impatient to receive a letter from you from London. Those we have had do not please me too much, seeing that Monmouth keeps the field every day. Perhaps the danger appears

---

[1] " Mémoires de Monsieur de B."
[2] " Clarendon Correspondence," vol. i. p. 124.

greater at a distance than it does near at hand. I imagine that the King has need of more regular troops, and that I should not be quite useless to him in England." [1]

About a week later William writes :

" I hope soon to hear of the defeat of the rebels, but the small number of Feversham's troops leaves room for disquiet, as I cannot imagine that Monmouth will be as easy to overcome as Argile. I much fear that they despise him too much, and that thus they may be deceived, but people who reason at a distance as I do are still more easily deceived." [2]

Monmouth himself bears witness to William's innocence; for, in his despairing letter to James, with the scaffold before him, he says :

" The Prince and Princess of Orange can bear witness to you of the assurances that I gave them that I would never lead any rising against you." [3]

In fact the evidence for William's ignorance of Monmouth's intention to invade England is so strong that we may safely suppose that on this occasion Fletcher made a mistake. Possibly he gave credence to vague statements on the part of Monmouth who was " excited," another witness tells us, " by the Scotch lords." [4]

If James's words are true, and Bentinck really showed " terrible anguish " [5] when he heard that James had granted Monmouth an interview, his fear of possible disclosures was probably referable to interviews between William and Monmouth of earlier date, when much had doubtless passed which William would not wish to reach James's ear.

Monmouth was executed on Tower Hill on

---

[1] Letter from Hounslaerdyck, July 6, 1685, in the possession of the Duke of Portland.

[2] *Ibid.*, July 14, 1685, in the possession of the Duke of Portland.

[3] " Mémoires de Jacques II.," vol. iii. p. 48.

[4] " Mémoires de Monsieur de B."

[5] " Mémoires de Jacques II.," vol. iii. p. 87.

July 6, 1685 ; and his death was followed by merci-
less reprisals conducted by Judge Jeffreys in the
west of England. James protested later that he
had not been aware of the brutality of his lieu-
tenant ; but in a letter to the Prince of Orange,
dated September 24, 1685, he says :

" As for news there is little stirring, but that Lord
Chief Justice has almost done his campaigne ; he
has already condemned several hundreds some of
which are already executed, more are to be, and
the others sent to the plantations." [1]

Thus, with what, we may be sure, he considered
judicious firmness, did James inaugurate his reign.

No doubt the Princess of Orange felt much
sorrow at the death of the one man with whom
she had been on terms of equality and intimacy,
certainly too she heard of Jeffreys's cruelty with
horror, as did many other people. The theory,
however, started by her enemies that the execution
of her fascinating cousin permanently alienated her
heart from her father, is quite untenable to any one
knowing her character or the story of her life.

We must not think that the bulletins from England
brought her only tidings of deaths and of insurrec-
tions. Lighter news sometimes came to her, provided
by Lady Mary Forester, who was for some time at
The Hague, and who used, when there, the Princess
remarks with amusement, to play basset every
evening, and then, not understanding Dutch,
to ask an interpreter to secure her winnings for
her. The Princess missed her very much when
she returned to England for the birth of her first
child, and recalled with pleasure their games of
hide-and-seek in the woods surrounding the palace.
When these frolics were in progress, Lady Mary had
been expecting to become a mother, though she
was too shy to inform the Princess of the fact,

[1] Sir John Dalrymple's "Memoirs of Great Britain and Ireland,"
vol. ii. p. 53.

and Mary remarks : " If I had then known your conditione you had never got the reputation of as good a walker as myself, at least we had never pased ditches as we did togethere." In the same letter the Princess alludes to her own increasing stoutness, saying that though she is not changed in her humour she is in her shape, but remarks : " I like this subject so little I shall say no more upon it." [1]

Lady Mary kept the Princess well informed about the gossip at the English Court; and the Princess, from her lively comments, evidently thoroughly enjoyed the budgets of news she received from her friend. After comments, which sound, to our modern ears, strangely outspoken, on sundry contemporary scandals, the Princess continues :

" I am extremely delighted with all the news you write me, but as everything is but nine days wonder so I hope strange marriages will now be laid aside to make rome for some new marvells, therefore I dare not speake of such old things for fear of seaming as old fashioned as they." [2]

She goes on later :

" I don't love the wedings of people I am not acquainted with, yet I shall wish myself at Lord Morpeth's to see how you woud behave yourself, I phansie that imployment will not become you unlesse you woud put on a forehead cloath like Lady Danby to which if you will ad a good large mufler so as to hide your face you might pass for as old a lady as she and then you may give instructions with authority. I have bin but once in the little wood where we played hide and seek since I came hithere, the ill wethere will not suffer much walking."

In the end of her letter she cannot repress a little sigh at the difference between the gay Court in which her correspondent found herself, and the quiet of her own life at The Hague.

[1] Stopford Sackville MSS., vol. 1. p. 29
[2] *Ibid.*, vol. 1. pp. 29 *et seq.*

" I am sory there are no wedings heer " [she says]
"when my maids marry I intend to act Lady " . . .
[here an initial has been erased by the recipient
of the letter] " exactly, I warrante they shall know
the matrimony by heart, and anssere to all with
an audible voice."

Evidently some of the English brides whose
adventures had been related to her by the lively
Lady Mary, had not distinguished themselves by
their knowledge of the marriage service.

However, the Princess was occasionally in the
position to preside at gaieties. On William's
birthday in 1686, a grand ball was given in the
House in the Wood in honour of the Great Elector
of Brandenburg, one of whose wives was the
Princess's aunt. His son, the young Prince Philip
of Brandenburg, had been sent on his travels in
charge of Jaucourt, who speaks with pleasure of a
" beautiful party given by the Princess in her house
in the wood."

To judge from an old engraving the scene must
have been very gay. The gallery and dome of the
octagonal ball-room were brilliantly lit by sconces
and chandeliers, which showed off to their fullest
advantage the priceless paintings with which the
room is panelled. Mary is represented as sitting
on the throne with the musicians opposite her, the
dancers ranged on one side of her and the spectators
on the other, while William and the Elector of
Brandenburg, who were supposed to be incognito,
stand near her.

Dancing had been one of Mary's favourite amusements—an amusement from which she gradually
weaned herself, as she considered herself inclined
to take an undue pleasure in it. She did not,
however, deny herself all enjoyment, for Jaucourt
tells us that the young Prince of Brandenburg used
to pay his court to Mme. la Princesse three times
a week, when he played cards with her, and that

CONTEMPORARY PRINT OF THE CEREMONY AT THE BANQUETING HALL
AT WHITEHALL.

In the possession of A. M. Broadley, Esq.

WILLIAM AND MARY.
In the possession of A. M. Broadley, Esq.

at the time of the "Kermesse" or Great Fair the
Princess enjoyed herself immensely. Then the
citizens, in costumes adorned with their coats of
arms, and wearing orange scarves as a compliment
to the House of Orange, passed in front of the
Palace, where they fired salutes in honour of the
Prince and Princess, who stood at the windows.
Shops were erected in the Bintenhof, which was
the principal square in the town, and people went
to them in masks and bought presents for their
friends. These they sent anonymously, the mys-
tification of the receivers being an essential part
of the excitement. Visiting these shops gave the
Princess much pleasure and a good deal of occupation, for she was so well known at The Hague,
that in order to conceal her identity she was obliged
to change her disguises continually. Jaucourt was
evidently pleased with his presents. "I got a
great many without knowing from whom they
came," [1] he remarks with satisfaction.

The Puritanical spirit was certainly strong in
Mary ; but in considering her life we must not forget the side of her character touched on by Burnet
in his "Essay" on her, written after her death,
when he says that she "carried that air of Life
and Joy about her, that animated all who saw
her." [2] Certainly our view of the Princess is very
imperfect if, in thinking of the many troubles of her
life, and of that indifference to death which seemed
caused partly by them, and partly by the deep
religious feeling which animated her, we do not
take into account the natural joyfulness of heart,
which had its origin in her sweetness of disposition,
and made her blind to fretting causes for annoyance, which might have poisoned life to any one
less soundly constituted.

[1] Fruin's notes to Droste's "Overblyffsels van Geheugchenis,"
p. 448.
[2] Burnet's "Essay on the Memory of the late Queen."

9

This characteristic causes a discrepancy which is often puzzling between the letters about the Princess, which mention the unhappy outward circumstances of her life, and her own memoirs, where she never complains, but speaks with humble surprise and gratitude—which, however, speak volumes—of the Prince's approval of any of her actions.

# CHAPTER VIII

Crisis in the married life of William and Mary—James's scheme—William
and Elizabeth Villiers—Mary's distress—William discovers James's
scheme—Covell to Skelton—Dismissal of the Princess's servants—
The Princess and Burnet—His description of her—The Princess's
views on the Succession—James II.'s folly—The Princess's resentment
at his measures—William and Mary and Lady Russell—Mary's letter
to her.

WE now approach a crisis in the matrimonial life
of William and Mary—a crisis brought about by
James II.'s efforts to separate the wife from the
husband.

In the autumn of 1685, soon after James's
accession, much excitement—echoes of which even
reached England—was caused at The Hague, by
the fact that Covell, the Princess's chaplain, Mrs.
Langford, her nurse or personal maid, and Miss
Trelawney, her chief maid of honour, were dismissed
from her service, and sent back to England.

The causes for this step were kept carefully
secret, for it was to the interest of the principal
agents in the affair on both sides that nothing
should transpire about it. However, from the
letters of the Dutchmen Huyghens and Witsen,
both of whom were well informed as to what
passed at the Dutch Court, we see that James II. in
his jealous hatred of his son-in-law, and his intense
dislike to the idea that, as husband of the presumptive heiress to the English throne, he would one
day, to all practical purposes, reign over England,
determined on an attempt to separate Mary from
him.

A summary remarriage would not of course

have been possible, but rumour whispered, and Huyghens and Witsen evidently believed, that James's plan included the kidnapping of the Princess, and her marriage to a Roman Catholic. They even named the King of France, or, as another account has it, a Popish Prince of France, as the possible bridegroom.

Dr. Fruin remarks [1] that though the fact that Huyghens, William's private secretary, as well as Witsen, attached faith to this story, forbids us to rule it out of court without due consideration, it is hardly possible to attribute to James and to his Government the mad idea of marrying the Princess of Orange to any one, while her marriage with William was not annulled. To any one, however, who possesses even a casual acquaintance with James's schemes, and his methods of carrying them out, it is not difficult to believe that without the knowledge of his Government, he might have planned to separate Mary from her husband, and to convey her, willingly or unwillingly, to England. Possibly he hoped that, if supported by France, it would be practicable for him to obtain from the Pope the annulment of the marriage, and to arrange an alliance between the heiress to his throne, and some one who would have continued the work of bringing the country back to the fold of the true Church. Some years earlier, in speaking of the marital relations between William and Mary, James gives a hint which shows that the idea of finding grounds for the annulment of the marriage was already working in his brain. Parental affection doubtless had its influence in deciding him to take this step, for it must be remembered that all the Englishmen who visited the Dutch Court, were indignant at William's treatment of his beautiful young wife. Mary's letter to James in 1688, in which she says

[1] Notes to Droste's "Overblyffsels van Geheugchenis," vol. ii. p. 261.

that she " is not in awe, and is happier than he thinks," [1] shows that, though the Princess, with her habitual caution, only refers casually to her state of subjection, the subject was in discussion between the father and daughter.

The possibility of finding a reason for separating Mary from William, was first disclosed to James by Skelton, who, we are told, " found out the secrets in the Princess's household." [2] In other words, he discovered the liaison between the Prince and Elizabeth Villiers, and further, the useful fact that, whatever the Princess may have suspected, she knew nothing for certain about her husband's infidelity. As Burnet remarked of William in the first draft of his history, [3] " if he has been guilty of any disorders too common to princes, yet he has not practised them as some to whom he is nearly related have done, but has endeavoured to cover them, tho' let Princes be as secret as they will in such matters, they are always known." Burnet goes on to say that William's want of generosity in money matters, " and another point too tender to be put in writing "—probably his rough treatment of his wife—are the only things that " hinder him from being the greatest King that has been for many ages."

At any rate, William's secret was on this occasion made use of by Skelton, for he, with James's knowledge, instructed Covell, the Princess's chaplain, who seems to have been the principal agent in the intrigue, to enlighten her about her husband's attachment to Elizabeth Villiers. Anne Trelawney, the Princess's favourite maid of honour, and Mrs. Langford, her nurse, were also privy to the scheme. Huyghens describes the object of William's affections—" the squinter," he calls her—in most

---

[1] Birch, Add. MSS., 4,163, British Museum.
[2] Fox's " Life of James II.," p. 128.
[3] Harleian Collection, 6,584, British Museum.

unfavourable colours, as utterly lacking in dignity, very unattractive, and in fact as the ordinary type of the "fast woman" of the period. Other contemporaries, however, speak of her wit and wisdom, and we may be sure she would not have exerted for so long a decided influence over William had she not possessed more remarkable qualities than are credited to her by William's secretary. The latter evidently shares in the affection and admiration for the Princess felt by every one who came into contact with her, and is indignant with his master for his neglect of her.

The Princess's misery at the news of her husband's infidelity was heartrending. For some time she refused to believe it; but, according to Daniel de Bourdon,[1] she was one night persuaded to watch on the staircase leading to the rooms occupied by the maids of honour. William had told her that he would be kept up late by business, and when he at last came to her at two o'clock in the morning he found her weeping. In his anger he refused to speak to her or to see her for several days.

Whatever truth there may be in this account of the matter, it is at any rate certain that the fact of her husband's infidelity was by some means brought home to her, that she was utterly miserable, and that many people were indignant with the Prince for his treatment of her. Even Bentinck, whose affection for his master was so great that for his sake he lived what a contemporary calls a life of slavery, and was only free while William was giving audience to other people, espoused her cause, and was for a time in disgrace in consequence. It is curious, too, to hear that Bentinck's wife, Anne Villiers, who was, unlike her sister, a woman of great gentleness and virtue, and was evidently sincerely attached to the Princess, also sided with her on this occasion.

[1] "Mémoires de Monsieur de B."

William, however, apparently soon managed to soothe the Princess, or at least to compel her to submit to his will. What happened exactly between them is of course a matter for conjecture. From subsequent events, however, it is clear that M. de Bourdon is not very incorrect when he says that William represented his attachment to Elizabeth Villiers as merely a temporary amusement, and that the Princess, though thoroughly miserable, appeared to see everything with her husband's eyes, professed herself satisfied with his professions of affection, and promised to submit to his will in everything.

It may be remarked however that Burnet, who came to the Court a few months later, was much struck with what he calls the one defect in the Princess's character, or at least the one peculiarity which might hide a defect. This is in his opinion [1] " her closeness, which is so very strange in one of her age, that it may give colour to fear there may be something sinister underneath." Later, Burnet changed this opinion, and it does not appear in his printed history. He realised that the Princess's extraordinary discretion, which led her, he remarks, to say the right thing to every one, never to offend anybody, and never even to make an intimate friend among her ladies, for fear of being thought to show favouritism, had been taught her by the difficulties of her position. William learnt this fact later about his wife, and told Lord Danby that he must not think the Queen always agreed with him because she did not contradict what he said. From Mary's subsequent attitude it seems probable that she was not really deceived as to the facts of the case, however much her wifely submission made her feel it a duty to submit to them.

Meanwhile the Prince, with his usual astuteness,

---

[1] Harleian Collection, 6,584, British Museum.

set to work to discover the instigators of the
plot. Knowing that much correspondence with
Skelton was going on, he pretended to go out
hunting, and placed people to intercept and to
search any one who left the Court with letters. A
servant was caught with a packet from the in-
triguers, giving assurances to James that their
efforts to alienate the Princess from her husband
were likely to be successful.

One of the letters in the packet was written by
Covell, the chaplain to Skelton, and ran as follows :

" *Dr. Covell to Mr. Skelton. Dieren Oct.* 1685.

" Your Honour may be astonished at the news,
but it is too true the Princess's heart is like to
break ; yet she, everyday with Mrs. Jesson and
Madame Zulestyn, counterfeits the greatest joy,
and looks upon us as dogged as may be.

" We dare no more speak to her. The prince
hath infallibly made her his absolute slave, and
there is an end of it. I wish to God I could see
the King give you some good thing for your life,
for I would have it out of the power of any revocation ; for I assure you I fear the Prince will for
ever rule the roast. As for Mr. Chudleigh, if his
business be not done beyond the power of the
Prince, before the King die, Mr. Chudleigh will be
in an illtaking. But I wonder what the devil
makes the Prince so cold to you. None but pimps
and bawds must expect any tolerable usage here.

" I beseech God preserve the King many and
many years. I do not wonder much at the new
Marchioness's [1] behaviour, it is so like the breed.
We shall see fine doings if we once come to town.
What would you say if the Princess should take her
into the Chapel, or in time into the bedchamber ?
I cannot fancy the sisters [2] will long agree. You

---

[1] Possibly Mme. Puisars, one of the Villiers sisters.
[2] The Villiers.

guess right about Mr. d'Allonne, for he is Secretary
in that as well as in other private matters. The
widow and maid [1] and I do often remember Your
Honour and your most excellent Lady with all
hearty and true respects. They both this minute
most passionately desired me to present their
most humble service to you ; and I beseech you
accept of mine. I never so heartily longed for
to come to the Hague : God send us a happy meeting. The Princess is just now junketing with
Madame Bentinck and Mrs. Jesson in Madame
Zulestyn's chamber." [2]

It will be remarked that Lady Inchiquin, the
Princess's principal attendant, is not mentioned in
this letter. She had left The Hague and gone to
England in 1682. After the death of Lord Inchiquin
she married again, but her second venture does
not seem to have been fortunate, as we are told
in 1694 :

" The Lord Howard of Escrick, who not long
since married the Lady Inchiquin, has left her
already for the sake of another woman who he was
in league with before, and it is said they are both
gone together for Holland." [3]

Mrs. Jesson, one of the maids of honour men-
tioned, had been very intimate with Ken when he
was the Princess's chaplain, and later he made use
of her in an attempt to communicate with the
Princess after she had become Queen of England.
She was at this time in high favour, but Elizabeth
Villiers and she had been in disgrace with the
Princess in 1682 " because of a scandal the two were
spreading about people of the highest rank." [4]
Possibly James II. was the victim of their gossip.

Abel Tassin d'Alone, the Princess's private secre-

---

[1] Mrs. Langford and Miss Trelawney.
[2] " Clarendon Correspondence," vol. i. p. 165.
[3] " Lexington Papers "—Vernon to Lexington, January 1, 1695.
[4] Fruin's note 5,330 to Droste's " Overblyffsels van Geheugchenis."

tary, who is mentioned in this letter, occupied, as is said here, a very confidential position with her. He was popularly supposed to be the illegitimate son of William II. of Holland. He accompanied the Princess to England, stayed on after her death at the English Court with no particular occupation, till Huyghens also died, when he stepped into his shoes and became private secretary to William III.

As a reason for demanding the recall of Skelton, William sent Covell's letter to Rochester. With characteristic diplomacy he explained that it had fallen by chance into his hands, and that, having cause to suspect Covell's fidelity, he had read it by means of a cypher found in the chaplain's desk.

William wisely identifies the Princess with himself in the affair, and says :

" The Princess and I have done nothing but to send him away from the house, any other punishment we have left to his Bishop. I consider I have much reason to complain of Mr. Skelton in this affair, for having kept up such a correspondence in my house ; after the way I have treated him since he came here, he should not have repaid me thus."

James must have been intensely disgusted and disappointed at the turn affairs had taken. He was, however, obliged to submit to his son-in-law, who certainly was in a position, in Covell's words, " to rule the roast " ; for, owing to the exigencies of the case, James was helpless. He objected, however, to the recall of his Minister while so much business was in his hands, but promised to send for him as soon as he conveniently could.

As to Dr. Covell, instead of being punished by his Bishop, he received preferment from James. Witsen, who visited England in 1689, and kept a diary, gives a curious account of the relations

between William when King, and his wife's former
chaplain.

He says :

" *7th Nov.* 1689.—Dr. Covel, Vicechancellor of
Cambridge, came to Newmarket to harangue the
King on his knees. It resembled an adoration.
He had been for three years Chaplain at the Hague,
and had been expelled, because at the instance of
James he had conspired with the maids of honour
to stir up strife between William and Mary, then to
kidnap her, and to marry her to a Popish French
Prince. For this reason he was sent back to
England. King James had made him his Chancellor. And now he came, without having spoken
to King William since, to praise him in a flowery
speech as a saint and saviour of his country, and
to execrate the late Government. It was noticed,
however, that he never looked the King straight
in the face." [1]

Great caution was shown by every one at The
Hague in speaking of the affair. Bentinck writes
to Sidney about it as follows, and it is probable
that William prompted the letter :

" You will be extremely astonished to hear of
the change which has taken place at our Court.
His Highness received by chance a letter which
shewed that for a long time Dr. Covel has been a
malicious spy in the house, who repeated a great
many things invented to do harm; therefore the
Princess sent him away, without inflicting on him
any further punishment because of his office;
and as it was clearly proved that Madame Langfort
and Miss Trelawney were in league with him, the
Princess sent them also away this morning. It is
a horrible thing that people should be wicked
enough to wish to do harm to those who feed them,
but even worse that the clergy should be capable

---

[1] Fruin's notes to Droste's " Overblyffsels van Geheugchenis,"
vol. ii. p. 461.

of it. The second chaplain Langfort is also in the intrigue. I do not complain of the malice those people have shewn about me, as I see that they betray their master and mistress. Please tell me whether anyone has repeated to you a story which has been charitably concocted at our expense as if we had not shewn proper respect to her Royal Highness on our arrival at Hounslaerdyke, so that I may know what people are saying."[1]

Constantine Huyghens wrote to his brother about the same subject on October 22 :

" You have already heard that our Dr. Covel, Mistris Langford and Mistris Trelawney have been dismissed, and will appear no more at Court. They have deserved it to a certain extent, especially the first."[2]

However, later, people began to be less cautious, and Huyghens writes in 1692 in his " Journal ":

" Dr. Hutton was talking to me for a long time. He says that Dr. Covel, Mrs. Langford, and Miss Trelawney were corresponding with the Envoy Skelton with the intention of marrying the Queen " [Mary, then Queen of England] " to the King of France, so that she might escape from William."

Jaucourt gives us another point of view in his " Memoirs," written at Geneva in 1708, when he says :

" The Princess shewed great respect for her husband, but he had not much consideration for her. As an example, when d'Alonne, the Princess's secretary, deciphered certain letters in which something was repeated about the intrigue between the Prince and Miss Villiers, she was obliged to her great regret to send away her Nurse, and a young lady who had been educated with her."

The poor Princess was certainly the sufferer all

[1] " Henry Sidney's Diary and Correspondence," vol. ii. p. 253.
[2] Fruin's notes to Droste's " Overblyffsels van Geheugchenis," vol. ii. 460,

round, for she was not only forced to submit with apparent complacency to the continuation of the intrigue between William and Elizabeth Villiers, but had also the sorrow of parting with two friends to whom she was warmly attached. The only comment she makes on the affair is to be found in a letter to Lady Bathurst (December 11, 1685), in which she asks her correspondent to pay £20 a year for her to Lady Prestwich, who would have been her "mother of maids" if this office had existed at the Dutch Court. The Princess does not explain the circumstances, but, apparently to make up for some disappointment Lady Prestwich had felt about the matter, the Princess had for some time made her a grant of £20 a year, and she asks Lady Bathurst to pay the money for her in the future.

" my Mam " [she says] " haveing put her self out of a conditione of ever doing any thing more for me of wch I have not spoke it being a thing for wch I was good natured enough remembering what she had bin to me to be sory for at first but her behaviour has bin such as has given me just cause to forget that. I will say no more upon this subject because I think when what is past cant be recaled the lesse one thinks of it the beter." [1]

That the Princess, however, continued to suffer acutely from her husband's infidelity, and that he did not succeed in deceiving her, is shown by Mme. de Zoutelande in her "Memoirs." What she says is also interesting as proving that at this time Mary was in confidential correspondence with her father, and that she did not scruple to appeal to him for help against her husband.

Speaking of the liaison between William and Elizabeth Villiers, Mme. de Zoutelande says :

" It did not fail to give umbrage to the Princess of Orange, who wrote about it to King James,

[1] Letter in the Bathurst Collection.

who was reigning at that time. One day when the Prince had gone out to hunt, the Princess made Mistress Villiers start for England, pretending that it was to carry a letter from her to her Father. When the Prince returned, they did not fail to tell him that the Princess had sent her away, but he had the discretion not to say anything about it.

" When Mistress Villiers arrived at Harwich, she began to suspect something, and pretended to wish to walk by herself, but finding a packet-boat which was going to Holland, she returned to the Hague while the Princess thought she was in England, where she had begged King James to keep her in confinement. Mistress Villiers went to live with her sister who had married M. Pisars, the eldest son of the Marquis de Thouars. She often went to see the Prince incognito, as I have frequently seen her pass, her head wrapped in a scarf in the Flemish fashion ; she passed through the Earl of Portland's apartments." [1]

Meanwhile, Mary was destined to make a new friend, to whose able and admiring pen we owe much of our knowledge of her. In the year 1686 Gilbert Burnet, afterwards Bishop of Salisbury, came by William's invitation to The Hague, and waited on the Prince and Princess. The former, he said,

" seemed highly dissatisfied with the King's conduct. He apprehended that he would give such jealousies of himself and come under such jealousies from his people, that these would throw him into a French management, and engage him into such desperate designs as would force violent remedies. There was a gravity in his whole deportment that struck me." [2]

Burnet was much struck by the Prince's belief

---

[1] Fruin's notes to Droste's " Overblyffsels van Geheugchenis," vol. ii. p. 538.

[2] Burnet's " History of My Own Times," vol. iii. p. 131.

in predestination, and in the fact that all things
spring from the absolute will and providence of
God. This belief was a practical one, for William
refused to be alarmed when Burnet told him that
an attempt was to be made to seize him when
he went on the sands at Scheveling, and to convey him to France. The Princess, on the other
hand, was much alarmed; and doubtless was grateful to Burnet for this intimation of her husband's
danger, which led to his being induced with much
difficulty to accept the attendance of a guard.

The picture Burnet gives of the Princess at this
time is very charming. She was now a beautiful
woman of four-and-twenty, her growing stoutness
being her only defect. She had evidently inherited
the Stuart power of fascination; and in contradistinction to her husband, her sweet, graceful
deportment, vivacity, and cheerfulness charmed
all who met her. Burnet was also much struck by
her understanding. She had read a great deal,
had reflected on what she read, and had very
decided opinions; though she expressed them with
the utmost gentleness. For instance, she considered that in writing history, kings and queens
should be treated impartially and without flattery;
and added that,

" if princes would do ill things, they must expect
that the world will take revenges on their memory,
since they cannot reach their persons : that was but
a small suffering, far short of what others suffered
at their hands." [1]

When she penned these words, Mary had travelled
far from the doctrine of divine right of kings, to
which her father was at this time acknowledging
allegiance.

The Princess soon became on terms of intimacy
with Burnet; and one day, evidently at the Prince's
instigation, he put to her a question which had

[1] Burnet's " History of My Own Times," vol. iii. p. 135.

agitated William's mind ever since his marriage,
though he had been too proud to approach his wife
on the subject. If the Princess were to inherit the
throne, Burnet asked her, what position did she
intend the Prince to hold? At first she could not
understand what was meant by the question, for
she had always thought that what belonged to her
would consequently belong to her husband. Burnet told her that this would not be the case, and
cited to her the instance of Henry VII., who had
reigned, by his wife's right only, after her death,
and on the other hand, that of Philip II. of Spain,
who had been completely excluded from the administration of affairs in England.

"I told her" [continues Burnet, who had evidently noticed the Princess's unhappiness about the
position Elizabeth Villiers held in the Prince's
affections, and was anxious to be a peacemaker]
"that a titular kingship was no acceptable thing
to a man, especially if it was to depend on another's
life : and such a nominal dignity might endanger
the real one that the prince had in Holland. She
desired me to propose a remedy. I told her the
remedy, if she could bring her mind to it, was to
be contented to be his wife, and to engage herself
to him, that she would give him the real authority
as soon as it came into her hands, and endeavour
effectually to get it to be legally vested in him
during life : this would lay the greatest obligation
on him possible, and lay the foundation of a perfect union between them, which had been of late a
little embroiled : this would also give him another
sense of all our affairs : I asked pardon for the
presumption of moving her in such a tender point,
but I solemnly protested that no person living had
moved me in it, or so much as knew of it, or
should ever know it, but as she should order it.
I hoped she would consider well of it for, if she
once declared her mind, I hoped she would never

CONTEMPORARY PRINT OF THE CORONATION PROCESSION.

In the Collection of A. M. Broadley, Esq.

144]

go back, or retract it. I desired her therefore to take time to think of it. She presently answered me, she would take no time to consider of anything by which she could express her regard and affection to the prince, and ordered me to give him an account of all that I had laid before her, and to bring him to her, and I should hear what she would say upon it. He was that day a hunting and next day I acquainted him with all that had passed, and carried him to her when she in a very frank manner told him, that she did not know that the laws of England were so contrary to the laws of God, as I had informed her : she did not think that the husband was ever to be obedient to the wife ; she promised him, he should always bear rule ; and she asked only that he would obey the command of ' Husbands love your wives,' as she should do that, ' Wives be obedient to your husbands in all things.' From this lively introduction we engaged into a long discourse of the affairs of England. Both seemed well pleased with me, and with all that I had suggested. But such was the Prince's cold way, that he said not one word to me upon it, that looked like encouragement. Yet he spoke of it to some about him in another strain. He said, he had been nine years married, and had never the confidence to press this matter on the queen, which I had now brought about easily in a day. Ever after that he seemed to trust me entirely." [1]

Thus Mary showed her willingness to give up everything to her husband. However, though the devotion she showed on this occasion may have served to increase the love he undoubtedly felt for her, and manifested at her death in a passion of remorseful regret which almost killed him, he could not rise to the height of sacrificing his infatuation for Elizabeth Villiers for her sake.

[1] Burnet's " History of My Own Times," vol. iii. p. 138.

10

That cross was to accompany her to the end of her life.

Meanwhile, in England, matters were going very badly, James having embarked on the senseless course of tyranny which was to lose him the crown. Mass was celebrated publicly in the chapel of St. James's Palace, a Jesuit School was established in London, monasteries were built, and monks, in the habits of their different orders, were seen about the streets, while Romish chapels began to spring up not only in London, but in different parts of the country. The Bishop of London was suspended for refusing to punish Dr. Sharp, who had spoken against Popery, and when the Princess of Orange, whose religious education had been conducted by the Bishop and her marriage ceremony performed by him, wrote a remonstrance to James on the subject, he reprimanded her for interfering in his concerns. However, the Princess continued to show her sympathy with the Anglican Church; and when the King, in his determination to force Popery on his people, trampled on the rights of Oxford University, she subscribed £200 to the ejected Fellows. This action on her part was necessary, for efforts were continually made by James to represent his daughter's views as different from those of her husband; whereas, whatever her private troubles might be, the Princess had now taken her line decidedly, and had determined to throw in her lot with William, and to fight with him for the preservation of what she considered the true religion.

James now broke the Test Act, which the English nation considered their defence against the re-establishment of the Romish faith, and admitted Roman Catholics into the Army. He also promulgated the speciously liberal Declaration of Indulgence, which removed all penal laws against both Roman Catholics and Dissenters,

and authorised them to perform their worship
publicly.

James tried in vain to obtain William's consent to
these measures, and was very angry when it was
refused. While William spared no pains to obtain
success, his father-in-law continued his senseless
system of misgovernment. The Quaker William
Penn, was sent by him to Holland to interview the
Prince of Orange, with whom he had two or three
long audiences ; but though the Prince assented
to a toleration both of Dissenters and of Papists,
provided this were legalised by Act of Parliament,
he still refused, without Parliamentary consent, to
have any part in the revocation of the Test Act.[1]
The Princess, who was appealed to separately,
was equally decided, and expressed resentment on
receiving the request. She was, like William, strong
in her opinion " that no violence should be done
to the conscience of any Christian and that no one
should be persecuted for differing from the dominant
and established religion."

A document signed by the Prince and Princess
embodying these views, was drawn up by the
Pensioner Fagel, translated by Burnet, and was sent
into England, where the King showed it to the
Cabinet Council, but nothing further followed.
However, William's emissaries in England were
tireless in impressing on every one that the Prince
and Princess of Orange took the popular side.

In March, 1686, over a year after her husband's
execution—the length of time after the event gives
the occurrence special political significance—Rachel
Lady Russell received a visit from Dyckvelt the
Dutch Ambassador. He came to condole with
her on the loss of her husband, and to assure her,
from the Prince and Princess of Orange,

" That if it ever came to be in their power there
was nothing I could ask that they should not find

---

[1] Oldmixon's " History of the Stuarts," vol. ii. p. 722.

content in granting. That for the re-establishment
of my son what I should at any time see reason to
ask would be done in as full and ample a manner as
was possible. That he did not deliver this message
in a private capacity, but as a public Minister." [1]

These protestations were followed in about three
months by a letter from the Princess, which ran as
follows :

" I did not expect so many thanks my Lady
Russell, as I find in your letter by Mr. Dykvelt,
who has said so much to me of all the marks of
kindness you showed both to the Prince and myself,
that I should be ashamed not to have answered it
sooner, but that you know one is not always provided with an opportunity of sending letters safely,
of which indeed I am as much to seek now as ever,
but hoping Mrs. Herbert will sooner find one than I,
I resolve to leave this with her, not knowing when
it may come to you, but whenever it does, pray do
me the justice to believe, that I have all the esteem
for you which so good a character deserves, as I
have heard given you by all people both before I
left England and since I have been here. And
have had as much pity as any could have of the sad
misfortunes you have had, with much more compassion when they happen to persons who deserve
so well, and yet those are they we often see the
most unlucky on the world, as you find by experience ; but I hope your son will live to be a comfort
to you, which, under God, I believe will be the best
you can have. As for myself, I can only assure
both you and my Lord of Bedford, that I should be
very glad it lay in my power to do you any kindness ; the same I can answer for the Prince ; and
indeed you have expressed so much for us both to
Mr. Dykvelt, that if it were possible it would increase
the esteem I had before for you which I shall be very

[1] " Lady Russell's Correspondence," vol. i. p. 204.

glad of any occasion to shew, and more to be better known to you, that I might persuade myself of the desire I have that you should be one of my friends.

"MARIE.

"HONSLERDYKE,
"*July 12th*, 1687." [1]

In February, 1688, the Princess wrote again, this time to congratulate Lady Russell on her daughter's engagement to Lord Cavendish;

"And since I wish so well to my Lord Devonshire" [she says] "I cant but be glad it is his son, believing you will have taught your daughter, after your own example, to be so good a wife, that Lord Cavendish can't choose but be very happy with her, I assure you I wish it with all my heart, and if that could contribute anything to your content, you may be sure of as much as it is possible for you to have; and not only my wishes, but upon all occasions, I shall be glad to show more than by words the esteem I have for you.

"MARIE.

"HAGUE,
"*Feb.* 13, 1678–8." [2]

Meanwhile James was claiming as his royal prerogative the right to break all laws at will, and his chronicler remarks naïvely :

"A great power was thus committed to the King, and it was reasonable to consider that he would never make an unreasonable use of it, for there existed no point in the prerogative which the King if he chose to do so could not abuse to the ruin of the people." [3]

Here James evidently considered that he was

[1] "Lady Russell's Correspondence," vol. i. p. 224.
[2] *Ibid.*, vol. i. p. 238.
[3] "Mémoires de Jacques II.," vol. iii. p. 131.

uttering a truism, and we cannot be surprised when he says ruefully that :

" the disposition to murmur among the clergy and the people began to take up much of His Majesty's time, and to exercise his patience considerably." [1]

Nevertheless, a certain respect is due to James's sincerity, whatever we may think of his understanding. Probably—though under a different name—he shared William of Orange's belief in predestination. Therefore, as William considered himself raised by Providence to protect Protestantism in Europe, James thought that, having risked his crown for his faith, his having safely ascended the throne contrary to all expectations, was a proof of special Divine protection, and that he was destined to fulfil the sacred duty of bringing back heretic England to the fold of the Mother Church of Rome.

[1] "Mémoires de Jacques II.," vol. iii. p. 139.

# CHAPTER IX

JAMES II. saw clearly that if he intended to make
his efforts for the conversion of England to Roman
Catholicism permanently efficacious, it was necessary that the heiress to the English throne should
embrace the true faith. The effort to bring about
this happy consummation by separating her from
her husband having failed ignominiously, he now
set about a method to gain his ends which was less
fantastic, but almost as impossible. He would
use the same means that—reinforced, as we know,
by certain circumstances of her life—had succeeded
in the case of the Duchess of York. Mary, like
her mother, must be convinced by argument. The
hope showed a cheerful disregard of difficulties,
which was eminently characteristic of James.

He opened the campaign on May 3, 1687, by
telling his daughter that the unpopular measures
he had brought forward had all been for the good
of the monarchy. To this she replied on June 17 :
"When you will have me speak as I think I
cannot always be of the same mind as Your Majesty.
What you do seems too much to the prejudice of
the Church I am of for me to like it."[1]

On November 4, 1687, James wrote the Princess
a long letter which he despatched to her by d'Albe-

[1] Birch's Add. MSS., 4,163, vol. i., British Museum.

ville, an Irish Jesuit, whose real name was White, but who had been honoured with the title of Marquis as a reward for acting as a spy in the service of the Spaniards. He had been sent by James with instructions to induce the Prince of Orange to consent to the abolition of the Test Act,[1] and to assure him that James had never wished to prevent the succession of the Princess of Orange to the English throne, and that the report that he intended to confer the crown at his death on the Duke of Berwick was quite untrue. D'Albeville was also charged, as he had often been before, with messages begging the Prince and Princess to have nothing further to do with Burnet—messages to which, as to most of those addressed to them by James, they paid no attention.

James began his letter by saying that, from what d'Albeville told him, the Princess wished to know his reasons for being converted to the Roman Catholic faith. He had been brought up, he said, very strictly in the Anglican religion by Dr. Stuart, and had been so zealous about it that, when the Queen Henrietta Maria tried to force the Duke of Gloucester to become a Roman Catholic, he withstood her—though he is careful to add that he did this with proper respect. The first thing, to quote from his letter, which led him to consider the question seriously was

" the great devotion I remarked among Catholics of all sorts, in all places where I found myself among them, the great charities they have to keep up, and that every day I meet people of my acquaintance who becoming of this religion, abandoned their licentious life, and led one suitable to good Christian although several of them remained in the world." [2]

James goes on to say that he then considered the

[1] Sir John Dalrymple's " Memoirs of Great Britain and Ireland," vol. ii. p. 15.

[2] " Lettres et Mémoires de Marie Reine d'Angleterre," edited by Countess Bentinck, p. 4.

reasons for the Reformation, and read Heyling's
" History of the Reformation " and the preface to
Hooker's " Ecclesiastical Polity," but found nothing
satisfying in them. He next turned his attention
to books written to prove the infallibility of the
Roman Church, and " soon found the truth of them
could not be denied without upsetting the founda-
tions of Christianity." James then quotes our
Lord's words to St. Peter and to His disciples on
founding His Church and feeding His sheep. He
goes on to declare the right of the Church to be the
interpreter of the Bible, which she had declared to
be canonic, and here his premises seem rather weak,
for he says : " Now it is impossible to think that
anyone can be as capable of interpreting the Holy
Scriptures as the person who has assured us
of their correctness and authenticity." The Reformers, he argues, were more concerned with tem-
poral than with spiritual affairs, and were not inspired by the Holy Spirit. An infallible Church
must exist, or our Lord would never have said that
the gates of hell could not prevail against her, and
he remarks with some reason, and a reference to his
recent experiences, that he is confirmed in this belief
by the practice of the Anglican Church,
" which has always acted since the time of the
Reformation as though she believed herself to be
infallible, though she refuses to allow it, but otherwise why should she have been so severe towards
those who differed from her from the beginning of
the Reformation, and have made such rigorous laws
against them, which from time to time have been
executed even more rigorously, as is generally
known, and those against the Protestant Nonconformists as well as the Romans."
The English Church can have no grounds, James
asserts, for disapproving of those who leave her,
when she has herself left the Catholic Church.
Burnet tells us that, as d'Albeville had to wait in

England to collect despatches, this letter did not reach the Princess till late on the evening of Christmas Eve, 1687. On Christmas Day she received the sacrament and spent most of her time in church, yet he remarks, with a pride in the capacity of his beloved Princess which her husband evidently shared, that the Prince sent him, on December 26, the rough copy with the amended draft of the Princess's answer to her father, and that the rough copy had been very little altered.

In this answer, after a few preliminaries, the Princess said that she had indeed wished to know James's reasons for his change of religion, and that in spite of this change she would always ask for his prayers and his blessing. She was always grateful, she said, to her instructors in the Anglican Communion ; but they had never hidden from her that much good existed in the Roman religion. Reading in the Scriptures that it was her duty to work out her own salvation with fear and trembling, and that each person must give account for his own works, she " thought it her duty, to have a care for her soul herself, and had therefore read much, and could say that she was a Protestant, not because she had been brought up as one, but because she was convinced by her own judgment that she was in the right path." The reproach that Protestants led a life of less devotion than did Roman Catholics had evidently distressed her, and she begs the King not to censure a Church because of the disordered lives of those who profess it. Those who behave thus are a scandal ; and " assuredly it is not the principles of their religion which makes them live like that."

After expressions of humility on her disability to defend her Church, the Princess speaks with no uncertain voice; and as her self-abnegation and submission to the Prince have sometimes caused her to be considered a person of little ability, it seems advisable to translate the letter *in extenso* from the French, in which it was written. It shows plainly the strength and clearness of Mary's religious views, and enables us to estimate her much criticised attitude towards her father with fairness. Though the Princess had been well instructed in controversial questions, and the errors of the Roman Church had doubtless been strongly insisted on by the English clergy who took charge of her religious instruction during her youth, any one reading this letter, and knowing the circumstances in which it was written, would, I think, allow it to be a remarkable composition, and one which showed reasoning power and intellect of an unusually high order.

"As to the infallibility of the Roman Church" [1] [the Princess writes], "I have never heard that it was decided, even by Roman Catholics, in what it consists, and it remains a matter of dispute whether it is in the Pope alone, or in a General Council, or in the two together, and I hope that Your Majesty will allow me to ask where it was when there were sometimes three Popes at the same time, each having his Council, which he styled General, and one fulminating anathemas against the other? Was not the succession at least a little interrupted? It is not necessary to read much history to discover that all Popes have not been guided by the Holy Spirit, and I do not know, whether they have nevertheless continued to be successors to St. Peter, when their lives were so openly opposed to his doctrine. However the passage in Matthew 16th, which I know is generally alleged to prove St. Peter's authority above the other Apostles, is differently interpreted by us. We think that the question Our Saviour repeats three times, 'Simon, son of Jonas, lovest

[1] "Lettres et Mémoires de Marie Reine d'Angleterre," edited by Countess Bentinck, p. 13.

you Me ? ' was only put to him because of his
triple denial, so that by this triple confession he
might be re-established after his fall, and that
this passage is (as it has pleased Your Majesty
to mention himself) said to all the Apostles ; otherwise St. Paul would not have been aware of the
Saviour's intention, when he claims the same
privileges ; and not only does this, but resists
St. Peter to his face because he was blameable,
and if he (St. Peter) could not himself support this
authority, I do not see how his successors can lay
claim to it. No Christian would deny that the
Apostles were infallible in their doctrine, being
manifestly guided by the Holy Spirit. But
nevertheless the gifts, as well as the other miracles,
have ceased for a long time, and the present Roman
Church is so different from the primitive Church,
that all those of the last-named party are very
glad to separate themselves from the other (the
Roman Church). And the principal object of the
Anglican Church which obliged it to form itself
into a separate body was only to efface all the
abuses which had crept into the Church and to preserve its primitive purity, as far as that is possible
in this corrupt period of the world. As to the reading of the Holy Scripture, I wish only that Your
Majesty may remind yourself that the Saviour
himself commanded the Jews to search diligently
in the Scriptures. St. Paul orders his Epistles to
be read to all the holy brothers, and says :
' I speak to you as to wise men ; judge what I say
to you.' And under the Mosaic law, when the
Scriptures were publicly read, it was not ordered
that only the Scribes and Doctors and Lawyers
should be present, but even women and children.
I could mention several passages of Scripture on
this subject, but I should be too tedious ; all I
will add is that God, who has created us reasonable
beings, assuredly wishes that we should use the

reason given us on religious matters. For though our faith is above our reason, it is nowise contrary to it, and Our Saviour does not make use of any other method to convince us of St. Thomas's incredulity, than by making him put his fingers in the print of the nails in his hands, and his hand in his side, and allowing him to be convinced by his own reason, and not by that of his fellow disciples, who were already convinced. It is certain that some people make a bad use of the Scriptures, and most of the sects find something in them which with great difficulty they twist to bear out their view. But it seems to me that is not a sufficient reason for forbidding the free use of them to the rest of mankind. However, it is certain, as Your Majesty himself remarks, that, provided one believes in the infallibility of the Roman Church, all the rest becomes a necessary consequence, because then her decrees must be believed as such, and the Scriptures mean nothing, or anything, just as it pleases her to construe them. But I have already stated my opinion on this. The Roman Church allows no contradiction. The English Church certainly sets up no claim to infallibility ; but she is very unfortunate when all the persecution against the Nonconformists is laid to her charge, as it is notorious that all these severe laws have been promulgated against State crimes, and that it is the Government, and not the Church, who has judged them necessary. Since the Reformation our enemies have always endeavoured to raise dissensions among us, and unfortunately have succeeded only too well. But if Your Majesty would please to consider the matter, you would find a great difference between the separation of the Anglican Church from the Roman Communion, and our Nonconformists leaving us. However, it would take up too much time for me to say more on the subject than I have already done, and I

have only wearied Your Majesty too much already
by the length of this, but I have written it solely
to show the reasons which keep me firmly to my
religion.  This, and more besides, with which I
have not wished to trouble Your Majesty, seems so
convincing in the truth it contains, that I have
confidence in God that he will keep me believing it
for the rest of my life, and I support myself with
much trust in Our Saviour's words that the gates
of Hell will not prevail, as he will be with his
Church till the end of the world.  I hope, Sire, that
in writing my feelings so freely, you will consider
that I have kept the respect I owe to you, and
shall never lose.  Nevertheless I trust you will
pardon me for troubling you with so long a letter,
and will believe that no change of religion will alter
my duty, the religion I profess teaching me how
much I owe to you.  I shall always endeavour to
prove myself, with all imaginable respect,

" Your Majesty's

" Very obedient daughter and servant,
" MARIE."

To this letter the King answered by return of
post, that, as the Princess's letter showed that she
understood controversy better than did the greater
number of her sex, he hoped that she would use
the capacity God had given her to guide her into
the right path.  James sent several books for her
instruction, and advised her to read the letters of
the late King, and of the Duchess, her mother.
He also wished her to be interviewed by Father
Morgan, a Jesuit priest at The Hague.

The Princess tells us that she answered her
father's letter with all imaginable respect and
promised to read the books he recommended ; but
that she objected to seeing Father Morgan.  D'Albeville, who had either seen James's letter or a copy
of it, and who was, she says, quite " forward enough

himself," was delighted to have the King's authority to uphold him, and came to her asking what he should answer his master. The Princess told him what she had written, and d'Albeville was obliged to agree that as long as she was satisfied with her religion, it would be useless for her to receive Father Morgan.

James's next letter showed a diplomacy which was generally foreign to him, and which was therefore most probably inspired by his priestly advisers. He would not, he said, allow himself to be discouraged; for if she had been quite certain of herself and of her religion, she would not have refused to hold a conference with the Jesuit father he had recommended to her.

Mary was quite intelligent enough to realise the danger of an interview with Father Morgan, which would be bruited abroad by the Roman Catholic party, who would raise reports in England that the Princess was contemplating a change in her religion. She was soon able to prove the correctness of her prognostications, for directly after her first conversation with M. d'Albeville, she heard from several people that he was triumphantly telling every one of the liberty with which she allowed him to speak to her about religion. He boasted also about the order he had received from the King, not only to speak to her himself about religion, but also to introduce Father Morgan to her with the same object. Infinite harm might be done if this talk were to continue. Indeed Mary suspected that, though the King was doubtless sincere in his intentions for her conversion, the Jesuits' main object in pretending to attempt it was to spread reports which would induce the English nation to believe that there was no hope of a Protestant reaction, and so to become amenable to the impending change of religion.

The Princess at once informed her sister that

there was not the slightest truth in any report
she might hear about her change of religion, and
she also wrote to Dr. Compton, the Bishop of
London, her former instructor in the faith of the
Anglican Church, and gave a letter to her chaplain,
Dr. Stanley, to be sent to Sancroft, the Archbishop
of Canterbury. The letter to Sancroft is dated
from Loo, October 1, 1687, and runs as follows :

" Though I have not the advantage to know you,
my Lord of Canterbury, yet the reputation you have
makes me resolve not to lose this opportunity of
making myself more known to you than I could
have been yet. Dr. Stanley can assure you that I
take more interest in what concerns the Church of
England than myself, and that one of the greatest
satisfactions I can have, is to hear how that all
the clergy show themselves as firm to their religion
as they have always been to their King, which
makes me confident God will preserve his Church,
since he has so well provided it with able men. I
have nothing more to say, but beg your prayers,
and desire you will do me the justice to believe I
shall be very glad of any occasion to show the
esteem and veneration I have for you.

"MARIE."[1]

The Princess showed this letter to the Prince,
and her words of naïve delight at his approval are
touching ; so happy is she when he is kind to her,
and so unused is she to any expressions of praise
from him.

" The Prince " [she says], " to whom I read the
letter I had written to Dr. Stanley, seemed so
pleased at it, and was even so much astonished
with it, not believing me capable of writing so,
that I will allow that my vanity was not a little
flattered. But praise be to God I soon realised

[1] " Clarendon Correspondence," vol. ii., appendix, p. 484.

160]

A CONTEMPORARY PRINT OF THE CORONATION.

In the possession of A. M. Broadley, Esq.   From the Fraser Collection.

my folly, and discovered the few reasons I had for pride. I considered what the Apostle says, ' Let him that thinketh he standeth take heed lest he fall,' and reflecting on the punishment due to pride and to vanity, I could not fail to feel very much humiliated, so that the Lord might not leave me to myself. That is why I became more fervent in my prayers and more assiduous in the service of my God. When the first Sunday in February came I prepared myself for the Sacrament, and praise be to God, I was so much aware of my want of merit, and so much touched by all the grace and pity of God towards me in particular, that I approached the Table as is commanded, resting only on my Saviour's merit, and found all the spiritual consolation my soul could wish for, and thus strengthened myself greatly." [1]

This careful self-examination, this anxious survey of her faults, and earnest desire to amend them by divine help, enable us to realise the perfection of character described by Dr Burnet, when he says that praises of anything she had done or said seemed hardly to be heard by the Princess :

" They were so little desired that they were presently past over ; without so much as an Answer, that might seem to entertain the Discourse, even when it check'd it ; She went off from it to other subjects as one that could not bear it." [2]

The Princess had been suffering from weak eyes, and had therefore not been able to fulfil her promise to her father of reading the reasons left by Charles II. for his change of faith. When, however, she was able to study them, she found in them nothing which loosened her adhesion to the English Church ; while she read the replies made by the English Church twice, and with the greatest satis-

---

[1] " Lettres et Mémoires de Marie Reine d'Angleterre," edited by Countess Bentinck, p. 61.
[2] Burnet's " Essay on the Memory of the late Queen."

11

faction. She then went on to examine her mother's papers, and found her reasons for becoming a Roman Catholic

"as strange as astonishing in a woman whom I had always heard to have been endowed with much intellect, so that I was terribly grieved to find that the Lord had given her up to such blindness."[1]

The Princess next turned her attention to the book James had sent her by d'Albeville. It was called "Reflections on the Different Forms of Religion," and on the subject of it she wrote a second long letter to her father. In this she says that she does not look upon herself as one of the people for whom the book sent her was intended; for though she is not clever enough to be able to argue, she yet has enough knowledge for the satisfaction of her mind and for the repose of her conscience, so that she has only read it to show how much she wishes to please her father. She considers the book easy and agreeable in style, and even very serious and religious, as the writer constantly asks for divine benediction of his work. He also recognises the rightful methods of dealing with people, as he says that "no one has ever yet been convinced by abuse."

These concessions on the Princess's part are only intended to smooth the way, so that her principal attack may be made with all the more effect.

"I am led to believe" [she says] "that the first edition of this book must have been published before the King of France began to convert by means of dragoons."

Here the Princess had touched on a matter on which she felt most strongly. The Revocation of the Edict of Nantes, which had driven thousands of Huguenots out of France, and the cruelties practised by the dragonnades, had roused the

---

[1] "Lettres et Mémoires de Marie Reine d'Angleterre," edited by Countess Bentinck, p. 61.

indignation of Europe ; and Louis XIV., instigated by Madame de Maintenon, had done infinite harm not only to France, but also to the Roman Catholic cause generally. In England, and in Holland in particular, the greatest indignation was caused by accounts of French cruelty towards the Protestants, and if Louis had wished to make the impossibility of James's task of converting England doubly sure, he had certainly chosen the right means of doing so. The Princess expressed herself most strongly on the subject of the barbarities practised by the French troops, and related a horrible story to the effect that a fire had been lit under two Huguenot girls to torture them into recantation. D'Avaux, the French Ambassador, who must have hated the Revocation, for his endeavours to tempt the Dutch from their allegiance to William of Orange, and to persuade them that France was their best friend, were made doubly difficult by its consequences, went to William of Orange and complained that the Princess should repeat such stories. However, William merely answered drily that he could not prevent this, and d'Avaux was helpless.

Returning to the Princess's letter, we see that after this practical illustration of the political results of the creed which her father was trying to inculcate, she went on to doctrinal matters, and here her reasoning seems slightly at fault. Simple faith in a Church's system without examination will not save a man, she says, because the devils also believe and tremble—a remark which shows some confusion about the difference of meaning between the words faith and belief.

The Princess's letter is too long to quote from fully, and is only interesting because it shows her faith in the English Church, her love for it, and incidentally the acuteness of her intellect, and her power of consecutive reasoning.

After arguing at length against the infallibility of the Roman Church, and in favour of a free use being made of the Scriptures, she touches on a point which is interesting, as it is much insisted on nowadays, and may seem to some to be of recent growth. "The Reformers," she says, "did not leave the true Catholic Church, but only the errors which have crept into it."

The Princess handed this letter over to d'Albeville and had a long conversation with him. He had been enjoined to justify James in his daughter's eyes, as Dyckvelt and Bentinck had complained of his want of affection for her. This was shown, they said, by the fact that though she was presumptive heiress to the English throne, she received no allowance from him, all his generosity being concentrated on the Princess Anne. With her usual highmindedness, Mary waved the monetary question, but Louis XIV.'s sequestration of the principality of Orange without any interference from England, was in her eyes a severe count against her father. She said with a certain haughtiness : "The only thing I ever asked the King, my father, to do, was to use his influence with the King of France to prevent the seizure of the Prince of Orange. But my father preferred to join with the King of France against my husband."[1] This point of view was hardly encouraging, and her opinions on the religious question were hardly more so.

D'Albeville brought her the second volume of "The Different Forms of Religion" and a manuscript purporting to be taken from the writings of St. Cyprian, which was read to her by Dr. Stanley. After a preliminary study of the writings of St. Cyprian, Stanley was able to inform the Princess that the manuscript was not a genuine work of antiquity, for nothing had been translated in order, but that sentences had been picked here and there, and

[1] "Mazure, Révolution de 1688," vol. iii. p. 44.

strung together with interpolations to suit the object of the compiler. However, St. Cyprian even thus wrested does not, the Princess says, show the partiality and conceit of the priests.

The King's answer to the letter of the 17th showed that he was angry. He prayed God to touch his daughter's heart as he had touched her mother's,[1] he was sorry that books had had no effect on her, and that she refused to consult Father Morgan, and he said that he would send her no more books or writings.

"That is what I wished" [she says] "for I found that in reading these books I had wasted a great deal of time, and had gained but very little profit, though thanks be to God, I found in them only attempts to seduce those of weak mind : no solid reasoning, nothing at all that could shake me in the least in the world, so that the more I learn of this religion, and the more I reflect on my own, so many more thanks have I to render to my God, for his mercy in keeping me in the true religion. For all thy mercies and thy goodness, Oh my Saviour not to me, not to me, but to Thy Holy Name be glory and praise."

The Princess felt that great and terrible events were approaching, and later on in her meditation she says :

"I must also thank my God that with all my fear and the reason I have to feel it ever increasing, when I think of the goodness and of the wisdom of God I am afraid of nothing. I know that he can overthrow the wisest counsels, and can preserve his Church, and that if it pleases him to make use of the Prince and of me as instruments to perform his will, he can preserve us, if not His Will be done. I bless his Goodness for having given me so much

---

[1] Birch's Add. MSS., 4,163, British Museum.
[2] "Lettres et Mémoires de Marie Reine d'Angleterre," edited by Countess Bentinck, p. 65.

resignation to his good pleasure, that I hope never to murmur, and that he has bestowed on me so much confidence in his Mercy, that I can fear nothing ; when I think about the advantages I may gain from my anxiety for the Prince's safety and for my own, I hope it will help to prepare us so well for death, that when it comes it may be to both of us only the Gate of Heaven." [1]

[1] " Lettres et Mémoires de Marie Reine d'Angleterre," edited by Countess Bentinck, p. 68.

# CHAPTER X

MEANWHILE the crisis in England was approaching its culmination. This was brought about finally by two almost simultaneous events—the birth of the Prince of Wales, which assured the continuance of Roman Catholic rule in England, and the trial of the Bishops for their refusal to enforce the reading of the King's second Declaration of Indulgence, which proved that the Roman rule in James's hands would mean subversion of law and the ruin of the English Church.

James's view of his own actions is instructive. In one of his letters, after informing his daughter that Mary of Modena's confinement was to take place at St. James's Palace, he excuses himself for his action in imprisoning the Bishops who had presented him with the " strange petition," and says that he is " sorry about it, but was forced to it by their behaviour." [1]

James's subjects, on the other hand, argued that he had broken his word to them, had set at nought the laws of the land, and had proved himself utterly untrustworthy. They also declared that as the

[1] Add. MSS. Birch Papers, British Museum, 4,163, vol. i.—Letter, June 8, 1688.

faith of the heiress to the throne was unshakeable, it was necessary to the success of his scheme for subjugating England that he and his bigoted Italian wife should have a son to be educated in the Popish faith. Therefore they believed that Mary of Modena was not in reality expecting to become a mother, but that a supposititious child was to be palmed off on the nation as Prince of Wales. Under the circumstances this belief was excusable, and James had only his folly to thank for it.

When, however, we look at the matter from the point of view of William of Orange, of Mary, and of Anne, and consider whether they really believed that the unfortunate baby afterwards known as the Old Pretender was not the child of James II. and of Mary of Modena, the question becomes more complicated.

It is difficult after reading the evidence sent by Anne to The Hague to suppose that the clearsighted William believed in the plea of a supposititious child. Anne, however, was not a woman of quick wits, and was evidently so blinded by indignation at her father's attacks on the religion she practised, that all gratitude for his undoubted indulgence towards her was obliterated. Her prevailing feeling therefore seems to have been malignant hatred of him and her stepmother, and this obscured the small reasoning powers she naturally possessed. Her anger was natural, if she really considered that the King was tampering with the rights of her own offspring. Mary, on the other hand, had been separated early from her father, had no special cause for gratitude towards him, and, though not blinded with passion, was completely under the influence of his bitterest enemy ; while, independently of that fact, she had good cause to mistrust him.

In the private "Memoirs" intended for her own

eye alone, and in which she may be considered to
have given her real opinions, she writes thus on the
Queen's expectations of becoming a mother :

" As soon as I arrived at the Hague, she mentioned something about it to me in writing, but in
very doubtful terms. Two or three posts later the
King did the same, but in quite a different way,
talking of it so certainly, and that at a time when
no woman could be certain, that there was ground
for some slight suspicion. I give thanks to God,
that this news does not trouble me in any way,
God having given me a contented mind, and no
ambition except that of serving my Creator and of
keeping my honour stainless. What the Lord has
done for me is sufficient for me, and in my present
condition I can serve him better than if I were in
a more eminent post, so that if it were only for myself, I should wish as much as the King himself
that he should have a son. But while I am so
indifferent for myself, I find I cannot remain so
any longer when the interest of the Protestant
religion depends on it, so that whoever wishes it
well (as it is the duty of every member of it to do)
must necessarily be alarmed at the idea of a Papist
successor. This, then, destroys the soft and satisfying tranquillity I was enjoying, and makes me see
how much I ought to wish to come to the throne.
Besides the Church's interests, the love I have for
the Prince makes me wish for him all he deserves.
And though I regret to have only three crowns to
bring him, I am not blinded by love ; no, I can
see his faults, but I say this because I also know
his merits. I continue to be of this mind, so that
other people's interests cause me a trouble which
I should never feel for my own. But thanks be to
God, I put my trust in him, and am so sure that his
Church will be in safety, provided the sins of the
Nation do not call Divine vengeance down on her,
that even if a son be born, I shall not be discouraged,

though I fear the consequence of this birth on the weakminded. My greatest difficulty is writing about it to the King and Queen." [1]

Meanwhile the poor Queen, though aware of the idle gossip of the multitude, like her husband, considered it of little account, and apparently never realised the suspicions of her stepdaughter. She therefore continued to inform Mary about her health in a confidential and affectionate strain, and when we have the knowledge of what was to follow, her letters have a pathetic ring. She writes from Whitehall on February 21, 1688, "Am already very big, tho' I don't reckon myself gone above twenty weeks"; and on May 15 she says, "Soundly frighted—I am now within six weeks." [2]

Even Lord Danby seemed to consider a fraud likely. In a letter to William he says:

" I hope the Princess " (Mary) " will take care that the Princess Ann may be alwaies within call, and especially to see (when the time is near) that the midwife discharges her duty with that care which ought to be had in a case of so great concerne." [3]

He was evidently determined that Mary's rights should be safeguarded.

In a letter written a few days earlier Danby gives a graphic account of James's condition at this time. Danby's daughter, Lady Plymouth, was most anxious to enter the Princess's service, and his son was at the same time desirous of paying William a visit at The Hague. However, on asking for James's permission, both requests were refused, and when Danby remarked that the Dutch were astonished that James should be raising three more regiments, James replied angrily that they would be " surprised and more before

---

[1] "Lettres et Mémoires de Marie Reine d'Angleterre," edited by Countess Bentinck, p. 62.

[2] Birch's Add MSS., 4,163, British Museum.

[3] Danby to William, King William's Chest, Record Office—Letters, March 27 and 29, 1688.

he had done with them ! " Next day he apologised for his heat, and explained that he had received news which had disordered him, and that
Danby must not notice what he had said. The
young man could travel where he wished, though
if his only object was to satisfy his curiosity, he
might as well go elsewhere. Danby took the hint,
and answered that as the boy was too young to
be useful to William, it would perhaps be best
to send him to Flanders, and that possibly Lady
Plymouth might be received into the Princess's
service later, if the King would allow this.

During this time the Princess Anne was bom-
barding her sister's ear with letters full of doubts
of the reality of the Queen's condition ; her views
on this subject being mingled with expressions of
hatred for Lord and Lady Sunderland. Anne was
so inert a woman that when she takes a decided
line, as she does on the subject of the Sunderlands,
it is safe to attribute this to outside influence,
most probably to that of Sarah Lady Marlborough,
who was no doubt jealous of the Sunderlands.
Lord Sunderland was meanwhile playing a double
game, for though ostensibly James's Minister, he
was in reality working to secure the confidence
of William of Orange, while Lady Sunderland's
correspondence with the Princess was not, as she
announces, solely conducted with the object of
sending her recipes for treacle-water.

" Roger's wife " [Roger is Sunderland] " plays
the hypocrite more than ever " [writes Anne], " as
she goes morning and afternoon to St. Martin's
Church, because there are not enough people to
see her at the Chapel at Whitehall ; she goes
there half an hour before everybody and remains
half an hour after everyone has gone out, for her
private devotions."

Further abuse of both husband and wife follows,
Sunderland being described, possibly without much

undue exaggeration, as " the most wily rascal in the world." Anne's letters are not attractive—they give the impression that we are listening to the railing of a bad-tempered, common-minded woman ; and the gulf between the two sisters in intellect, taste, and good feeling is very apparent. Anne was extremely indignant with Lord Sunderland because, after James had given leave for her and her husband to travel in Holland, the permission was suddenly withdrawn, and she considered this due to the machinations of the Minister.

In her letters, she strongly advises the Prince and Princess of Orange not to come to England on a visit if they are invited to do so,

" as though I dare sware that the King could not have such a thought against either of you, still as it is possible to say one thing and yet do another, one cannot help being afraid, if one or other of you were to come here. I shall be delighted to see you, but really if you or the Prince were to come here, I should go out of my senses with fear that something should happen to either of you." [1]

The question, however, which agitated the Princess Anne to the exclusion of everything else was that of the Queen's condition.

" I cannot help thinking " [she says] " that the ' grossesse ' of Mansel's wife " [so the Princess designated the Queen in confidential communications] " is rather suspicious. It is true that she is very big, but she looks better than she has ever done, which is not usual in the case of women as far gone as she pretends to be, as they generally look very ill. Besides this, it is very strange that the baths, which, according to the opinion of the most celebrated doctors, should have done her a great deal of harm, have had such a good effect, and

[1] " Lettres et Mémoires de Marie Reine d'Angleterre," edited by Countess Bentinck—Letter of March 13, 1688.

so promptly, that she became ' grosse ' from the
first moment that Mansel and she met after her
return from Bath.   The certitude she has that it
will be a son, and the principles of her religion
being such that nothing will stop her, however
impious may be the means of which she makes use,
provided they advance its interests, causes one
to think that some trickery is intended.   I do all
I can to discover what is being done, and if I discover
anything, I will not fail to let you know." [1]

In another letter Anne remarks with some
justice that, considering the current stories, she
considers that the Queen should allow her personally some convincing proof that the baby is
really on his way into the world.

Anne's dislike for her stepmother shows itself
violently in these letters.   The unfortunate Mary
of Modena is, she tells her sister, the most hated
woman in the world.   It is she who is supposed
to urge the King on to violence, and she is so proud
that ladies of quality only go to Court when it is
absolutely necessary that they should do so.   On
one thing Anne is absolutely determined—the baby
shall be born in her presence, or she will refuse to
believe it to be its mother's child.

After all these asseverations, it must have been
a humiliation for Anne to be obliged to allow in
a letter written on June 18, that she had been
absent at Bath when her little brother was born
at St. James's Palace on June 10.   According to
James's "Memoirs," [2] which, however, are not always
trustworthy, he had implored his daughter to
remain in London, and she had declared that the
Bath waters were necessary for her health.   He
says : " The Princess Anne contrived to go to Bath,
in order to be absent when the Queen was brought

---

[1] " Lettres et Mémoires de Marie Reine d'Angleterre," edited by
Countess Bentinck—Letter of March 14, 1688.
[2] " Mémoires de Jacques II.," vol. iii.

to bed." [1]  Anne, for her part, complained that
she had been purposely deceived as to the date
of her stepmother's confinement.

The appearance of the unfortunate baby was
not greeted generally with much pleasure.  Like
the infant grandson of Louis XVIII., his advent
in the world sounded the knell of a dynasty.
Apart from any question as to his being the
genuine son of the King and Queen, the importance of the birth of a Roman Catholic heir to
the throne of England is shown by the caricatures
and broadsides of the time.  There the unfortunate baby is represented in all sorts of positions,
sometimes issuing from a warming-pan, but more
often in his mother's arms surrounded by priests,
cardinals, and the devilish crew who, in the popular
Protestant mind, were supposed to accompany these
dignitaries.  " The birth of the Prince, which caused
such great joy to the King and Queen and all
those who wished them well, excited extreme sorrow
throughout the Kingdom," says the chronicler of
James's " Life."  The whole nation was indeed in a
state of mourning, for at the time of the infant's
birth the Bishops were incarcerated in the Tower,
and the cause of liberty and of the rights of the
English Church seemed in an almost desperate
condition.

Meanwhile the Princess of Orange had been
leading her usual life, travelling with the Prince
from The Hague to the Palace at Loo, attending
many services, and blaming herself severely if her
thoughts were unduly occupied with worldly affairs.
An occasion which, in her opinion, showed her
weakness in this respect occurred about six
weeks before the birth of her brother, when, on
April 22, she and the Prince received the Elector
and Electress of Saxony at Loo.  Then, the trouble

---

[1] " Mémoires de Jacques II."  Macpherson's " Memoirs," p. 151.

the Prince made his wife take about decking herself with all her jewels, distracted her mind so much from her devotions, that she realised herself not to be as firmly fortified against the vanities of the world as she had hoped to be.

She was much distressed about this time by the Prince's cough, for which it was difficult to induce him to take remedies. She says in her " Memoirs," that at the beginning of June she began to feel in a better frame of mind than formerly, and that this was a comfort, for she had great need of all her strength, as in sending the seven Bishops to the Tower, the King had begun to show himself in his true colours.

" The people thought " [writes the Princess] " that it was a great risk to do this before he knew whether he would have a son or not. But the son coming so suddenly afterwards gave cause to suspect foul play. For it was the 8th of June old style, that the Bishops were imprisoned in the Tower, and on the 10th the Queen was delivered of a son. This was much too early, as there was a month still to her full time. . . . This circumstance, with the absence of my sister, shewed something strange. But I am so strongly persuaded, that if there be any trickery, God will not permit it to remain hidden for long, that I do not trouble myself much about it, and I give thanks to God, for the Prince and for myself, that neither of us trouble about our own interests, our only care is for the Church of God, but in what has to do with that we put our trust in him."

Even if we doubt the truth of these words when applied to William, I think we may assume that Mary used them with absolute sincerity.

There was much to justify the Princess's mistrust of her father, who had certainly never given his daughter much cause for belief in his affection for her. Though she was presumptive heiress to his throne, and he possessed a larger revenue than his predecessors, and allowed her younger sister an income of thirty or forty thousand pounds, he had never helped his elder daughter pecuniarily, and had excused himself by saying that he did not intend to give money to be used against himself.   Her marriage had not in the least modified his bitter hostility to her husband, and from the time of his accession to the throne of England reports had been rife as to the possibility of passing over the Princess of Orange, and putting a Roman Catholic in her place.   When confronted with one of the many pamphlets on the subject James showed much indignation, but the French Ambassador seemed to think that he was likely to be favourable to the project.   In fact, after the attempt to separate William and Mary, James, incited by the English Roman Catholics, had seriously entertained the idea of converting the Princess Anne to the Roman Catholic religion, and of altering the succession to the throne in her favour.

Another scheme which James certainly had in view when he sent Tyrconnel into Ireland was to separate that country from England and Scotland :

" I know with certainty " [1] [writes Bonrepaux to Seignelay] that the King of England's intention is to lose Ireland to his successor, and to fortify it so that all his Catholic subjects may find a safe asylum in it."

Knowing the lengths to which James's enthusiasm for his religion would carry him, the introduction of a supposititious child did not doubtless seem unlikely to his daughter.   At first the infant was prayed for in the Princess's chapel, a course to which Dr. Stanley objected, but of which the Prince approved.   Zulestein was sent to congratulate the King on the birth of a son, and with

[1] See Macaulay's " History of England," vol. iii. p. 44.

FROM A CONTEMPORARY DUTCH PRINT OF THE CORONATION OF
WILLIAM III. AND MARY II.

In the possession of A. M. Broadley, Esq.

FROM A DUTCH CONTEMPORARY PRINT REPRESENTING THE SCOTCH
CONVENTION PRESENTING THE CROWN TO WILLIAM AND MARY.

In the possession of A. M. Broadley, Esq.

private orders to discover the truth of the matter, and to sound the feeling in England as to the Prince's proposed expedition. Meanwhile reports that a fraud had been practised multiplied ; and Mary, having consulted her husband, decided that the prayers for the child should be stopped in her chapel. D'Albeville was naturally at once on the alert, and complained of this neglect, and also of the fact that the Court did not make an appearance at the festivities given to celebrate the birth of the Prince of Wales.

At first the baby was extremely delicate ; and the Princess Anne wrote to her sister on July 9 :

" The Prince of Wales has been ill these three or four days ; and if he has been so bad as some people say, I believe it will not be long before he is an angel in heaven." [1]

Hoping, therefore, as James's chronicler insinuates, [2] that all difficulties might be ended by the death of the child, William decided to temporise ; and gave orders that prayers should again be offered for him, a course which Mary says was much against her principles, as it was showing dissimulation towards God.

She consoles herself, however, by saying that for her and the Prince to show their suspicions too soon might prove their ruin, a consideration which sounds strangely utilitarian from her pen. She was at this time most miserable, and thoroughly believed that a fraud had been practised.

" To think that my Father should be capable of so horrible a crime, and that humanly speaking there is no other way of saving the Church and State than that of my Husband going to dethrone him by force, are the most afflicting reflections, and would be unbearable without the help of God,

---

[1] Sir Dalrymple's " Memoirs of Great Britain and Ireland," Book V., appendix, p. 176.

[2] "Mémoires de Jacques II.," vol. iii. p. 236.

and a firm and unshakeable confidence in him, his grace extending over all he has made. That is the only thing that supports me, but I only speak openly about it to the Prince who has seen my tears and is sorry for me." [1]

On July 21 Mary sent a string of medical questions to her sister,[2] with the object of trying to find out whether the child was supposititious or no. On the 24th, Anne answered these categorically, and her answers seem sufficient to persuade an impartial reader of the truth of the fact that Mary of Modena had indeed been delivered of a child. Mary was not, however, by this time impartial; she, like the majority of her countrypeople, was convinced that a fraud had been practised.

Meanwhile the Princess had been further agitated by the sudden resignation of her chamberlain, Verace, whom she represents as a rude, rough man, not at all suited for intercourse with ladies. Before he left, he begged the Princess to persuade William to take precautions about his safety. The Prince, who professed much astonishment at his retirement, told her that he had been warned against a man named Bude de Verace, who intended to kill him, but that he had refused to believe in the danger.

However this may be, it is certain that Verace was acting as one of Skelton's spies, and that he actually discovered William's schemes against James. After his resignation, he wrote from Geneva (1688) to inform Skelton of them. Skelton passed on the information to Sunderland, who is accused, justly or unjustly, of concealing the facts from James. Verace left The Hague so hurriedly, that he omitted to take with him the cypher in which

---

[1] "Lettres et Mémoires de Marie Reine d'Angleterre," edited by Countess Bentinck, p. 75.

[2] Sir John Dalrymple's "Memoirs of Great Britain and Ireland," Book V., appendix, p. 177.

he corresponded with his brother, and which, as the Princess remarks, " being for all the names of the Kings and Princes in Europe, shewed that it was not for use in private affairs." [1] Possibly he felt that the crisis was approaching and that his position was dangerous, or at least that it would be easier to make use of the information he had received when he was at a safe distance from The Hague. Certainly the reason he gives for his withdrawal, as reported by Jaucourt in his " Memoirs," [2] would not account for the hurry with which he left The Hague—a hurry which filled the Princess with apprehensions, as concealing some mysterious attempt against William's life.

Skelton is described by Burnet as " the haughtiest and at the same time the weakest man James could have found, and one who apparently could never keep a secret, so that he soon became the scorn of all Holland." [3]

This is manifestly an *ex parte* statement. Skelton was apparently a faithful servant to James. He was the one person who discovered the Prince of Orange's scheme, and it was not his fault, but the over-confidence or the treachery of others, which prevented James receiving any warning of his danger. Skelton was recalled and sent to the Tower, for publicly announcing a treaty between England and France, and thus trying to strengthen James's almost desperate position. This was of course an extraordinary step for an Envoy to take unauthorised, though it might have saved James ; and as Louis XIV. remarked pertinently : " This envoy rather deserves a recompence, than a disgrace so public as that of being obliged to return immediately to England to give an account of his

---

[1] " Lettres et Mémoires de Marie Reine d'Angleterre," edited by Countess Bentinck, p. 167.

[2] Fruin's notes to Droste's " Overblyffsels van Geheugchenis," p. 467.

[3] Burnet's " History of My Own Times," vol. iii. p. 13.

actions." [1] However, James, who had been ready to intrigue with France when connection with that country was prejudicial to his interests, refused all Louis XIV.'s offers of assistance when they might have saved him.

At this time William was in good health, except that his cough inconvenienced him ; but the Princess was in a state of constant anxiety, fearing that he would be assassinated by his enemies, and she speaks several times of plots, or suspected plots, against his safety.

" I do not know at present " [she says] " what will happen to me or the Prince, or where, or in what situation we may possibly be several months hence, and the aspect of everything is so sad that I do not know what I ought to expect or what I ought to hope."

She opened her heart, she says, " to no one but the Prince," and to the world at large she appeared " as joyful and happy as possible." This pretence at lightheartedness, intended apparently to prove to every one that the Princess was at one with her husband and thoroughly agreed with all his actions, was a mistake, and a repetition of it later on was to do her much harm in general estimation.

The Princess does not, however, appear to have thought it necessary to keep on her mask of cheerfulness before Gilbert Burnet, who went to see her a few days before he left The Hague with William, and who, with his usual openness, warned her that if there should appear at any time to be any " disjointing between the Prince and her, that would ruin all."

" She answered me " [says Burnet] " that I need fear no such thing : if any person should attempt that, she would treat them so as to discourage all others from venturing on it for the future. She

---

[1] Sir John Dalrymple's " Memoirs of Great Britain and Ireland " —Louis XIV. to Barillon, Sept. 30, 1688.

was very solemn and serious, and prayed God
earnestly to bless and direct us." [1]

The day before the Prince left, he advised the
Princess, in case of difficulty during his absence, to
consult the Prince of Waldeck, Pensionary Fagel,
or Mr. Dyckvelt.   Then he began to think of other
contingencies, and of one which must have seemed
to him very likely at the moment, though, as the
expedition was accomplished without bloodshed,
it is difficult after the lapse of years to realise his
feelings.

"He said to me also" [says the Princess] "that
in case it should please God, that I should never
see him again (words which pierced me to the heart,
and caused me such a shudder, that at the time
I write this it has hardly passed), if that should
happen, he said, 'it will be necessary for you to
marry again.'   If his first words struck me cruelly,
these surprised and horrified me terribly, and put
me in a state as though someone had pierced my
heart."

"'It is not necessary,' continued he, 'that I should
tell you that it must not be a Papist.'  He could not
himself pronounce these words without shedding
tears, and during the whole of the interview he
shewed me as much tenderness as I could wish for,
so that I shall never all my life forget it.  But I
was so much amazed at this proposition that I was
a long time without being able to answer.  He
protested that it was only the anxiety he felt about
the Protestant religion which made him speak
like this.  I do not in the least remember what I
said.  The trouble I was in made me answer in a
confused manner, but I assured him that I had
never loved anyone but him, and should never be
able to love anyone else.  Besides this, having
been married for so many years without its having
pleased God to bless me with a child, I thought

[1] Burnet's "History of My Own Times," vol. iii. p. 311.

that would be enough to prevent me from ever thinking of what he proposed to me. I told him, that I prayed God not to allow me to survive him ; if nevertheless I must do this, as it had not pleased God to grant me a child by him, I should not wish to have one by an Angel. Oh my God! If I have sinned in this passion, as I fear to have done, I pray Thee to pardon me. But praised be Thy holy Name, for having prevented me from murmuring against Thee." [1]

The following day, October 26, 1688, the Princess accompanied her husband to the Palace at Hounslaerdyke, where they dined together, and after dinner she accompanied him to the bank of the river, where he was to embark for Brill. There they said good-bye, not knowing whether they should ever meet again, and she remained motionless, and as though deprived of her senses, not even being able to give any orders to the coachman, as long as she could see her husband in the distance. In the evening she returned to The Hague in a condition of misery, though she thanks God that she was enabled not to repine at his will.

The day after the Prince's departure, was observed as a fast-day by all the States of Holland, even the Jews keeping it ; while it is curious to note that Coloma the Spanish Envoy, as if to show that he considered the Prince's expedition directed not against the Roman religion, but against the French nation, had masses said for its success.

On October 29 the Prince embarked at Brill, and on the 30th he set sail. However, a tempest arose, and the whole fleet was disordered, while several horses were stifled by want of air. At five o'clock next morning the wind changed, and blew with such vehemence from the west, that, fearing for the fate of his vessels, the Prince was obliged

[1] "Lettres et Mémoires de Marie Reine d'Angleterre," edited by Countess Bentinck, p. 80.

to return into port. In the storm several of the ships were separated from the rest, but eventually they all returned into port. The news of the disaster was exaggerated in London, where reports of the destruction of the Prince of Orange's fleet lulled James to a false security. The Prince's letters during this time of anxiety showed, the Princess tells us, the utmost resignation to the will of God. She, however, suffered inexpressibly during the tempest. As she remarks naïvely: " I found it a very hard and disagreeable thing to love so much when the person one loves is away." [1]

Meanwhile, William had returned to Helvoetsluys. The English packet-boat brought him news that, as a defence against his invasion, the lights along the English coast had been extinguished, and the marks on the sands to guide incoming vessels obliterated. The captain also told the Prince of the King's conference with the Bishops, and of the concessions made by him in view of the expected invasion. William wrote this news to his wife, told her that he shared her anxiety for a meeting, and promised not to sail without seeing her again. Meanwhile the trouble and anxiety she had gone through had affected her health, so that she was unable to meditate and to pray as was her wont, and felt so stupid that she could not collect her ideas to receive the Communion with due devotion. She tortured herself with the fear that, the wind being now favourable, William might break his promise, and start without seeing her again. She could not sleep ; but after she had been bled she felt better, and a letter from her husband, summoning her next day to Brill, caused her such joy that she was not able to listen with due attention to the sermon preached before her.

[1] " Mémoires et Lettres de Marie Reine d'Angleterre," edited by Countess Bentinck, p. 84.

On November 10 she arrived at Brill, where,
she says, with the humility she always shows when
William is in question, " the Prince had the goodness to come though only for two hours, his presence being very necessary at Helvoetsluys." [1]  The
road between there and Brill was so bad that it
was difficult for a chariot to plough its way along
it, and, from our knowledge of the relations between William and his wife, he would doubtless
enhance his condescension and goodness by making the most of the difficulties of locomotion.

This separation, Mary tells us, she felt even more
than the former one, and she remained in the
room where her husband left her for an hour and
a half, not having power to move, and hardly able
to weep ; but praying God to spare her much-
loved husband. Her first action when she felt
equal to making any movement was characteristic,
for, going to the door, she questioned her ladies,
and hearing that a sermon was being preached in
the town, she went at once to listen to it.

The next day the Prince was to set sail, and,
having attended public prayers for his success, the
Princess mounted a tower to see the fleet ; but
though the tower was a high one, she could only
catch sight of the sails.  There was a favourable
wind, and the Prince embarked at Helvoetsluys at
one o'clock.  The Princess arrived disconsolately
at The Hague that night, after three hours on the
water, and having been surrounded by an enormous
crowd at Maeslandsluys, where the Prince was
much beloved by every one.

A few days later, d'Albeville sent to say that he
had something to communicate to the Princess.
She consulted Dyckvelt as to what she had better
do, and, following his advice, asked d'Albeville to
excuse her from seeing him, and to send a message,

[1] " Lettres et Mémoires de Marie Reine d'Angleterre," edited
by Countess Bentinck, p. 84.

because, during the Prince's absence, she was receiving no company. In reply, d'Albeville despatched to her the depositions of the witnesses
before the Privy Council summoned by King
James, proving that the Prince of Wales was
really his and the Queen's son. Mary, who apparently still conscientiously believed that a fraud
had been practised, sent by her secretary to say
she was not surprised that the King should consider it necessary to make some explanation about
the matter, of which the Parliament, and not she,
was the proper judge.

During this time of intense anxiety she spent
most of the day at her devotions. Each morning
she was present at a French service in her private
chapel, and at twelve o'clock she attended Common
Prayer. At five o'clock she made her way again
to the chapel either for prayers or to listen to a
sermon, and at half-past seven she assisted at
Common Prayer, while every Wednesday an English sermon was preached before her. Her over-
scrupulous conscience now gave her trouble, by
suggesting that all this devotion might be caused
by vanity and a desire to attract the praises of
men. On the other hand, she considered that if
she were to lessen the number of the services she
attended, she would not be setting a good example
to other people. In the end she took the sensible
course of deciding to continue the services, and to
consider that if she were doing her duty, she must
not mind what people might say. We are told by
a Dutchman, Ortumnis, who visited her at this time,
that he found her " turmoil'd with many cares
and deep cogitations. 'What a severe and cruel
necessity,' said she, ' now lies upon me, either to
forsake a Father whom my Grandmother[1] first
ruin'd, or to forsake a husband, my country,
character, nay, God Himself ; and my Soul, my

[1] Henrietta Maria.

nearest and dearest pledge ? ' " [1]  So the matter appeared to the Princess. However, at this time she hoped fervently that her father would still wear the crown—at least, nominally—and that William would be appointed Regent during his lifetime.

The Princess was struck with the extreme kindness of every one during William's absence. The States of Holland in particular showed themselves most solicitous for her safety, and begged her to be specially careful of attempts on her person at the hands of Papists. From fear of tempting Providence, she consented to take more precautions than she did generally, but her dependence on God caused her to feel no real anxiety as to her future. However, she found it impossible to feel a like placidity about her husband's fortunes. In her solitude and profound melancholy, the words the Prince had used to her on the subject of his death and of her second marriage, acquired a fatal significance ; she thought of them as prophetic, believed that she would never see him again, and felt as though her heart would be broken.

Scandalous gossip has sometimes connected William of Orange's name with Elizabeth Villiers's sister, Madame Bentinck. References to his distress at her delicate health occur constantly in William's letters ; he was certainly on most intimate terms with all the Villiers family, and lavished on them thought and attention which might better have been bestowed on his gentle uncomplaining wife. However, a paragraph in Mary's " Memoirs " effectually clears William of the reproach of having betrayed his friend's honour. This paragraph records the death of Madame Bentinck, at which the Princess was present, and which took place during William's absence.

" She bore all her illness with much patience " [writes the Princess], " but felt much distress at

1 Royal Diary, 1705.

leaving her husband and five little children, and
though she had led an innocent life, she lamented
her sins continually, and at least a week before her
death I never went to see her, that she did not tell
me how she felt she offended God by her want of
resignation, as she could not feel as much as she
wished about leaving so good a husband and five
poor children, the eldest of whom was not yet nine
years old."

We can plainly see by Mary's attitude to Elizabeth Villiers, that, though she was a good and
long-suffering woman, she had considerable pride ;
and it is certain that she would never have written
in this strain about one who had been her husband's
mistress.

These children Madame Bentinck specially recommended to the Princess's care. Mary promised
to do what she could for them, and next day,
she tells us, Madame Bentinck died, as gently as
though she had fallen asleep.

On November 5 William landed at Torbay ; but
his wife did not hear this till the 19th of the month,
when she received letters from London apprising
her of the fact. William, however, did not write
to her—an omission she felt deeply. The fact that
he allowed her to have the account of his success
from many different sources, friendly, inimical, and
indifferent, before he condescended to inform her
of it, is on a par with William's ordinary behaviour
to his wife ; but apparently, from the affection he
had shown her at their parting, Mary had hoped for
better things, and she was bitterly disappointed.

# CHAPTER XI

WHEN the Princess heard that her husband had landed safely in England, she relaxed her rule of leading a life of complete seclusion, and began, as of wont, to receive The Hague ladies four times a week, though she still refused to engage in her favourite dissipation of playing cards. News reached her from England of the success of the expedition, of the flight of the Queen with her "supposed" son, and later, of the arrest of the King, as he also was preparing to escape. The Prince then wrote saying she must be prepared to move into England. This summons gave her much sorrow, as she had become so much attached to her adopted country that her Calvinistic conscience made her feel sometimes that so much affection for it must surely be a sin. In her return letter to the Prince she warned him of a reported design on his life, set on foot by an apothecary in Paris who had undertaken to poison him. She was terribly alarmed at this rumour, and found her only comfort in paraphrasing the 91st Psalm. She finishes her journal for the year 1688 with the words :

" And so waiting to hear what the King is doing, and fearing to be sent for ever out of this country,

though I long to see the Prince, I finish in these
various expectations the year 1688, which has been
a year of several strange events in the world and
of special mercies and spiritual blessings of God to
my soul, for which I shall glorify his name as long
as I live." [1]

In the early part of May, 1688, the Sieur de
Bodelschwing had arrived at The Hague as Envoy
from Brandenburg to acquaint William and Mary
with the death of the Great Elector, who was
William's uncle by marriage ; and Mary, in her
letter of condolence, mentioned the different con-
nections she had " with the house of Brardenburg "
and the " affection which the late Elector had
always shewn her." Now his son, Frederick III.
of Brandenburg, came to pay his first visit to
Holland since he had assumed the position of
Elector, and it was naturally necessary to show
him due honour. The Princess considered him
very odd-looking, while, of the many good qualities
with which he was credited, she had no opportunity
of judging. The Electress she thought very agreeable, but she was shocked at her want of religion.
When left to observe for herself, Mary's judgments
were critical, and seem generally to have been acute.

The Princess's visitors were evidently a welcome
change after the anxiety and solitude she had
undergone, and though afterwards she reproached
herself severely for her enjoyment of their society,
and of the little bustle entailed by receiving them,
we can discern through the measured language of
her journal that it gave the Princess much pleasure
to entertain the Elector and Electress in her
different houses. She played cards till two o'clock
in the morning, " out of complaisance," she is
careful to add, and was so much taken up with the
amusing duty of entertaining her guests that she

[1] "Lettres et Mémoires de Marie Reine d'Angleterre," edited by
Countess Bentinck, p. 4.

had no time for anything else, and even neglected going to church in the afternoon. When she ruefully contemplated her backslidings, her only consolations were that, however late she sat up at night, she never missed both French and English morning prayers, and that even when she saw the Electress dance, she felt no temptation to follow her example.

" So that I believed I had overcome that which used to be one of my prettiest pleasures in the world and that I feard might be a sin in me for loving it too well." [1]

Again there was a long pause in any communication with England, and every one wondered why the Princess heard nothing. In Holland there was much cause for anxiety, as the French were massing on her frontiers, so that the Prince of Waldeck was obliged to go to the army. Dyckvelt had been despatched to England by the States; and the Princess now had her first experience of public affairs, for the States deputed some one to give her an account of all their proceedings. " She indeed answered little, but in that little she gave them cause often to admire her judgment." [2]

Meanwhile respect for his wife's feelings, combined with policy, prevented William from pursuing the methods advised him by the Earl of Clarendon, and incarcerating his father-in-law in the fortress of Breda. " He knew the Princess's temper well, and he was sure she would never bear it," [3] he said. Though judgment was as usual the principal factor in dictating his course, and he would doubtless have disregarded his wife's wishes if they had run counter to it, his words help to exonerate Mary from the charge of want of filial affection often levelled at her.

[1] Doebner's " Memoirs of Queen Mary."
[2] Burnet's " History of My Own Times," vol. iii. p. 314.
[3] *Ibid.*, vol. iii. p. 356.

After James had smoothed his son-in-law's way by leaving the kingdom and taking refuge in France, a Convention assembled to discuss the political situation. Tories who could not make up their minds to break the succession, and yet dreaded a continuation of James's misgovernment, especially as he would be followed by a Popish successor, wished that William should assume the position of Regent, while James, though powerless for all practical purposes, should still keep the title of King. The Princess, in her anxiety for her father, favoured this view. Others, in their desire to keep within the bounds of legality, declared that James's flight entailed abdication, and that grave doubts existed as to whether the Prince of Wales were in reality his son. They therefore announced that the crown had now devolved on the Princess of Orange. The famous wit, Sir Charles Sedley, contributed a jest to the discussion. His daughter, James's mistress, had been created Countess of Dorchester, and he said bitterly that he " wished to make the King's daughter a Queen, in return for his Majesty's having made his daughter a Countess." [1] Lord Danby favoured this proposal, while a strong party, headed by Halifax, wished to make William King. The Prince's views on this subject were, as we know, very decided, but it was difficult for the Englishmen surrounding him to gauge his opinions, for he listened to everything almost in silence, and never committed himself to any expression of his convictions. The line he affected to take was that of disinterested and magnanimous inaction. He had been invited, he said, to come over to England to save the English nation, and when the people had settled on a free and representative government, he would be well satisfied to return to Holland.

[1] Sir John Dalrymple's " Memoirs of Great Britain and Ireland," vol. ii. p. 271.

A meeting was eventually held at the Earl of
Devonshire's house, and Lord Halifax, in despair
at the impossibility of learning William's real
sentiments, attacked one of his adherents on the
subject. The Dutchman, probably Zulestein,[1] after
evading an answer for a long time, said that,

" he knew nothing of the Prince's mind upon that
subject, but if they would know his own, he believed
the prince would not like to be his wife's gentleman
usher." [2]

Lord Danby at once broke up the meeting, declaring passionately that now they all knew enough,
and that, for his part, he knew too much. Still he
did not despair of making Mary Queen, and sent
an Envoy to Holland as bearer of a letter asking
what her wishes were about the matter, and saying
that if she desired to reign as Queen alone, he was
sure that he could manage to bring this about.
Mary, we are told, proved to him the truth of the
old adage that it is dangerous to interfere between
husband and wife, for she answered sharply that she

" was the prince's wife, and would never be other
than what she should be in conjunction with him
and under him; [3] and that she should take it
extreme unkindly if any, under a pretence of
their care for her, would set up a divided interest
between her and the prince. And, not content
with this, she sent both Lord Danby's letter and
her answer to the prince."

William received these communications " with
his usual phlegm," and continued to employ Lord
Danby and to advance him in his service. How-

---

[1] Burnet names Fagel, but he had died a few months earlier;
and Macaulay suggests Dyckvelt or Zulestein. Dyckvelt, however,
according to Mary's "Memoirs" ("Lettres et Mémoires de Marie
Reine d'Angleterre," edited by Countess Bentinck, pp. 80, 87), remained in Holland.

[2] Dartmouth's note to Burnet's "History of My Own Times,"
vol. iii. p. 394.

[3] Burnet's "History of My Own Times," p. 393.

WILLIAM III. WITH QUEEN MARY ON ONE PILLAR, AND EMBLEMATIC
FIGURES SUGGESTING THE BENEFITS OF HIS REIGN.

From a very rare print in the possession of Charles Edward Stewart, Esq.

ever, a few weeks later, he summoned Shrewsbury,
Halifax, and Danby, and, speaking in his usually
impassive manner, he informed them that unless
he were offered the crown he would return to
Holland. This was plain speaking ; and the effect
of William's words was heightened by the fact
that, with his tacit permission, Burnet, whose bab-
bling, sometimes inconvenient, had, after all, its
uses, told of the interview he had had with
the Princess in Holland, and of her resolution
always to take a subordinate position to that held
by her husband.

"Those" [says Burnet] "to whom I gave the
account of that matter were indeed amazed at
it, and concluded that the Princess was either
a very good or a very weak woman."

Parliament now assembled to discuss the matter,
and eventually it was settled that William and
Mary should be declared King and Queen for their
joint and separate lives, the administration of the
government being in William's hands alone. After
their deaths, Mary's children were to inherit the
throne, next in order Anne's posterity should
succeed, and then William's by any other wife but
Mary.

Meanwhile the Princess was left to bear this
crisis in her life alone. On February 1, before
Parliament began to sit to discuss the Succession,
Admiral Herbert arrived in Holland with a letter
from the Prince, ordering her to come to him at
once. She was already prepared for the summons ;
but she was full of trouble that night and could
not rest, thinking of her father's misfortunes, and
of how she would suffer in taking his place. Perhaps the letters from her unfortunate stepmother,
written about five weeks before William landed in
England, may have haunted her during her
sleeplessness : "The first moment that I have
taken a pen in my hand since I was brought to bed

13

is this to write to my dear Lemon."[1]    And later,
" Even in this last letter by the way you speak of
my sonne and the formal name you call him by
I am confirmed in the thoughts I had before that
you have for him the last indifference "—to which
cry of anguish Mary, full of doubt and suspicion,
had answered, " All the King's children will have
as much affection and kindness from me as can be
expected from children of the same father."[2]

On receiving the news of William's intended
invasion of England, Mary of Modena writes :

" The second part of this news I will never believe,
that is that you are to come over with him ; for I
know you to be too good, that I don't believe you
could have such a thought against the worst of
fathers, much less perform it against the best, that
has always been kind to you, and I believe has
loved you better than all the rest of his children."[3]

It was certainly Mary's fate to find herself en-
compassed with dilemmas.

Life seemed dark to her, as she thought of her
past happiness in her adopted country, and dreaded
a strange position in what was to her now an unknown
land.    Her reiterated complaint that here she
had " the esteem " of the inhabitants is pathetic,
when we consider how, owing to the invidious
position she involuntarily occupied as her father's
supplanter, and to her efforts to satisfy the behests
of her husband, the few years she had yet to live
would be darkened by detraction and misunderstanding.    Distracted between her duty and affection to her husband and her father, religion was
her only consolation :

" I saw my husband in a prosperous way "[4] [she
says] " and blessed God for it, and was sorry I

    [1] Birch's Add. MSS., 4,163, vol. i., July 16, 1688.
    [2] Ibid., Letter, September 28, 1688.
    [3] Ellis's " Original Letters," first series, vol. iii. p. 349.
    [4] Doebner's " Memoirs of Queen Mary," p. 1.

could not so much rejoice as his wife ought ; neither
was I so sad as became the daughter of a distressed
King.  I bless my God who decided between the
daughter and the wife, and shewed me when
Religion was at a stake I should know no man after
the flesh, but wait the Lord's leisure and trust his
goodness for the event."

She prayed for resignation, and tried to busy
herself in preparations for her journey, but found
that she could settle to nothing till she had confessed her feelings to her faithful " Memoirs."  She
managed to find time for this, and then came a
perpetual hurry, for she was besieged from early
morning till night-time by crowds of her adorers,
miserable at the idea that they were about to lose
their beloved Princess.  Their trouble at parting
from her increased hers ; and in the bustle and the
distraction of her feelings she omitted to receive
the sacrament, although it was the first Sunday in
the month, and her chaplain, Dr. Stanley, told her
that an important crisis was not the suitable time
to neglect devotion.  This was a great crime, and
she considered she was punished by contrary
winds which delayed her embarkation, but at least
enabled her join in the Holy Communion on the last
Sunday she would spend at The Hague.

Mary embarked in the yacht brought over for
her use on February 18, but a violent storm arose,
and she was obliged to remain in the Maas all day.
On Sunday at noon the yacht at last set sail, and,
though the sea was absolutely calm, reached Margate
the next day about twelve.  The Princess tells us
that she arrived in her native country with very
mingled feelings.  It was more than eleven years
since she had left it, and her heart was sore with the
thought that she might never see Holland again.
Nevertheless, she confesses to a

" secret joy, which doubtless proceeded from a
naturall simpathy, but that was soon checked with

the consideration of my father's misfortunes which came immediately into my mind. The joy of seeing the prince again, strove against that melancholly and the thoughts that I should my husband see owned as the deliverer of my country, made me vain ; but alas, poor mortal ! thought I then, from who has he delivered it but from thy father. Thus were my thoughts taken up, and while I put the best face on, my heart suffert a great deal, but at last I came." [1]

When the Princess landed at Whitehall Stairs, she was clad, according to a contemporary picture, in a low bodice draped with muslin, and a purple robe over an orange petticoat, wore many strings of pearls round her throat, and had her hair dressed high and adorned with yellow ribbons. The costume sounds chilly for the middle of February. She found her husband looking very ill, and suffering from a terrible cough. They were delighted to see each other, and even the self-controlled William shed tears of joy when they were alone together, though they wished that their meeting had taken place in Holland, for they felt that they were beset with difficulties and dangers, and that their liberty was over for ever.

The portraits of William taken at the time seem to show that he was experiencing a reaction after the toil and anxiety of the great enterprise. His is the face of some one in permanent ill-health. There are deep lines between the nose and mouth, and the whole expression is weary and sickly, as of one in continual suffering. Evelyn writes in his "Diary" of March 29, 1689 : " Things far from settled as was expected, by reason of the slothfull sickly temper of the new King." The reader, however, of certain passages in William's letters to Bentinck, is more disposed to marvel at the strength of mind which enabled the King to work at all, than

[1] Doebner's "Memoirs of Queen Mary," p. 10.

to comment, as did his contemporaries, on his sloth-
fulness. In one of these William writes :

" Backwardness and neglect are beyond amendment, although I work assuredly harder than I
ought to on the ground of health. I have been
troubled 3 or 4 days with sickness. This unfits
me for doing what is necessary at this juncture,
and makes me utterly prostrate." [1]

The Princess was now to have her first experience
of unfriendly criticism. Her anxiety about her
father's condition was so great, that those who surrounded her in Holland could not fail to notice
her low spirits. Reports of her unhappiness were
carried by busybodies to England, where William
realised that they would do much harm to his
cause, as every one would consider that she did not
approve of her father's dethronement. He therefore wrote telling her that she must appear at first
so cheerful, that " nobody might be discouraged by
her looks, or be led to apprehend that she was uneasy
by reason of what had been done " ; [2] and doubtless,
in his first interview with her, he enjoined the same
conduct. The result of his admonitions was most
unfortunate, for, in her anxiety to obey him, she
appears to have sadly overacted her part, with
disastrous consequences for her future reputation.

The Duchess of Marlborough writes thus of her
behaviour when she reached Whitehall :

" I was one of those who had the Honour to wait
on her to her own Apartment. She ran about it,
looking into every Closet and Conveniency, and
turning up the Quilts upon the Bed, as People do
when they come into an Inn, and with no other sort
of Concern in her Appearance, but such as they
express ; a Behaviour which, though at that time
I was extremely caress'd by her, I thought very
strange and unbecoming. For, whatever Necessity

---

[1] Letter, February ₁⁴₇, 1690, Welbeck Abbey.
[2] Burnet's " History of My Own Times," vol. iii. p. 406.

there was of deposing King James he was still her
Father, who had been so lately driven from that
Chamber and that Bed; and if she felt no tender-
ness, I thought she should at least have looked
grave or even pensively sad, at so melancholy a
Reverse of his Fortune." [1]

This was the testimony of a bitter enemy, as
we shall see hereafter; but John Evelyn bears witness to the same thing, and there is no doubt that
he voices the feeling of the best-minded of the nation
when he says in his " Diary " for February 21, 1689 :

" It was believed that both, especially the
Princesse, would have shew'd some (seeming) reluctance at least, of assuming her father's Crown,
and made some apology, testifying by her regret,
that he should by his mismanagement necessitate
the Nation to so extraordinary a proceeding, which
would have shew'd very handsomely to the world
and according to the character given of her piety;
consonant also with her husband's first declaration,
that there was no intention of deposing the King,
but of succouring the Nation; but nothing of all
this appear'd; she came into Whitehall laughing
and jolly as to a wedding so as to seem quite transported. She rose early the next morning, and in
her undresse, as it was reported, before her women
were up, went from roome to roome to see the convenience of Whitehall; lay in the same bed and
apartment where the late Queene lay, and within a
night or two sate down to play at basset, as the
Queene her predecessor used to do. She smil'd
upon and talk'd to everybody, so that no change
seem'd to have taken place at Court since the last
Queene's going away, save that infinite crowds of
people throng'd to see her, and that she went to
our prayers. This carriage was censur'd by many.
She seemed to be of a good nature, and that she
takes nothing to heart."

[1] " Conduct of the Duchess of Marlborough."

Readers of Mary's "Memoirs," are fully aware that this is not a correct view of her character; and before her death Evelyn changed his opinion of her; but his words show what a serious mistake her lively behaviour was.   She told Burnet, who was surprised at this apparent failure of feeling in one who had hitherto seemed to him perfection, that " she was obeying directions and was possibly going too far, because she was acting a part which was not very natural to her."

Mary suffered to the end of her short life from the consequences of her untimely high spirits; and the reader cannot help feeling a certain indignation against William, who in his anxiety to reign and to reign alone, compelled her to a course of conduct which intensified the bitter detraction to which she was already exposed, as the supplanter of her unfortunate father.   The Jacobite poems and pamphlets of the time abound in allusions to Mary's heartlessness:

"Yet worse than cruel scornful Goneril, thou;
She took but what her monarch did allow,
But thou, more impious, robbest thy father's brow." [1]

In another poem Mary is designated as the elder Tullia, and sarcastic allusion is made to her increasing stoutness.   In a third we find a reference to the allusions continually made by William and Mary to King Charles II., James II. being, according to the writer, ignored by them.   The pasquinade, which is quoted by Miss Strickland, runs thus:

"Your royal uncle, you are pleased to own,
But royal father, it should seem, you've none.
A dainty mushroom, without flesh or bone,
We dare not call you, for it seems you are
Great Charles' niece, o' the royal character,
Great James's daughter too, we thought you were.
That you a father had you have forgot,
Or would have people think that he was not;

---

[1] Miss Strickland's "Mary II," p. 224.

The very sound of royal James's name
As living king, adds to his daughter's shame.
The Princess Mary would not have it known,
That she can sit upon king James's throne." [1]

Gone were the love and admiration which had
surrounded the Princess in Holland, and Mary
missed them very much ; though, with the pluck
and reserve characteristic of her, she did not allow
her feelings to influence her demeanour, and her
cheerfulness never abated.   In her "Memoirs" she
says :

" I found myself here very much neglected, little
respected, censured of all, commended by none.
This was a great trouble at first, but when I considered the thing right I saw it was from the
Lord, and I resolved to bear patiently whatever
he should lay upon me.   I wanted to be humbled,
and I was it sufficiently.   Tis hard to flesh and
blood to bear neglect, especially coming as I did
from a place where I was valued too much." [2]

All this did not show itself at first ; and in spite
of her reluctance to reign, Mary must have felt a
certain exultation, at any rate for her husband's
sake, when, the day after her arrival, the great Banqueting Hall at Whitehall was thronged by a large
assemblage, and deputations from the Lords and
Commons came to do homage to her and to William.

The Declaration of Rights, the provisions of
which had been settled by the joint deliberations
of the two Houses acting together as a Convention,
was then read.   It reasserted the rights of the
Constitution which had been infringed by the late
King ; and it was noticed that, when mention was
made of his misdoings, Mary looked down and
seemed troubled. [3]   Then Halifax, in the name of
the Estates of the Realm, offered the crown to

---

[1] Strickland's "Mary II.," p. 215.
[2] Doebner's "Memoirs of Queen Mary," p. 14.
[3] Lady Cavendish's letter, "Lady Russell's Correspondence,"

William and Mary.  The Prince, in reply, accepted
the position for himself and the Princess, and
promised that he would faithfully observe the laws
of the land.  The Lords and Commons then retired ; a procession was formed ; and

" Within Temple Bar and all along Fleet St.
the Orange Regiment of the City Militia lined
both sides of the way, so did the Green Regiment
within Ludgate and St. Paul's Churchyard ; the
Blue Regiment in Cheap-side, and the White in
Cornhil." [1]

Marching between these troops, the procession
made its way first to the Great Gate of Whitehall,
next to Temple Bar, where it was joined by the
Lord Mayor, then to Cheapside, and last to the
Royal Exchange.  At each of these stations, amid
the acclamations of the multitude, Garter King at
Arms performed the ceremony of proclaiming
William and Mary King and Queen of England.

This was the showy side of the picture.

" The next day after I came " [says the Princess
in her " Memoirs "] " we were proclaimed, and the
government put wholy in the prince's hand.  This
pleased me extreamly, but many would not believe
it, so that I was fain to force myself to more mirth
than became me at that time, and was by many
interpreted as ill nature, pride, and the great delight I had to be a Queen.  But alas, they did
little know me, who thought me guilty of that ; I
had been only for a regency, and wisht for nothing
else ; I had never desired [2] being queen (liking
my condition much better and indeed I was not
deceived) ; but the good of the public was to be
preferd and I protest, God knows my heart, that
what I say is true, that I have had more trouble

[1] " The Manner of the Proclaiming of King William and Queen
Mary," February 13, 1689.
[2] " dreaded " is the word used in the " Memoirs," but this must
be a mistake.

to bring myself to bear this so envyed estate then I should have had to have been reduced to the lowest condition in the world. My heart is not made for a kingdom and my inclination leads me to a retired quiet life, so that I have need of all the resignation and self denial in the world, to bear with such a condition as I am now in. Indeed the Princes being made king has lessend the pain, but not the trouble of what I am like to endure." [1]

Many were the difficulties with which Mary was surrounded, and anomalous was the position in which she found herself. The nation generally were not cognisant of the letters in which James II. definitely claimed subsidies from Louis XIV., because, knowing the people's hatred for the Roman Catholic religion, it was his intention to introduce it into England against their will. Therefore, the danger over, a reaction necessarily took place, and people thought their fears exaggerated. Many whose consciences were outraged when William seized the throne from his father-in-law would have subscribed to a Regency ; though their ideas must have been vague as to how this could be worked satisfactorily. Nevertheless, the best of the nation kept itself aloof from William and Mary, and they both felt this bitterly. On one occasion, Bentinck remarked to William that

" the English were the strangest people he had ever met with ; for by their own accounts of one another, there was never an honest nor an able man in the three kingdoms, and he really believed it true. The king told him he was very much mistaken, for there were as wise and honest men among them, as were in any part of the world (and fetched a great sigh) but they are not *my* friends." [2]

---

[1] Doebner's "Memoirs of Queen Mary," p. 11.
[2] Dartmouth's note to Burnet's "History of My Own Times," vol iv. p. 219.

In consequence it is very evident that the Queen thought poorly of the English nation, and that she remembered the happy times she had spent in Holland with regret and longing. Writing to a Dutch friend she says:

" I cannot hear that you still weep at my departure without being very sorry to give you this occasion for sadness, but if it is any consolation to know that often I myself wish to be able to cry about it, I will tell you the fact in confidence, not daring to allow here how much I shall all my life love Holland, and the more I am worried here and overdone with people the more I regret the happy time I spent with so much quietude in your country, and what troubles me is the small hope I have of ever again being so happy. When you see Madame de Rosendale think a little together of me, and now while Madame de Stirum is at the Hague, take your memory back to that happy time when we were at Loo or Dieren, we working and you reading aloud, all the walks in the neighbourhood which amused us then and which I regret now more than you will be able to believe, but there is no remedy, and I lose myself in these thoughts which makes me change the subject; you give me plenty of new subjects in your letter of the 19th of July, but it is my misfortune to be continually interrupted. One of the misfortunes of this place is to have no time to oneself, which obliges me to finish, assuring you that the esteem I have for you will never end.

" MARIE R." [1]

Mary was, unlike her husband, much beloved by those who knew her ; but in the popular imagination she was painted in even more lurid colours

[1] "Lettres et Mémoires de Marie Reine d'Angleterre," edited by Countess Bentinck—Letter to Baronne de Wassenaer d'Obdam, August 20, 1689.

than he. Her relation to the dethroned King formed the climax of the terrible unnaturalness of the situation.

Bitterest blow of all, what was best in the English Church, that Church which Mary loved with all her heart, and for whose defence—in her view at least—the Revolution had been consummated, turned against her. Among the seven Bishops who had been sent to the Tower for refusing to allow King James to defy the law, only Lloyd of St. Asaph waited on Queen Mary II., and when she sent to ask for the blessing of Sancroft, Archbishop of Canterbury, he replied, that " she must ask her father's, for his would not otherwise be heard in heaven." [1]

Even a woman like Lady Dorchester, James II.'s late mistress, dared to treat the Queen with insolence. When told that she would be received by her on no higher footing than what was due to her as her father's daughter, and that no account would be taken of the title bestowed on her by the late King, she answered, " Then I will treat her as her mother's daughter." As the Queen received her coldly, she remarked with the utmost impudence : " There is no occasion for this ; for if I have broken one of the commandments with your father, you have broken another."

The Queen's relations with her mother's brothers, Lord Clarendon and Lord Rochester, were also very difficult, and gave rise to much unfavourable comment. The two Hydes were, like many others in those troublous times, in a most awkward position. Sunderland had tried to entrap Rochester to his destruction, by pretending to James that he showed some inclination to become a Roman Catholic. When Rochester showed that he had no intention of departing from the tenets of the

---

[1] Sir John Dalrymple's " Memoirs of Great Britain and Ireland," Part II. Book I.

English Church, James was very angry; while, in omitting—by James's wish—to pay his respects at The Hague on the way to Spa, he offended William. Clarendon appears to have been a weak and violent man, who had the unfortunate faculty of pleasing neither party. He had been one of the malcontents in James II.'s time, for, after entrusting him with the government of Ireland, James had sent the Roman Catholic Tyrconnel to harass and finally to supersede him. During James's misfortunes Clarendon had lectured him with a bluntness which shocked many of those present. He was, on his side, horrified at the callousness shown by the Princess Anne, who joked and made merry with her ladies over her father's misfortunes.

To the honour of both brothers it must be allowed that, however strongly they may have disapproved of their brother-in-law's misgovernment, they had no hand in intriguing with the Prince of Orange for his downfall, and this inactivity naturally did not stand them in good stead when William and Mary ascended the throne. Neither had they the least notion of acting with diplomacy. When the Revolution was a *fait accompli*, and the question of putting William and Mary on the throne was under debate, Evelyn says that it was

" opposed and spoken against with such vehemence by Lord Clarendon, that it put him by all preferment, which must doubtless have been as great as could have been given him. My Lord of Rochester, his brother, overshot himself by the same carriage and stiffnesse, which their friends thought they might have well spar'd when they saw how it was like to be over rul'd, and that it had been sufficient to have declared their dissent with lesse passion, acquiescing in due time."[1]

Clarendon also endeavoured to rouse the Princess

[1] Evelyn's " Diary," February 21, 1689.

Anne against the Succession as settled, telling her
that she and her children ought to reign at Queen
Mary's death, instead of leaving the crown to
William for his life. Nevertheless, he seems at
first to have paid assiduous court to William, in the
hope that the government of Ireland might be
entrusted to his charge; a hope which, under the
circumstances, showed either a strange optimism, or
a disproportionate sense of his own importance.

As soon as Clarendon heard that the Princess was
on her way up the Thames, he went into the country,
as, being uncertain about his reception, he had all
along settled to do. He left Lady Clarendon to
give a letter from him to the Princess and to bear
the onus of the first interview. She reported that
she had been " civilly received," but that, as the
Princess was surrounded by a crowd of people,
it had been impossible to have any private talk
with her; and that Lord Rochester had advised
that his brother's letter should not be given to
the Princess.

However, next day the Queen—as Mary now
was—had a private talk with Lady Clarendon,
and told her that she was much dissatisfied with
her husband. " What had he," she asked, " to
do with the Succession ? "[1]  When Lady Clarendon
declared that all he had done had been in Mary's
interests and in those of her sister, and that if she
would appoint a time to see him, he would be able
to justify himself, she answered imperiously that
she would not appoint any time. In reply to
further entreaties from Lady Clarendon, Mary
replied that " she had nothing to do to forbid anybody coming into the withdrawing room; but she
would not see me anywhere else, nor speak in
private with me." She refused also to see Lord
Rochester or his children.

William had received both brothers with polite-

[1] Clarendon's "Diary," February 16, 1689.

ness,—and we know that Mary was guided in everything by his wishes. We may therefore presume that her behaviour was intended to further that policy of conserving an appearance of perfect unity between husband and wife by putting the latter in the forefront of the battle, which William looked on just now as necessary to the success of his schemes. So, while *he* affected an indifferent pose, Mary was to be delighted at his triumphs, grieved at his reverses, and intensely indignant with his enemies. No one knew of the long course of training in self-abnegation and submission she had gone through, and it is impossible to wonder at the popular verdict that, though charming and amiable, she was cold and heartless.

One pleasant meeting at least awaited Mary on her arrival on her native shores. The Princess Anne, though in an advanced condition of pregnancy, came to Gravesend to meet her sister ; and Mary remarks that she was " really extream glad to see her." [1] The union between the two was not destined to be durable ; but it is pleasant to imagine that, before alienated by outside interference, Mary had a soft place in her heart for the sister who had been her constant companion during her youth.

[1] Doebner's " Memoirs of Queen Mary," p. 10.

# CHAPTER XII

ON April 11, 1689, William and Mary were crowned
in Westminster Abbey.

The day chosen was Ash Wednesday, a fact
which, we are told, displeased many good Churchmen.

There were many cogitations as well as preparations before the ceremony. Sancroft, the Archbishop of Canterbury, refused to assist; for to
him a Coronation while James was still alive was
an impious mockery. Therefore Mary's old governor, Compton Bishop of London, acted in his stead,
and the form of the Coronation Service which was
drawn up by him, has been the basis of all similar
services which have followed it. A change, which
was certainly necessary on this occasion, and
which has been kept to during all the later Coronations, is the substitution of the words " the undoubted King of this Realm," for " the rightfull
inheritor of the Crown of this Realm," when the
King is presented to the people by the officiating
Bishop.

The words in which the actual Coronation Oath
was to be administered were, however, the most
important question in debate, and some time
beforehand the House of Commons formed itself
into a Committee to discuss the matter. As a

CHARLES TALBOT, DUKE OF SHREWSBURY.

British Museum.

result of the Committee's anxiety to safeguard the Constitution, and to insist that the laws of the Realm must not be broken by the Sovereign, the Oath was completely reframed. References were introduced to the " Statutes in Parliament agreed on," and the " Protestant Reformed Religion established by law." The ceremony of the presentation of the Bible as an emblem of the Protestant religion, which had been abolished by Mary I., was reintroduced, and has been performed at all subsequent Coronations.

Other smaller innovations were requisite at this unique Coronation. It was necessary for Mary, as Queen-Regnant, to be invested with a regalia corresponding as far as possible with her husband's. After the Coronation she held in her right hand the " sceptre with the cross," as do also the Queens-Consort, but in her left hand she—like the King—held the " sceptre with the dove," who represents the spirit of power and wisdom, instead of the " ivory rod with the dove," with which the Queens-Consort are invested. Curiously enough, the sceptre with the dove, which had been made specially for Mary II., and was of great value, disappeared for many years, and was only found in 1814.[1]

It was also necessary to make a second chair, and an orb surmounted by a cross to be presented to the Queen before the Coronation, with the words : " And when you see this Orb set under the Cross, remember that the whole world is subject to the Power and Empire of Christ our Redeemer."

It is curious to read Queen Mary's reflections before the Coronation. Reading between the lines of her undoubtedly pious sentiments, it is not difficult to realise that she enjoyed the idea of the ceremony—" that was to be all vanity "—immensely. Here the indignant Jacobites were right

[1] *Times,* June 19, 1911.

14

in their judgment of her—she had apparently no
feeling of remorse about the dethronement of her
father.  That William and he should be in active
conflict gave her intense distress ; that he should be
in danger or in suffering caused her acute anxiety.
She seems, however, to have felt no pangs of conscience because of William's usurpation of the
crown, her view of the Revolution being that her
husband had been raised by God to deliver England
from her father's misgovernment.

She writes on June 3, 1689, to the Electress
Sophia :

" You will allow me to pass over the beginning of
your letter in silence, it is very kind to me, but my
misfortune is such that it is best to pass over many
things in silence about which other people can
speak.  I have no doubt of the correctness of your
opinion, and I hope that mine is reasonable.  I
have much to suffer in my Father's misfortune, but
that does not prevent me from rejoicing in the
public good, and the satisfaction of having a
husband who has done his duty and not to have
failed in it myself is great enough to give me great
repose of mind." [1]

Again and again this feeling—expressed in different ways—occurs in Mary's correspondence with the
Electress.  She was to suffer—she was to continue
to suffer—for her father's misfortunes.  Calamities
were to visit her and her family because of their
breaking of the Seventh Commandment.  Yet—
and in this her Calvinistic idea of God as a stern
Schoolmaster seems to ally itself to the Greek
belief in an overmastering Fate—though she must
bear punishment, she was doing God's will, and
was helping her husband to perform his allotted
task of saving England.

Mingled with this feeling was the natural one of
delight at that dear husband's exaltation, a feeling

[1] Doebner's "Memoirs of Queen Mary."

which she expressed in her "Memoirs" as Princess
of Orange when she said :

"In addition to the interests of the Church, the
love I feel for the Prince makes me wish for him
all he deserves. And though I am sorry only to
have three crowns to bring him, I am not blinded
by love ; no, I can see his faults, but I say this
because I know also his virtues." [1]

The Queen was not without reminder of her father
at this time, for Lord Nottingham notes that on
April 9, two days before the ceremony, a letter
came to her from King James, in which he said
that he had

"up till this time been willing to make excuses
for her, considering that her obedience to her
husband and compliance with the nation might
have accounted for her conduct ; but that her
being crowned was in her own power ; and if she
did it while he and the Prince of Wales were living,
the curses of an angry father would fall on her,
as well as of a God who commanded obedience to
parents."

The Princess of Denmark had a letter also.
King William declared : "There is nothing he has
done, but he had the Queen's advice and approbation." [2]

It must have been a time of great stress and
strain for William. A short time before the Coronation, news had reached the Court of the arrival
of James II. at Kinsale on March 12, and Ireland,
which William had allowed to remain in the background of his mind as a country of small importance, to be dealt with when affairs of greater
interest had been arranged, leapt suddenly into
disquieting prominence.

Some talebearer informed the unhappy James

---

[1] "Lettres et Mémoires de Marie Reine d'Angleterre," edited by
Countess Bentinck, p. 62.

[2] "Mémoires de Monsieur de B."

that Mary, seeing her husband terribly disturbed by the untoward news, cried impetuously that " it was his own fault for having allowed the King to leave England "; and James considered that he realised " his children's loss of all feeling, not only of filial affection, but even of natural compassion." [1]

Judging from the tone of Queen Mary's intercourse with her deeply adored and admired husband, and from her feeling for her father, we can hardly believe that the words were really said as reported to James. His only consolation is characteristic if justifiable.

" But Providence gave the Princess also her share of the sorrow of the occasion " [writes her father's amanuensis]," for the news having arrived just before the Coronation, threw a melancholy shade over the joy which had left no place in her heart for the memory of a father so loving and so tender. Like a second Tullia, under the pretext of sacrificing everything to her country's liberty, she sacrificed her honour, her duty, and religion to chase away the peaceful Tullius and to put Tarquin in his place." [2]

Here was one point of view, and one held by many, as Mary was already finding to her cost.

To Anne, the eventful day brought qualms of conscience. She did not appear publicly at the Coronation, as the state of her health would not allow her to take part in any fatiguing ceremony. However, while dressing to look on at it, she sent for " Mistris Dawson," who had been present at her own birth, and asked her whether the child known as her brother were in reality the son of the Queen. " Mistris Dawson assured her positively that she was as sure of the fact as that Anne herself was daughter of the late Duchess of

[1] " Mémoires de Jacques II.," Guizot edition, vol. iv. p. 66.
[2] *Ibid.*, Guizot edition, vol. iv. p. 67.

York "; and, according to James's "Memoirs," she reminded Anne that Mary of Modena had given her proof positive that she was actually enceinte.

If this conversation took place as reported by James—we must remember that his "Memoirs" are not always trustworthy—Anne must have gone to the ceremony with no enviable feelings.

While the new Queen looked forward to the Coronation as conferring fresh honour on her adored husband, she also regarded it as an act of devotion, and a solemn entry upon new and important duties.

She composed a prayer which she used constantly beforehand to fit herself for the solemn occasion, and also some ejaculatory petitions which she offered during the ceremony. The Bishop of London spoke most seriously to her about the nature of the service, representing to her its devotional character, and telling her that the alterations made in it were intended to intensify the religious side of it. She was much averse to the reception of the sacrament as part of the ceremony, as she considered that the excitement and gaiety attendant on it were not fit adjuncts to the rite.

" One thing " [she says] " was to be done which I was much against, it was receiving the Sacrament, this all I could say they would have it, because it had been left out by my father, and worldly considerations prevailing, it was done ; but I confess myself much to blame in the matter ; and never had any thing so much troubled me as that did ; for there was so much pomp and vanity in all the ceremony that left little time for devotion, and my thought there was so much . . .[1] and so little true devotion in the matter, that I must reproach it my self as long as I live." [2]

The King and Queen went separately to the

[1] Blank in the MS.
[2] Doebner's "Memoirs of Queen Mary," p. 13.

Coronation. William set off at 10.15 and travelled
by barge from Whitehall to Westminster Hall.
Mary did not start till eleven, and was carried in
her chair.[1] By half-past eleven they had both
arrived in Westminster Hall, had taken their
places on the thrones prepared for them, and had
been presented by the Keeper of the Crown Jewels
with the sword of State.

Meanwhile, the Peers had been called over in
the House of Lords, the Peeresses had gone through
the same ceremony in the Painted Chamber, and
they were all assembled in Westminster Hall to
meet their Majesties. Some delay took place—
not because, as Miss Strickland states, the news
of James's landing in Ireland then reached William
and Mary for the first time, for that fact had been
known before, but because the Duke of Norfolk,
who was Earl Marshal, had forgotten to summon
the Dean and Chapter ; and they, not liking to
come without an invitation, kept the King and
Queen waiting for an hour.[2]

At last they appeared, and a procession was
formed, which started about one o'clock, and proceeded on foot to the Abbey. It was preceded
by heralds, who announced its approach. Then
followed "Drums and Trumpets, Quire, and Pour-
suivants, Chaplains, Sheriffs, Bishops, Peers, Peeresses, and Great Officers of State, walking upon
two bredths of Blew Cloth,"[3] which were railed
in, and guarded by horse and foot soldiers. Thus
they passed from Westminster Hall through New
Palace Yard into King Street, which is now de-
molished, to Broad Sanctuary—a distance of about
twelve hundred and twenty yards.[4]

[1] "An Account of the Ceremonial at the Coronation of King
William and Queen Mary, 1689."
[2] Lamberty's "Mémoires de la Révolution," vol. ii.
[3] "An Account of the Ceremonial at the Coronation of King
William and Queen Mary, 1689."
[4] Canon Perkins's "The Coronation Book."

Lady Cavendish, Lady Russell's daughter, who was an onlooker, remarks on the wonderful acclamations of joy. Thinking possibly of similar rejoicings which had greeted public events strangely opposed to each other, in the course of the preceding fifty years, she goes on naïvely,

"Though they" [the acclamations] "were very pleasing to me, yet they frightened me, too ; for I could not but think what a dreadful thing it is to fall into the hands of the rabble—they are such a strange sort of people." [1]

The Queen's sceptre was carried by the Duke of Bedford, the King's by the Duke of Rutland; the Queen's crown by the Duke of Somerset, the King's by the Duke of Devonshire. The Bishop of Rochester held the chalice, the Bishop of St. Asaph the gold patine, and the Bishop of London the Bible.

The tall Queen and the tiny King followed; walking side by side under a canopy held over them by the Barons of the Cinque Ports. Both were robed in crimson velvet edged with ermine; their wax effigies in Westminster Abbey are still clothed in the garments, and hold models of the orb and sceptre. The King wore a red velvet cap, while the Queen's hair was surmounted by a gold circle. Difference in height was not the only contrast between them, for the onlookers, who crowded the balconies and thronged the stands erected on the route, said that " it would be impossible to see an uglier King or a more beautiful Queen." [2] "Hook-nose" was their nickname for the unfortunate William, whose health was at this time in a very precarious state, and whose sickliness and apathy seem to have struck all those who came into contact with him.

Much of the usual splendour of the ceremony

---

[1] " Lady Russell's Correspondence," vol. i. p. 270.
[2] " Mémoires de Monsieur de B."

in the Abbey was dimmed by the absence of several of the clergy and the great officers of State, who would in the ordinary course of events have been present.

The Bishop of London, as we have seen, took the principal place in the performance of the ceremony ; and it was a long one, for it was not till four o'clock in the afternoon that the actual Coronation took place.

On the arrival of their Majesties, an anthem was sung. They were next allowed a short time for their private devotions, and the Bishop of London then performed the formality of asking in three places in the Abbey whether the people would receive William and Mary as their King and Queen. The answer was " The Recognition," a mighty shout from every one present.

After this their Majesties performed their first oblation. Here an awkward contretemps took place, for when the time came for the customary presentation of the purse and the roll of silk, it was discovered the King's purse had been stolen on the way to the Abbey. Fortunately, Lord Danby was able to come to His Majesty's assistance with a loan of twenty guineas.

Then followed the chanting of the Litany, and the first part of the Communion Service. The next item in the service must have given the Queen satisfaction, for she was, as we know, extremely fond of sermons, and certainly the one preached by Burnet, Bishop of Salisbury, on this occasion, was very fine. It lasted, Evelyn tells us, about half an hour, and was received with " greate applause."

The text was taken from 2 Samuel xxiii. 3, 4 : " The God of Israel said, the Rock of Israel spake to me, He that ruleth over men must be just, ruling in the fear of God. And he shall be as the light of the morning, when the sun riseth, even

a morning without clouds; as the tender grass
springeth out of the earth by clear shining after
rain."

Burnet began his sermon by saying that it is a
rule over men, not an arbitrary power without
laws or measures, which is here commended to us.

"Man is indeed born free, and so he has a right
to liberty; but he is born likewise with so much
frailty in his composition, that he wants conduct,
and must be kept under rule."

As was inevitable, reference was made to the
last reign: "The being given up blindly to a
Confessor, the breaking of Faith, the persecution
of Heritics, to signify a zeal for the Holy Church,
can serve with some to cover a multitude of sins."
It is the King's prerogative to convert the world,
" not by dragoons, sanguinary laws, or cruel edicts;
but by examples of true religion, a true life."

Burnet's peroration rises to a great height of
eloquence.

"You" [he said, addressing the King and Queen
directly] "have been hitherto our hope and our
desire; you must now become our glory and crown
of rejoicing; ordinary virtues in you will fall so
far short of our hopes, that we shall be tempted almost to think them vices. It is in your persons, and
under your Reign that we hope to see an opening
to a Glorious Scene, which seems approaching.
May you not only accomplish, but exceed even our
Wishes. May you be long happy in one another.
May you reign long in your persons, and much
longer in a glorious posterity. May you be long the
support of the Church of God, and the Terror of all
its enemies. May you be ever happy in obedient
Subjects, in wise Counsellors, and faithful Allies.
May your fleets be prosperous, and your Armies
victorious. But may you soon have cause to use
neither; by settling both at home and abroad a
firm and just peace, and by securing the Quiet of

Europe from those who have so often, with so little
regard to the Faith of Treaties, and now at last
beyond all Examples, disturbed it. In order to the
obtaining of all these Blessings, and in Conclusion a
Sure, tho' a late admittance to the Kingdom Above,
where you shall exchange these Crowns with a more
lasting, as well as a more glorious One. May not
only this Auditory, but the whole Nation, join with
united voices and inflamed Hearts, in saying God
Save King William and Queen Mary ! "

We are sure that the Queen listened to these
eloquent words with an uplifted heart, and a prayerful desire to do all in her power to fulfil the ideal
held up to her. We are sure too that in her humility
she would consider herself totally unable to do anything alone for the good of England, and would turn
with affectionate pride to her husband, its noble
deliverer.

James would be forgotten for the moment, the
sense of the difficulties of her position would recede
into the background, and England alone would
fill her thoughts and swell her heart—England saved
from Papacy, from despotism, from destruction;
England free and prosperous, her Church snatched
from the fangs of the devourer.

The reality was, alas, to be very different from the
vision evoked by the preacher's eloquence ; the un-
clouded sky, the plain easy way softened by general
approval, were not to be hers, any more than were
the joys of the " glorious posterity " and of the
peaceful and prosperous kingdom. The path before her was to be short and troubled—so troubled
that when in the plenitude of her youth and beauty
she was confronted with death, she greeted him as
the friend she had long hoped for, who had wearied
her by tarrying on the way.

After the sermon followed the Coronation Oath,
which, under the peculiar circumstances, was the
most important part of the ceremony. William and

Mary promised to govern the people of the kingdom and of the countries depending on it, according to the laws and customs established by Parliament, to maintain the divine laws and the profession of the Gospel according to the Protestant religion as established by law ; and to conserve to the Bishops and Clergy, and to the Churches committed to their charge, all the privileges which according to law belong to them.

These words must have been heard with intense interest by the people thronging the church. Next the King and Queen took their places for the Anointing, on chairs covered with cloth, after which they were arrayed in rich sacerdotal clothing, and the King doffed his sword and belt and put them on the altar, whither Bentinck (now Earl of Portland), brought back the sword with some pieces of gold, and carried it for the rest of the ceremony. The King and Queen were presented with the sceptre and cross, the sceptre and dove, and the golden orb. Now the actual Coronation took place, and as the symbols of their Sovereignty were put on the heads of the King and Queen by the Bishop of London and Bishop of Rochester, a general shout was raised through the Abbey, and was joined in with energy by the " Parliament men," who were seated with their Speaker in the North transept of the Abbey. Drums beat, trumpets sounded, Peers and Peeresses put on their coronets, and guns were fired in St. James's Park.

After this the Bible was presented to William and Mary, who kissed it and then ascended the throne, where they received the obeisance of the Bishops and also of Prince George.

The next ceremony cannot have been dignified, for the Treasurer threw about Coronation medals, and there was a general scramble for them. The design of these does not seem to have been selected with great tact or delicacy of feeling, while " the

sculpture " was, according to Evelyn, "very meane."
On one side were the figures of the King and Queen
inclining towards each other, and on the reverse
Jupiter was throwing a bolt at Phæton—an
allusion which, under the circumstances, might
well have been omitted. The motto, " *Ne totus ab-
sumatur*," does not meet with Evelyn's approval,
as he says that something more apposite might have
been chosen from the poet.

The reception of the Holy Communion, which
was so dreaded by the Queen, was the finish of the
ceremony, and then the weary King and Queen,
their work not yet fully accomplished, went into St.
Edward's Chapel, where they were divested of their
Imperial cloaks. Then, clad in the purple velvet
and ermine robes in which they had started, they
returned to Westminster Hall, where a great dinner
was given. The first course of this was served to
their Majesties with much ceremony, the Lord High
Steward, Lord High Constable, and the Earl
Marshal preceding it on horseback. The Duke
of Norfolk rather spoilt the effect of the entrance
by falling from his horse, which was frightened at its
unusual surroundings.[1] As it was his mistake which
had caused the delay in the morning, he cannot be
said to have performed his duties as Earl Marshal
with striking success. Lady Russell, however, tells
us that she hears that this Coronation is

" much finer and in better order than the last, and
that though the number of ladies in attendance
was fewer, they looked more cheerful than they had
when in attendance on Mary of Modena."

Before the second course of the banquet, Sir
Charles Dymoke, the Royal Champion, appeared
clad in a full suit of armour and performed on horseback the ceremony of the Challenge. He demanded,
according to usage, whether there were present any
person of any quality who would dare to declare

[1] Lamberty's "Mémoires de la Révolution," vol. ii. p. 253.

that William and Mary were not the legitimate King and Queen of the Realm, or that they had no right to wear the Imperial crown, as, if so, he defied them to single combat. Crying this out, he flung down his gauntlet, but it was by this time so dark that nothing could be seen when the steel gauntlet clattered on the pavement.

The Barons of the Cinque Ports were extremely indignant on this occasion, as, besides the privilege they enjoyed of carrying the royal canopy, they were entitled to sit in Westminster Hall at a table to the right of the King and Queen, and on this occasion they were ousted by certain of the Bishops. These Barons were, however, accustomed to a struggle for their rights, as, at the Coronation of Charles II., " they only succeeded in gaining possession of their canopy after a desperate tussle with the Royal footmen." [1]

" The feast, however, was magnificent," says Evelyn, after making sundry derogatory remarks about the rest of the ceremony, and he tells us that " the Parliament men were feasted in the Exchequer Chamber, and had each of them a gold (Coronation) medal given them, worth five and forty shillings." According to Lamberty, the Commons were again feasted next day in the Banqueting Hall, when their Majesties were present, and speeches were made on the Coronation.

At eight o'clock in the evening the company at last broke up, and the weary King and Queen returned to Whitehall. There was no repose for them, however, as in the evening they held a Court.

" At night " [writes Lady Cavendish, Lady Russell's daughter, from whom we have already quoted, and who was naturally delighted at the downfall of one whom she considered her father's murderer] " I went to Court with my Lady Devonshire, and kissed the Queen's hand, and the King's

[1] Perkins's " The Coronation Book," p. 112.

also. There was a world of bonfires, and candles almost in every house, which looked extremely pretty. The King . . . is a man of no presence, and looks very homely at first sight, but if one looks long on him, he has something in his face both wise and good. But as for the Queen, she is really altogether very handsome, her face is very agreeable, and her shape and motions extremely graceful and fine. She is tall, but not so tall as the last Queen. Her room was mighty full of company, as you may guess." [1]

On the Coronation Day a Proclamation was made at the Mercat Cross in Edinburgh, where it was announced that

"the sole and full exercise of the Regal Power be only in, and exercised by the said King, in the names of the said King and Queen, during their joint lives." [2]

Whitehall was not to be William and Mary's permanent abode; in fact, a few days after the Coronation, William found the London air so pernicious to him, that he moved to Hampton Court, and after that he only came up to town on Council days. This change of residence was not at all agreeable to his subjects, who were used to a gay Court, presided over by a Monarch who was easily accessible.

The Queen, writing about this time to a Dutch friend, describes Hampton Court as a place in the country, which is much neglected, and says that though it contains four or five hundred rooms, it possesses none of the conveniences of the palace at Dieren. From Evelyn's description nearly thirty years earlier, when Charles II.'s bride, Catherine of Braganza, arrived there, Hampton Court certainly sounds an attractive residence.

"Hampton Court is " [he says] "as noble and

---

[1] "Lady Russell's Correspondence"—Lady Cavendish's letter.
[2] "The Manner of the Proclaiming of King William and Queen Mary."

uniforme a pile, and as capacious as any Gotig
architecture can have made it. There is incomparable furniture in it, especially hangings designed
by Raphael, very rich with gold ; also many rare
pictures, especially the Caesarian Triumphs of
Andr. Mantegna, formerly the Duke of Mantua's ;
of the tapessrys I believe the world can shew nothing
nobler of the kind than the storys of Abraham and
Tobit. The gallery of hornes is very particular for
the vast beames of staggs, elks, antelopes etc. . . .
The greate hall is a most magnificent roome. The
chapell-roof excellently fretted and gilt. I was also
curious to visit the wardrobe and tents and other
furniture of state. The park formerly a flat naked
piece of ground, now planted with sweete rows of
lime trees ; and the canall for water now neere
perfected ; also the hare park. In the garden is a
rich and noble fountaine, with syrens, statues, etc.,
cast in copper by Fanelli, but no plenty of water.
The cradle walk of horne beames in the garden is,
for the perplexed turning of the trees, very observ-
able. There is a parterre which they call Paradise, in
which is a pretty banquetting-house set over a cave
or cellar. All these gardens might be exceedingly
improved as being too narrow for such a palace."[1]

There, on March 31, with the Bishop of London
as officiant, the King and Queen received their
Easter Communion. Queen Mary was much distressed by the pomp and ceremony, and by the
fact that she and the King received the elements
almost alone—a custom which seemed to her to
infringe the laws of humility.

The Palace did not please William, being " very old
built," [2] and irregular ; and when it was discovered
that large sums of money were to be lavished on
building, and that the principal royal residence
was to be established at a distance from the capital,

---

[1] Evelyn's "Diary," June 9, 1662.
[2] Burnet's "History of My Own Times," vol. iv. p. 3.

the discontent was general. " The misfortune of
the king's health which hindered him from living
at White Hall, put people out of humour, being
here naturally lazy," says Queen Mary in her
" Memoirs." [1]

To Sir Christopher Wren was entrusted the task
of arranging the alterations and additions ; but he
was obliged to consult the King in everything.
In " Anecdotes of Painting," Sir Horace Walpole
says that Wren had first submitted to His Majesty
a design approved of by Queen Mary, which was
in better taste than the one ultimately chosen by
His Majesty ; but that the Queen's wishes were, as
usual, overruled.[2]

Architecture and gardening were Mary's principal
amusements—she seems to have had a natural talent
for both ; in fact her desire to be " well housed "
is one of the failings for which, in her " Memoirs,"
she rebukes herself. Wren had a great admiration
for what his biographer calls her " exquisite judgment." He submitted everything to her about the
building of Hampton Court, when she would inspect the " drawings, mechanism, and whole progress of the works." Besides this, he had many
conversations with her, not only on architecture,
but on other branches of science and learning, and
was much impressed with her knowledge.

The Queen collected many rare plants at great
expense and put them under the charge of Dr.
Plunkenet, whom she appointed her head gardener
at a salary of £200 a year. The long arbour of
wych-elm is still known as Queen Mary's Bower,
and Mr. Law, in his book on Hampton Court, tells
us that three catalogues of her botanical collec-
tions are to be found in the British Museum.

William's idea at Hampton Court seems to have
been to build a second Versailles, and by July 16

---

[1] Doebner's "Memoirs of Queen Mary," p. 15.
[2] Law's " Hampton Court Palace," vol. ii. p. 28.

ELIZABETH VILLIERS, COUNTESS OF ORKNEY.

From a portrait by Sir Peter Lely.   In the possession of the Earl of Orkney.

Evelyn notes that " a greate apartment and spacious garden with fountaines was beginning in the parke at the head of the canal."

During the process of building, the Queen established herself in the edifice near the river known by the name of the Water Gallery. This is the only part of the Palace she ever occupied, for at the time of her death the State Apartments for the royal habitation were still unfinished. However, thanks to her taste, the Water Gallery soon became a charming abode.

" The decoration of the rooms was superintended by Sir Christopher Wren, and included painted ceilings and panels, richly carved doorways and cornices, with festoons of fruit and flowers in limewood by the delicate hand of Grinling Gibbons, oak dados, hangings of fine artistic needlework, and corner fireplaces with marble mantelpieces surmounted by diminishing shelves, on which were placed many rare and curious pieces of oriental and blue and white china. The taste for this she was the first to introduce into England, and for her choicest specimens she had cabinets specially made by Gerrard Johnson, a clever cabinet-maker of the time, which were placed in a room called ' the Delft Ware Closset,' and many of which may now be seen in various State rooms. Other rooms of hers in the Water Gallery were: ' the Looking Glass Closett,' which she engaged James Bogdane, the fashionable painter of animals, to decorate for her ; her ' Marble Closett' in the same suite, which was likewise finely painted and decorated; and her ' Bathing Closett,' fitted with a white marble bath, made very fine, suited either to hot or cold bathing, as the season should invite. She had also here a dairy, with all its conveniences, in which Her Majesty took great delight, being once heard to say that she ' could live in a dairy.' " [1]

[1] Law's " Hampton Court Palace," vol. ii. p. 28.

The Queen, too, had her Gallery of Beauties
painted by Sir Godfrey Kneller, in emulation of
Lely's Beauties of the Court of Charles II. The
famous Lady Dorchester advised the Queen against
the plan : " Madame," she said, " if the King was
to ask for the portraits of all the wits in his Court,
would not the rest think he called them fools ? " [1]

The Queen, however, persisted in her undertaking, which did not increase her popularity with
the denizens of the Court. The process of building
was a long one, and the King saw the absolute
necessity of having some residence near London,
as his Ministers grumbled continually at the loss
of time entailed by their journeys backwards and
forwards, and in the summer or autumn of 1689
he bought Nottingham House from Lord Nottingham.

This country villa, which stood in about 150
acres of meadow and park—now part of Kensington Gardens—had been built by Sir Heneage Finch,
formerly Lord Chancellor, and first Earl of Nottingham. King William bought it from the second
Earl for £18,000. Being only a simple house, with
a small clock-tower built round a courtyard, it
required many additions before it became suitable
for a royal residence, and on October 1, 1689, the
work was put into the hands of builders and
architects. "Thomas Lloyd, paymaster of their
Majesties Workes and Buildings," arranged the
account with " Sir Christopher Wren, Knight,
Surveyor of the workes ; William Talman, Comp-
troler ; John Oliver, Master mason ; and Matthew
Bankes, Master Carpenter." The agreement was
copied by the hand of "Nicholas Hawkesmore,
clerke of the said workes, according to the ancient
usual and due course of the office or their Majesties
workes." [2]

[1] Walpole's "Anecdotes of Painting."
[2] Law's "Kensington Palace."

It is sad to be obliged to record that, in spite of the imposing array of worthies—Christopher Wren among the number—who were engaged in the alterations, in the second week of November a great part of the new building " suddenly fell flat to the ground, killing seven or eight workmen and labourers. The Queen had been in that apartment but a little while before."

Perhaps the Queen was partly responsible for the accident. As it was necessary that William should have some residence nearer London than Hampton Court while the alterations at what the Queen calls " Kinsington " were in progress, he had borrowed Holland House from the Rich family. There the Queen found herself " very ill accomodated all manner of ways,"[1] and she was therefore very anxious to move to Kensington.

" This made me" [she says] "go often to Kinsington to hasten the worckmen, and I was to impatient to be at that place, imagining to find more ease there. This I often reproved myself for and at last it pleased God to shew me the uncertainty of all things below ; for part of the house which was new built fell down. The same accident happen'd at Hamptoncourt. All this as much as it was the fault of the worckmen, humanly speaking, yet shewed me the hand of God plainly in it, and I was truly humbled."[2]

William, whose views were more mundane than those of his wife, insisted, it may be remarked, on an inquiry into the causes of the accident at Hampton Court.

Though the alterations at Kensington were not nearly completed, it was possible to move there on December 2, 1689, and Mary records with joy in her "Memoirs":

" Blessed be God who has at last after more

<hr />

[1] Doebner's " Memoirs of Queen Mary," p. 15.
[2] *Ibid.*, p. 17.

than nine months being in England and never setled, brought me to a place where I hope to be more at leisure to serve my maker and to worck out my own salvation with fear and trembling."

On February 25, 1690, Evelyn records in his "Diary":

"I went to Kensington, which King William had bought of Lord Nottingham, and alter'd, but was yet a patch'd building, but with the garden, however, it is a very sweete villa, having to it the Park and a straight new way through this Park."

During William's absence in Ireland in 1690, the Queen lived at Whitehall, but continued to superintend the alterations at Kensington, the varying progress of which she records from time to time in her "Memoirs."

# CHAPTER XIII

WHEN Queen Mary arrived in England, the Prince
and Princess of Denmark went to meet her at
Greenwich and travelled down the river by barge to
Whitehall with her. As we have heard, Mary was
" really extream glad " to see her sister. She had
indeed good reason to feel well satisfied with Anne,
for she and her husband had at once thrown in
their lot with the Prince of Orange. This action
was doubtless much to their advantage, as, in the
probable event of Mary continuing childless, Anne's
progeny, instead of her brother, would inherit the
throne ; but Anne had consented to waive her
right to inherit the crown on her sister's death,
and to leave it to William for life. This cannot
indeed have seemed to involve any practical abandonment of her rights, as, on William's arrival in
England he appeared to be almost in a dying condition, and the chances that he would survive his
wife were so remote as to be almost negligible.
Besides, on this point Anne apparently made a
virtue of necessity, for Lady Marlborough allows
that she did her best to rouse the Princess against
submission to the change in the Succession, and
only desisted when she discovered that " the settle-

ment would be carried in Parliament whether the
Princess consented to it or not." Still, it would
have been unpleasant had Anne objected, even if
uselessly, and she no doubt felt that she deserved
well of her sister.

Soon, however, a coldness was observed between
the sisters, and after considerable friction, there
was complete estrangement between them—estrangement which lasted till Mary's death.

Lady Marlborough [1] comments in light and airy
fashion on a breach to which she was largely instrumental, and of the real causes of which she was
certainly not ignorant. She says

" a visible coldness ensued, which I believe was
partly occasioned by the persuasion the King had,
that the Prince and Princess had been of more use
to him than they were ever like to be again, and
partly by the different characters, and humours of
the two sisters. It was indeed impossible they
should be very agreeable companions to each
other, because Queen Mary grew weary of anybody who would not talk a great deal ; and the
Princess was so silent that she rarely spoke more
than was necessary to answer a question." [2]

The first serious dispute took place soon after
the King's arrival at Whitehall. The Princess,
who had been treated by James II. with the utmost
indulgence, was now to feel the difference between
being under the rule of a kindly father, and that
of a brother-in-law whose gifts did not lie in the
direction of endearing his relations to himself.
She wished to change her lodgings at Whitehall.
The sisters met every day, and the Princess found
the way between the Queen's apartments and the
Cockpit, which she had hitherto occupied, very
inconvenient. She was already accommodated

---

[1] Afterwards Sarah Duchess of Marlborough. During Queen
Mary's lifetime she was only Lady Marlborough.
[2] "Account of the Duchess of Marlborough's Conduct," p. 25.

with lodgings at Hampton Court, and she now petitioned to be allowed to occupy the rooms at Whitehall which had, in Charles II.'s reign, been assigned to the Duchess of Portsmouth. This was agreed to by the King, but when the Princess requested that certain rooms near these should be assigned to her servants, some difficulty was made, as it transpired that the Duke of Devonshire was anxious to have the rooms which Anne had selected.

"The Duke of Devonshire took into his head" [says Lady Marlborough, Anne's all-powerful favourite] "that could he have the Duchess of Portsmouth's lodgings, where there was a fine room for balls, it would give him a magnificent air." [1]

This way of putting the matter certainly gives the impression that the Duke of Devonshire's wishes were preferred to those of the Princess of Denmark. However, the author of the incisive criticism on the Duchess of Marlborough entitled, "The Other Side of the Question," remarks with some justice that it was not the rooms the Princess required for her own use which were denied her, but those demanded for her servants, and that this is elsewhere allowed by the Duchess herself. Therefore, as the Duke of Devonshire was then Lord Steward, the matter really resolved itself into a question whether the King's or the Princess's servants were to have precedence of lodging.

After many conversations on the subject, the Queen told the Princess that

"she could not let her have the lodgings she desired for her servants, till my Lord Devonshire had resolved whether he would have them, or a part of the Cockpit. Upon which the Princess answered She would then stay where she was, for she could not have my Lord Devonshire's leavings. So she took the Duchess of Portsmouth's apart-

[1] "Account of the Duchess of Marlborough's Conduct," p. 27.

ment granted at her first and used it for her children, remaining herself at the Cockpit."

To an unprejudiced reader it seems as though Anne had really managed the affair very well; for she ended apparently by keeping the whole of the Cockpit, in addition to the Duchess of Portsmouth's apartments, except the rooms she had required for her servants. However, another grievance was almost at once started by the Princess— or rather by Lady Marlborough, whose hand can plainly be seen prompting Anne to put a request which would, she knew, be most unpleasant for William to grant. The house at Richmond inhabited by Anne in her youth was now the abode of Lady Elizabeth Villiers's sister, Mme. Puisars. The Villiers family and the Churchills hated each other, and everything the Churchills did which could possibly anger the King was repeated to him by Elizabeth Villiers. Possibly out of revenge, Lady Marlborough persuaded Anne to ask to be given Mme. Puisars' house, a request which was at once refused. The Queen was evidently unconscious at this time of having given any cause for offence to her sister; for she makes no mention in her "Memoirs" of any quarrel; while the Princess, according to her friend and confidante, "notwithstanding these mortifications, continued to pay all imaginable respect to the King and Queen."[1]

However, from the tone of Lady Marlborough's remarks on the subject, it is easy to see that she would not allow the Princess to forget that she had been slighted by the King and Queen. As Anne was completely in her hands, and was, moreover, in a state of health which may have tended to make her irritable, it was doubtless easy to prevent the grievance from being forgotten. It must be allowed, too, that William's manners in

[1] "Account of the Duchess of Marlborough's Conduct," p. 29.

private life were—to put the matter indulgently—hardly conciliatory ; and that a scene which took place about this time, when the Princess dined with him and the Queen, was not calculated to soothe her injured feelings.

" It was in the beginning of his reign " [says the Duchess of Marlborough] " and when she (Anne) was with child of the Duke of Gloucester. There happened to be a plate of pease, the first that had been seen that year. The King, without offering the Princess the least share of them, eat them everyone up himself. Whether he offered any to the Queen I cannot say ; but he might do that safely enough, for he knew she durst not touch them. The Princess confessed, when she came home, she had so much mind to the pease, that she was afraid to look at them, and yet could hardly keep her eyes off them." [1]

On July 24, 1689, a son was born to Anne at Hampton Court, and there was general rejoicing throughout the country. On August 27 he was christened, the King and the Earl of Dorset being godfathers and Lady Halifax godmother. For the first fifteen days after his birth, the Queen spent nearly all her time with either her sister or the infant. " It was necessary," she said, " to keep her sister company." [2] The baby was named William, and the King conferred on him the title of Duke of Gloucester.

The birth of Anne's son was most satisfactory, as helping to secure the Succession ; and the King and Queen both became extremely fond of the little boy, while Anne's position gained importance as mother of the presumptive heir to the throne. No doubt the state of affairs was extremely difficult for the Queen to bear with equanimity. In

---

[1] " Account of the Duchess of Marlborough's Conduct," p. 115.

[2] "Lettres et Mémoires de Marie Reine d'Angleterre," edited by Countess Bentinck—Letter to Baronne Wassenaer d'Obdam.

Holland she had been the one beloved Princess,
whereas in England she found herself

"very much neglected, little respected, censured
of all, commended by none. Tis hard to flesh and
blood to bear neglect, especially coming as I did
from a place where I was valued too much."

Her temper suffered from the strain, so that she
grew peevish, and was very grateful when Dr.
Stanley, her chaplain, told her of this fault. It
may well have seemed to her hard that Anne, while
reaping the benefits of the Revolution, did not
share in the obloquy which fell on her and William.
It is true that, in the Jacobite ballads, Anne is
attacked as savagely as her sister and brother-in-
law. Nevertheless, with the bulk of the nation,
Anne, the English Princess, who had always lived
among the people, was popular as William never
could be; and Mary felt bitterly any belittling or
misunderstanding of her beloved husband. Then
Anne never confided in Mary or allowed herself
to be influenced by her or by William; for Lady
Marlborough, working for her own ends, scheming,
cajoling, even bullying, stood between the two
sisters. Therefore Anne, poor stupid, slow Anne,
dominated by forces stronger than herself, soon
assumed the likeness of a hostile power, and one
whose influence was enormously increased by
being mother to the heir to the throne. Mary's
longing for a child increased, and became a sick
yearning against which she felt it her duty to
struggle. About two years later she writes pathetically in her "Memoirs":

"Thy prayer is granted and thy wife Elizabeth
shall bear a son. Those are the Angel's words to
Zachariah. Joyful words certainly and the accomplishment of which was much more so. Why
art thou so troubled oh my soul? dost thou not
know that the Lord does all he pleases in heaven
and on earth? and do you not realise that the

Lord is just in all he does ? and as it is not his
will to bless you with a child you must submit to
it. Though I have been married about thirteen
years, I know that the Lord can still give me one, or
several, if he finds it right ; while in the interval of
waiting I must have patience, I must even remember
that humanly speaking there is no probability
that I should be thus blessed after such a long
sterility, and that I should be contented, knowing
that man does not see as the Lord sees." [1]

She tries sadly enough to console herself with
the idea that if she had had children she would
never have been able to bear her husband's continual absences and the dangers he incurred. These
had always caused her terrible anxiety, but at
any rate the suffering had only fallen on herself,
and if she had had children who might have been
left fatherless, her anguish would have been
infinitely deeper.

" That is why " [she says] " I look on my child-
lessness as a sign that the Lord wishes that I should
be so much the more detached from the world,
and more ready to leave it when it pleases him to
call me to him. Why then, oh my soul, do you
allow yourself to be again troubled about this ? "

The Queen was sincerely grieved when, at five
weeks old, the little Duke of Gloucester was seized
with violent fits of convulsions, and it was thought
that he could not possibly live. In commenting
on this she shows plainly her Puritanical spirit,
and also the feeling which with her—in the popular
opinion, absolutely gay and indifferent to her
father's downfall—amounted almost to an obses-
sion, that she and her sister must in their persons
expiate the sin they had involuntarily and of
necessity committed, in breaking the fifth Commandment.

[1] " Lettres et Mémoires de Marie Reine d'Angleterre," edited
by Countess Bentinck, p. 92.

" In this " [the child's recovery] " blessed be God,
I saw the grace of God in my heart, for tho'
I can truly say I was as heartily sorry for the
child as I could be, yet I looked further; I considered it as a continuance of the righteous judgment of God upon our unhappy family and these
sinfull nations, and that made great impressions
upon me, which, praised be God, I turned to the
good of my soul, and had abundant reason to
thank my good God for the recovery of the child,
as also for the wonderful relief of Londonderry
which happened some time before." [1]

The next difference of opinion with Anne was
more serious than the question of her abode; and
the Queen writes about it with bitterness. The
question of the royal revenue was now under
discussion in Parliament. The hereditary revenue,
amounting to between four and five hundred thousand pounds, had passed with the crown to William
and Mary for their joint and separate lives, but of
the money accruing from the duties of excise and
customs, which had been granted to James for his
life, and which made an income of nine hundred
thousand pounds, only a portion was settled permanently on the King and Queen. [2]

William was not pleased with this arrangement.
He was even more disgusted when it transpired
that Anne, instigated by the Marlboroughs, was,
without consulting him or the Queen, setting on
foot a party in the House of Commons to obtain a
separate settlement on herself; and that £70,000
a year was the sum her friends thought a suitable
income for her. The Queen's account of the matter
in her " Memoirs " is as follows:

" I had a very sensible affliction also at this
time, which was to see how my sister was making
parties to get a revenue settled, and said nothing

[1] Doebner's " Memoirs of Queen Mary," p. 15.
[2] " Macaulay," vol. iii. p. 557.

of it to me. The King did not think fit I should say anything of it to her, and indeed she avoided carefully ever since I came from Hampton Court all occasions of being alone with me. This bussiness went on till there were great heats in the House of Commons about it, at last in a Committee it was carried against her; upon which the King the next morning sent her a message by the Lord Shrewsbury to desire that she would put an end to all this, and that he would for this year give her 50,000 p. and when his own revenue was settled would take care that the sum should be settled on her, and being sensible she must be in debts he offered to pay her debts besides. This the Lord Shrewsbury first proposed to the Lord Marlborough, who begged he would not own he found him, his wife would by no means hear of it, but was like a mad woman, and said the Princess would retire if her friends would not assist her; and when he spoke to my sister herself, the answer was, she had met with so little encouragement from the king, that she could expect no kindness from him, and therefore would stick to her friends."

The Queen was now naturally on the warpath.

"When I heard this" [she says] "I thought it no longer time to be silent, but upon her coming to me next night I spoke to her. She could tell me no one thing in which the king had not been kind to her, and would not own herself in the wrong for not speaking to either of us, so that I found as I told her she had shewd as much want of kindness to me as respect to the king and I both. Upon this we parted ill friends, and she will make no advance to me not having once been at Kinsington since, so I came hither the day before Christmas eve, and tis now the last day of the old year. But the King thought it an ungenerous thing to fall out with a woman, and therefore went to her and told her so, upon which

she said, he should find by her behaviour she
would never give him cause. But neither upon
this did she say any thing to me." [1]

Lady Marlborough says that she had never seen
the Princess so angry as when she returned from
her interview with the Queen; who was also
heated, as we can see from her "Memoirs." According to Anne, the Queen opened the subject
by inquiring the meaning of the proceedings that
were going on, a form of introducing the matter
which was hardly conciliatory, but which the
Princess bore with meekness, answering only that
she heard her friends "had a mind to make her
some settlement." This pretended innocence on
a subject in which the Princess was known to be
deeply implicated, naturally did not soothe the
Queen, who said imperiously : " Pray, what friends
have you but the king and me ? " [2]

According to Lady Marlborough, the next move
on the part of the King and Queen was to send
Lady Fitzharding to try to induce the powerful
favourite to persuade the Princess to give up the
idea of the settlement. Lady Fitzharding—one of
the Villiers sisters—seems to have held a unique
position at Court. She was in Anne's service, enjoyed the advantage of the friendship of Lady
Marlborough, and the Queen felt much affection
for her. This fact—considering the relations between her sister and William—seems to argue some
special claim on the Queen's affection. The Villierses
were not always a united family ; and it is possible
that she, like her sister, Countess Bentinck, may
have stood by her royal mistress in some time of
trial. She was evidently a woman of great tact
and discretion ; but she could prevail nothing with
the imperious Sarah. It would indeed have been
strange if she had ; for Sarah held the Princess's

---

[1] Doebner's " Memoirs of Queen Mary," p. 17.
[2] " Account of the Duchess of Marlborough's Conduct," p. 29.

purse-strings, and was fighting for what was as
dear to her as life itself. William's parsimony
was notorious; and no one, I think, can blame
Lady Marlborough, whatever her ulterior motives
may have been, for the actual fact that she wished
to make Anne's maintenance secure, and beyond
the possibility of revocation.

William, on the other hand, surrounded by
dangers, tricked and betrayed on all sides, had no
wish to increase his difficulties by making his
sister-in-law (and, through her, the powerful and
slippery genius, Marlborough) independent of him.
Who could tell whether the money settled on Anne
might not be used to undermine her brother-in-
law's throne ? However, as Anne was completely
the Marlboroughs' tool, the only way to prevent
this was to gain over Lady Marlborough; though
the necessity for this must have irritated the King,
and have hurt Mary's feelings. For this purpose
Lord Shrewsbury, one of William's Secretaries of
State, was the chosen envoy.

Lord Shrewsbury is a curious figure in the history of those times. He had been one of the
" Immortal Seven " who had invited William over
—a fact which shows that he was not lacking in
initiative courage. He had done more than this—
he had mortgaged his estates to raise money, and
had taken his sword and his purse with him to
Holland, to be used in William's service. William
called him the " King of Hearts," and felt warm
affection for him. He became Secretary of State
before he was thirty; and though the fact that
he had lost one eye detracted from his good looks,
his charm of manner, his amiability, and agreeable
conversation made him a most fascinating personage. Foolish gossip credited him later on with
being the only man besides the King who had ever
touched the Queen's heart. Possibly she enjoyed
talking with him, but, as we know, her love was

so wholly given to her husband that all men but him were shadows to her. The undoubted fact that she singled out Shrewsbury for special attentions, was because William was most anxious to keep him attached to himself, and hoped that the Queen's amiability to him would further this object.

All William and Mary's endeavours in this direction were, however, useless. By the spring of 1690, Shrewsbury was in correspondence with James II., and as a proof to the latter of his sincerity, just before William started for Ireland, after many vacillations and at the cost of much mental anguish, he relinquished his seal of office.

This was later. When Shrewsbury visited Lady Marlborough, he was still in William's service. He told her that he had been sent by the King to offer the Princess £50,000 a year if she would desist from demanding a settlement, " and that he was confident his Majesty would keep his word ; that, if he did not, he was sure he would not serve him an hour after he broke it." To which Lady Marlborough replied rather pertinently—she was evidently proud of the repartee—that " such a resolution might be very right as to his grace " [here Lady Marlborough, writing long afterwards, makes a mistake, as Shrewsbury was not created Duke till later], "but that I did not see it would be of any use to the Princess, if his Majesty did not perform the promise." [1]

Here was plain speaking with a vengeance ; and when Shrewsbury interviewed Anne, she would not move from the position held by her friend. From the time when Anne as a child had insisted that a tree was a man, and, because she had once said it, had refused to look when she would have been obliged to allow herself in the wrong, her principal characteristic had not changed. "*J'y*

[1] " Account of the Duchess of Marlborough's Conduct," p. 33.

DANIEL FINCH, 2ND EARL OF NOTTINGHAM.

From a painting by Houbracken. British Museum.

*suis, j'y reste,"* might have been her motto. Here
was Lady Marlborough's vantage-ground. When
once Anne had been put into a position and given
a certain point of view, the operator could at least
feel that the exertion had not been useless, for
there would be no vacillations, and no change in
the Princess's mind.

Anne now gave full vent to her feelings
of annoyance, and showed much coldness to the
Queen. She would not receive the sacrament with
her, but had the service celebrated in her own
chapel, which was so unusual a course that Mary
complains that every one remarked on it. To
oppose William and Mary as much as possible,
she sided with the High Church party, and made
fun openly of the afternoon sermons so dear to
her sister's heart. Mary would have liked to have
spoken openly to her on the subject, but she says
sadly: " I saw plainly she was so absolutely
governed by Lady Marlborough that it was to no
purpose." [1]

However, before long a change took place in
Anne's behaviour, as, after conferring with the
Speaker of the House of Commons, and also with
Lord Rochester, Anne—or rather Lady Marlborough
—realised that it would be difficult to get the
£50,000 settled by Parliament, in direct opposition
to the King and Queen. Therefore Mary records
in her "Memoirs":

" There happened that day a thing which did
not a little contribute to the content I had ; which
was that my sister came and asckt both the King
and I pardon for what was past, and desired we
would forget it. I was very willing to live well
with her, and therefore past over all and would
say nothing of it, and when I assured her, I would
ever be reddy to shew her all the kindness I could,
she presently laid hold on that to tell me, I had

[1] Doebner's " Memoirs of Queen Mary," p. 24.

16

now a fair opportunity in consenting that 20,000 p.
yearly should be added to the 30,000 she formerly
had; and that it might be settled in the same
manner."

When the Queen discovered the real object of
this pretended reconciliation, she was much disappointed; especially when she found that Anne
now disingenuously declared that the proposal
that she should have the allowance of £50,000 had
in the first instance come from the King. Mary
guessed that Lady Marlborough, finding the measure "could be carried no other way, had with
much ado, rather than lose it, brought her self to
give my sister this advice." She consoled herself
with the idea that people would think the King
very good-natured for the proposal, and was very
glad to "live easy" with Anne; "tho' this gives
me no hopes of a lasting kindness, since it seems
on her side to depend so much on another's humour;
but one thing I am certain of, it shall never be
broken." [1]

Anne had triumphed; for though the Parliament
were aghast at the idea of £70,000, which Lady
Marlborough had endeavoured to obtain in the
first instance, the sum of £50,000 was eventually
granted her. In addition the King agreed to pay her
debts, as James II. had often done, and had traced
the cause of them to its true source, "someone
about her, for whose sake she had plunged herself
into these inconveniences." [2]

Meanwhile everything attempted by the King
and Queen seemed doomed to failure. William,
of course, had never been a member of the English
Church; and Mary, though considering herself one
of its most devoted adherents, was naturally much
under his influence, and was certainly not what
an orthodox High Churchman of the present day

[1] Doebner's "Memoirs of Queen Mary," p. 26.
[2] Ralph's "The Other Side of the Question."

would call a " good Churchwoman." Much of the ceremonial observed at the reception of the sacrament was abhorrent to her.

" One of my grievances " [she says] " was the pomp and stir observed at receiving the Sacrament. There was an old custom left since the time of Popery, that the kings should receive almost alone ; this had been always observed, this I could not resolve to do, but told the Bishop of London, who I found unreasonable upon that, and would keep up the foolery but at last I got the better, and the king being of my mind we resolved to make it a matter of as litle state as possible, yet there is to much left." [1]

An object which was therefore very near Mary's heart was what was called the Comprehension Bill. This Bill, which was introduced by Lord Nottingham, was intended to make certain changes in the liturgy of the English Church with a view to conciliating moderate Presbyterians. Its principal clauses were to the effect that the clergy should no longer be required to subscribe to the Thirty-nine Articles, and that any Nonconformist minister might enter the English Church without re-ordination after the imposition of hands by a Bishop. The Bill pleased no one. It was referred to Convocation, which was to sit in October, 1689, but Convocation would have none of it, and the High Church majority in the Lower House refused even to allow the matter to be discussed.

The Queen was much disappointed at this failure of her hope to unite the English Church with the Dissenters.

" I have had likewise an other mortification " [she says, after relating her failure to influence her sister about the settlement], " which was seeing the convocation go on so ill, but I hope God in

[1] Doebner's " Memoirs of Queen Mary," p. 13.

his good time will make all things succeed to the glory of his name." [1]

The year 1689, after opening joyously, was closing in trouble. William was personally unpopular, and the English nation hated the incursion of Dutchmen, who, they said, obtained all the best places in the kingdom, and were alone admitted to the King's intimacy. Even James II. had been accessible ; but when William was obliged to appear in public he looked stiff, and had nothing to say; his conversation, his liveliness, his confidences were reserved—his subjects complained bitterly—for the small circle of Dutch friends with whom he retired to drink beer.

The statesmen surrounding him felt his reign to be precarious, and made the matter safe for themselves by opening communications with James. Danby told Sir John Reresby that, " if King James could quit his priests, he might still retrieve his affairs." [2] Indeed, it was difficult to tell what might happen ; and statesmen as well as ordinary mortals have a liking for keeping their heads on their shoulders. Therefore, most of them deceived William as they had deceived James, and it is little wonder that his Dutchmen were the only people in whom he felt any confidence.

William was utterly discouraged. He could trust no one ; and he did not understand or sympathise with the English system of party government. Affairs in Ireland were still undetermined, the armies of Schomberg on the one side and of James and Lauzun on the other, faced each other without decisive action, while the ultimate issue hung in the balance. William was indignant at the ingratitude of the English, who had, he considered, summoned him to their aid and then had betrayed him ; and he determined to make a feint at any-

---

[1] Doebner's " Memoirs of Queen Mary," pp. 18, 19.
[2] " Memoirs of Sir John Reresby."

rate of returning to Holland, and of leaving them
to be governed by the Queen in his absence.

In all probability William was absolutely certain
that the English would never allow him to go,
and only used his intention of doing so, as a lever
to compel them to allow him to conduct the Irish
campaign in person.  This supposition is strengthened by the fact that in his confidential letters to
Bentinck at this time, there is nothing at all about
any idea of abandoning England, but a great
deal about his anxiety to go to Ireland, and the
reluctance of the English people to allow it.[1]  It is
an instructive commentary on the relations between
husband and wife, that William's purpose of leaving the government to her and retiring to Holland,
was not confided to Queen Mary till long afterwards.  The separation would have caused her
bitter anguish, might almost have killed her; but
she was only a pawn in the game, and her feelings
were negligible qualities.

Having called a few of his counsellors together,
William broke to them the news that a squadron
was in waiting, and that he was about to return
to his native country, and would leave them to be
governed by the Queen.  There was general consternation at his words, and every one implored him
not to abandon England.  He then announced with
determination that if he did not return to Holland,
he would go to Ireland, and would lead the troops
in person against James.

Though William's resolution to command his
army himself had not yet been expressed openly,
it was already rumoured abroad; and the Queen
had been approached by two prelates on the
subject.  Burnet, the Bishop of Salisbury—who
appears, in his intense admiration for the Queen,
to have occasionally felt qualms for the part he
had been induced to play in assuring her subser-

[1] Letters at Welbeck.

vience to her husband—came, she says, " in great
concern about the government, to know if it were
not to be left in my hands." [1]   About this point
Mary felt the utmost indifference ; but the discourse held to her by Lloyd Bishop of St. Asaph
touched her very nearly. He

" told me all that I but too well knew before of
the sadness of such a bussiness, to see my husband
and my father personally engaged against each
other."

The Queen therefore approached her husband
timidly on the subject.   His answer, as recorded by
her, does not sound peculiarly consolatory, though
she appears to have been satisfied with it.   The
King

" told me in general, that he should go, if he saw
the necessities of affairs required it, and that I
thought so reasonable that I endeavoured to prepare
my self for the thought of it as well as I could."

Matters were for some time in abeyance ; for
it seemed likely that the King and Queen would
have to visit Scotland first, " things going so ill
there, that the King's presence was absolutely
necessary."   This delay of the Irish expedition
must have been a relief to Mary, though she says :
" I confess this journey troubled me, yet seeing
it must be I set about to prepare myself every
way, and began to give over the hopes of ever
being settled more."   Her longing was intense for
a "comfortable lodging " in the charming suburban
palace at Kensington, where she would be surrounded by her china, her Grinling Gibbons carv-
ings, above all by her garden, and her rare
exotic plants.   Travelling was not luxurious in
those days ; and the Queen loved a home, and
was fascinated by the employment of making one.
She also enjoyed the amusements of the capital.
She was, as we know, fond of music, and played

[1] Doebner's " Memoirs of Queen Mary," p. 21.

several instruments, and one of her favourite recreations was to go in her barge to the Chelsea reach of the river, where a " consort of musick " [1] was provided for her entertainment. At that time, when coaches were heavy and streets narrow, uneven, and often extremely muddy, the Thames had an importance as a means of transit from one part of London to the other, which it has lost in these days of wide, smooth roads, and quick means of locomotion.

The Queen was also devoted to the theatre. Mountjoy, a popular actor of the time, often performed before her at Whitehall ; and she specially admired him in the title part of *The Rover*, though she considered it a poor play. There was a theatre in Lincoln's Inn Fields, and the Queen ordered Congreve's witty, immoral *Double-dealer*, with Kynaston in it, to be acted before her.[2] Dryden's Prologue to *The Prophetess* was, however, forbidden during the King's absence in Ireland. Perhaps this was a case of the burnt child dreading the fire, for one of the performances specially ordered by the Queen during her husband's Irish campaign was distinctly unfortunate. She was most anxious to see Dryden's beautiful play, *The Spanish Fryar*, which had been a special favourite with Charles II., but which James had forbidden because it contained reflections on the Roman Catholic clergy. A gossiping unknown writer thus describes the scene in an amusing, though decidedly spiteful letter to a friend :

" The only day that her Majesty gave herself the diversion of a play, and that on which she designed to see another, has furnished the town with discourse for near a month. The choice of the play was ' the Spanish Fryar,' the only play forbid by the late King. Some unhappy expres-

---

[1] Luttrell's " Relation of State Affairs," vol. ii., June 13, 1690.
[2] Colley Cibber's " Apology," p. 79.

sions, among which those that follow, put her in
some disorder, and forced her to hold up her fan, and
often look behind her and call for her palatine and
hood, and anything she could think of, while those
who were in the pit before her turned their heads
over their shoulders, and all in general directed
their looks towards her, whenever their fancy led
them to make any application of what was said.
In one place, where the Queen of Aragon is going
to church in procession, 'tis said by a spectator:

" ' Very good ! she usurps the throne,
    Keeps the old King in prison, and at the same time,
    Is praying for a blessing on the army.'

" And when 'tis said:

" ' 'Tis observed at court who weeps, and who wears black,
    For good King Sancho's death.'

" Again:

" ' Who is it that can flatter a court like this ?
    Can I soothe tyranny ? seem pleased to see my royal master
    Murdered, his crown usurped,—a distaff on the throne ? '

" And:

" ' What title has this Queen but lawless force ? and force
    Must pull her down.'

" Twenty more things are said, which may be
wrested to what they were never designed ; but,
however, the observations then made furnished
the town with talk, till something else happened
which gave us much occasion of discourse ; for
another play being ordered to be acted, the Queen
came not, being taken up with other diversion.
She dined at Mrs. Graden's, the famous woman
in the Hall, that sells fine ribands and head-dresses ;
from thence she went to the Jew's that sells Indian
things, to Mrs. Ferguson's, De Vetts, Mrs. Harrison's
and other Indian houses ; but not to Mrs. Potter's,
though in her way, which caused Mrs. Potter to
say, that she might as well have hoped for that

honour as others, considering that the whole
design of bringing in the Queen and King was
managed at her house, and the consultations held
there ; so that she might as well have thrown
away a little money in raffling there, as well as
at the other houses ; but it seems that my Lord
Devonshire has got Mrs. Potter to be laundress ;
she has not much countenance of the Queen ; her
daughter still keeping the Indian house her mother
had."

As the " Indian houses," though occasionally
used for unsatisfactory purposes, were the fashionable shops of the day, it is hard to censure the
Queen for her visits to them ; and we may suspect
the writer of those strong party prejudices which
distort everything. Queen Mary's next visit, if
the unknown writer be to be trusted, was certainly
indiscreet.

" The same day the Queen went to Mrs. Wise's,
a famous woman for telling fortunes, but could not
prevail with her to tell anything, though to others
she had been very true, and has foretold that
King James shall come in again, and the Duke of
Norfolk shall lose his head ; the last I suppose
will naturally be the consequence of the first.
These things, however, innocent in themselves,
have passed the censure of the town.   And beside
a private reprimand given, the King gave one in
public, saying to the Queen, that he heard she
dined at a b'—y house, and desired the next time
she went he might go too.  She said she had done
nothing but what the late Queen had done.  He
asked her if she meant to make her her example.
More was said on this occasion than ever was known
before, but it was borne with all the submission
of a good wife, who leaves all to the direction of
the King, and diverts herself with walking six or
seven miles a day, and looking after her buildings,
making of fringes, and such like innocent things ;

and does not meddle in government, though she has better title to do it than the late Queen had." [1]

The writer goes on to inform us that the Queen had told Lord Shrewsbury that her being in love with him was the talk of the town, and remarks that his Lordship had refused many good matches that had been proposed to him. The gossip about the Queen being in love with Shrewsbury apparently originated with the Princess's vice-chamberlain, who may have concocted it with the help of Lady Marlborough. William's warm affection for Shrewsbury, and Mary's adoration for William, are sufficient disprovals of this calumny.

On January 27, 1690, Parliament was prorogued, as it was beginning to be very troublesome, and at the same time the King declared his resolution of going in person to Ireland.

" This resolution being taken, I fell into great melancholy " [says the Queen]. " I told the King all my trouble, he said there was no help, that it was but the same thing he had begun before and must now be finisht ; he said much to satisfy me, but desired to talke no more upon so sad a subject." [2]

That William fully realised his wife's unhappiness, and sympathised with her, is evidenced by one of his letters to Bentinck, written just at this time. " I pity the poor Queen who is in terrible straits," [3] he says.

Eventually the journey to Scotland was put off because there was no time for it before the Irish expedition, and the first six months of the year 1690 were busy ones, for the King had not only to make preparations for the war in Ireland, but also to arrange efficient machinery for government during his absence.

[1] Add. MSS., 14,195, 100, 101, British Museum. This letter is entered in the catalogue as written by Lord Nottingham, to whom much has apparently been credited for which he is not responsible. The handwriting is not his, and the style is totally unlike his.

[2] Doebner's " Memoirs of Queen Mary," p. 22.

[3] Letter at Welbeck.

# CHAPTER XIV

The Queen's unhappiness during the Irish campaign—Her letters to William
—Elizabeth Villiers—Jacobite intrigues—The Queen's Council—Her
opinion of them—Admiral Torrington—An anxious month—Plots—
French fleet seen off Plymouth—Alarm and indignation—The Queen's
letter to Torrington—The Council's resolution—The battle of Beachy
Head—Indignation with Torrington—Patriotism roused—The Queen's
calmness—The battle of the Boyne—The Queen's letters to her
husband—French sarcasm.

PROBABLY the first six months of the year 1690
were the most anxious Mary had ever experienced.
Fears that her husband might lose his life in the
Irish campaign haunted her continually, and almost
as terrible was the dread that her father might
be killed while fighting against him. She writes
openly on the subject to the clever Electress Sophia,
for whom—though the two never met—she seems
to have felt a strong liking, though she is, as usual,
rather shy about expressing her feelings. She says :
" Vous jugeres bien que si j'ay toute la raisson
du monde estre en paine pour un marry et j'ose dire
une tele mary, je suis pourtant encore fille et ne
scay quel souhaits je dois faire pour une pere.
Vous avez bien voulu entre dans mes sentiments,
ce qui me donne le courage de vous en escrire
a present." [1]
The Queen indeed was so anxious about her
father's safety, that we are told that she spoke to
some of the officers who were going to Ireland
with William, and, with tears in her eyes, implored
them to watch over him.[2] She was so miserable

[1] Doebner's "Memoirs of Queen Mary "—Queen Mary to Kur-
fürstin Sophie, p. 78.
[2] " Mémoires de Monsieur de B."

that she committed a sin for which she blames
herself severely—she longed to die, because " of
all the crosses I met with in this world."

In April, while the King was busied with preparations for his departure, she became ill with
a sore throat. This would not yield to treatment,
and, hoping she should die of it, she set her affairs
in order, and spent her time in prayer and meditation.

" I had often " [she says naïvely] " wished to dye
of a consumption, but now I thought this yet better ;
for I thought I should see my self dye and have
my senses, which I imagined to be the happiest
death that could be."

Her only concern was the fact that some of her
debts were unpaid. However, as Luttrell notes
succinctly in his diary : " The queen being lately
indisposed was lett blood, and is since pretty well
again."

We cannot help wondering whether another
trouble—a trouble which pressed on Mary continually, though there is no mention of it in her
" Memoirs " or " Letters "—had not a large share in
causing her extreme unhappiness. After all, though
the suspense was wearing and must give her much
anxiety, Mary was a brave woman, and there was
no reason to despair. William might return victorious, and yet James be saved, as was actually
the case. But one matter seemed hopeless of
remedy—William's liaison with Elizabeth Villiers
continued ; with all her goodness, sweetness, and
devotion, Mary could not keep her husband's
heart to herself. The brilliant Elizabeth Villiers,
clever, keen, and tactful, born of a stock among
whom scruples were not rife, was to be her rival
to the end. William no doubt found in her a
piquant contrast to Mary, and however little he
would have borne the like qualities in a wife ;
in a friend, a comrade, a mistress dependent on

his will for her position, he liked independence of judgment, possibly even contradiction. Besides, Elizabeth was useful to him, he could entrust her with commissions for which Mary's situation as Queen rendered her useless. Swift gives us one or two glimpses of Elizabeth Villiers in her old age, but it is difficult to find out much about her, for William spared his wife's feelings by keeping her in the background, and exercised a secrecy about his love-affairs, which is most unlike the publicity shown in like matters by his royal contemporaries.

The Queen's letters to her husband during the Irish campaign are love-letters in the best sense. While they show a power of observation, discrimination, and a tact in dealing with men which prove the truth of Burnet's opinion that the Queen was capable of great affairs, we can see from them the absolute wholeheartedness with which she worked for her husband, and her complete dependence on his judgment, as well as the generosity of her anxiety that he should claim credit for suggestions which she had really originated. Her exiled father showed an acumen unusual to him when, speaking of his daughters one day at supper at St. Germains, he remarked that he felt no resentment against Mary, for she had no will or sentiment but her husband's.

On the last night of her life the Queen burnt all William's letters to her, so that on his side is a blank, a wall of silence. The one fact known to us which reveals anything of his feelings during the Irish campaign, is that on his return he settled large Irish estates on Elizabeth Villiers; and this certainly introduces a discordant note into the idyll.

Nevertheless William was genuinely fond of his wife.

" The day before he left " [says Burnet] " he

called me into his closet, he seemed to have a great
weight upon his spirits, from the state of his
affairs, which was then very cloudy : he said, for
his own part, he trusted in God, and would either
go through with his business, or perish in it ; he
only pitied the poor queen, repeating that twice
with great tenderness, and wished those who
loved him would wait much on her and assist
her." [1]

The next day (June 14, 1690) the King started
for Ireland,

"which was the terriblest journey to me that ever
he took" [says the Queen in her "Memoirs"].
"When he came out of Holland, there was hope a
Parliament might decide all, but here was no room for
any thing to flatter one self.  Nothing but a battle
could decide here, and what the event of that
might be, God only knew.  Then the concern for
his dear person who was so ill in health when he
went from hence, the toil and fatigue he was like
to endure, the ill air of the country he was going to,
his humour when I knew he would expose himself
to all dangers, then again the cruell thought that
my husband and my father would fight in person
against each other, and if either should have
perished in the action, how terrible it must have
been to me ; these were the cruel thoughts I had
upon his going, which none can judge of that have
not felt the like." [2]

The Queen, the Princess Anne, and the little
Duke of Gloucester now took up their abode in
Whitehall.  The sisters might have been a comfort to each other had not Lady Marlborough come
between them, with the result that the Queen
dared not confide in the Princess, who was, she
said, absolutely reserved to her.  Therefore, surrounded by strangers, she felt quite alone; and

[1] Burnet's "History of My Own Times," vol. iv. p. 83.
[2] Doebner's "Memoirs of Queen Mary," p. 29.

certainly few people can ever have been more in need of a tried friend.

Public affairs were in a most disturbed condition. The defection of Lord Shrewsbury, in whom the King had recommended her to confide, filled the Queen with dismay. A letter, too, written by Lord Clarendon, which proved him to be in correspondence with James II., had lately been intercepted, and it was believed that Somerset House, the abode of Charles II.'s widow, was a hotbed of intrigue. William had been careful to warn both the Queen's uncles of his knowledge of Clarendon's intrigues. He told Rochester that he could show a letter in Clarendon's handwriting proving his treason, and had been inclined to leave him out of the act of grace, but, for the Queen's sake, would not do this. However, Clarendon had best be careful, for if this had to be done, " it would be no jesting matter." [1]

Lord Preston, a Scotch peer, was known to be deeply involved in the conspiracy, but it was impossible to say who was or was not implicated in it, so widespread were its ramifications. William and Mary were surrounded by men who felt no scruple about holding office under them, while at the same time plotting for the return of James. Shrewsbury's resignation of the seals when he began to intrigue with the exiled King showed, for those times, a high standard of morality.

An Act of Parliament had been passed, empowering Queen Mary to govern when the King was out of the kingdom, and before his departure he presented her to the nine men who were to act as her Cabinet Council during his absence.

" She wants experience " [he said] ; " but I hope that by choosing you to be her counsellors, I have supplied that defect. I put my kingdom into your hands. Nothing foreign or domestic

[1] Clarendon's "Diary," May 30, 1690.

shall be kept secret from you. I implore you to be diligent, and to be united."[1]

William had done his best, without success, however, to conciliate both Whigs and Tories, and to bind both to his interests, by his selection of the nine who were to form the Council for government during his absence. Caermarthen, Pembroke, Nottingham, Marlborough, and Lowther were Tories; while the other four, Devonshire ("Lord Stuard," Mary always calls him, from the office he held), Dorset, Monmouth, and Russell, were chosen from among the Whig ranks.

Lord Caermarthen, formerly Lord Danby, who had been chiefly instrumental in bringing about the marriage between William and Mary, was to be the Queen's principal adviser. "He was one to whom I must ever own great obligations, yet of a temper I can never like,"[2] comments the Queen. Certainly his physiognomy, with its astute, crafty eyes, and small, thin-lipped mouth, is not agreeable.

Lord Devonshire, who as Lord Steward had been the occasion of the Princess Anne's disappointment about the "lodgings" at Whitehall, had also been recommended by the King as trustworthy; "but he," says the Queen incisively, "I found weack and obstinate."

Lord Marlborough was to take charge of the army, and the Queen remarks that she will say nothing of him, "because 'tis he I could say the most of, and can never deserve either trust or esteem." Marlborough, who was at this time about forty years of age, must have passed beyond the stage of the superb youth, the conquering hero, of his earlier portraits. It is difficult, however, to realise how far he had assumed the traits of his later likenesses of Queen Anne's time, when,

[1] Macintosh MSS.—See Macaulay.
[2] Doebner's "Memoirs of Queen Mary," p. 29.

CHARLES MORDAUNT, LORD MONMOUTH, AFTERWARDS EARL OF
PETERBOROUGH.

British Museum.

though now in reality the conquering hero, he had
lost all appearance of it, his mouth had become
pinched, thus giving a mean look to the lower part
of the face, and his only beauty is his fine eyes,
which are deep and brooding, as though he were
pondering over the mysteries of strategy.

Dorset, the Lord Chamberlain, is " to lazy to
give himself the trouble of bussiness."

" Lord Monmouth is mad ; and his wife, who is
mader, governs him." Monmouth was indeed to
give the Queen much trouble. His portraits,
which represent a handsome man with an aquiline
nose, delicate mouth, and keen eyes, partly over-
shadowed by the forehead-bone, give the idea of a
keen, active personality, full of life and fire. There
was something incalculable in it, as the Queen
would discover.

Lord Pembroke, according to his royal mistress,
" is as mad as most of his family tho' very good
natured, a man of honour, but not very steady " ;
while Lowther, the chief Lord of the Treasury, she
considers " very honest, but weack."

Admiral Russell the Queen seems to have liked
best among her nine advisers, but he " had his
faults."[1] He had been specially recommended to
her by the King for sincerity—a recommendation
he certainly did not deserve, though his round,
pugnacious face with its pouched eyes, his general
stoutness of demeanour, and his bluff, downright
manner, seemed to denote that he belonged to the
type of brave and honest seaman of whom our
nation is justly proud.

In Lord Nottingham, the son of a great lawyer,
a great lawyer himself, the man to whom William
owed the adherence of the bulk of the Church
party, Mary felt a certain trust, and she says
that William considered him an honest man. The
difficulty was, however, that though, as the only

[1] Doebner's " Memoirs of Queen Mary," p. 30.

Secretary of State since Shrewsbury's defection,
it was necessary that he should " know all, and do
all," he was suspected of not being true to the
Government, because, being privy to the Prince of
Orange's proposed invasion, he drew back at the
last. When once William was on the throne,
however, he owned allegiance to him, saying that
though he could not make kings, he could obey
them when made, and, unlike others who made
more profession than he did, he kept his word.

Nottingham indeed—"Don Dismal" he was
called by his contemporaries, with his swarthy
complexion, thin, falling cheeks, thick nose and
lips, a face the ugliness of which was only redeemed
by his bright eyes with their direct look—was, in
this age of corruption, one of the few instances of
an honest man.

It will be observed that the Queen does not view
her Council through rose-coloured spectacles. It
must be remembered in estimating the difficulties
of her position that hitherto William had never
spoken to her about State affairs, and that the
Treasury was in an impoverished condition, while
Lord Torrington, she says indignantly, "lay drinking and entertaining his friends till the French
appeared upon the coast, and had like to have
surprised him."

The Queen was doubtless surrounded by men
who were hostile to the offending Admiral—"Lord
Tarry-in-Town " he was nicknamed, but the reputation he bore with his contemporaries makes her
statement likely ; though it is difficult to reconcile
with Admiral Colomb's statement that Torrington
was kept in town by the Government till his orders
were signed on May 29, and that he left for the
fleet next morning.[1]

To guard the country itself, only 6,000 men
were available, and a great conspiracy was in pro-

[1] Admiral Colomb in "United Service Magazine," May, 1899.

gress, planned to a large extent by men avowedly favourable to the Government. In Macaulay's opinion, " the month which followed William's departure from London was one of the most eventful and anxious months in the whole history of England " ; [1] and though writers with Jacobite sympathies minimise England's danger at this time, and declare that the scare was simulated by the Government to make an excuse for severities against the Jacobites, to any one reading the Memoirs and Letters of the time, there seems little doubt that the alarm and the peril also were real.

A few hours after the King had left England, Crone, who was deeply implicated in the Jacobite plot in progress, and had been caught carrying despatches from Mary of Modena to England, was had up for trial at the Old Bailey. He was condemned to death, but was respited in the hope that he would betray his confederates. For a time he held firmly to his decision that he would rather die than confess ; but Lord Clarendon, who was naturally watching his doings with painful interest, records in his " Diary " that a friend who had visited him in prison said

" she had been to see Crone; that he was in a rage to think of death ; that he said, he was too young to be a martyr ; and that she did believe, rather than die, he would tell all he knew." [2]

Eventually Crone did indeed give important information to the Government, and as a result many arrests were made.

At this crisis the Queen showed the strength of her personality, and proved that Burnet was right in his opinion that she was " fit for great affairs." When Lord Caermarthen (Danby) asked her what she would do in the very probable case of an insurrection in the City, she told him that at any rate she would

---

[1] Macaulay's " History," 1862 edit., vol. iii. p. 601.
[2] Clarendon's " Diary," June 8, 1690.

not be governed by her fears; and, taking warning by her father's fate, she says that in private she determined that nothing should induce her to leave Whitehall. Mary received many compliments on her conduct at this juncture, and a little unwonted complacency may be discerned in her "Memoirs," when she relates what happened. She wrote to William almost every day; and her first letter is full of anxiety about the intrigues at Somerset House, which was a favourite meeting-place for Lord Clarendon and those engaged in the present conspiracy, and which it was therefore necessary to keep under observation.

Lord Feversham, the Queen Dowager's chamberlain, had given orders that prayers for William's success in Ireland should be discontinued in the Protestant chapel at Somerset House. The omission was, under the circumstances, ominous, and the chaplain was summoned to account for it, and was examined by Lord Nottingham. He explained that Lord Feversham had advised him to omit the prayer, because the chapel was under the jurisdiction of the Queen Dowager, and the reading of it might give her an excuse to cancel her permission for Church of England services to be held there.

On hearing this, the Queen herself interviewed Lord Feversham, who " seemed extreamly concerned, lookt as pale as death, and spoke in great disorder." The fact that he was a Frenchman, and could only express himself with difficulty in English, and that he used " abundance of words," made his excuses and apologies very difficult to follow, and the Queen found it impossible to understand his confused explanation. However, he assured her that the Queen Dowager knew nothing of what had happened, and " implored her to pardon him as God pardoned sinners."

The Queen, however, had either a prejudice against

Catherine of Braganza, or good reasons for mistrusting her, and she writes to the King :

" I pity the poor man for being obliged thus to take the Queen Dowager's faults upon him, yet I could not bring myself to forgive him. This I remember I did say more, that if it had been to myself, I could have pardoned him, but when it immediately concerned your person, I would, nor could not." [1]

To add to her worries the Queen was suffering from a swollen face, to cure which leeches were applied behind her ears, and one of her eyes gave her a good deal of pain.

" I have still the same complaint to make " [she writes], "that I have not time to cry, which would a little ease my heart ; but I hope in God I shall have such news from you as will give me no reason ; yet your absence is enough, but since it pleases God, I must have patience ; do but continue to love me, and I can bear all things else with ease." [2]

The next day (June 22, 1690) Mary had very grave news to communicate. The French fleet, under Admiral Tourville, had been seen from Plymouth, and was making its way slowly along the coast of Devonshire and of Dorsetshire. On the 22nd, writes Luttrell in his diary,

" The queen received an expresse that the French fleet was arrived in the channel, and seen off Plymouth sailing eastward, consisting of 70 odd men of war, 80 fireships, and several tenders ; being joined by the Thoulon squadron."

This was serious news ; for, of the portion of the British fleet which had sailed to Spain and the Mediterranean, only part had returned, and that

<hr />

[1] Sir John Dalrymple's " Memoirs of Great Britain and Ireland," vol. iii. p. 71.

[2] Sir John Dalrymple's " Memoirs of Great Britain and Ireland," vol. iii. p. 73.

part was blocked up at Plymouth. The ships were "so foul" that it would be impossible to "avoid the enemy if he should come up the channel; and the difficulty therefore of joining the fleet is almost insuperable." [1] The ships which had attended the King to Ireland had not yet returned from there ; and only a few of the Dutch squadron had joined the English, so that, "Tis said our fleet and the Dutches consists of 50 odd men of war and 20 fireships."

The matter was urgent ; and the Lords of the Admiralty met at three in the morning and despatched an express messenger to Lord Torrington, who was lying with his fleet off Spithead, and had no search boats out, to inform him of his adversaries' position.

Torrington had from the first shown himself difficult to manage.

On April 19, Luttrell says :

"The Earl of Torrington is disgusted, and seems inclined to lay down his commission as Admiral, declaring he will not hold it by commission from the lords of the Admiralty unlesse he may have a particular commission from his majestie constituting him admiral."

However, on April 30, the same informant tells us that this not very enthusiastic sailor

"is now better satisfied, and hath his commission for admiral to putt in or turn out any officer as he thinks fitt; and the king hath given him a promise of a grant of 3000 per ann. of the lands belonging the late Queen Mary."

Apparently, Torrington, who had, as Admiral Herbert, commanded the squadron which brought the Prince of Orange to England, and to whom later the duty of conveying the Princess over to join

---

[1] Sir John Dalrymple's "Memoirs of Great Britain and Ireland," vol. iii. p. 63—Lord Nottingham to William.

[2] Burnet's "History of My Own Times," vol. iv. p. 89.

her husband had been entrusted, considered that his part in helping to bring about the Revolution had been far from unimportant. He was therefore extremely angry at being left out of the naval administration, especially as his rivals Russell and Pembroke were among the Nine to whom the government had been entrusted during the King's absence.

To do Torrington justice, he appears to have been more aware of the strength of the French navy than were his advisers on land, and to have endeavoured unsuccessfully to impress on Nottingham the need for adequate preparation. Now, however, he seemed hardly conscious of the imminence of the danger, and great was the Queen's impatience at what she considered to be dilatory behaviour on his part.

He had been ill; for Luttrell notes in his diary, "The Lord Torrington, since his being on board the fleet, hath been very ill"; and the Queen wondered whether this indisposition were his excuse for inaction, or whether he were waiting to be joined by Lord Pembroke's regiment. The crisis was alarming. "Certainly," writes the Queen in her "Memoirs," "if any rising had happen'd upon the apeering of the French fleet . . . I had been in a very bad condition." [1]

The fate of England hung in the balance; for London swarmed with disaffected people—a rumour, a blunder, the whole city might be in a ferment, and William and Mary dethroned. No one even among the chosen Nine was enthusiastic about William's Government; it was at the best the only possible expedient, and several of those in office were already making themselves secure with James, in view of a possible counter-revolution. Nevertheless, the news that the French fleet was off the coast roused the true patriotic spirit. A Great

[1] Doebner's "Memoirs of Queen Mary," p. 31.

Council was held at Whitehall, and the arrest of any person of whose guilt the Government had proofs was decided on. "All Papists and reputed Papists were ordered to depart from the cities of London and Westminster," and Popish recusants were ordered to remain within five miles of their dwellings.

At the Council, Sir H. Capel did his best to defend his brother-in-law, Lord Clarendon, from imputations of complicity in the plot for restoring James. As no one attempted to controvert his statements, the Queen, thinking that the silence was caused by the respect the company felt for her, spoke out boldly, saying that "there was too much against him to leave him out of the list that was making"; and Lord Clarendon was, in her quaint phraseology, "clapt up" with the others. At the same time she tells the King that she "is sorryer, than it may be will be believed, for him, finding the Dutch proverb true which you know, but I should spoil in writing."[1] What was this proverb? Perhaps the Dutch equivalent of "Blood is thicker than water."

Meanwhile, great agitation prevailed among the Queen's advisers, for—after facing the French fleet off the shores of the Isle of Wight, and being joined there by a Dutch squadron under command of Evertsen—Torrington, fearing an engagement, began to retreat towards the Straits of Dover. The French fleet consisted of 78 men-of-war, and 22 fireships, and they carried 4,702 pieces of cannon; while the united Dutch and English fleets made up only 56 men-of-war, and possessed between them 3,462 guns.[2]

However, the Council hourly expected to hear that an engagement had taken place, and the Duke of Devonshire, who was especially indignant at the delay, proposed that Torrington should not

---

[1] Sir John Dalrymple's "Memoirs of Great Britain and Ireland," vol. iii. p. 75.
[2] Ralph's "History of England," vol. ii. p. 226.

be left in sole command, but that some one should be put into commission with him.

This scheme the rest of the Council considered untenable; and the hot-headed Monmouth suggested going to the fleet as a volunteer, accompanied by some one who should take the command if Torrington were killed in the engagement.

The Queen would not give her consent to this suggestion, as she doubted whether it would meet with William's approval. She thought, moreover, that, Monmouth being one of the Council of Nine appointed advisers, it would not be right for him to be sent away. At this, Nottingham, who had a well-founded dislike and mistrust of Monmouth, laughed bitterly, and said that Her Majesty was indeed paying Lord Monmouth a great compliment, when she said that she could not use his arms, because she needed his counsels.

Caermarthen's advice at this juncture was to send Admiral Russell to the fleet; but the Queen objected strongly to this proposition. She thought, with good sense, that "Lord Torrington being in the post he is in, and of his humour, ought not to be provoked."

The Queen was not fond of Caermarthen, who did not, she considered, consult her as it was right that she should be consulted, and she suspected him of thinking "by little and little to do all." She therefore thought that his desire to send Admiral Russell to the fleet was caused by jealousy, and appears to have clung to Russell as a counterpoise to his overmastering influence.

She writes to William:

"And now I have named Mr. Russel" [the title of Admiral seems to have been unknown to the Queen]. "I must tell you that at your first going, he did not come to me, nor I believe to this hour, would not have asked to have spoke with me, had I not told Lady Russel one day, I desired it. When

he came I told him freely I desired to see him sometimes, for being a stranger to business I was afraid
of being too much led or persuaded by one party.
He said he was very glad to find me of that mind
and assured me since I gave him that liberty he
would come when he saw occasion, though he would
not be troublesome, so I hope I did not do amiss in
this, and indeed I saw at that time nobody but
Lord President" [Caermarthen] "and was afraid
of myself."

Possibly Mary's trust in Admiral Russell was
partly due to the fact of his relationship to Lady
Russell, for whom she had a great admiration, and
with whom, as we know, she kept up a correspondence.

However, matters were precipitated by the arrival
of a letter from Torrington to the Queen, in which
he enunciated his policy. After a consultation
with his Council of War, he proposed to decline a
general action, and to sail, if possible, to the west
of the French, thus endeavouring to join with the
other sections of the English fleet. Torrington
was evidently not at all happy in the situation in
which he found himself, and he did not hesitate
to reproach the Council with his unheeded warn-
ings anent the strength of the French navy. He
warned them that if he were unable to pass the
French to the westward, he might be driven east
behind the gun fleet, where he would wait for re-
inforcements to enable him to drive them out of
the Channel.[1]

This communication appears to have been received with a cry of indignation. Caermarthen
was with the Queen when the letter was brought
to her by Nottingham, and he reiterated his advice
to send Russell to the fleet. A Council was summoned, and met that night, when, expressing the
general exasperation against Torrington, Devonshire

[1] Admiral Colomb in "United Service Magazine," May, 1899,

declared that it was not safe to leave the fate of three kingdoms to his sole keeping, and that some one must at once be joined in commission with him. Russell, knowing Torrington's haughty nature, cried : " Then you must send for him as a prisoner ! " As, to imprison the commanding admiral in face of the enemy, seemed hardly a safe proceeding, this suggestion was abandoned ; and it was settled that a letter should be written in Council commanding Torrington to fight.

The first draft of this letter was drawn up by Russell, and was considered too strong for the purpose. The amended version, which was eventually signed by the Queen, and despatched in a covering letter written by Nottingham, told Torrington that if any advantage of the wind should offer, he was to attack the French, and that in any case he must never lose sight of them, lest they should either make an attempt on the shore, or should sail away without fighting.

After this letter had been despatched, the anxious Queen retired to bed ; but she was soon roused by Nottingham, who brought a message from Monmouth. Monmouth had not been able to make his appearance sooner, but had now arrived in a great state of excitement. He was most anxious, if the Admiralty would only confer on him the commission of a captain, to go at once to Portsmouth, to fit out the fastest ship there, and to join Torrington, " and being in a great passion, swears he will never come back more if they do not fight." The Queen found four other of the Council assembled in her ante-room, who were all agreed that this course was expedient, and as they formed two-thirds of the Committee, the matter was carried by vote.

The Queen had lately changed her mind about Monmouth. There were grave suspicions that Wildman, the Postmaster-General, who was one of his creatures, was not to be trusted. Expected

answers to letters did not arrive; and it was
necessary for the Council, with many precautions,
to send express messengers to inform their correspondents that no news had been received from
them. Meanwhile Monmouth continued to bring
the Queen the communications known as the
"lemon letters." These were written in lemon-
juice and were addressed to a correspondent in
Amsterdam. They seemed to prove that some one
among the Nine was a traitor, for they gave an
exact account of what had passed at the different
Councils. Naturally these letters had at first impressed the Queen, and had increased Monmouth's
importance by bringing him into direct contact
with her; but equally naturally the rest of the
Council were infuriated by them, especially when
it was suspected that Monmouth himself was the
author of them. He often found opportunities
for interviews with the Queen, and on one of
these occasions he made a serious mistake in
tactics. After condoling with her on the fact
that public affairs were going badly, and that
everything said at the Council was, according to
him, known the next day in France, he began
to insinuate suspicions of the Tory Nottingham.
"I don't believe," he said, "'tis he, but 'tis some
in his office"; and he then began to speak of the
unsatisfactory administration of the government.
This criticism reflected indirectly on William, and
Mary was at once on the warpath.

"I told him" [she says] "that I found it very
strange you were not thought fitt to choose your
own ministers; that they had already removed
Lord Halifax, the same endeavours were used for
Lord Carmarthen, and wou'd they now begin to
have a butt at Lord Nott. too?"

The Queen's natural perspicacity led her to
suspect Monmouth's good faith when she saw how
he endeavoured "to fright" her; and she was

glad of the opportunity of sending him away to
the fleet, as she was anxious to see whether the
" lemon letters " would cease during his absence.

Torrington received the Queen's letter on June 29,
when anchored off Beachy Head, and wrote back
at once to Nottingham promising obedience, but
saying at the same time that, as he intended to
keep the French fleet in view, it would be impossible
for them to make any attack on the coast, whereas
" if we are beaten, all is at their mercy ! "

He called together his Council of War, consisting
partly of Dutch and partly of English officers,
and communicated to them the contents of the
Queen's letter. The interpretation generally put
on her orders was that if the wind held, the attack
was to be made next day ; and though the Dutch
wished that they were in stronger force, they submitted to the necessity of obeying Her Majesty's
orders.

At three o'clock next morning (June 30, Old
Style) it was light enough to see the French fleet,
and Torrington quitted the coast, and went into
the open sea to meet the enemy. The Dutch
Admiral Evertsen commanded the van, and Torrington himself took charge of the main body of the
fleet. There was a fresh gale when Torrington bore
down on the French, who were standing towards
the shore ;

" and about 8 o'clock, being come within a league
of them, he hoisted the red flag, the signal
to engage ; upon which the French fleet immediately braced their head-sails to the mast, and
lay in their line to receive them." [1]

At about nine o'clock the Dutch began the
battle. Torrington's plan, according to his own
account, was to give battle to the French leader,
and then to start a ship-to-ship encounter towards
the centre ; while Delaval, one of the English com-

[1] "Memoirs relating to Lord Torrington," p. 44.

manders, was to attack the ships from the rear towards the centre. Meanwhile Torrington himself was to undertake the office of watching and keeping in check the French centre, so that the enemy should be prevented from making use of their superior numbers to overlap, and thus to surround the English.

This plan existed only in the Admiral's brain, or at least was never made clear to his subordinates; and the Dutch, hurrying to the attack, passed several of the French ships without firing a shot, and left a wide space between themselves and the English main fleet, which was at once filled with French ships.

Torrington, in his first account of the encounter,[1] does not mention this reason for the disaster, and speaks of the Dutch with much admiration, but imputes the defeat to the fact that he could not make his way to them, because after " we had fought two hours it fell calm, which was a great misfortune to us all, but most to the Dutch." Only when obliged to defend himself against accusations of treachery, did he blame the latter for their hurry. Whatever the reason may have been, it is certain that when his allies began to get the worst of the encounter, he left them unsupported, so that three of the Dutch ships were burnt, two of their admirals were killed, and the rest of their vessels were totally disabled.

The French Admiral Tourville, in his account of the battle, says : " Herbert would not engage with me, and did not fight with any of my ships." Macaulay, however, seems unnecessarily vindictive when he remarks :

" It was evident that the vessels which engaged the French would be placed in a most dangerous situation, and would suffer much loss ; and there

---

[1] Sir John Dalrymple's "Memoirs of Great Britain and Ireland," Book V.—Torrington to Caermarthen.

is but too good reason to believe that Torrington was base enough to lay his plans in such a manner that the danger and loss might fall almost exclusively to the share of the Dutch." [1]

The next day the English and Dutch declined a second engagement, and retired towards the Thames with the object of defending London.

The indignation when the news of the defeat and the circumstances of the battle reached London was intense. The Queen felt the abandonment of the Dutch by the English very deeply, and the Dutch were naturally furious at the English admiral's behaviour. Bad news had come from the Continent, where the French General Luxembourg had beaten the Prince of Waldeck at the battle of Fleurus. This defeat, though of comparatively little importance in the opinion of the English, was a great misfortune to William and Mary, and seemed to prove that French arms were everywhere invincible. Hopes began to revive at the Court of St. Germains, and Mary of Modena told the French admiral that, were they to return to England in triumph, they would owe their restoration to him.

Nevertheless, there is no sign of panic in the letters Mary wrote to William after the disaster. She says :

" As for the ill success at sea I am more concerned for the honour of the nation than any thing else ; but I think it has pleased God to punish them justly, for they really talkt as if it were impossible they should be beaten, which looks too much like trusting in the arm of flesh : I pray God we may no more deserve the punishment ; that same God who has done so much can still do what is best, and I trust he will do more than we deserve." [2]

[1] Macaulay's " History," edit. 1855, chap. xv.
[2] Sir John Dalrymple's " Memoirs of Great Britain and Ireland," vol. iii., appendix to Book V.

According to Burnet,

" Though she " [the Queen] " was full of dismal thoughts, yet she put on her ordinary cheerfulness when she appeared in public, and shewed no indecent concern ; I saw her all that while once a week ; for I stayed that summer at Windsor ; her behaviour was in all respects heroical : she apprehended the greatness of our danger ; but she committed herself to God ; and was resolved to expose herself, if occasion should require it ; for she told me, she would give me leave to wait on her, if she was forced to make a campaign in England while the king was in Ireland." [1]

The Queen's conduct was, however, judged with much bitterness by a section of the community. These critics, though obliged to allow that she took every possible measure to protect England and to refit the fleet, and ordered " 12 great ships " to be at once provided, took exception to the fact that she despatched a special Envoy to the States with a message of condolence, and with regrets that " the Dutch had not been seconded as they ought to have been." The sending of this to the gentlemen they sarcastically call " Their High Mightinesses," they deemed unworthy of the dignity of the English people.

They were also irritated by the fact that Nottingham wrote at the same time a letter to the States laying all the blame of the disaster on Lord Torrington, and that this was translated into the Dutch Gazettes.

The disabled Dutch ships were refitted at Her Majesty's own charge, the Dutch seamen who had been obliged to leave them received conduct money from the Commissioners of the Navy, and the sick were tended till their recovery.[2]

To an impartial mind it would seem that the

[1] Burnet's " History of My Own Times," vol. iv. p. 98.
[2] Ralph's " History of England," vol. ii. pp. 228, 229.

WILLIAM III.'S STATE ENTRY INTO HOLLAND AFTER BECOMING
KING OF ENGLAND.

In the possession of A. M. Broadley, Esq. From the Fraser Collection.

Queen was only doing what was wise as well as generous, but though like orders had been given about the English wounded, the complainants, intensely jealous of the Dutch, declared that they were given precedence in the hospitals, and that the measures taken were those of a vice-regent of the States rather than the head of an independent State. They looked on Torrington as a scapegoat for the mistakes of the Government, especially for those of Nottingham, who made insufficient preparations for a war by sea, and then forced the Admiral to fight against his better judgment.

Fortunately, however, the measures Queen Mary and her advisers had taken for the protection of the nation now stood them in good stead. The heads of the Jacobite party, having been " clapped up," the rising which was to have followed a French naval victory did not take place, and the only harm done by Tourville was the burning of the little town of Teignmouth. Therefore William, who had been on his way to Limerick after the victory at the Boyne, and receiving urgent messages, was beginning to retrace his steps towards England, returned to his work in Ireland, and left the protection of England to his consort and her advisers.

The gloom and alarm were general, and were intensified by the fact that the Queen forbade the usual circuits to be made in the counties, so that at this perilous crisis each person was left in a state of isolation. However, the spirit of the country was braced by the alarm-call of danger, differences were forgotten, and the whole nation banded together to resist any attempt at a French invasion.

The arrival of the news of the victory of the Boyne, which followed quickly on the steps of the naval disaster, roused the nation to enthusiasm,

18

and people suspected of Jacobite tendencies " kept out of the way, and were afraid to being fallen on by the rabble." [1]

Offers of help came to the Queen from many quarters. Marlborough brought a proposal from Shrewsbury—who seems always to have been to the fore when money was required—Montagu, Godolphin, and two others, to raise 1,200 men immediately at their own expense, if the Queen would promise to reimburse them as soon as convenient. The Queen and Marlborough discussed this proposition, and decided that, as the loyalty of several of the proposers of the scheme—Montagu being notably of the number—was not above suspicion, it would be wise to decline the offer. They did this on the grounds that the regiment could not be raised for three weeks, and that then William would be back and the crisis over.

The Lord Mayor, the Aldermen, and the Lieutenancy of London waited on the Queen to state that it was " the unanimous Resolution of the City to defend and preserve their Majesties." [2] They told her that in addition to the nine thousand City militia, the Lieutenancy would raise at their own expense six new regiments, and the Lord Mayor and Corporation a large regiment of horse and a thousand dragoons.

Ten thousand Cornish tinners too made a protestation of allegiance to their Majesties; in fact, the unfortunate defeat of Beachy Head, possibly in conjunction with the battle of the Boyne, seemed to have done good instead of harm to the cause of William and Mary.

The Queen heard of the fact that William was wounded before news of the result of the battle reached her, and she writes on July 6—the battle having taken place on the 1st:

[1] Burnet's " History of My Own Times," vol. iv. p. 97.
[2] Ralph's " History of England," vol. ii. p. 228.

" Whitehall,
"*July* ¹⁄₆, 1690.

" I can never give God thanks enough as long
as I live for your preservation ; I hope in his
mercy that this is a sign he preserves you to finish
the work he has begun by you ; but I hope it may
be a warning to you, to let you see you are exposed
to as many accidents as others ; and though it
has pleased God to keep you once in so visible a
manner, yet you must forgive me if I tell you that
I should think it a tempting God to venture again
without a great necessity : I know what I say of
this kind will be attributed to fear ; I own I
have a great deal for your dear person, yet I hope
I am not unreasonable upon the subject, for I do
trust in God, and he is pleased every day to con-
firm me more and more in the confidence I have
in him ; yet my fears are not less, since I cannot
tell, if it should be his will to suffer you to come
to harm for our sins, and when that might happen.
. . . This morning when I heard the express was
come, before Lord Nott. came up, I was taken with
a trembling for fear, which has hardly left me yet,
and I really dont know what I do. Your letter
came just before I went to chapell ; and though
the first thing Lord Nott. told me was that you
were very well, yet the thoughts that you expose
yourself thus to danger, fright me out of my wits,
and make me not able to keep my trouble to myself."

Writing next day to William, the Queen confesses that when Lord Nottingham brought the
letter containing the news that William had been
wounded, she wept before him, a weakness " which
I have hindered myself from before every body
till then, that it was impossible."
The Queen's anxiety was soon to come to an end,

¹ Sir John Dalrymple's " Memoirs of Great Britain and Ireland,"
vol. iii.

for on the 7th came the news of the battle of the
Boyne, which was magnified into an enormous
victory, and which, if hardly more than a skirmish,
had, at least, decisive results, for it drove James
out of Ireland.  The Queen writes joyfully :

" WHITEHALL,
"*July* $\frac{17}{7}$, 1690.

" How to begin this letter I don't know, or how
ever to render God thanks enough for his mercys ;
indeed they are too great, if we look on our deserts ;
but, as you say, 'tis his own cause : and since 'tis
for the glory of his great name, we have no reason
to fear but he will perfect what he has begun :
For myself in particular, my heart is so full of
joy and acknowledgment to that great God, who
has preserved you, and given you such a victory,
that I am unable to express it.  I beseech him to
give me grace to be ever sensible, as I ought, and
that I and all may live suitable to such a mercy
as this is.  I am sorry the fleet has done no better,
but 'tis God's providence, and we must not murmur, but wait with patience to see the event.  I
was yesterday out of my senses with trouble, I
am now almost so with joy, so that I can't really
as yet tell what I have to say to you, by this
bearer, who is impatient to return.  I hope in
God, by the afternoon, to be in a condition of
sense enough to say much more, but for the present
I am not.  When I writ the foregoing part of this,
it was in the morning, soon after I had received
yours, and now 'tis four in the afternoon ;  but I
am not yet come to myself, and fear I shall lose
this opportunity of writing all my mind, for I am
still in such a confusion of thoughts, that I scarce
know what to say, but I hope in God you will
now readily consent to what Lord President wrote
last night " [Caermarthen had written urging William to return to England] " for methinks there is

nothing more for you to do. I will hasten Kensington as much as it's possible, and I will also get ready for you here, for I will hope you will come before that is done. I must put you in mind of one thing, believing it now the season, which is, that you wou'd take care of the church in Ireland, Everybody agrees that it is the worst in Christendom : There are now bishopricks vacant, and other things, I beg you would take time to consider who you will fill them with. You will forgive me that I trouble you with this now, but I hope you will take care of those things which are of so great consequence as to religion, which I am sure will be more your care every day, now that it has pleased God still to bless you with success. I think I have told you before, how impatient I am to hear how you approve what has been done here ; I have but little part in it myself, but I long to hear how others have pleased you. I am very uneasie in one thing, which is want of somebody to speake my mind freely to, for its a great constraint to think and be silent, and there is so much matter that I am one of Solomon's fools, who am ready to burst."

Towards the end of her letter, Mary shows another side of her mind :

" This morning, when I heard the joyfull news from Mr. Butler, I was in pain to know what was become of the late King, and durst not ask him ; but when Lord Nott. came, I did venture to do it, and I had the satisfaction to know he was safe. I know I need not beg you to lett him be taken care of, for I am confident you will for your own sake ; yet add that to all your kindness, and, for my sake, let people know you would have not hurt come to his person. Forgive me this. . . . I do flatter myself mightily with the hopes to

see you, for which I am more impatient than can
be expressed ; loving you with a passion which
cannot end with my life."

It was rumoured in France that William had
been killed at the battle of the Boyne, and the rejoicings at this news were hysterical. The French
exultation at the supposed removal of their enemy
is depicted in several caricatures of the time. One
of these represents William being carried to the
grave by Halifax, Burnet, Shrewsbury—who is
represented as an old man—Dyckvelt, and Portland ; while Queen Mary walks behind weeping.
The verses which accompany the picture are addressed to her, and are hardly consolatory ; though
in the magnanimity of victory the poetaster has
treated the supposed widow with less acrimony
than might have been expected :

> " Ton superbe Tarquin vomit son ame impure ;
> Tullie, il faut calmer tes pleurs and ton effroy,
> Jacques est ton Pere et il est ton Roi,
> Ecoute encore ton sang, et son secret murmure,
> Malgré ton crime il est je crois
> De grands retours a la Nature." [1]

These rejoicings were, as we know, premature,
and the French merrymakers must have felt a
little foolish, when it transpired that their hated
and dreaded enemy was not only alive, but trium-
phant, and that their joy at his supposed demise
had been the greatest compliment they could
possibly have paid him.

[1] Caricature, British Museum.

# CHAPTER XV

Elizabeth Villiers and Irish estates—The Queen's feelings—Disputes in
Council—The Privy Council—The Queen's anxieties—The Scotch
conspiracy—The Queen's interviews with Ross and Montgomery—
Her overburdened condition—William's return—He goes to Holland
—Conspiracies—Ashton—Preston and Crone—Discontent among
Ministers.

In the midst of her anxieties and distractions,
the great trouble of the Queen's married life kept
up an undercurrent of pain. William's intention
of handing over much of the confiscated land in
Ireland to his mistress, Elizabeth Villiers, had
doubtless reached her ears, or was at least suspected by her, for though she does not mention the
real cause of offence, she writes to him on the
subject with a sternness of tone which is strangely
alien to her usual sweet submissiveness. Though
Mary was proud and reserved, and only once
apparently during her married life spoke to her
husband of his unfaithfulness to her, she never
deviated from her view of the subject. William's
relations with Elizabeth Villiers were not only an
injury to her, they were a sin against God, a stumb-
ling-block and a cause of scandal to the people
for whom he was the Almighty's instrument for
salvation.

She writes :

"Whitehall,
"*July the* ½, 1690.

" I have been desired to beg you not to be too
quick in parting with confiscated estates, but
consider whether you will not keep some for
public schools, to instruct the poor Irish ; for my

part, I must needs say that I think you would do very well if you would consider what care can be taken of the poor souls there ; and indeed, if you give me leave, I must tell you, I think the wonderfull deliverance and success you have had should oblige you to think upon doing what you can for the advancement of true religion, and promoting the Gospel." [1]

Could a rebuke have been more delicately worded ? However, as might have been expected, the Queen's remonstrances were in vain, and William settled on Elizabeth Villiers over 90,000 acres of James II.'s Irish estates. This land was valued at £26,000 a year, but owing to the rent-charges for James's discarded mistresses, the real income from it only came to £5,000 a year, and the whole grant was revoked by Parliament in 1699. Considering the huge sums that had been lavished by Charles II. and by Louis XIV. on their mistresses, this was a small outlay ; but it was looked on by the nation with far less indulgence than had been accorded to the weaknesses of the Merry Monarch.

The Queen cannot, however, have had much time for brooding over her matrimonial wrongs, for the crisis which had brought the Council into unity of action, if not of object, being surmounted, their divergent aims again became strongly marked. These, except in the case of Nottingham, who was abused by all parties, were to a great extent egotistical. This was apparent in the discussions which took place directly after the battle of Beachy Head, on the choice of an Envoy to deprive Lord Torrington of the command of the fleet, which was to be put for the present into the hands of his subordinate, Sir John Ashby. Admiral Russell, during whose absence the Queen seems to have felt much uneasiness, had not been long away, as he heard of the

[1] Sir John Dalrymple's "Memoirs of Great Britain and Ireland," vol. iii.—Mary to William.

battle of Beachy Head before he reached Canterbury, and, to the Queen's regret, Monmouth was
also back, so the Nine were again reunited—in body
if not in spirit !

Monmouth was related to Torrington, and said
he did not therefore wish to present himself before
him on so disagreeable an errand.  This was, however, a scruple which the Queen was intended to
overcome, for when she chose two other members of
the Nine to fufil the embassy, Monmouth was
evidently disconcerted, and remarked that the
King had once thought of entrusting him with the
command of the fleet.  In fact Monmouth was
determined to be made the commanding admiral,
and the rest of the Council were equally determined
that he should not have the post.   At last he took
the bull by the horns, and, going to Caermarthen
(Danby), begged his advice as to whether it would
be wise on his part to propose himself for the
command.  Caermarthen,

" as a friend " [says the Queen], " counsel'd him
not to ask it alone, not judging any one man fit
for it ; T'other pretended to thank him, but in a
passion begged not to be named as one who would
go in commission ; so that was over." [1]

Admiral Russell expressed reluctance to super-
seding Torrington, and was evidently sincere in his
resistance, for he assured the Queen

" he could not go any way even though he had
those with him who could help him with their
advice. He said the blame must still fall upon
him, if any thing happened, though merely ac-
cidental, yet he said the minds of all men were
so exasperated now that it would be his ruin.  You
may believe I could not press him after that."

The rest of the Nine offered their services, except
Nottingham and Marlborough, who remarked with

[1] Sir John Dalrymple's "Memoirs of Great Britain and Ireland,"
vol. iii.—Mary to William.

some justice that their appearance at the fleet as commanders would be absurd. Whereupon the Queen, using her own judgment for the first time, suggested that Lord Pembroke, Secretary to the Admiralty, and Lord Devonshire, the Lord Steward, should be the two to go.

Lord Caermarthen (Danby) looked black at this, and so evidently wished to have been chosen, that when the rest of the Council had gone, the Queen felt obliged to remind him how very useful and necessary he was to her, and to tell him that the King had advised her to rely on his counsel on all occasions. To this appeal he replied that "he did not look on himself as so tied, but he might go away upon occasions." [1]

Many were the Queen's difficulties; and the only way of deciding them seemed to be to put the fleet under the command of a commission of three, two of them being seamen, and the third "a man of quality."

For the two seamen the Queen chose Sir R. Hadock, of whom William had a great opinion, and Sir J. Ashby, the two first in precedence in the fleet, now that Torrington had been committed to the Tower to await his trial. It was left for William, on his return, to select the "man of quality." Lord Shrewsbury, with the curious vacillation which characterised him, after giving up his seals of office as Secretary of State, had been so far roused by the crisis, that he had proposed himself for this post. The Whigs on the Council were most anxious that the Queen should nominate him; but she hesitated, for though William, she knew, loved and trusted him, she could not forget that he had freed himself from his responsibilities at a time when any one who had the King's interests at heart, would have remained at his post. Lord

[1] Sir John Dalrymple's "Memoirs of Great Britain and Ireland," vol. iii.—Mary to William.

Pembroke was also named as a suitable choice, but eventually it was settled that the decision should be left till the King's return.

There were difficulties, moreover, about the appointment of the two seamen, for when the Admiralty appeared before the Queen and heard of the proposed nominations, they refused to obey her.

" Sir T. Lee, their spokesman, grew as pale as death, and told me " [says the Queen] "that the custom was that they used to recommend, and they were to answer for the persons, since they were to give them the commission ; and did not know but they might be called to account in Parliament." [1]

As the Queen discovered later, there was a strong feeling against Sir R. Hadock because he was backed up by Nottingham.

It was in vain that Caermarthen argued with the Admiralty ; Sir T. Lee, who was certainly not lacking in courage, said it could not be ; that the Queen might, if she pleased, give the two candidates a commission ; but they could not. The Queen then spoke with spirit. To quote her own words :

" I said, I perceived then the King had given away his own power, and could not make an admiral which the admiralty did not like ; he answered, No, no more he cant." [2] This was at any rate downright, and the Queen felt so angry that she was tempted to say, with something of her father's spirit, that the King would transfer the position of Commissioners of the Admiralty to people who would not dispute his will. However, she fortunately refrained from replying to defiance with counter-defiance, and the representatives of the Admiralty withdrew.

Caermarthen was left in a state of extreme

[1] Sir John Dalrymple's "Memoirs of Great Britain and Ireland," vol. iii.—Mary to William.
[2] *Ibid.*

indignation, in which "he talkt at a great rate," and the Queen was obliged to calm him, saying, with much good sense : "I was angry enough, and desired he would not be too much so, for I did not believe it a proper time." Admiral Russell, on the other hand, being a Whig, and objecting to Hadock's nomination because brought about by Nottingham, excused Lee, and refused to believe that he had said what was imputed to him.

Devonshire, also a Whig, took the same line ; and brought the Queen an apology from Sir Thomas Lee, who excused himself by saying that the Admiralty only objected to Hadock because he was recommended by people they did not like. The Queen answered indignantly that she thought the better of Hadock, if that was the only accusation that could be adduced against him.

Eventually the plan of the Commission of Three, to include a "man of quality," was abandoned ; and after many debates and much squabbling, Hadock and Ashby were sent to the fleet ; the question of their mutual precedence still causing much dissension.

Another naval question caused a fresh quarrel. Marlborough, backed by Nottingham, but opposed by the rest of the Council, considered that, as the French had returned to their ports, and the Channel was open, it would be the right time to despatch an English fleet with five thousand men on board to reduce Cork and Kinsale. William approved of this scheme, and gave orders that it should be carried out ; but though Caermarthen, who was very jealous of Marlborough, abstained from open opposition, he raised all the difficulties he could, and represented to the Queen the danger of leaving England exposed to France when her fleet and part of her army were in Ireland.

Besides the difficulty of contending with dissensions among the nine chosen advisers, the Privy

Council, or the Great Council, as the Queen calls
it, gave her a good deal of trouble by insisting
that she should be present at its sittings ; and when
she refused to attend, the members complained
that she was shut up by the Nine, and that no one
could get at her. Indeed it was a general and,
possibly, well-founded opinion that the Queen
would do nothing without asking Caermarthen's
or Nottingham's advice.

At last the matter came to a climax, and at an
extraordinary meeting held to acquaint the Privy
Council with William's victory at the Boyne, a
general disturbance took place, and some among
the Council declared that, as Privy Councillors
established by law, they refused to speak except in
the Queen's presence.[1]

To calm them, Devonshire and Monmouth came
to the Queen in her private room—a liberty which
she considered extraordinary—and begged her to
go at once to the meeting. This she refused to do,
as the King had told her to take the advice of the
Nine as to whether she should preside at the Privy
Council or not, and they had informed her that
her attendance was not necessary. As they
pressed her, she began to get vexed, and was much
relieved when Nottingham appeared and upheld
her resolution.

New to political affairs, distracted by diverse
counsels, not knowing whom to trust, and ner-
vously anxious to satisfy the husband whose word
was law to her, the Queen was in a position which
would have been trying to the strongest nerves.
Great was her disappointment when she heard
that, instead of coming home, William had undertaken the siege of Limerick.

" It will be vain to undertake telling you of the
disappointment 'tis to me that you do not come

---

[1] Sir John Dalrymple's "Memoirs of Great Britain and Ireland,"
vol. iii. p. 98.

so soon," she writes, and later in the same letter
she goes on : " I will endeavour as much as may
be to submit to the will of God and your judgment ;
but you must forgive a poor wife, who loves you
so dearly, if I can't do it with dry eyes ; yet since
it has pleased God so wonderfully to preserve you
all your life, and so miraculously now, I need not
doubt but he will still preserve you ; yet let me
beg you not to expose yourself unnecessarily, that
will be too much tempting that providence which
I hope will still watch over you." [1]

The Queen was terribly anxious about the
crossing of the Shannon, and writes : " This
passage of the river runs much in my mind,
and gives me no quiet night nor day ; I have a
million of fears, which are caused by that which
you can't be angry at." [2] She finishes this letter
with the words : " But I hope all is well, especially
your dear self, who I love much better than life."

Another anxiety was pressing on the Queen.
Ever since William's accession, Scotland had been
in a disturbed condition, and though the more
honest of James's adherents shrank from the
perfidy of the action, some of those who took the
oath to William did this merely with the object
of being in a better position to intrigue for James.
The leader of the particular plot which was exer-
cising the minds of Queen Mary and her advisers
was Sir James Montgomery, a restless, unscrupulous man, who did not hesitate to deceive those
with whom he was plotting. [3] Among those asso-
ciated with him were Lord Ross and Lord Annandale. Even if we look with sympathy on the
honest Jacobite who wished to bring back his
rightful Monarch, we cannot but regard these three,

---

[1] Sir John Dalrymple's " Memoirs of Great Britain and Ireland,"
appendix, vol. iii.—Letter, August $\frac{12}{2}$, 1690.

[2] *Ibid.*—Letter, August $\frac{19}{9}$, 1690.

[3] Ralph's " History of England," vol. ii. p. 210.

as unworthy representatives of the cause they espoused.

After a time Montgomery's perfidy to his associates became patent, and Ross, alarmed for his own safety, determined to turn King's evidence. Therefore, pretending that, in spite of his innocence, he was afraid of imprisonment if he remained in Scotland, he applied to the Lord High Commissioner for a pass to London, where he asked for permission to have an interview with the Queen. Lord Melville, the King's representative in Scotland, who seems himself to have been hardly a trustworthy personage, wrote thus about him to Queen Mary:

" MAY IT PLEASE YOUR MAJESTIE
" The bearer hereof, who desires not to be named till he wait on your Majestie, was desirous I should wrett to you with him. He has been engaged in a very badd design, and seems to be convinced to the ill of it, and saies he is willing to make a free discovery of all he knowes in relation too it." [1]

The Queen was advised to satisfy Lord Ross's desire for an interview, and saw him on June 28, 1690, when he was brought by the " bake stairs " to the eating-room. There she received him alone, and he delivered to her a letter from Lord Melville, but would reveal nothing to her. When she pressed him, he promised to tell all he knew on condition that his honour should be secured, and that the fact of the interview between him and the Queen should be kept absolutely secret. To ensure this, he begged that he might be allowed to kiss her hand in public, and to state in the hearing of all present, that, knowing himself to be falsely accused, he had come to justify himself. He requested the

---

[1] " Leven and Melville Papers," p. 456.

Queen to write her questions, and he would answer
them.

This was on a Saturday, and on Sunday and
Monday the Queen heard nothing of him. On
Tuesday, July 1, she sent for him again, and gave
him a list of written questions, which were intended
to discover the scope of the conspiracy. She asked
him to write his answers. He had now changed
his tone, declared the conspiracy was over, and
strongly objected to writing the answers, and thus
revealing his identity. Eventually, he took the
questions away with him ; and at his next audience
with the Queen he dictated answers to some of
them. To many, however, he refused response,
and she writes : " He is very sory he canot
ansere all these questions ; frivolous excuses."
The principal thing, from his point of view, was
his statement that he was falsely accused of complicity in the plot.

" He believes I may justly suspect he does not
deal fairly ; but he says upon his honour, and the
word of a gentleman, over and over, that he knows
no more the reason, because he never liked the
thing, and so kept much in the contre."

His answers were most unsatisfactory, as the
Queen told him plainly. She further remarked
that, as he had not kept his word to her, she was
discharged from the necessity of keeping hers to
him ; and Nottingham, having secured him, asked
the Council for leave to send him to the Tower.
This was granted by the majority of the Council,
but the Duke of Bolton, the Earl of Devonshire,
and Lord Montagu refused to sign the warrant.
Meanwhile, the ever-active Monmouth showed
himself most anxious for Ross's arrest, and also
that Montgomery should be prevented from seeing
the Queen. He said, perhaps with no very clear
conscience, that if Montgomery were to come to
London, he would be sure, in his malice and

JOHN TILLOTSON, ARCHBISHOP OF CANTERBURY.

British Museum.

cunning, to tell lies, and to accuse people whom he thought might do his party harm. Ross remained in the Tower for a few months, and was then liberated ; in fact the leaders of this conspiracy escaped very easily.

Meanwhile Montgomery, " who knows more of the affaire, haveing been a chife manager in it," was also most anxious to wait upon Her Majesty, and insinuated that many men in " chife employment " [1] in England were implicated in the plot, which he would do his best to crush. At this juncture the Queen, with her usual good sense, refused to give way to panic. In a letter to Lord Melville on July 3, 1690, she said that she had seen " the scrupulouse persson " (Lord Ross) " several times, but "—to his credit, be it said—" had obtained no fresh information from him." She goes on : " but I confesse I canot be so aprehensive of the dangers. God has of his goodnes revealed enough to make us stand upon our guard ; and if it please him to blesse the King with successe, I dont dout but all may in time be well setled."

Ross's arrest naturally alarmed Montgomery ; and before he would trust himself in London, he insisted on a safe-conduct, if he promised to reveal everything to the Queen. A pardon was therefore deposited by Melville in a friend's hand to be delivered to him ; " upon his dealing freely and ingenuously with Your Majesty." [2]

When he did arrive in London, he was in no hurry to see the Queen, as he wished to assure himself that even if he did not agree with her as to the reward for his treachery, he should not be detained. He announced to his fellow Jacobites that he had never received a pass from Melville, but had forged one in order to get away from Scotland, and was now forging another to get a letter conveyed to King James.

---

[1] " Leven and Melville Papers," p. 456.     [2] *Ibid.*, p. 479.

Lord. Annandale, being, he said, afraid of the
perfidy of his two associates, had also turned
informer, and had seen the Queen several times.
During these interviews he had seemed to her to
have the merit—surely a doubtful one under the
circumstances—of "dealing sincerely" with her,
which means that he revealed more about his
associates than Lord Ross had done.

Meanwhile the leader of the conspiracy, who,
with the use of superlatives fashionable at the
time, is variously designated by his fellow Scots-
men as "the greatest of villains," "the worst
and most restless man alive," or by the favourite
term of abuse, "the worst man in the whole world,"
was summoned to the Queen's presence.

He started by mumbling something which she
could not hear about his circumstances, and paid
her compliments about the good that her administration had done, because she, being "more afable
than the King," had gained more adherents. He
then named Marlborough as one of the Englishmen who was still true to the Stuart cause, and
said one other was spoken of. "After scruples he
named Lord Nottingham, but did not believe it."

The Queen was evidently inclined to think well
of the arch-rogue, who deceived all with whom
he came into contact. He made many protestations of zeal and service, was troubled when, in
reply to his query whether she thought him sincere, she answered that he had been reserved ; and
asked for leave to kiss her hand in public. She
said she must take time to consider the matter,
and wrote to recommend Montgomery to William,
who, having had communication with him before,
felt for him such an abhorrence that he would
not hear of employing him.[1]  The plotter therefore
retired to France, where he employed his time in
writing libels, and starting abortive plots.

[1] "Balcarres Memoirs," p. 66.

When it is remembered that the Queen, without
any previous training or experience in politics,
was interviewing the leaders of the Scotch Conspiracy, in the midst of the crisis caused by the
defeat of Beachy Head, and while William was in
peril, we can realise the truth of her lament to him :

" I never do anything without thinking now, it
may be, you are in the greatest dangers, and yet
I must see company upon my sett days ; I must
play twice a week ; nay, I must laugh and talk,
tho' never so much against my will : I believe I
dissemble very ill to those who know me, at least
'tis a great constraint to myself, yet I must endure
it : All my motions are so watch'd, and all I do
so observed, that if I eat less, or speak less, or
look more grave, all is lost in the opinion of the
world ; so that I have this misery added to that
of your absence and my fears for your dear person,
that I must grin when my heart is ready to break,
and talk when my heart is so oppressed I can
scarce breathe. In this I don't know what I
should do, were it not for the grace of God which
supports me : I am sure I have great reason to
praise the Lord while I live for this great mercy,
that I don't sink under this affliction ; nay, that
I keep my health ; for I can neither sleep nor
eat. I go to Kensington as often as I can for air,
but then I can never be quite alone ; neither can
I complain, that would be some ease ; but I have
nobody whose humour and circumstances agrees
with mine enough to speak my mind freely to.
Besides I must hear of business, which being a
thing I am so new in, and so unfit for, does but
break my brains the more and not ease my heart." [1]

However, on September 7, 1690, news came that
the King had landed, and on the 9th the Queen
went to Kensington to wait for his arrival. How-

---

[1] Sir John Dalrymple's " Memoirs of Great Britain and Ireland,"
vol. iii. p. 127.

ever, hearing from her that, though she had done
her best to hurry everything, there had been unavoidable delays, and that his rooms were not yet
ready,[1] the King went to Hampton Court, where
Mary met him on the 10th, and "found him,
blessed be God, in perfect health." The Queen
was very happy.

"Now I saw my self" [she says] "in a very
happy condition ; my husband returned and in
good health with great glory, which got him the
admiration and esteem of all ; I rid of all the
troublesome bussiness I was so little fit for, and
at liberty to praise my God, and at liberty to perform those vows I had made in my trouble to
serve him more lawfully hence forward. I had
found how impossible it was to pray much when
one has so much bussiness ; therefore now thought
my self the more obliged to pray, because I knew
my husband had so little leisure. And tho' at
first I let my self spend much time idle in going
about to see several things, yet my heart was still
right before my God ; and now I gave my self
wholy up to that, and minded so little bussiness,
that I can't but wonder at what I have often heard
said, that when any body was once used to it,
they could not give it over. For my part I quitted
it willingly, and knew by experience the trouble
it is to be askt about it, which makes me unwilling
ever to ask the king any thing. And the fear I
had the people would think I still affected it,
made me afraid ever to speack to the Lord President or Lord Nottingham. Yet the king would
be often talking before me and talckt more freely
to me of such matters, being to go to Holland,
where his presence was so very necessary. That
journey had nothing in it of the dismalness of the
Irish one, yet I am very sorry for it, for I love my
husband to well to be very easy in his absence,

---

[1] Doebner's " Memoirs of Queen Mary," pp. 33, 34.

and I love my own ease and quietness to well to
be glad to have any thing to do with bussiness ;
but since it must be so, I prepare my self for it
by prayer, which is the only way to succeed, or
not to sinck under it ; for as little as I love it, yet
since it pleases God to call me to it, I will by the
help of his grace do my best." [1]

There were great rejoicings at William's return,
and both he and the Queen received complimentary
addresses from the Lords and the Commons. The
Commons' eulogy of the Queen showed a warmth
and genuine affection which are not usual on
State occasions, and which prove that she had
succeeded where her husband had failed, and had
won the hearts of her subjects.[2]

William's birthday, November 4, was kept as a
holiday ; all the shops were closed, the great guns
at the Tower were fired, bells rung, and bonfires
lit at night. On this occasion their Majesties
dined in public at Whitehall, being surrounded by
nobility and gentry, and in the evening gave a
grand concert followed by a play. The next day,
the anniversary of Gunpowder Plot and also of
the King's landing in England, there were great
rejoicings. Birthdays were much observed at this
time, for ten days later the Queen Dowager's was
celebrated, and the Tower guns were again discharged, there were festivities at Court, and the
King and Queen went to Somerset House to congratulate Queen Catherine. Even the anniversary
of Queen Elizabeth's natal day was celebrated by
the ringing of bells.

The King was again going to Holland, where an
important Congress of the Powers opposed to France
was to take place. Just before he left England,
another Jacobite plot was discovered. This time,
instead of being engineered by rascals who did not

[1] Doebner's " Memoirs of Queen Mary," p. 34.
[2] Ralph's " History of England," vol. ii. p. 246.

scruple to betray their own associates, men of importance and standing in the country were implicated in it. The conspirators belonged for the most part to the English Church, Dartmouth, Clarendon, and Turner Bishop of Ely being among them. Meetings were held in England, and messages were sent asking James for guarantees that he would safeguard the rights of the English Church. If he would promise to rule England as a Protestant country, a great effort in his favour might be made in the spring. The proviso was, however, made that, though a French force must necessarily accompany His Majesty, he must announce that it was only there for the defence of his person, and must dismiss it as soon as he was reinstated on his throne.

The fact that William, who generally refused to be alarmed at plots, said he would not for a hundred thousand pounds have had this one remain undiscovered till he had left England, speaks volumes for the importance of this conspiracy in his eyes. Much sympathy is due to the leaders of it, though their credulity was great when they supposed, after their late experience of James—and several of them had been brought into close contact with him—that once on the throne he could be trusted to keep the promises he had made in adversity.

It was decided that Lord Preston, Major Elliot, and Mr. Ashton should convey these resolutions to France. They started down the Thames on January 1, 1691, but their smack was seized, their papers were confiscated, and they were conveyed to the Tower.

On January 6 the King "took coach for his journey to Holland,"[1] but the winds being contrary he only went as far as Canterbury, and returned to Kensington till the 16th. He started again in tempestuous weather, and was in so great a hurry to land in Holland that he spent the night

[1] Luttrell's "Relation of State Affairs."

in a small boat. From this adventure he, " by the mercy of God escaped only with a cold," [1] and arrived safely in his own beloved country, where he had a brilliant reception.

That was hardly over when the news reached him that Mons was besieged by the French, and the anxious Queen was agonised by hearing that, instead of being engaged in receiving congratulations on attaining the position of King, William was straining every nerve in the endeavour to reach Mons in time " to venture or hazard his person." Though he did not arrive in time, the " endeavours he used made me almost out of my wits for fear, coming so unexpected," [2] says the Queen. She was now mixing with society. She had been to the theatre, had played every night at the fashionable games of comet and basset, had given a dance on her sister's birthday, and, whatever her private troubles might be, had done her best to hide them, and to show a cheerful front to the world. When alone, however, the Queen allowed full course to her melancholy. Sitting in her private room at Kensington, where she had looked forward to serving God without interruption, she thought sadly on her solitude in a place where she had often been happy with the King, and her mind was filled with doubt and anxiety about the future.

The fate of the prisoners involved in the conspiracy was, in the absence of her husband, left to a great extent in the Queen's hands. As usual in those times, those who were of least importance were punished more severely than their betters, and as a general rule showed a fortitude which might well have put those betters to shame. In a letter written by Caermarthen to William on January 23, 1691, he says that the Queen " does not think fit to defer Ashton's execution beyond

[1] Doebner's "Memoirs of Queen Mary."     [2] *Ibid.*, p. 35.

Monday or Wednesday next."[1] Ashton died bravely, and incriminated no one.

Meanwhile, Lord Preston was reprieved for three weeks in the hope that he would reveal something, and these weeks must have been agonising to the unfortunate waverer. He tried to gain time by asking for his notes, and, when alone in the mornings and evenings, he felt that he could not face execution, but must tell everything. In the middle of the day, however, when his friends came in to dinner, he was sure that he, like Ashton, could die heroically.

The Queen, meanwhile, was suffering intensely at the idea of having to order further executions. The terrible position in which circumstances had placed her, must have been borne in upon her most painfully, when Preston's young daughter, possibly prompted thereto by wiser heads than her own, one day gazed for some time fixedly at King James's portrait which hung at Kensington. When Queen Mary asked her what she was doing, she replied : " I am thinking how hard it is that my father should be put to death for loving your father."[2]

Eventually, Preston confessed the names of his confederates, and his life was spared, as was the life of Crone, who had been a long time in prison. These reprieves were an immense relief to the Queen. She writes :

" In the mean while Lord Preston and Master Croon were giving in papers to deserve pardon, which I as heartily wisht they might obtain as themselves could do, having had the misfortune to have had one man suffer already in the time of my administration, which was Mr. Ashton ; and that which made his death the worse to me, was

---

[1] King William's chest, Record Office.

[2] Sir John Dalrymple's " Memoirs of Great Britain and Ireland," vol. iii. p. 149.

the great endeavours were used all manner of wais
to obtain at last a repreive. But I was persuaded
he was justly condemned, and that at this time
the necessities of affairs were such I must let the
law take its course. So I forced my own inclinations, and refused all the instances were used, so
that at the time appointed he was executed. And
tho' I had very well examined the thing before hand,
and was perfectly satisfied in my mind, yet I lookt
on it as a misfortune to be obliged to refuse a
man's life. . . . I was very desirous mercy might
be shewn to Lord Preston and Croon. And tho'
they have not deserved it since, yet I cannot be
sorry, but am glad they were pardon'd." [1]

The Queen was at this time surrounded by
malcontents, a general " peevishness and Sylle-
ness " [2] being shewn by all her admirers except Lord
Sydney. Certainly, Sydney's letters to the King,
with their undercurrent of humour, are a pleasant
change from the backbitings and complaints William received from most of his Ministers, and we
can realise why, even if Sydney's indolence was a
decided disadvantage in a time of stress, he was
yet a favourite with both King and Queen. Caermarthen, Mary's principal adviser, was particularly difficult to manage. He " hath been of late,"
says Sydney, " very peevish and continually com-
plaining ; I am now his confident, and he hath
almost told me that he would retire in a little
time." [3]

This was hardly grateful of Caermarthen, as the
Queen had just ordered the Treasury to allow him
the arrears of his pension for twenty-one years, an
order which made Godolphin, who was First Lord
of the Treasury, furious ; especially as Lord Bath's

---

[1] Doebner's " Memoirs of Queen Mary," pp. 39, 40.
[2] " Sullenness." (?)
[3] Sir John Dalrymple's " Memoirs of Great Britain and Ireland,"
vol. iii. p. 180.

arrears were also to be paid. Godolphin's wrath
seems excusable, as money was urgently needed for
Ireland, where troops could not be sent for the
want of it. He does not scruple to speak very
plainly to William on the subject,[1] telling him
that he would have refused the Queen's order had
he dared to do so. Perhaps his disgust at these
" unseasonable grants " helped to make him start
secret communications with the exiled Monarch.

Ireland seems to have loomed as large in the
minds of statesmen of the seventeenth century as
it does in those of the twentieth, and Caermarthen's
representations that everything there was going
on as badly as it possibly could, were most depress-
ing to the Queen. She was also worried by reports
of plots not only to restore King James, but to
establish a Commonwealth, or to set the Princess
Anne on the throne.

The idea of this last design was peculiarly painful to the Queen, and her nerves were evidently
suffering from a reaction after the strain she had
undergone when, during William's absence, the fate
of England seemed quivering in the balance. She,
hitherto calm and courageous in the face of danger,
now writes :

" I confess my weackness was so great, that I
was heartily troubled and frighted, but I kept it
to myself. I loockt over all my meditations, and
burnt most of them fearing they might fall into
hands I did not like. The journals I had kept, I
put in a bag and tyed by my side resolving if
anything happend to have them ready to burn. . . ."

She says also—and the words have a pathetic
ring in them—that she hurried up to Whitehall,
as it seemed to her to be safer than Hampton
Court, or at least she thought there would be more
people to share her sufferings, if the worst should
happen.

[1] Godolphin to the King, March 23, 1691, Record Office.

# CHAPTER XVI

By an anomaly which shows the irony of the Queen's circumstances, she, who had rejoiced in being the Defender of the English Church, was now looked on with horror by many of its most devoted adherents. The Bishops and clergy who refused to swear allegiance to William and Mary, were believers in the divine right of kings. They therefore considered that James was still the rightful Monarch, and that, in seizing his throne, William had committed an act of wicked usurpation —an act in which he was aided and abetted by Mary, in whose case the sin was aggravated by a filial impiety which would assuredly bring down punishment on her head.

This feeling was strong among them, and Frampton, one of their number, who had travelled in Egypt, told Lloyd, Bishop of St. Asaph, that as Her Majesty's almoner it was his duty to rouse her conscience as to her duty towards her father, who was now dependent on Louis XIV.'s charity. When Lloyd assured him that the Queen never spoke about her father without weeping, Frampton muttered disrespectfully something about " crocodile's tears." [1]

The point of view among the non-jurors varied : some of them wished to recall James; others—

---

[1] Plumptre's " Life of Ken," vol. ii. p. 80.

Sancroft among the number—would have been
satisfied if William had assumed the title of Pro-
tector or President, and had governed in James's
name. Apart from any question of taking the
oath, it is impossible to believe that High Churchmen like Ken and Frampton would have complied
with William and Mary's views on the abolition
of forms and ceremonies, or that their Majesties'
favourite scheme of uniting the English Church with
the Dissenters, could ever have commended itself
to them.

The Government did their utmost to persuade
the non-juring clergy to take the oath of allegiance ;
and, till the summer of 1691, left them in undisputed
possession of their endowments. Indeed, so important in the opinion of the King and Queen was
the avoidance of a breach in the Church they had
come to protect, that the non-jurors were promised
exemption from taking the oath of allegiance, if
they would promise to perform their usual duties
quietly. As, however, to read the Church services
meant an acknowledgment of William and Mary
as King and Queen, they felt this course to be impossible ; and after Preston's conspiracy, in which
Turner, the deprived Bishop of Ely, was implicated,
it was impossible to allow them to remain in possession of their dioceses and livings. Great was the
popular indignation against them. Even quiet and
holy men underwent persecution, and, when they
met to discuss religious matters, were nicknamed
"The Holy Jacobite Club," or "The Lambeth
Club," and were suspected by the populace of
assembling to conspire against the Government.

They had sufficient sympathisers, however, for
the matter to be likely to cause considerable
trouble ; and the Queen writes in her "Memoirs " :

"Besides what I have said already, we were like
to have a great division in the Church ; for not
only some would stick to their old Bishops, but

all our High Churchmen and the Bishop of London were ready to joyn with them and form a party. All imaginable care was taken to remedy these evils which seemed so incurable that it almost discouraged the endeavours."

The right filling of the new Bishoprics was a matter very near the Queen's heart, and much of the fortnight William spent in England in April, 1691, was occupied by consideration of the subject.

"The only thing of bussiness I concerned my self in" [the Queen writes] "was the filling of the Bishopricks which was now done ; and I am sure the king made it a point of conscience to do it well, which I thinck he has."[1]

Tillotson, for whom Mary always felt a warm affection, and who had, it may be remembered, come to her and to William's assistance at Canterbury soon after their marriage, was made Archbishop of Canterbury. This choice was popular, for Tillotson was a good and upright man with many amiable qualities, and was well known in the City as an eloquent preacher, having in 1689 been made Dean of St. Paul's by King William.

On the occasion of this first appointment, Tillotson wrote in a letter to Lady Russell, "the King spoke plainly of a great place, which I dread to think of, and said, it was necessary for his service and he must charge it upon my conscience."[2]

Tillotson accepted the Archbishopric of Canterbury with much reluctance, which would not have been shown by the Queen's old preceptor, Compton, who was deeply disappointed that the preferment had not been offered to him, though he was largeminded enough to remain on good terms with the new Archbishop.

[1] Doebner's " Memoirs of Queen Mary," p. 37.
[2] Birck's " Life of Tillotson," p. 205.

The Queen was delighted with Tillotson's appointment, and he says :

" The King I believe has only (just) acquainted the Queen with it ; as she came out of the closet on Sunday last, she commanded me to wait on her after dinner, which I did ; and after she had discoursed about other business (which was to desire my opinion of a treatise sent to her in manuscript out of Holland tending to the reconciliation of our differences in England), she told me that the King had with great joy acquainted her with a secret concerning me, whereof she was no less glad ; using many gracious expressions, and confirming his Majesty's promises." [1]

He says further that " the Queen's extraordinary favour to me, to a degree much beyond my expectation, is no small support to me."

The Queen's thoughts were, as we know, centred on religion, and she was

" incessantly employed in possessing her mind with the best schemes, that were either laid before her by others, or suggested by her own thoughts, for correcting everything which was amiss, and improving everything that wanted finishing." [2]

Burnet, who was warmly attached to Tillotson, was also of much assistance to the Queen, and drew up under her patronage a " Discourse of the Pastoral Care," which was, we are told, Tillotson's favourite tract.

Some of the Queen's plans for the betterment of the Church seem rather arbitrary, though possibly they were beneficent. She writes :

" Another thing I did at that time, was to propose to the king that of the Bishops revenues he should let them have 2gn and himself 3, for there were now 5 dew. This he consented to, as likewise the ways I with the Archbishop found for laying it

¹ Birch's " Life of Tillotson," p. 249.
² Ibid., p. 263.

out in charitable uses, that none of it might be made another use of."

Perhaps one of the "charitable uses" was the building of the Hospital at Chelsea for the maintenance of old and maimed soldiers, which was finished by the Queen during the summer of this year (1691), and was provided with a chapel, a burial place, and two chaplains.

The Queen's charities were not confined to this country, for she founded the William and Mary College in Virginia to educate the planters.

"All possible objections were made to the project" [says Burnet], "as a design that would take our planters off from their mechanical employments, and make them grow too knowing to be obedient and submissive."

The Queen, however, refused to heed these objections—which sound strangely modern—as she hoped that the planters might be improved by education, and might then spread the Gospel among the natives.

The hopes raised by the foundation of this College were, however, doomed to destruction, for it incurred the fate of many of the edifices built by William and Mary, and was burnt down soon after its erection.

The Queen was most anxious about the morals of the nation, and on July 9, 1691, she ordered the justices of the peace in Middlesex to put into force the laws already in existence against swearing, drinking, and profanation of the Lord's Day. She did not forget her adopted country in her charities, for we read of her sending "dix mille livres" to her friend and correspondent the Baronne de Wassenaer d'Obdam for the benefit of the French Protestant refugees in Holland, who had escaped to Holland after the Revocation of the Edict of Nantes. She says in another letter that she is much grieved at their suffering, but that the King does not see how he can grant them a lodging especially as England is likely to be soon crowded with Irish refugees.

Another society in Holland in which she took much interest, was one she had started for the support of French girl refugees of good family. While she was in Holland she went to see them often, worked with them, and entered into the details of all their little wants, which she supplied with a charming goodness which won all their hearts.[1]

Now that she was at a distance, this community gave her a good deal of trouble. It consisted of seventeen ladies; and about this time these ladies seemed to wish for a directress. However, when the Queen proposed that her friend the Baronne Wassenaer d'Obdam should take this post, it transpired that only five out of the seventeen had made the request, and that the others objected strongly to being under any one's government. On informing her friend of this, the Queen, with much tact, told her that she would, she was sure, be most acceptable to the ladies as their directress, and that they had, in her opinion, only objected to the creation of the post, because they feared that one of their number would be asked to fill it. The Baronne, however, who appears to have been a downright and decided person, told the Queen that the ladies had only proposed her as directress, because they wanted her to know the straits they were put to, in the famine prevailing in Holland. She proposed that some of the money the Queen subscribed to charities in London, should be transferred to the sustenance of the French ladies.

At the same time, having been asked by the Queen to inquire into the cause of certain dissensions among them, she wrote them a severe exhortation, telling them that

"their quarrelsomeness did not answer to the

[1] "Mémoires de Monsieur de B."

JOHN, 1ST DUKE OF MARLBOROUGH.

From a portrait by Kneller. British Museum.

expectation one would have of people who had shewn so much zeal for religion that they had abandoned their country and their property for its sake." [1]

We hear nothing further of these unfortunate ladies, who had been for a time in a half-starved condition, which would most probably induce irritability. Let us hope that they took the lecture in good part, as it was sweetened by an increase of three or four hundred francs to their income, and returned to a state of as much peace and harmony as is possible in this wicked world.

One clerical appointment made by Queen Mary seriously displeased her lord and master. The Deanery of Canterbury was vacant, and the King sent the Queen three names to choose from, one of them being that of Dr. Hooper, her former chaplain at The Hague. Her power of choice was, however, only nominal, for when she chose Dr. Hooper, whom William had always disliked,

" she was chid by the King for giving him the Deanery, and it had cost her some tears, which was too often her case after she came into England, but in Holland it was daily so " [2] [says Hooper, with what we may hope is exaggeration].

However, according to Hooper, the Queen was always on friendly terms with him, and often sent for him and asked him " many questions concerning men and things, as of one that would not deceive her." At one time she wanted to know why the Archbishop Tillotson was called a Socinian, at another she was distressed, because it had been reported to her that Hooper and his wife, did not visit the Archbishop and Mrs. Tillotson as they ought to do. Once Burnet made mischief by

---

[1] " Lettres et Mémoires de Marie Reine d'Angleterre," edited by Countess Bentinck, pp. 137 et seq.

[2] Trevor's "Life of William III.," p. 471, appendix, "Hooper Memoirs."

20

saying that Hooper always chose Sundays for travelling, but when he defended himself from this charge, the Queen

" told him in a very gracious manner that she had never believed what she then accused him of, but she would always let him know his faults and what was told her concerning him." [1]

On one occasion, the Queen accompanied the King part of the way to Margate, and when the wind changed, so that he could not embark, he proposed that, instead of returning to Whitehall, as had been intended, she should spend the night with him at Canterbury. "This," says Hooper, sarcastically, " was too great a favour to be refused." However, when they arrived at Canterbury, the unnamed lady of " of great birth and equal merit " whose hospitality they intended to claim, had, in her dislike for the King, left Canterbury, having first emptied her house of every convenience.

Dr. Hooper was also absent, but some one offered the Queen the Deanery for the night, and Hooper was much pleased when she told him, in her pretty, gracious way, that it was the cleanest house she had ever been in, and that she had heard an excellent sermon on Sunday. " But," says she, " I thought myself in a Dutch church, for they stood on the communion table to see me."

The Queen noticed that the altar hangings and the covering of the Archbishop's throne were dirty, and provided the Dean with new ones. Her only trouble was that, because of the height of the Deanery windows from the ground, and the fact that a walnut-tree grew in front of them, she was not able to please the people by showing herself to them, though they assembled in crowds to get a glimpse of her.

[1] These anecdotes can be found in Trevor's " Life of William III.," appendix, " Hooper Memoirs."

The Queen paid Hooper one compliment of which he was justly proud :

" Just after the Archbishop died " [he says] "a lady who came into the Queen's apartment told her Majesty that she believed there was all the dignified clergy in town come to Court that day to shew themselves. The Queen immediately replied that she was sure she knew one that was not there, and that was the Dean of Canterbury, some of the party not seeming to think any was missing on that occasion, a lady who knew the Dean was sent out to see, and upon her return saying he was not there, No, says the Queen, I was sure he was not there. I can answer for him, or words to that effect."

Tillotson's intercourse with the Queen was very close. After his death, which took place about five weeks before hers, she could not speak of him without tears ; while William said : " I have lost the best friend that I ever had, and the best man that I ever knew."

Ken, who had been, as we know, Queen Mary's chaplain in Holland, was treated by her with special leniency, and she is reported to have said of him, and of his friend Frampton, the deprived Bishop of Gloucester, that though they wished to be martyrs she would disappoint them. The Queen waited a year before making a new appointment to the See of Bath and Wells, in the hope that Ken would yield, and at one time he did waver in his resolution to refuse taking the oaths. When the year was over, the Bishopric of Bath and Wells was offered to Beveridge, who refused it, and eventually Kidder became Ken's unpopular successor.

The other appointments were filled after much prayerful consideration by the Queen.

A letter written by her to Lady Russell on July 30, 1691, gives the same impression of sadness that her " Memoirs " do.

"You are very much in the right" [she says] "to believe I have cause enough to think this life not so fine a thing, as, it may be, others do, that I lead at present. Besides the pain I am almost continually in for the King, it is so contrary to my inclination, that it can be neither easy nor pleasant. But I see one is not ever to live for oneself." [1]

In spite of the cheerfulness, buoyancy, and evenness of temper praised by Queen Mary's contemporaries, it is difficult to imagine how, with the inherent thirst for affection and approval for which she sometimes blames herself, she could have been happy. She knew what people were saying about her relations to her father, and some of the violent Jacobites—Sir John Fenwick being conspicuous among them—did not scruple to insult her publicly, by staring rudely and refusing to doff their hats to her when she walked in Hyde Park. That Mary felt these insults keenly, is shown by the vengeance William, usually forgiving and pacific, took on Fenwick after Mary's death, when any ill treatment of her had assumed in his sight the proportions of a crime.

The King did not return from Holland till late in the autumn of 1691, and though there was no serious plot to contend with, as in 1690, the Queen passed through a most anxious time.

For one thing, the year was singularly fruitful in accidents. On April 9, 1691, the Palace at Whitehall caught fire, and burnt from eight o'clock till four in the morning; the Queen being only rescued with difficulty. "I was heartily frighted," she says, "but blessed be God, it was stopd and all went over." The next misfortune was that a floor in the Tower fell down and many barrels of gunpowder with it, but fortunately, except for the spilling of the powder, no damage was done. Worst of all, on November 9, one side

[1] "Letters of Lady Russell," vol. ii. p. 89.

of the house at Kensington which the Queen
had been longing to occupy, was burnt down,
so that, as she says sorrowfully, " I was weaned
from the vanities I was most fond of, that is ease
and good lodgings."

The Queen's ordinary duties as Head of the State
during her husband's absence, caused her much
anxiety.  She had managed to get rid of Wildman,
the Postmaster-General, who had been one of those
engaged in the " lemon-letter " plot, but as he was
succeeded by a Whig and a Tory, who were expected
to work together, the result was far from peaceable.

However, the Queen was most popular with the
bulk of the nation, as is proved by a fact which
seems to have astonished her contemporaries.  It
is recorded that on February 20, 1691, the Queen
in Council asked for a loan from the City for the
seamen, and that on February 27, " The Citty lent
threescore thousand pounds." [1]

Her actions were at least dictated by a strong
sense of duty, which overcame with her all other
considerations.

" I had also an other tryall" [she says] "which
was seing a poor unfortunate mother whoe's son
was condemned for attempting to kill his master.
which made the poor woman almost distracted.
I never saw so moving a sight in my life as she was ;
yet the fears I had of the threats in scripture
about a land defiled with blood, and the theme
from thence, ones eye must not pity a murderer,
this made me stop my ears to all that could be
said in his behalf." [2]

Meanwhile the Queen found something to blame
in her own conduct.  One of her ladies-in-waiting
was ill, and she could not help "coming near to
wishing" that she might die, and thus make
room for Lady Nottingham.  Unfortunately, the

---

[1] " State Papers," Record Office.
[2] Doebner's " Memoirs of Queen Mary," p. 40.

unpopular lady recovered, and a vacancy was
made for Lady Nottingham by the death of Lady
Dorset, to whom the Queen was warmly attached,
and whose demise she looked on as a punishment
for her wicked thoughts.

Lady Nottingham became lady-in-waiting on
August 15, 1691, and was so fond of her royal
mistress that, when the latter died, Nottingham
was obliged to break the sad news to her gently,
and was afraid to leave her alone for some time
afterwards. She appears to have been a gentle,
amiable woman, whose rapidly increasing family
gave her much occupation. We are told by her
husband that, when in waiting at Kensington, " she
eat at supper a piece of hog's pudding which was
so hot that she fell into a swounde " [1] for half an
hour. Then her husband heard of the disaster,
and hastened to the spot with " a chirugeon ";
but fortunately the lady recovered without being
bled !

If we return to public affairs, it is interesting
to note the difference of feeling in the years 1690
and 1691. In 1690 the outside danger had
been pressing, but in spite of Jacobite plotting,
the spirit of the nation had rallied to meet it.
In 1691, though the bulk of the nation felt safe and
happy under William's rule, disaffection for his
government was strong among his Ministers, and it
was impossible to know who was trustworthy.

In truth there were not enough rewards to go
round. Each man who had invited William over,
had corresponded with him, or had gone to The
Hague to offer assistance to his cause, considered
that he had risked his life and his fortunes in the
new King's service, and aspired to stand on a
pinnacle above his fellows.

As this was clearly an impossibility, there was
general discontent. Besides, as the astute Sun-

---

[1] Add. MSS., 29,594, British Museum.

derland pointed out later to William, his policy of
dividing important posts as far as possible equally
between Whigs and Tories, pleased neither party.
In addition to these causes for disaffection, William
was singularly without the power of inspiring
devotion in those with whom he came into contact.
Therefore, as he had overturned the principle of
the hereditary right of kings, the impelling motive
in the minds of most of his Ministers seems to have
been a mixture of personal ambition, and anxiety
to secure their lives and fortunes, in the likely
case of his overthrow.

William's want of personal magnetism, or whatever it is which endows a man with the power of
drawing others to himself, is very noticeable.
Even Bentinck, who was deeply attached to him,
deserted him before the end, and it is strange to
see that he, perhaps the greatest man in Europe,
generally lavished his affection on some one extremely inferior to him, begged for a return,
and generally begged in vain. Shrewsbury, who,
like Henry Sidney, was of the type of charming,
good-looking, rather feminine men who seem always
to have appealed to William, was treated by him
with the utmost gentleness. His waverings towards the Jacobite cause were forgiven, and the
King did all he could to attach the young man
to himself, and felt deep affection for him. This
is evident from a letter written by Tillotson, while
he was hesitating to take the Archbishopric, to
Lady Russell, in which he says that he would not
dare to cause the King the trouble with which
he " saw him affected," [1] when Shrewsbury, in
spite of all his endeavours, insisted on resigning
the seals of office.

Shrewsbury had now for some time corresponded
with James II. ; so had Godolphin ; while Halifax
had received the communications from St. Ger-

[1] Birch's " Life of Tillotson," p. 223.

mains with complacency. Bluffness and a down-right manner do not always denote sincerity, and Mary's favourite, Admiral Russell, who had lately accepted the position of commander of the united fleets of England and Holland, with the title of Admiral of the Fleet, was also in secret correspon-dence with the exiled Monarch. It is interesting to compare James's account of Russell's declara-tion that if he were to meet the French fleet he would be obliged to fight, even if James himself were on board, but that he would help the latter by keeping the English fleet out of the way and allowing him to land,[1] with Mary's words in her "Memoirs" :

"At sea the French did the same as by land, avoided fighting, so that Mr. Russell could not so much as get sight of them, and after endeavouring it in vain a long time, being unwilling to come home without doing some thing, went over to the French coast, where he was taken with a storm which might have been fatal, had not the same providence preserved the fleet which has still watched over us, and that in small as well as great things, so that I can never enough praise my God for it."[2]

William evidently suspected the truth, for he writes to Bentinck from Brussels about this time : "I confess that the proceeding of Admiral Russel is very extraordinary."[3]

Possibly Russell did not contemplate open treachery, but thought that, according to the signs of the times, a counter-revolution was imminent, and considered that it would be wise to protect himself against the vengeance of the reinstated King. If James had had a Sunderland beside him to guide his policy along the lines of conciliation

---

[1] "Mémoires de Jacques II.," Guizot edition, vol. iv. p. 303.
[2] Doebner's "Memoirs of Queen Mary," p. 41.
[3] Letter of May, 1692, at Welbeck.

and forgiveness, there seems little doubt that
the Jacobites might have been right in their prognostications of triumph.   But the exiled King
still breathed out fulminations about the outraged
Absolute Monarchy, and therefore William and
Mary, though surrounded by attacks, continued to
wear the crown.

On October 19, the Queen's government of State
affairs came to an end for the time, as the King
returned from Holland.  He landed at Margate,
and was upset in his coach at Gravesend, but,
fortunately, not hurt.  The Queen went to meet
him at Whitehall and they at once proceeded to
Kensington.  " The whole town was filled with
bonfires and illuminations in the windows, ringing
of bells, and the guns at the Tower were discharged." [1]  For a time the Queen's anxieties and
troubles had come to an end, and she had a little
leisure to amuse herself with her gardening, and with
the building operations at Hampton Court.

[1] Luttrell's "Relation of State Affairs," October 19, 1691.

# CHAPTER XVII

The Princess Anne and Lady Marlborough—William and Mary's dispute with Anne—Marlborough—His disgrace—The Queen's letter to her sister—William's departure to Holland—State perils—Mary and Anne—Continued breach between the sisters—Ken's letter —The Queen and the Navy—Battle of La Hogue—Grandval—The Queen's distress—William's return.

THE Princess Anne was completely in Lady Marlborough's hands, and, even if Mary did her best to conciliate her sister, it must be allowed that William's behaviour to his brother-in-law was hardly polite. Poor " Est-il possible ? " was a remarkably dull man, and no one could certainly be expected to find pleasure in his society. Charles II. had "tried him drunk and tried him sober and could find nothing in him." Nevertheless, the Prince had wits enough to resent the fact that when he accompanied the King to Ireland, he was not allowed to drive in the same coach with His Majesty, and that "the King never took more notice of him than if he had been a page of the backstairs." [1] Anne, too, was naturally very indignant at this slight to her husband. It was therefore decided—no doubt by the Marlboroughs, and possibly with ulterior motives unknown by Anne—that to avoid such indignities in the future, when the King went to Flanders in 1691, the Prince should ask for leave to serve at sea as a volunteer.

In his farewell interview with the King, the Prince mooted the project. Diplomatically dissembling, William made no answer, but embraced

[1] "Account of the Conduct of the Duchess of Marlborough," p. 38.

him in silence by way of adieu. He left, however, orders with the Queen—to whom, it may be remarked, many disagreeable tasks were entrusted—that Prince George was not to be allowed to go to sea, but that she was only to forbid him as a last resort, and was to try to manage the matter so that every one should think that he stayed at home by his own wish.

Meanwhile, Prince George, taking silence for consent, made preparations for a sea expedition. Hearing this, the Queen sent to beg Lady Marlborough to induce the Princess to prevent the Prince from going to sea, without, however, mentioning her name in the matter. Lady Marlborough refused to obey Her Majesty's behests, and eventually the Queen was obliged very reluctantly to send Lord Nottingham with a formal refusal of permission. This order naturally made the Princess Anne extremely indignant, and the Queen was angry and frightened, for rumours about Anne's ambitions—or rather the ambitions of the Marlboroughs through her—were rife ; and, according to report, a party had been formed in England to set the Princess on the throne.

" I was told " [the Queen says in her " Memoirs "] " of many designs against the government by severall parties which were thought would join ; and Jacobites as they call them, were to be assisted, or would assist my sister, and the Commonwealth men would help neither of them for her, but both against me, in hopes by that disturbance each to carry on their own designs. This was very grievous to me to thinck my sister should be concerned in such things ; yet 'twas plain there was a design of growing popular by the princes resolution of going to sea without asking leave, only telling the king he intended it, which I had order to hinder, and when perswasions would not do, was obliged to send word by Lord Nottingham he should not, which was desired by them as much as avoided by me, that they might have a pretence to raile, and so in discontent go to Tunbridge." [1]

No idea roused the Queen's terror and indignation as did the one that Anne might be brought forward to supersede William on the throne. There was some justification for her alarm, though the Princess was in all probability quite innocent of any design of seizing the crown from her brother-in-law. The Dutch were hated in England ; William was personally unpopular. Anne, on the other hand, was loved as the English Princess *par excellence*, the mother of the heir to the throne ; while Prince George was conveniently negligible, he would not, like William, aspire to sovereignty, or bring his foreign favourites to insert themselves in lucrative and important posts, which should have been occupied by honest Englishmen.

Like many other prominent men in England, Marlborough had for some time written letters to James expressing remorse for his past treachery. In one of these he declared that "his crimes seemed so horrible to him that sorrow prevented him from eating or sleeping," [2] and begged for a letter from James without signature promising his forgiveness. Under the influence of Marlborough, Anne wrote on December 1, 1691, to her father expressing sorrow for her past conduct, and when he received this, James, knowing the Princess's absolute dependence on the Marlboroughs, began to believe in Marlborough's sincerity.

As James complains in his "Memoirs" that his correspondence with Marlborough brought him eventually nothing but expense, it is possible that the latter merely intended to follow in the footsteps of most of the statesmen of his day, and to

[1] Doebner's "Memoirs of Queen Mary," p. 38.
[2] "Mémoires de Jacques II.," Guizot edition, vol. iv. p. 236.

ensure his safety with James in the case of a second Restoration. The next step he contemplated was, however, strongly inimical to William ; for in 1692 he undertook to move an Address in the Lords, and to induce some one to move a similar Address in the Commons, requesting that all foreigners should be dismissed from the King's service.

Marlborough's object in this, may have been merely to oust the hated foreigners from the posts they had usurped in the English Army. There is, however, no doubt, from James's own words, translated by Macpherson, and quoted by Macaulay, that the exiled King was not ignorant of the scheme, and considered that Marlborough, in undertaking it, was knowingly furthering the Jacobite interests. James wrote regretfully in November, 1692 :

" This scheme was already in action, and a large number had been gained over, when some indiscreet faithful subjects, thinking to serve me, and imagining that what Milord Churchill was doing was not for me, but for the Princess of Denmark, had the imprudence to reveal everything to Benthing, and so to turn away the blow." [1]

The plot therefore came to nothing, and there is no direct proof that Marlborough had ever wished to put Anne on the throne. Probably, he had too much common sense to think this possible, for, though William was disliked by those who came into contact with him, the bulk of the English people, without feeling any personal enthusiasm for him, were satisfied with his rule, as assuring them immunity from attacks on their religion. Nevertheless, Marlborough was intensely discontented with William's treatment of him, and after his treachery in the last reign, it would, from his

---

[1] Macaulay's "History," 1862 edition, chap. xviii., vol. vi. p. 171.

point of view, have hardly been safe to restore
James—the man of abiding resentments—to the
throne. Therefore he may well have toyed in-
determinately with a dazzling prospect, for with
a Queen, who was a puppet in the hands of his
devoted wife, he would have become practically
dictator.

Everything was stopped, however, by the fact
that the alarmed Jacobites informed Portland of
Marlborough's intended motion, and the latter was
summarily deprived of all his appointments.

It would have been well for William's, and certainly for Mary's fame, had it not in the disturbed
condition of affairs, been thought necessary to conceal the details of Marlborough's real or supposed
treachery. To the public, who did not realise the
alarm the Queen felt for her husband's crown, and
thought that Marlborough had been dismissed for
having " us'd words against the King " ;[1] for his
insistence on an allowance being settled in Parliament on the Princess Anne,[2] or merely because he
had excited the " jealousy of the King's Dutch
Favourites," [3] Mary's subsequent behaviour to
her sister seemed like petty persecution.

A few people, however, must have known the
truth ; and it is interesting to note that Burnet
was among the well-informed. In his printed
" History," indeed, he says that Marlborough had
censured the King, and had reflected on the
Dutch, but that the real cause of his disgrace was
his wife's part in obtaining a settlement for the
Princess. This version of the affair, was certainly
what would be useful to the Marlboroughs in
Queen Anne's reign. Read, however, what Burnet
wrote before assailed by fear of the imperious and
all-powerful Duchess of Marlborough, and it will

---

[1] Evelyn's "Diary," February 28, 1692.
[2] "The Other Side of the Question."
[3] Ralph's "History of England," vol. ii. p. 329.

be seen that he knew more than he dared to disclose in his later edition. He says :

" The King said he had good reason to believe that Marlborough had made peace with James, and was engaged in a correspondence with France. It was certain that he was doing all he could to get a faction in the army and the nation against the Dutch and to lessen the King." [1]

Before the announcement of Marlborough's disgrace, the Queen had an interview with her sister, and says in her " Memoirs " :

" I heard much from all hands of my sister. Whether she was wronged in it or no I can not well judg, but am apt to believe by the way I have seen since of her doing, that Lord Marlborough was so sure of the prince and she when he would, that 'tis not likely he would acquaint them so far at first ; so that when I told her the rapports and she denyed them 'tis probable she was sincere." [2]

The Queen hoped that after this she and her sister would live together on better terms than before, and apparently considered that Anne would herself dismiss Lady Marlborough, or would at least ask what she should do about the matter. However, directly after Marlborough's disgrace, the Princess brought Lady Marlborough with her to Kensington. Next day the Queen wrote the following letter, which was no doubt either dictated by the King, or was at least submitted to him for approval. The responsibility for what was done at this time must be shared equally by both William and Mary—in fact, it appears that Mary's rôle, if it could be separated from that of her husband, was rather that of the moderator than of the aggressor.

The Queen's letter ran as follows, and I think no one can accuse it of harshness :

[1] Burnet MSS., British Museum.
[2] Doebner's " Memoirs of Queen Mary," p. 45.

" Having something to say to you, which I know will not be very pleasing, I chuse rather to write it first, being unwilling to surprize you ; though, I think, what I am going to tell you, should not, if you give yourself the time to think, that never any body was suffered to live at court in my lord Marlborough's circumstances.  I need not repeat the cause he has .given the King to do what he has done, nor his unwillingness at all times to come to such extremities, though people do deserve it.

" I hope, you do me the justice to believe it is as much against my will, that I now tell you, that, after this, it is very unfit lady Marlborough should stay with you, since that gives her husband so just a pretence of being where he ought not.

" I think, I might have expected you should have spoke to me of it.  And the King and I, both believing it, made us stay thus long.  But seeing you was so far from it, that you brought lady Marlborough hither last night, makes us resolve to put it off no longer, but tell you, she must not stay ; and that I have all the reason imaginable to look upon your bringing her, as the strangest thing that ever was done.  Nor could all my kindness for you (which is ever ready to turn all you do the best way, at any other time) have hindered me showing you that moment, but I considered your condition, and that made me master myself so far, as not to take notice of it then.

" But now I must tell you, it was very unkind in a sister, would have been very uncivil in an equal, and I need not say I have more to claim. Which, though my kindness would make me never exact, yet when I see the use you would make of it, I must tell you, I know what is due to me, and expect to have it from you.  'Tis upon this account,

QUEEN MARY II.

From a portrait by Wissing.  In the collection of Earl Bathurst.

I tell you plainly, lady Marlborough must not continue with you in the circumstances her lord is.

"I know this will be uneasy to you, and I am sorry for it; and it is very much so to me to say all this to you, for I have all the real kindness imaginable for you, and as I ever have, so will always do my part to live with you, as sisters ought. That is, not only like near relations, but like friends. And, as such, I did think to write to you. For I would have made myself believe your kindness for her made you at first forget that you should have for the King and Me; and resolved to put you in mind of it myself, neither of us being willing to come to harsher ways.

"But the sight of lady Marlborough having changed my thoughts does naturally alter my stile. And since by that I see how little you seem to consider what even in common civility you owe us, I have told it you plainly; but withal assure you, that let me have never so much reason to take any thing ill of you, my kindness is so great, that I can pass over most things and live with you, as becomes me. And I desire to do so merely from that motive. For I do love you, as my sister, and nothing but yourself can make me do otherwise. And that is the reason I chuse to write this, rather than tell it you, that you may overcome your first thoughts; and when you have well considered, you will find, that though the thing be hard, (which I again assure you I am sorry for) yet it is not unreasonable, but what has ever been practised, and what you yourself would do, were you in my place.

"I will end this with once more desiring you to consider the matter impartially, and take time for it. I do not desire an answer presently, because I would not have you give a rash one. I shall come to your drawing-room to-morrow before you play, because you know why I cannot make one:

21

At some other time we shall reason the business calmly ; which I will willingly do, or anything else that may shew, it shall never be my fault if we do not live kindly together. Nor will I ever be other by choice, but your truly loving and affectionate sister,

"M. R." [1]

The Princess wrote a letter in answer, which she requested Lord Rochester to convey to the Queen, and, on his refusal to do this, it was taken by one of her servants. It contains the following passages :

"Your Majesty was in the right to think your letter would be very surprizing to me. For you must needs be sensible enough of the kindness I have for my lady Marlborough, to know, that a command from you to part with her must be the greatest mortification in the world to me ; and indeed of such a nature, as I might well have hoped your kindness to me would have always prevented. I am satisfied she cannot have been guilty of any fault to you. And it would be extremely to her advantage, if I could here repeat every word that ever she had said to me of you in her whole life. I confess, it is no small addition to my trouble to find the want of your Majesty's kindness to me upon this occasion ; since I am sure I have always endeavoured to deserve it by all the actions of my life." [2]

Later in her letter the Princess announced that "there was no misery she would not rather resolve to suffer, than that of parting with Lady Marlborough."

The reply to this missive was merely an order that Lady Marlborough should at once leave the Cockpit. The Princess, being still determined not

---

[1] "Account of the Duchess of Marlborough's Conduct," pp. 43-7.
[2] *Ibid.*, p. 55.

to part from her friend, asked the Duchess of Somerset to lend her Sion House, and Lady Marlborough informs us that the King tried in vain to prevent the Duchess from acceding to this request.

Before leaving London, however, the Princess went to visit the Queen at Kensington, and, according to Lady Marlborough, did her best to be conciliatory, though, as she still defied the King and Queen, it is difficult to see in what her complaisance consisted. According to the same authority, the Queen " received her sister like a statue." On her side, the Queen says in her " Memoirs," that she did her best to bring about a reconciliation, and that it was only when she saw the Princess's coldness and indifference towards her, in contradistinction to her passion and kindness for Lady Marlborough, that she began to feel, or at least to endeavour to feel, indifference towards her.

On February 20, 1692, the Princess, who was enceinte, was moved in a sedan-chair to Sion House, Lady Marlborough, of course, accompanying her. A few days later, when the Prince of Denmark came to town to attend the House of Lords, much comment was caused by the fact that no guards were allowed by the King to ride on either side of his carriage, and that as he drove through the Park the drums were not beaten in his honour.[1]

The King now sent a peremptory message to Sion House ordering the Princess to part with Lady Marlborough; but the only answer to this command was that Anne removed the little Duke of Gloucester to Sion from Kensington, where he was staying with the Queen, who was extremely fond of her nephew.

Four days later—on March 4, 1692—William left for Holland. He had been completely worsted by his sister-in-law and Lady Marlborough, a

[1] Luttrell's "Relation of State Affairs," February 23, 1692.

situation which, to one with his views on women,
must have been peculiarly galling.

Before his departure the King had taken leave
of the Queen Dowager, who was returning to
Portugal, but it was noticed that he paid no farewell visit to the Prince and Princess of Denmark,
though the Prince went to pay his respects at
Kensington.   The fact that, though no honours
were shown Prince George on his entrance, when
he came out, " the guards ran to their arms, and
beat their drums as formerly," [1] was remarked with
much interest.

The Queen accompanied her husband to Harwich, and returned in the afternoon to Kensington.
She remained there till the announcement reached
her that he had put to sea, when she went to
Whitehall to take up the reins of government.
She was much pleased that her uncle, Lord Rochester, who was a conspicuous actor in the dispute
between the royal sisters, and excited Lady Marlborough's indignation by his supposed partiality for
the Queen, was a member of her Council.   At first
she employed her intervals of leisure from business
in preparing herself for receiving the sacrament
at Easter, and in altering her apartments at Whitehall.   She was not in any special anxiety about
William, as, though he had " spit blood for a day
and a night " before leaving, he was at any rate
not engaged in a campaign, but was staying quietly
at his palace at Loo.

At the beginning of April the Queen was taken
ill with a severe cold, which caused " inward feaver
and very great weackness," [2] so that she resigned
herself to death, and missed going to church on
the Lord's Day for the first time in twelve years.
This fact caused her the greatest trouble.   It is
instructive, as showing that William was the prin-

[1] Luttrell's " Relation of State Affairs," March 5, 1692.
[2] Doebner's " Memoirs of Queen Mary," p. 47.

cipal actor in the contest with Anne, that one of
Mary's reasons for not wishing to die at this time
was fear of " what might happen between the king
and my sister."

Lord Dartmouth takes a view which seems
reasonable when he contends that William was
mainly responsible for what has often been imputed solely to Mary. He complains that Burnet,
who, in Queen Anne's reign, had, as we know, revised
his account of what passed to suit the views of
the lady who was then Duchess of Marlborough,
" very unjustly endeavours to throw all the scandalous treatment of the princess upon the queen ;
though he knew she did nothing but as she was
ordered by the king." [1]

Even Lady Marlborough, who hated Queen Mary,
allows that it was the King, and not she, who tried
to influence the Duke of Somerset to refuse the
Princess the asylum of Sion House.

Mary's reflections on the subject are illuminating,
as showing her peculiar point of view. She says :
" But in all this I see the hand of God, and look
on our disagreeing as a punishment upon us for the
irregularity by us committed upon the revolution.
My husband did his duty and the nation did theirs,
and we were to suffer it, and rejoice that it pleased
God to do what he did. But as to our persons it
is not as it ought to be, tho' it was unavoidable
and no doubt that it is a just judgment of God,
but I trust the Church and nation shall not suffer,
but that we in our private concerns and persons
may bear the punishment as in this we do." [2]

It has been usual to separate the quarrel between
Mary and Anne from its context, and to treat it
rather as a piquant relief from the consideration
of State affairs, than as itself a part of them.

---

[1] Dartmouth's note to Burnet's " History of My Own Times,"
vol. iv. p. 164.
[2] Doebner's "Memoirs of Queen Mary," p. 46.

To Anne, the order that she was to be torn from
her beloved Lady Marlborough, was merely an un-
justifiable attempt to interfere with her private
rights, for, as we have seen, Mary, even when most
indignant with her, acquits her of any participa-
tion in the designs for her advancement with which
the Marlboroughs were credited. Therefore the
tenacity inherited from her father was roused, and
she determined that, whatever happened, she would
not yield to tyranny.

Besides, the Princess seems to have been completely hypnotised by Lady Marlborough.

" There is no misery I cannot readily resolve
to suffer, rather than the thought of parting from
you. And I do swear I would rather sooner be
torn to pieces, than alter this my resolution."

In another letter, speaking of Lady Marlborough
leaving her, she writes :

" And should you do it without asking my
consent (which if I ever give you, may I never
see the face of heaven) I will shut myself up, and
never see the world more, but live where I may
be forgotten by human kind." [1]

Where can doting subserviency sink lower than
in extracts like these from the Princess's letters to
her favourite ?

However, while feeling sympathy with Anne, it
is unfair to forget that, during most of the time
when the Queen has been most severely blamed for
harshness to her sister, she held the reins of government at an unusually anxious period in our history, when William, no undue alarmist, wrote
from Holland that he was in " extreme anxiety." [2]
If we remember that Anne, unless separated from
the Marlboroughs, was in Mary's eyes a more
dangerous rival to William in his possession of
the English crown, than even the unfortunate

[1] " Account of the Duchess of Marlborough's Conduct," p. 76.
[2] Letter, May, 1692, at Welbeck.

King in exile, her stringent measures seem excusable.

The Queen had hardly recovered from her indisposition when the most alarming news arrived. The French were planning an invasion of England. This was to take place before the end of April, while at the same time Louis XIV. intended to march into Flanders with a large army. The time was well chosen; for, as Ralph says: "The reins of Empire were in the hands of a woman, whose Councils were embarrassed with the feuds of two rival parties."[1]

In addition to this, grave fears were entertained about the loyalty of the Navy. The King was very busy in Holland with preparations for meeting the French forces, but he sent by Portland a message to the Queen, telling her that he would come himself, if he heard that James had actually landed on the English coast.

"That was" [says the Queen] "the greatest trouble of all; this was the only thing I dreaded to thinck my father and husband might once more meet in the field; and the fears that my father might fall by our arms, or either of them fall where t'other was present, was to me the dreadfullest prospect in the world."[2]

It was while the State was in deadly peril, and the Queen, only convalescent, did not know whom to trust, and counted her sister in the hands of the Marlboroughs as not the least of the perils surrounding the State during William's absence, that the scene took place which has shocked many of Mary's admirers as showing an unwomanly harshness. Our only authority for it is Mary's bitter enemy, Lady Marlborough, who wrote long afterwards, and did not scruple to descend to falsehood, as can be vouched for by any one who reads her

---

[1] Ralph's "History of England," vol. ii. p. 346.
[2] Doebner's "Memoirs of Queen Mary," p. 46.

book, and is acquainted with the times she professes to describe. As the judicious author of " The Other Side of the Question " observes on this subject, " The Evidence of a Party was never yet admitted by any equitable judge."

However, as there is no possibility of checking Lady Marlborough's account, it must be accepted with reservations. According to her, when the Princess discovered that her confinement was at hand, she sent Sir Benjamin Bathurst, husband to the Queen's friend and correspondent, to acquaint Her Majesty with the fact, and to tell her that the Princess considered herself much worse than usual on these occasions. To this intimation the Queen returned no answer, an action which seems heartless, unless we suppose, as we safely may from what we already know, that she was acting under orders from William, who was determined to force his unruly sister-in-law to obey his commands.

William's attitude to his sister-in-law is sometimes surprising, when we think of the patience and magnanimity he generally showed, even when his life was threatened. It must be remembered, however, that Elizabeth Villiers hated Lady Marlborough, and doubtless repeated to him all the coarse epithets used about him by Anne and her Court.

When, a little later, a daughter was born to Anne, and died a few minutes after her birth, the Princess sent Lady Charlotte Beverwaert to apprise the Queen of the fact. There was still delay, for Lord Rochester was absent, and the Queen evidently did not dare to visit the Princess without first consulting him. After seeing him, she sent for Lady Charlotte and told her she would go that afternoon to visit the Princess. Attended by Lady Derby and Lady Scarborough, she arrived at Sion almost as soon as did Anne's returning messenger, and went up to her sister's room.

There, without inquiring after her health, or even taking her hand, she said :

" I have made the first step by coming to you, and I now expect you should make the next by removing my Lady Marlborough."

The Princess answered that

" she had never in all her life disobeyed her, except in that one particular, which she hoped would, some time or other, appear as unreasonable to her Majesty, as it did to her." [1]

Therefore, on Anne's as well as on Mary's side, there was to be no surrender. The interview was now over, and the Queen went away, repeating the same words to the Prince as he conducted her to her carriage.

The Queen had evidently received orders not to hold any communication with the offender till she submitted to royal authority. However, when she reached home, her heart smote her, and she said she was sorry she had spoken like that to the Princess, who trembled and became as white as the sheet she lay on, when the subject was re-opened.

Shortly after this (May 5, 1692) Marlborough was taken into custody on charge of high treason. His accuser was a man named Young, who, as it afterwards transpired, had invented the plot ; but knowing of Marlborough's communications with the Court of St. Germains, and of the impending French invasion, the Government was seriously alarmed. Certainly, with a crisis at hand on which the fate of England depended, it was wise to have a man as clever, unscrupulous, and powerful as Marlborough, safely under lock and key.

Anne was now deprived of her guards, and forbidden to receive company, though this command cannot have been very strictly observed, as we hear that the Queen Dowager went to wish the

---

[1] " Account of the Duchess of Marlborough's Conduct," p. 70.

Princess good-bye before her departure to Portugal.
The Queen, too, visited Catherine of Braganza,
and in spite of her suspicions that the Queen
Dowager favoured Jacobitism, she must have felt
a certain affection for her, as we read in Luttrell's
accurate though uninspired " Diary " : " The Queen
and Queen Dowager both wept at parting." [1]
However, the latter did not leave the country for
some time, but waited at Dover for favourable
weather.

Later, Anne wrote to Stillingfleet, Bishop of
Worcester, to ask the Queen's permission to wait
on her, and received the following answer:

### " *To the Princess.*

" I have receiv'd yours by the bishop of Worcester, and have very little to say to it ; since you
cannot but know, that as I never used compliments,
so now they will not serve.

" 'Tis none of my fault, we live at this distance,
and I have endeavoured to shew my willingness
to do otherwise. And I will do no more. Don't
give yourself any unnecessary trouble : for be
assured it is not words can make us live together
as we ought. You know what I required of you.
And I now tell you, if you doubted it before, that
I cannot change my mind, but expect to be complied with, or you must not wonder if I doubt of
your kindness. You can give me no other marks,
that will satisfy me. Nor can I put any other
construction upon your actions than what all the
world must do, that sees them. These things
don't hinder me being very glad to hear you are
so well, and wishing you may continue so ; and
that you may yet, while 'tis in your power, oblige
me to be your affectionate sister

"MARIE R." [2]

---

[1] March 31, 1692.
[2] " Account of the Duchess of Marlborough's Conduct," p. 78.

The quarrel caused much talk and stir. The unity between the sisters had been their strength at the time of the Revolution, and the Jacobites rejoiced at a breach which alienated many people from Mary ; for Anne, the English Princess, was extremely popular. In March, 1692, everything seemed to smile on James's cause, and a curious proof of the Jacobite confidence in approaching victory, is afforded by the action of Ken, the ejected Bishop of Bath and Wells, who had been warmly attached to the Queen ever since the time of his chaplaincy at The Hague.

Ken wrote to Mrs. Jesson, a lady-in-waiting, who had, since Mrs. Trelawney's disgrace in 1685, obtained a high place in Queen Mary's affections, and whom he had known and liked at The Hague. His letter was enclosed in another, in which Ken told his " Good Friend " that though his epistle was ostensibly to her, it was in reality intended for her " Royall Mistris," and that he would incessantly pray God to impress on Queen Mary's mind what his zeal had prompted him to utter.

The enclosed letter ran as follows :

" ALL GLORY BE TO GOD.

" GOOD MISTRIS JESSEN,

" Being to leave ye towne, God willing, to morrow, if my service is any way acceptable to your Excellent Mistris, (for such she is in her native and unblended disposition) I entreat you to lay it at her feet. If not, say nothing at all of me. I verily believe she will find at long run, yt those very persons who pretend ye most reall concerne for her service, will at ye first appearance of danger wholly abandon her. I dread to thinke, yt there is any probability of my living to see our Mistris calamitous, and I earnestly beseech God to be propitious to her, to direct her ye right way, and to guard her from evill Counsellours, from treacherous flatterers, from Unchristian Casuists, from all Unnaturall opposition to her most tender and Royall father, whenever he returns to assert his right, and from ye guilt of all bloodshed wch will be ye unavoidable consequence of such an opposition, and wch will loudly cry to Heaven for vengeance. I doe with a bleeding heart deplore ye condition in wch I apprehend your Mistris to be, and I humbly beg of God to open her eyes yt she may see in this her day, a Day wch, I fear, is very short, and will soon be irrevocable, ye things which belong to her peace, lest they be hid from her eyes. If I had a regular call to preach before your Master and Mistris, who have been both gratious to me heretofore, this passage of ye Prophet Jeremy shoud be ye subject, wch I should very passionately recomend to their consideration. ' Say unto ye King and ye Queen, Humble yourselves, sitt downe, for your principalitys shall come downe, even ye Crowne of your Glory.' If my Zeale has transported me, tis from no temporall motive, but from a sincere and most affectionate desire of my Mistrisses happinesse in this world, and in ye world to come, wch has occasiond this excursion, and wch, at ye worst, is, I hope, veniall. I beseech God of His Infinite Goodness to give you ye grace of true Repentance, to restore you to your health, to fill you with His Reverentiall love, and to keepe you in his favour, wch is of all things under Heaven most desirable.

"Your faithful and affectionate servant
"THO. BATH AND WELLS.

"*Ap.* 27th 1692." [1]

Ken waited two days. Then, receiving no answer, and evidently fearing that he had not per-

---

[1] Plumptre's "Life of Ken," vol. ii. p. 306.

formed his duty towards his royal mistress as a
Bishop, and also as her former servant, he wrote
again to Mrs. Jesson. In his second letter, he said
that he longed to know whether she had given
his letter to the Queen, and that, fearing she might
have been afraid to do this, he now enclosed a
sealed letter to the Queen herself, and begged her
to choose a fit opportunity for presenting it. The
letter runs as follows :

### " *To Queen Mary.*

" ALL GLORY BE TO GOD.

" MADAM,
" I writ a letter very lately to Mrs. Jessen,
wch I desired her to lay before your Royall Highnesse, but fearing yt her heart might have failed
her, and having had no opportunity offered me
of waiting on you, and being inexpressibly jealous
and sollicitous for your good, I presume to write
to you my selfe. I doe not give you the title of
Majesty not daring to doe it, because I thinke it
justly belongs to your royal ffather, and to his
Queene, and my encouragement to make this
address to you, is ye persuasion wch possesses me
yt you have of late acted from an Intention, wch
is rather misguided than wilfully evill, and ye
entire confidence I have of your wisdome, and ye
goodness of your nature, wch will be better pleased
with sincerity, than with flattery. I am willing to
believe yt your Royal Highnesse thinkes me at
least an honest man, and you cannot but be sensible yt I, having never had any personall obligation to King James and having had ye honour
to have been your servant, and to have received
particular markes of your favour (of wch I shall
alwayes retaine a most gratefull Remembrance)
my worldly interest, and my owne naturall inclination for ye service of so gratious a mistris,

whose Happinesse temporall, as well as eternall,
I allways most passionately desired, would, from
ye beginning, have very readily determined me,
to have followed all your measures, but my Conscience would not permit me to comply then, and
it will as little permit me to be silent now. I
thanke God I had rather suffer your utmost severity,
than be disregardfull of your wellfare at such a
time as this, when ye possible apprehensions of
danger, may by Gods grace, soften you into yt
relenting, and awaken those serious reflections, wch
successe and prosperity, even in devout persons,
are to apt to stifle and to lay asleepe, and when I
may reasonably hope, yt you will hearken to a
word spoken in due season.

" Madam, I most humbly, I most importunately
beg of you to consider, yt ye dutys you owe to a
Husband, to a ffather, and to a brother, are not
at all inconsistent, yt ye duty you owe to God is
superiour to them all, yt no one comand of God
is to be violated to gratify either, yt such a vio-
lation is a publick scandall to our Christianity,
yt no evill is to be done to promote our most holy
Religion, yt there can be no true Repentance
without Restitution, yt if King James once setts
up his standard in his kingdome, ye arguments
now urged against him, will then all turne for him,
and be generally urged on his side, yt you yourself will tremble at ye thoughts of drawing your
sword against your owne Royall Father, and against
God's Anointed, and if you should not tremble,
yt ye nation will tremble to follow you. For my
owne part I wish my head waters, and my eyes
fountaines of teares, to bewaile ye sins of ye late
Revolution, and I will gladly sacrifice my life, to
heale those wounds, wch you yourselfe have
given to your own conscience, and wch at one
time or other will fall a bleeding. God out of
ye multitude of his most tender mercys give you

grace to weep much, to love much, and withall
to be much beloved of God.

"Madam,
"Your Royall Highnesses most humble servant
and Intercessor at ye throne of Grace,
"THOMAS BATH AND WELLS.

"*Ap*. 29*th* 1692."[1]

We do not know whether the reading of this
letter ever added to the perplexities of the unfor-
funate Queen at this time of trial. Perhaps
"Mistris Jessen" was advised not to present it,
or the Queen, seeing who had written it, refused
to read it.

It was a letter penned under the impulse of duty
by a pious and honest man. But no less pious
and honest was the woman who wrote just at this
time :

"I am naturally extream fearful and now found
I had so much reason for it that had I not been
supported by God's special grace, I had dyed
almost with the apprehensions. But I gave myself
to prayer and fortified my self so well, that I
believed I could dye, considering God could preserve my husband, and would certainly take care
of his Church. So having no children to be in
pain for I committed my self to God, and waited
not without impatience for the end."[2]

It now seemed as though nothing could stay
the invasion which threatened England, and James
was extremely active, though, fortunately for
William and Mary, his activities did not always
run in a judicious direction. Mary of Modena
was expecting a child, and he wrote to eight
Privy Councillors requesting their presence at
her lying-in, which was expected about the end of
May. Various ladies also received intimations of

---

[1] Plumptre's "Life of Ken," vol. ii. p. 308.
[2] Doebner's "Memoirs of Queen Mary," p. 48.

the expected event. This was a sensible proceeding ; but the Declaration James now issued, which,
in anticipation of victory, gave a long list of people
and categories of people on whom his vengeance
was to fall, was the most impolitic composition
that could be imagined. In fact so disastrous did
sundry of James's party consider it, that they
issued another Declaration which they pretended
to be the genuine one ; while the Queen did great
service to her cause by having James's Declaration
reprinted, and widely circulated with severe comments.

The known disloyalty of the Navy was now the
principal danger to be feared, but, instead of
showing suspicion of any of the naval officers,
the Queen executed a masterly stroke of policy.
Just before the fleet commanded by Russell started
to meet the French, a despatch came to them from
her, in which, says her father discontentedly,

"pretending by affected generosity not to believe
in what she could not prevent, she told them that
she trusted with absolute confidence in their zeal
and faithfulness, and that she looked on all reports
to the contrary as inventions of her enemies. This
brought her an address from the Fleet in which
the sailors promised to defend at the utmost peril
of their lives the incontestable rights of their
Majesties (so they called the Prince and Princess
of Orange) as well as the liberty and religion of
their country, against the attacks of all foreign
papists whoever they might be."

To this address, which Russell, conscious of his
own want of integrity, did not sign, the Queen
answered : " I had always this opinion of the
commanders ; But I am glad this is come to satisfy
others." [1] In thus rallying the patriotism of the
nation, the Queen certainly deserved well of her
countrymen.

[1] *Gazette*, May 16, 1692.

EDWARD TENISON, ARCHBISHOP OF CANTERBURY.

From a portrait by Kneller. British Museum.

Her condition of mind at this time was not enviable.

" In the meanwhile " [she says] " I heard Namur was besieged, and the king of France come in person, my husband gone there to raise the siege, so that in all likelihood some decisive action was to be expected. I never was in that condition in my life ; the kings person which was dearer to me than my own, exposed on one hand ; the fate of England on the other depending on our success at sea ; if the king should fall, all humanly speaking would fall with him ; if our fleet was beaten we knew there was an army ready to devour us from abroad, and a strong faction to help it at home, which would make quick worck, and not have given the king leisure to have helped us, could he have been spared where he was." [1]

The Queen betook herself to prayer as her only refuge, but on May 21 came joyful news, for the combined English and Dutch fleets, under Admiral Russell, had not only prevented the invasion of England, but had blockaded the bay of La Hogue, near which James and the chief part of his army were encamped.

Indignant at James's proclamation, and animated by the true spirit of a naval commander, Russell had done his best. Nevertheless, his loyalty was still doubtful, and he distressed the Queen by " his strange letters, wherein he seemed dissatisfied and did nothing but talck of retiring, and did really from that time hinder as much as he could, at least he forwarded nothing."

People seem sometimes astonished at England's want of success under a strong Monarch like William III. However, to the reader of the history of those times, who realises that the principal commanders, both by land and by sea, were always contemplating a desertion to the forces they were opposing, it

[1] Doebner's "Memoirs of Queen Mary," pp. 49-50.

appears as though any leader less cursed than
James with the fatal spirit of obstinacy and resentment, must infallibly have led the Jacobite cause
to victory.

Fifty surgeons were at once despatched to
Portsmouth, and the hospitals in London were
ordered to make room for the wounded. Great
was the jubilation throughout England at the news
of the victory, in which the English sailors had
borne themselves so bravely, that James, seeing
them scrambling from their boats up the high
sides of the French ships, cried out : " Ah, none
but my brave English could do that ! " [1]

He consoled himself for the defeat by the following reflection :

" The way in which the matter turned out shews
plainly a particular design by Providence to
punish the English by apparent successes, and
to sanctify the King by continual suffering." [2]

Meanwhile, Queen Mary protests : " I praised
God heartily and that before I did anything
else and spent the whole morning in that duty. [3]

A great joy and triumph which proves an enormous relief from anxiety, is reflected in all the contemporary caricatures, for La Hogue seemed to wipe
out the painful recollection of the defeat of Beachy
Head. Russell has become the popular hero, and
the universal domination of Louis, the " Christian Turk," with his harem of priests and his
Cardinals, is over for ever.

Even the fall of Namur, besieged by Louis XIV.,
did not appreciably affect the general satisfaction.
One of the caricatures of the time shews a
balance depending from the world, which is represented as a ball. This is being inspected by Louis

---

[1] Sir John Dalrymple's "Memoirs of Great Britain and Ireland,"
vol. iii. p. 247.

[2] "Mémoires de Jacques II.," Guizot edition, vol. iv. p. 505.

[3] Doebner's "Memoirs of Queen Mary," p. 50.

and his Court on one side, and by Russell and his officers on the other. In the scale on Admiral Russell's side are the French ships destroyed at La Hogue; in Louis' scale are Namur and the Pretender. But in spite of the fact that the Devil does his best to drag down the scale on the French King's side, the one on Admiral Russell's far outweighs it.

Queen Mary's view of the relative importance of the land and sea victories was not, however, the same as that taken by her subjects; for in her "Memoirs" she blames herself for waiting to hear what success the army had in Flanders, before ordering a public thanksgiving for the victory of La Hogue. "What did all my private prayers signify?" she says. "Oh my soul, this was a great sin, and such as I fear we still feel the effects of." [1]

She also reproaches herself with her vainglory in "fancying a thousand fine things of the king's victory." [2]

"And when the news came, first of the Namur Castle, then the towns being taken, I was to much troubled and disappointed so that I did not look on our deliverance and victory as I ought."

Then followed the battle of Steinkerk, in which the Allies were again unsuccessful, and after great preparations had been made by the Government for a descent on the coast of France, the attempt was abandoned. Therefore, as Queen Mary justly remarks, "all the expense was thrown away, the troops came back as they went, having made us rediculous to all the world by our great preparations to no purpose." [3]

Mary blames herself, apparently with no sufficient cause, for inadequate arrangements for this expedition, and says with touching humility: "a woman is seldom good for any thing and here it was plainly seen, and that vext me too much."

[1] Doebner's "Memoirs of Queen Mary," p. 51.
[2] *Ibid.*, p. 52.                    [3] *Ibid.*, p. 54.

And now the Queen underwent a fresh trouble. She had thanked God most heartily for the arrest of Grandval, a French officer who had been entrusted by the French War Office with the task of assassinating William. However, at Grandval's trial, which took place in the Netherlands, it transpired that before leaving Paris to execute his design, he had been presented to James and Mary of Modena at St. Germains, and that James was reported to have said : "If you and your companions do me this service, you shall never want." Mary's anguish at this news was terrible, and her comment is a veritable *cri du cœur.*

She says :

"The 10th of August I received Grandvals tryall, in which I saw that which must afflict me while I live, that he who I dare no more call father was consenting to the barbarous murder of my husband. 'Tis impossible for me to express what I then felt. I was ashamed to loock any body in the face. I fancied I should be pointed at as the daughter of one who was capable of such things, and the people would believe I might by nature have as ill inclinations. I lamented his sin and his shame ; I feard it might lessen my husbands kindness to me. It made such impressions upon me that I was uncapable of comfort. As for the printing of the tryal, I could not tell what I should do. The Lords all thought it necessary. I saw it was so, I knew it would be printed beyond sea, but I thought it was a hard thing on one hand for me to publish my own shame, and it might loock as ill on the other to conceal the mercys of God in saving my husband. But he was so kind as not to take it ill of me or not to love me less for that my great and endless misfortune."

It is only just to James II. to say that in the "Memoirs" written in his name, which are not, however, always trustworthy, he is represented as rejecting with horror the idea of assassinating his son-in-law. Mary, however, believed implicitly that her father had intended to murder her husband, and it is pathetic to see that she complains that after this blow, which she calls " my great afflic- tion," she could not pray for some time as she ought. However, she hopes that her inability was more owing to " the infirmity of my nature, which was perfectly tired, then to any ill disposition of my mind." [1]

In July the Queen retired from Whitehall to Kensington for about six weeks, to drink what she calls the " German Spaw " waters. How she employed herself there we do not know, but she evidently did not approve of her own doings, for she says that she misspent her time.

William returned from the Continent late in the autumn. There were great rejoicings on his arrival. The streets were illuminated, and a huzzaing crowd followed the coach which contained their Majesties from Whitehall to Kensington. Some of the crowd on their return, in the exuberance of their spirits, broke the windows which had not been lit up.

From this time happy little notices of visits with William to Hampton Court to see how the building was progressing, of accompanying him to Windsor when he was going to hunt, or of attend- ing the Lord Mayor's Show with him, are inter- spersed in Queen Mary's letters to the Electress Sophia with news of the old Duke of Richmond's marriage to the young widow of Lord Bellasis, or of the Duchess of Leinster having caught measles from her children.[2] She can walk from Kensing- ton to Whitehall, she tells her correspondent. Indeed, Luttrell notes in his " Diary " of Novem- ber 18, 1692 : " Yesterday the Queen walked on foot from Kensington to Whitehall."

---

[1] Doebner's "Memoirs of Queen Mary," p. 54.     [2] *Ibid.*, p. 98.

# CHAPTER XVIII

THE breach between the royal sisters continued;
and when the Princess moved from Sion to Berkeley House, the minister of St. James's, Piccadilly,
was forbidden to pay her the usual respect
shown to royalty. The Queen, too, refused to see
those who visited her sister, so that few dared to
do this except one or two Jacobite ladies; and
when the Princess visited Bath, the Mayor was
forbidden to receive her with the customary
honours.

The little Duke of Gloucester often went to see
the Queen, who gave him rattles and playthings,
and, when he showed a taste for carpentering, sent
him a box of ivory tools which had cost £25. One
day he brought the regiment of boys who were
supposed to act as his guards, to drill before
the King and Queen in the garden of Kensington
Palace, and made the Queen change colour by
remarking that his mamma once had guards and
now had none. The King, who was most anxious
to foster his heir's martial qualities, gave the boys
£20, and professed himself much pleased with the
performance. He came to see his nephew on one
occasion and the child said to him: " My dear
King, you shall have both my companies to go
with you to Flanders "; a remark which no doubt
delighted William.

Sometimes the boy was used by his elders as a

vehicle to obtain their desires, as on the occasion
when the Princess Anne and the Marlboroughs
wished him to fill the vacant place among the
wearers of the Garter, and as a gentle hint he was
sent to the King and Queen wearing a broad blue
scarf. This manœuvre did not meet with success,
for the Garter was conferred on the Duke of
Shrewsbury. The Queen on this occasion offered
the little Duke a beautiful blue bird belonging to
her, but he refused it, saying politely : " Madam, I
will not deprive you of it." On the Queen's birthday, he was sent to congratulate her, and asked
what the carpenters were doing in the Gallery of
Kensington. He was told by the Queen that they
were repairing it for fear it should fall ; "Let it
fall, let it fall," said he, " and then you will soon
scamper away to London." [1] This seems to have
been merely a child's inconsequence, or love of
sensation, as he was very fond of his aunt.

Mrs. Pack, the Duke of Gloucester's wet-nurse,
was one of those who helped to keep up the bad
feeling between the sisters, by repeating to the
Queen's ladies what had happened at the Princess's
Court.

William and Mary's intercourse with their nephew
did not in the least help to soften them towards
his mother. Lady Marlborough, whose words cannot, however, be believed without reservation, tells
us that when the Queen sent to inquire during
the Duke's illness—a frequent occurrence, for the
poor little boy had a sickly childhood—the messenger would come into the room without any
ceremony, pay no more attention to the Princess,
if she were present, "than if she were a rocker,
go directly up to the Duke, and make her
speech to him, or to the nurse, as he lay in her
lap." [2] Anne had worsted William over the Settle-

---

[1] Jenkins Lewis's " Memoirs of the Duke of Gloucester."
[2] " Account of the Duchess of Marlborough's Conduct," p. 104.

ment, and he had determined that as she had
again defied him, she should suffer severely for
her disobedience.   However, the brunt of the blame
for the quarrel, which rejoiced the Jacobites,
and did much harm to the cause of William and
Mary, fell on the Queen ;  for the matter was popularly supposed to be merely a dispute between the
sisters.

Writing in her " Memoirs " at the end of the year
1693, the Queen says :

" When I begin to reflect on this year I am almost
frighted, and dare hardly go on ;  for 'tis the year
I have met with more troubles as to publick matters
then any other."

The general disaffection of the nation towards
William's administration seemed to be on the
increase, and the nobility showed, in the Queen's
opinion, their corruption, by their shameful partiality in the acquittal of the dissipated young
Lord Mohun, who had, in consequence of a love-
affair, murdered the actor Mountford.  When,
towards the end of March, William left for the
Continent, the Queen says :  " the publick were as
angry with me as I could be with them."

In truth, the strain of the wearing position in
which the Queen was placed by her husband's
long absences from the country, was beginning to
tell on her ;  and there are constant references to
illnesses in her diary and letters.  Sometimes she
is merely suffering from her chronic trouble of
inflamed eyes, sometimes she has a bad cold, an
attack of fever, or a swelled face ;  and though she
is hardly over thirty, she begins already to feel
old.

To the Queen's great comfort Nottingham was
still Secretary of State, but she says sadly :

" The man I found the most constant in serving
the king his own way, and who was the only one
who really toock the most and greatest pains to

do so, more and more disliked, and people were inveterate against him."

It had been found impossible for Nottingham and Russell to act together, so the latter had been obliged to retire, and Killegrew and Delaval, with disastrous results, were put at the head of the Admiralty, and in command of the Channel fleet.

"Thus" [says the Queen] "I enterd into my administration which was all along unfortunate, and whereas other years the king had almost ever approved all was done, this year he disapproved allmost every thing." [1]

One of the Queen's actions which displeased the King, was her dismissal of Lord Bellamount from the post of Treasurer, a step for which the Queen justifies herself by saying that he had behaved impertinently. She allows that she was " censured for it by all, which was no small vexation to me ; but I could not be convinced I was in the wrong."

These words sound as though the Queen had deprived Lord Bellamount of his office on her own responsibility ; but Coxe tells us that Bellamount was dismissed because of his impeachment of the lords justices. This sounds more likely than the common report quoted by Luttrell, to the effect that Lord Bellamount had been deprived of his post because he had spoken for the Triennial Bill, which was to limit the duration of any Parliament to three years, and to which William objected as interfering with the royal prerogative.

England suffered two great misfortunes this year (1693). On July 19 William was beaten by Luxembourg at the battle of Landen, though, as his wife says proudly, " he got honour enough to flatter and please the vainest humour." [2]

Many people, however, who heard of William's defeat with indifference, or even, according to the Queen, with " malitious joy," received the news of

1 Doebner's "Memoirs of Queen Mary," p. 59.   2 *Ibid.,* p. 60.

the second great disaster with very different feelings. After the national pride in the battle of La Hogue, it was a terrible blow that the next important naval news should be that of a serious defeat.

England's trade with the Mediterranean was a principal source of her wealth, and early in 1693 about four hundred ships, forming what was known as the Smyrna fleet, were waiting in the Thames laden with cargoes, the value of which was estimated at several millions sterling. Hitherto, owing to French privateers, it had not been considered safe for this cargo to start, but now to Admirals Killegrew and Delaval was entrusted the task of conveying the treasure to the Mediterranean.

We may judge from a letter written by Killegrew after the disaster, in which he speaks of the " tottering and miserable condition of the nation," [1] and discusses James's chances of success in overthrowing the Government, that he was not one of William's enthusiastic admirers. There appears, at any rate, to have been much difficulty in getting the Admirals to start, and this caused great dismay among the merchants whose commodities were to be protected, and who petitioned the Queen continually that the expedition should embark.

On May 24, 1693, it was said that the fleet would have taken its departure had it not been becalmed, but on the 29th, although the weather had changed, it was still in the harbour; and the Queen wrote indignantly to inquire the reason of these continual delays "from day to day." There were apparently many postponements both in manning and in provisioning the ships, though it is difficult to judge how far the cause for this backwardness was bad management or want of good faith on the part of the Admirals, or how

[1] Letter, July 12, 1693, Record Office.

far it proceeded from the impoverished condition
of the Exchequer.

It was not till June that the immense fleet at
last set sail, and then, owing to faulty information,
Killegrew and Delaval considered that Tourville
was in the harbour of Brest, and therefore soon
insisted on returning to the Channel, leaving
Rooke, with only twenty men-of-war, to take
charge of the merchant vessels. Meanwhile, news
had reached England that Tourville had slipped
out of Brest Harbour, and was going south. This
news was at once sent to the Admirals, but they
received it too late for action, and Rooke encoun-
tered the whole French fleet off St. Vincent, and
was only able, by great efforts, to save the entire
squadron from destruction. The Dutch, to whom
all honour is due, sacrificed two or three of their
ships to save the fleet, but about three hundred of
the merchant ships under Rooke's guardianship
were scattered over the ocean, and many were
lost.

Terrible was the gloom in the City when the
tragic news reached England, for the loss to both
England and Holland was enormous, and a depu-
tation of merchants came to the Queen to represent their grievances. They were admitted to the
Council Chamber, and she commanded Somers to
address them in her name, and to inform them
that she had appointed a Committee of the Privy
Council to inquire into the causes of the late
disaster. In spite of the Queen's pessimistic view
of the relations between herself and the English
nation, she was evidently very popular, for in
answer to her address, the Lord Mayor came to
the Palace to assure her that the City would still
remain loyal, and would, in spite of its recent
losses, continue to defray the expenses necessary
to support the Government.

Killegrew   and   Delaval,   however,   met   with

general reprobation, and could only defend themselves by declaring that they were not sufficiently provisioned for the voyage to Lisbon to be practicable without starving their crews, and that the sailing of the fleet at all at that time had been done against the advice of all the flag-officers. They then showed insubordination by refusing to obey the Queen's orders to put Rooke at the head of the squadron, this being "the first time," says Rooke, "that an Admiralty order and the Queen's commands have been disregarded." [1] Eventually, William gave orders that neither Killegrew nor Delaval should appear at the Admiralty Board till further notice.

The Queen comments thus to the Electress Sophia on the disaster :

"You spare the sea maters as much as you can, tho, the litle you say is enough ; I wish I coud difer from you in that, but there is one of the misfortunes of the Kings long absence, that he canot at a distance take the nesessery care of so great a conserne, and a woman is but a very uselesse and helplesse creature at all times, espesiely in times of war and difficulty. That I find by my owne sad experience, that an old english inclination to the love and honour of the nation signifys nothing in a woman's heart without a mans head and hands."

She goes on to remark with her usual philosophy, that her correspondent knows how the English value themselves and their honour, especially in sea matters, and that it may be that they are to be taught a little humility, and not "to dispise the rest of mankind." [2]

An expedition on August 29 to the West Indies, under Sir Francis Wheelen, was equally unfortunate; for the fleet of merchant vessels, and their

[1] Letters, June 29 and August 23, 1693, Record Office.
[2] Doebner's "Memoirs of Queen Mary," p. 109.

" extraordinary wealth," fell into the hands of the French. On October 17, 1693, when what was left of this ill-fated squadron returned to England, the Queen sent most careful directions that, although all the sailors appeared to be in good health, they were to be kept in quarantine for a time, and their clothes washed for fear of infection.[1]

It is interesting to hear the Electress's opinion of Queen Mary from Lord Dartmouth, who visited Hanover about this time.

" She " (the Electress) "was very free in her discourse" [he observes], "and said she held a constant correspondence with King James, and his daughter, our Queen, with many particulars of a very extraordinary nature, that were great proofs of his being a very weak man, and her being a very good woman." [2]

After the naval disaster, Nottingham became more unpopular than ever, and on the King's return in good health on October 29, the Queen writes bitterly :

"All the world was almost despairing ; himself thought his case so bad that he was forced to part with Lord Nottingham to please a party he cannot trust."

The King was most anxious that Shrewsbury should take the place vacated by Nottingham, and he employed Elizabeth Villiers to persuade him to do so—a mission in which, till the beginning of 1694, she was not successful. Her letters to Shrewsbury are interesting, and show that her intercourse with William was frequent, and that he had much confidence in her judgment and powers of influence. On one occasion she begs Shrewsbury not to let the King know

---

[1] Letter, October 17, 1693, Record Office.  *L'Hermitage* Despatch, October 27, 1693.  Add. MSS., 17,677. P.P.

[2] Notes to Burnet's " History of My Own Times," vol. iv. p. 203.

that she has sent a messenger to him, as he had given her special instructions to go herself.[1] If these transactions came to Queen Mary's ears, she must indeed have felt that the times were out of joint. The King disapproved of all she had done during his absence, and on his return went to Elizabeth Villiers for help.

One sentiment the Queen expresses, gives us a human feeling of nearness to her, though there is little doubt that if she did not blame herself bitterly afterwards, it was only because she looked on the French as the powers of evil.

"Now" [she says joyfully], "since I have writ the foregoing I have heard one piece of good news, to make us end an unfortunate year really well, that our ships have taken severall ships of corn going for France, which must certainly be a great loss to them; this I heartily bless God for." [2]

This feeling about France is expressed with less seriousness in one of her letters to the Electress Sophia, in which she shows the vivacity often mentioned by eulogists. This is absolutely lacking in her "Memoirs," which are intended to be a record of her serious thoughts and religious feelings, and therefore, if taken alone, give a one-sided aspect of her character.

"I am very glad" [she says] "that you amuse yourself so well, and that you have so much reason to be happy. I wish with all my heart that this may continue, and that M. Danquelman may always wear his wig hindpart before, though, if he is like his brother, he will not be very handsome like that. I wish that you and I could turn the French wigs in the same way, I think it would be a good thing. I would not hurt them. I should be a good valet and not deprive them of any of

---

[1] "Shrewsbury Correspondence," p. 28.
[2] Doebner's "Memoirs of Queen Mary," p. 62.

their own hair, except what falls in front of their eyes and prevents them from seeing." [1]

The correspondents were evidently by this time on terms of considerable intimacy, for the Electress does not scruple to rally the Queen on the fact that the Elector of Saxony's promise to provide William with ten thousand men, was secured after he had been well plied with wine during a fête at The Hague, and was hardly responsible for his actions. The Queen defends herself in a light style, saying that she had never thought of gaining him that way, " but was bid hold my tongue, and not lose him by my scruples." [2] She hastens to protect William from any possible imputation of double-dealing, by saying :

" I think Ministers have some latitude allowed them, and must not stand so much upon things which othere honest men must scruple, a litle equivocation is dispensed with in them by all religions."

In the spring of 1694, the King set out again to the Continent, leaving the Queen for the last time at the helm. Before his departure he had appointed the Archbishop of Canterbury, Lord Caermarthen, the Earl of Pembroke, Lord Godolphin, and Lord Shrewsbury to form the Queen's Council, and had arranged for an attack to be made on Brest. As usual, however, there were traitors in the camp, and though Russell, in spite of his communications with James's Court, [3] kept the secret of the destination of the fleet, both Godolphin and Marlborough betrayed it to the French Court. As a result, the French fortified the harbour of Brest ; and Talmash, who had stepped into Marlborough's shoes at his disgrace, and was in command of the land forces, was killed, and with

---

[1] Doebner's "Memoirs of Queen Mary," p. 99.
[2] *Ibid.*, p. 106.
[3] "Macpherson Papers," p. 480.

him four hundred sailors and seven hundred soldiers.

As the Queen died before the end of 1694, there are no "Memoirs" to give us her feelings about this disaster, but we can judge of them by the fact that

"at her Majesty's command, the captain who brought the sad news was told not to divulge all the circumstances, which did not her Majesty thought redound to the credit of the officers." Treachery, however, was not suspected at the time.

In revenge for this defeat, the English devastated Dieppe, and injured Havre and Calais, but these exploits were hardly glorious.

The Queen was much worried about affairs in Flanders, and in a letter written to the Electress about the time of the Brest disaster, which she does not mention, she speaks of her anxiety about the chances of an engagement in Flanders. She says that while the campaign was going on, she could not settle to anything; as every day she feared to hear of an action.

" I am sure the expectation of it is very uneasy, so that a good peace grows every day more and more desirable, but I am so little used to have wat I wish that I dare not flater myself with any hopes of it, one woud think war coud not last much longer."

Her heart was, as usual, with William, though he could not be called a devoted husband. Lord Hardwicke says :

" Till her grace of Marlborough was pleased to publish her own very bad conduct, I can with great truth affirm, that I never heard an ill character given of her Majesty by any body. She was generally thought to submit to the King's ill humours and temper more than she had reason to do, considering the insolent treatment she frequently received from him, which she was never

**DEATH OF QUEEN MARY II.**

Contemporary print. In the possession of A. M. Broadley, Esq. From the Fraser Collection.

known to complain of herself, but I have heard most of her servants speak of it with great indignation."[1]

During the King's absence, the Queen was, as usual, worried by quarrels and discontents.

Lord Normanby declared that he had permission from William to be always present at the Queen's secret Councils. The Queen, on the other hand, insisted that the King had said that there was to be no regular Cabinet Council, and that, except in the case of those who could not be excluded because they held important appointments under the Crown, different lords should be summoned to attend according to the subject in discussion. Though Devonshire, who was in the same position as Normanby, showed an unexpected complaisance about the matter, this mode of government was very cumbrous, and, as Shrewsbury pointed out, would lead to constant dissatisfaction.[2] In fact, government by Ministry was becoming imperative in the near future.

The next trouble was about Admiral Russell, who had been ordered by the King to remain in the Mediterranean, but was not at all pleased with his position, and wished to return. Eventually the Queen signed an order giving him permission to do this under certain conditions; but to this the King objected, and wrote to Shrewsbury:

"I very much fear, that the last orders which the Queen sent him, leave him too much at liberty to return, if he wishes it, as I doubt not that he does."[3]

The matter led to much correspondence, and Russell, though exhorted by Shrewsbury—who calls him "dear Mr. Russell"—to "patience and submission," was not a striking example of these virtues, as he growled and grumbled continually.

[1] Note to Burnet's "History of My Own Times," vol. iv. p. 249.
[2] "Shrewsbury Correspondence," p. 34.  [3] *Ibid.*, p. 70.

" Really, I am not able to undergo the burthen "
[he says in one of the letters which Shrewsbury
answers with admirable suavity], " all my hours are
full of cares, and apprehensions that my labour
will be rewarded, as hitherto it has been, with
complaints and ill-usage." [1]

Russell, however, did good service in the Mediterranean, and earned the Spaniards' gratitude, and
when the King, on his return to England in November, addressed the Parliament, he was able to say :
" I am glad to meet you here, when, I can say,
our affairs are in a better posture, both by sea
and land than when we parted last."

A great sorrow now befell the Queen, for on
November 18, Tillotson, her adviser and dearly
loved friend, was suddenly taken ill while perform-
ing service in the Chapel at Whitehall, and died
on the 23rd. " The Queen for many days spoke
of him in the tenderest manner and not without
tears " ; [2] and the King showed his affection for
" the best friend he had ever had " by granting a
pension to his widow. Speaking of this lady, who
was apparently a very happy wife, it may be
mentioned that when her father, Dr. Wilkins, told
her that Tillotson wished to marry her, and she
" begged to be excused," he said to her: " Betty,
you shall have him ; for he is the best polemical
Divine this day in England " ; [3] and the matter
was settled. Thus summarily were affairs of the
heart arranged in those days.

Tenison, Bishop of Lincoln, was appointed Archbishop in Tillotson's place. He is described as
worthy and solid, without possessing the charm
of his predecessor. The Queen had been most
anxious for Stillingfleet, Bishop of Worcester, to be
made Archbishop, and had several conversations

---

[1] " Shrewsbury Correspondence," p. 203.
[2] Birch's " Life of Tillotson," p. 345.
[3] *Ibid.*, p. 417,

with Shrewsbury on the subject. The Whigs, however, considered, " both his notions and his temper were too high " ; [1] and his health being delicate, it was thought that he would not be able to cope with so onerous a charge.

[1] Burnet's " History of My Own Times," vol. iv. p. 244.

# CHAPTER XIX

Illness of the Queen—She burns her papers—The Triennial Bill—The Queen's illness declared to be smallpox—General sorrow—The King's distress—The Princess Anne—The Queen's danger—Question of her letter to the King—She receives the sacrament—Her death—General sorrow—The King's anguish—He carries out her wishes—James II.—The lying-in-state—The funeral—Ken's letter—The Queen's character—Greenwich Naval Hospital.

TENISON'S appointment to the Archbishopric was announced in the *Gazette* of December 10, 1694, and on the 20th the Queen was taken ill. Smallpox was raging in London, and as she had never had the illness, there was considerable alarm among those who surrounded her. Her indisposition, however, seemed to be but slight, for the next day she received people as usual ; and Burnet, who was with her for half an hour, said that she seemed in her usual health.[1] The following day she went out, but on her return felt so unwell, that it was impossible for her to disguise from herself the fact that her illness was serious. She was, as we know, well prepared for death, and in the last letter we have from her pen, which was written in September to her Dutch friend, the Baroness Wassenaer d'Obdam, she remarks that it is comparatively easy for people who have no children to leave the world.[2] So we see that she still longed for the great boon which had been denied to her.

That she already considered her disease dangerous, is shown by the fact that she shut herself up till late, tearing up and burning private papers,

[1] Burnet's "History of My Own Times," vol. iv. p. 244.
[2] "Lettres et Mémoires de Marie Reine d'Angleterre," edited by Countess Bentinck, p. 150.

and putting the rest in order. After her death, it was found that everything was arranged most methodically, " to the very least of her debts, which were very small, and everything in that exact method as seldom is found in any private person." [1]

Apparently, no physician was summoned, and the Queen merely took a dose of a cordial which she was in the habit of using whenever she was slightly indisposed. This, Dr. Harris, one of the physicians who was in the habit of attending her, considered to be the cause of her death.

On December 22, the second day of the Queen's illness, the King passed the Triennial Bill. In spite of the representations made to him, of the disastrous consequences of a struggle between him and his Parliament, he had hitherto refused to do this. Bishop Kennet sees a special providence in the fact that he was directed to pass the Bill before the Queen's death ; as, if he had deferred doing this till afterwards, the general opinion would have been that, his position being now precarious, he was forced to pass a measure which he detested.

The day following (Sunday, December 23) great alarm was caused by an eruption appearing on the Queen's skin. This the physicians said was small-pox. William, who, from the ravages that deadly disease had made in his family, had good cause to dread it,

" called me " [says Burnet] " into his closet, and gave a free vent to a most tender passion ; he burst out into tears ; and cried out, that there was no hope of the Queen, and that from being the happiest, he was now going to be the miserablest creature upon earth. He said, during the whole course of their marriage, he had never known one single fault in her ; there was a worth in her that nobody knew besides himself." [2]

[1] Evelyn's " Diary," March 8, 1695.
[2] Burnet's " History of My Own Times," vol. iv. p. 277.

However, on the evening of December 24, "the nurse who lives with my Lady Pulteney," and who had been called in to attend the Queen,[1] inspired fresh hopes by saying that she thought Her Majesty was suffering from measles. Dr. Radcliffe, who was considered the ablest man in his profession in England, agreed with her ; while Sir Thomas Millington, the other high authority, suspended his judgment. Burnet imputes the Queen's death to Radcliffe's mistake ; but it must be remembered that the latter, a strong Tory, as well as a conceited and insolent man, was not likely to be popular with the Whig historian.

The Queen slept several hours that night, and woke apparently better, so that the King became satisfied that she was suffering only from measles. The next day, however, the physicians changed their mind, and announced that the Queen was suffering from smallpox of a peculiarly malignant character. As soon as the Queen knew this, she sent away every one belonging to the Court who had not had the disease, a precaution which was quite unusual in those days, and which is mentioned as a sign of extraordinary consideration for others. She was perfectly conscious, and when she saw that those surrounding her were weeping, she said : "Why are you crying ? I am not very bad."

"Never was such a face of universal sorrow seen in a court or in a town as at this time," says Burnet ; "all people, men and women, young and old, could scarce refrain from tears." [2] When the minister prayed for the Queen in the Whitehall Chapel that Christmas Day, the congregation, as well as the King and Court, burst into tears. A gloom hung over everything ; customary festivities were omitted, and the road to Kensington was

---

[1] "Lexington Papers," p. 31.
[2] Burnet's "History of My Own Times," vol. iv. p. 247.

blocked with vehicles, riders, and foot-passengers, on their way to inquire after their beloved Queen.

On the morning of Wednesday, December 26, the nine doctors who were attending the Queen, met in consultation, and decided that she ought to be informed that her condition was hopeless. The King, who now never left his wife's room, gave permission that this should be done; and the task was entrusted to Tenison, the new Archbishop. It was a difficult one; and the Archbishop, with much hesitation, began to say something which, without abruptly disclosing the truth, would, he hoped, prepare the Queen's mind for it. However, she soon realised what he was endeavouring to tell her, and answered him that

" she thanked God she had always carried this in her mind, that nothing was to be left to the last hour; she had nothing then to do, but to look up to God, and submit to his will." [1]

The King, however, could not control himself, but broke out into a pitiful sobbing. In distress at this, the Queen begged him not to make her suffer the pangs of death twice, and reminded him that he must take care of himself for the sake of the nation. He replied that if God caused this blow to fall, everything would be over for him. Then the doctors appeared, and said that the interview must cease. It is curious to note that in all the accounts of the Queen's last illness, the mutual positions of William and Mary are reversed, and she is infinitely the stronger of the two.

The King now refused to leave the Queen's bedside; and it was only with much difficulty that he was persuaded to have a camp-bedstead put up in her ante-room, where he occasionally lay down, though he never slept. Meanwhile, in spite of the administration of " Sir Walter Raleigh's cordial," and " King Charles's drops," the Queen's

---

[1] Burnet's " History of My Own Times," vol. iv. p. 247.

pulse continued to grow weaker; and though
upon her taking "the bezoar cordial" she appeared to be "a little more lively,"[1] and Dr.
Radcliffe thought that her pulse was stronger, Sir
Thomas Millington could not perceive this. He
stated in a report to the other doctors that the
spots did not raise the skin, which continued (as he
represented it) "smooth like glass." One of her
physicians was so much struck with the serenity
with which she bore her sufferings, that he exclaimed: "She seemed to me more like an angel
than a woman."

The Queen and the Princess Anne had not met
for two years, but as soon as the Princess heard
of the Queen's indisposition, she sent a messenger
to ask how she was, and to say that, though
ill herself, she would come to see her if allowed
to do so. The messenger told Lord Derby
this, and an answer was brought that the King
would reply the next day, when the following
letter was received from Lady Derby, which was
addressed "to the same lady, who had brought
the message":

" MADAM,
      " I am commanded by the King and Queen
to tell you, they desire you would let the Princess
know they both thank her for sending and desiring
to come: But, it being thought so necessary to
keep the Queen as quiet as possible, hope she will
defer it.
                    " I am, Madam,
             " Your ladyship's most humble servant,
                         " E. DERBY.

      " Pray, madam, present my humble duty to the
Princess."[2]

---

[1] "Lexington Papers," p. 34.
[2] "Account of the Conduct of the Duchess of Marlborough,"
p. 105.

After this the Princess sent every day to inquire about her sister, and though Burnet says that the Queen sent Anne a kind message, Lady Marlborough declares that Lady Fitzhardinge, who forced an entrance to the Queen when she was dying, with a message from her sister, received only a cold " Thanks " from her.

As Lady Marlborough is the only actual witness as to what passed between the Queen and her sister, it is necessary to quote from her, but it must be remembered that she did not scruple to invent and to alter at her will. Even too, if her testimony as to actual facts is reliable, we may agree with what the author of " The Other Side of the Question " says indignantly : " Even the sinking Spirits, feeble Voice, and dying Manner of the Queen in her last Agonies, are misrepresented under the Term of a Cold Thanks." [1]

On hearing one day that his aunt was supposed to be better, the little Duke of Gloucester said— apparently without any prompting—" I am glad of it with all my heart." When the news of her death came, he varied the words " Oh ! be joyful " used by the attendant who had brought the news of her amendment, and exclaimed, " Oh ! be doleful " [2]—a remark which was much admired by those who surrounded him.

The Queen had much private talk with Tenison. " She had formerly wrote her mind in many particulars to the king ; and she gave orders to look carefully for a small scrutoir that she made use of, and to deliver it to the King ; and, having despatched that, she avoided the giving her self or him the tenderness which a final parting might have raised in them both." [3]

The letter, in which Mary " wrote her mind " in

---

[1] Ralph's " The Other Side of the Question," p. 141.
[2] Jenkins Lewis's " Account of the Duke of Gloucester."
[3] Burnet's " History of My Own Times," vol. iv. p. 248.

many particulars, is doubtless the one Lord Hardwicke mentions when he says :

" I have seen a letter of the queen's containing
a strong but decent admonition to the king for
some irregularity in his conduct. The expressions
are so general that one can neither make out the
fact or person alluded to. This was thought im-
proper to be published by Sir J. D(alrymple)." [1]

Jesse, in his " Memoirs of the Court of England," [2]
says :

" We are assured in the ' Account of the Death
of Queen Mary by a Minister of State,' that after
her decease a letter was found in her strong box,
addressed to the King, in which she affectionately
urged him to discontinue the intercourse which
she had so long bewailed. The appeal was rendered the more forcible, from its being enjoined by
the neglected wife that the letter should on no
account be delivered to the King till after her own
death."

Jesse, however, gives no reference to help us
to find the manuscript or pamphlet to which he
refers, and the present writer can find no trace of
its existence.

However, we are told in Whiston's " Memoirs "
that his patron, Bishop Moor, " who was one of
those sorrowful company of bishops, of whom
Burnet speaks a little before, who attended her "
[the Queen] " in her receiving her last communion,"
gave Whiston the following information :

" It was this : there was a Court lady, the lady
Villiers, with whom it was well known William had
been too familiar, and had given her great endowments. Upon the Queen's death the new
Archbishop, whether as desired by the Queen before
her death, or of his own voluntary motion, I do not

---

[1] Hardwicke's note to Burnet's "History of My Own Times,"
vol. iv. p. 249.
[2] vol. i. p. 243.

know, took the freedom, after his loss of so excellent a wife, to represent to him the great injury he had done to that excellent wife by his adultery with the Lady Villiers. The King took it wel and did not deny his crime, but faithfully promised the Archbishop he would have no more to do with her. Which resolution I believe he kept; I having heard another way that this lady wondred she could never see that king after the Queen's death." [1]

Tenison's sermon, preached at the King's desire on December 30, and printed afterwards by command, "Concerning Holy Resolution," was intended to strengthen William in his determination to break permanently with Elizabeth Villiers. On November 25, 1695, about eleven months after the Queen's death, the separation was confirmed by her marriage to Lord George Hamilton, who was created Earl of Orkney.

Queen Mary's long-borne sorrow at the existence of her rival ceased, however, before her death, for we are told that she detached her mind completely from all earthly things.

She passed most of her time in prayer, and begged twice a day to have the commendatory prayer, "For a sick person on the point of departure," read to her. Her usual thoughtfulness for others continued, and a few hours before her death she begged Burnet to sit down, as she was sure that he must be tired of standing.

On the 27th—the day before Queen Mary died—the King was at last persuaded to leave her, and to retire altogether to the ante-chamber. His condition was deplorable, and when he heard that the Queen's pulse was failing, he fell into a fainting fit, from which it was feared that he would not recover.

Meanwhile the Queen, and the Bishops in atten-

[1] Whiston's "Memoirs," vol. i. p. 100.

dance on her, received the Holy Communion. "We were, God knows, a sorrowful company," says Burnet; "for we were losing her who was our chief hope and glory on earth."[1] She was so drowsy, that she had feared she would not be able to rouse herself for the performance of the rite. "Others have need to pray for me, seeing I am so little able to pray for myself,"[2] she said. However, to her great relief, she was able to repeat the whole service after the Archbishop, and to swallow the bread, which she had feared would have been an impossibility.

When this was over,

"she composed her self solemnly to die, she slumbered sometimes, but said she was not refreshed by it; and said often that nothing did her good but prayer; she tried once or twice to have said somewhat to the king, but was not able to go through with it. She ordered the archbishop to be reading to her such passages of scripture as might fix her attention, and raise her devotion; several cordials were given, but all was ineffectual."[1]

"She was then upon the Wing. Such was her Peace that she hardly felt any uneasiness from symptoms. We first thought that the ease was from her mind, then, when she said she felt well inwardly, we saw it was a particular blessing."[3]

One more trial was left. For some hours the Queen lay silent. Then she began to speak, and it was evident that her mind was wandering. Her fancies took a characteristic turn. Begging every one but Archbishop Tenison to leave the room, she asked him to look behind the screen which stood near her bed:

"For" [said she] "Dr. Radclyffe has put a Popish

---

[1] Burnet's "History of My Own Times," vol. iv. p. 248.
[2] "Tenison's Sermon in Westminster Abbey, March 5, 1695."
[3] Burnet's "Essay on the Memory of the late Queen."

Nurse upon me; and she is always listening to what is said about me; that woman is a great disturbance to me." [1]

An hour before the Queen's death William, whose anguish filled all those around him with sympathy, again approached her. She motioned him away, and at a quarter to one in the morning of Friday, December 28, 1694, in the thirty-third year of her age, and the sixth of her reign, " after two or three small strugglings of Nature, without such agonies as are usual," [2] Mary II. of England breathed her last.

Luttrell says, speaking of her death: " The King is mightily afflicted thereat, and the whole Court, as also this citty, 'tis impossible to expresse the general grief upon this occasion." [3]

" It is impossible " [writes Auersperg to his Court] " to describe the desolation which this death has caused to the whole nation. For the love which every one had for the Queen is indescribable." [4]

" The terrible blow " [says Hoffmann] " is lamented by great and small, for the Queen had made herself inexpressibly beloved by her peculiar qualities and virtues, particularly by her benevolence to the poor." [5]

In Holland, the sorrow for the loss of Queen Mary was as great as in England. Prior, writing from The Hague, was astonished at its intensity. He writes :

" 'Tis impossible for me to tell you the sorrow that reigns universally in Holland. These people who never had any passions before are now touched, and marble weeps." [6]

The Electress Sophia shared in the general

[1] Ralph's " History of England," vol. ii. p. 540.
[2] " Tenison's Sermon in Westminster Abbey, March 5, 1695."
[3] " Relation of State Affairs," December 29, 1694.
[4] Klopp's "Fall des Hauses Stuart," vol. vii. p. 12.
[5] *Ibid.,*
[6] " Lexington Papers," p. 47.

sorrow, and writes that she is quite overcome by the death of the " incomparable Queen of England."[1]

" I never admired any person so entirely as I did her," cries Burnet with emotion. " The purity and sublimity of her mind were the perfectest thing I ever saw." Speaking of her death, he says : " I never felt myself sink so much under anything that had happened to me."[2]

William's condition was pitiable.

" He has scarce got any sleep or taken any nourishment, and there is hardly any instance of so passionate a sorrow as the King has been overtaken with, which seemed excessive while life yet lasted, and 'tis risen to a greater degree since ; so that he can hardly bear the sight of those that were most agreeable to him before. He had some fits like fainting yesterday."[3]

A few days later he was still wasted with sorrow, broke down if any one came to see him, and had lost the use of his legs, so that it was necessary to carry him into the garden to take the air. Burnet says : " The new Archbishop was long and oft with him ; " and he adds that the King now went to prayers twice daily ; and " entered upon very solemn and serious resolutions of becoming in all things a true Christian, and of breaking off all bad practices whatever."[4]

William was determined to carry out all the Queen's wishes, and to keep on all her charities.

" That he might pursue that designe which above all others was dearest to her, of encouraging pious and labourious clergy, he appointed a Commission consisting of the two Archbishops and of several of the Bishops, to select suitable men for preferment in the Church."

[1] Letter, January 13, 1695.
[2] Burnet's MSS., British Museum.
[3] "Lexington Papers," p. 35.
[4] Burnet's MSS., British Museum.

As we know, the King was not popular in England; but his grief on this occasion raised him in his subjects' estimation.

" This sad occurrence has effaced the bad impression people had about the King, for they thought he only loved the Queen because she had helped him to the succession, but now people are quite undeceived about that." [1]

He was not, however, spared by the wits of the period, who wrote :

> " So greatly Mary died and William grieves,
> You'd think the hero gone, the woman lives."

And

> " Sure Death's a Jacobite that thus bewitches,
> His soul wears petticoats, and hers the breaches;
> Alas ! Alas ! we've err'd in our commanders,
> Will should have knotted, and Moll gone for Flanders."

The writer of the last stanza, would apparently have agreed with the relative estimate of William and Mary held by Dr. Hooper. He

" would never allow any comparison to be made between his [William's] abilities and those of his Mistresse, which, he assured him, far surpassed anything in the King."

Hooper says triumphantly that, during William's first absence in Holland, Pelham, one of the Lords of the Treasury, who had evidently, in spite of Hooper's enthusiasm, been rather sceptical about the Queen's talents, told him

" he came to knock underboard, and to acknowledge that he had been in the wrong. Saying that she had so clear an understanding, and quick conception in all business that she was immediately misstresse of it, so as presently to despatch them, and that there was no need of attendance which they had always been used to." [2]

---

[1] Klopp's "Fall des Hauses Stuart," vol. vii. p. 9—Auersperg to Kinsky.

[2] Trevor's " Life of William III.," p. 476—" Hooper's Diary."

James II. did not wear mourning for his daughter, and forbade his Court to show her this mark of respect. Middleton, his Minister, says : " The King my Master does not consider her his daughter, because she had renounced her being so in such an open manner." [1] If James had been consistent, he should have wept bitterly for her as an impenitent sinner, for he says of himself :

" If anything had been capable of troubling the quiet which the King had found in his resignation, it would have been when he knew that his poor daughter was so much in error that she had declared at her death that her conscience troubled her in nothing, and that if she had done anything for which the world might blame her, she had followed the advice of the most learned men of her Church, so that they were responsible for it. The King, hearing this, cried : Oh miserable arguments, so fatal to those who deceive, and to those who allow themselves to be deceived ! " [2]

Some of the very violent Jacobites went further, and it is reported that a sermon was preached on the Queen's death by one of them, the text of which was : " Go now, see this cursed woman, and bury her, for she is a King's daughter." [3]

Auersperg, the Austrian Envoy, is, however, struck by the fact that the Tories and moderate Jacobites, were among those who showed the most sorrow at the Queen's death.

" They had up till now" [he says] "had cause for hope in the likelihood that the young and healthy Queen would outlive the asthmatic King, and that then their time would come." [4]

Wiser than James, they realised that his eldest daughter's death was in reality the knell of his

---

[1] " Macpherson Papers," p. 506.
[2] " Mémoires de Jacques II.," vol. iv. p. 354.
[3] Ralph's " History of England," vol. iv. p. 540.
[4] Klopp's " Fall des Hauses Stuart," vol. vii. p. 7.

THOMAS KEN, BISHOP OF BATH AND WELLS.

British Museum.

hopes of restoration to the throne of England. As we know, Mary had never wished to oust her father, but had hoped that during his lifetime William would merely act as Regent. It is a striking fact that Nottingham, the person most in her confidence, always declared that, had she survived William, she would have attempted— with proper safeguards for the liberties and religion of the people—to have restored the crown to James. The exiled King's estimate of his eldest daughter's feeling towards him, was one of his many mistakes.

Meanwhile a reconciliation—which may have been among Mary's last recommendations to William—had taken place between him and the Princess Anne. The latter now promised, at the King's request, to receive into her service some of the Queen's old servants, specially recommended to William's care in a paper found in the Queen's cabinet.

The Queen's body was at once embalmed, and was removed to Whitehall, where it lay for some days in the Great Bedchamber. A paper was afterwards found in her private desk, enjoining that her body should not be embalmed, and that there should be no great expenditure over her funeral; but by the time this had been discovered, preparations for it had already been made. "The funeral cost £50,000 against the Queen's desire," remarks Evelyn. Certainly, from what we know of Queen Mary, we can guess that she would have deprecated the needless expense of the ceremony, and would have wished the money lavished on it to have been used for the poor.

However, the King, Court, and Nation were determined to do ample honour to the much-loved and lamented Queen, and on February 21, 1695, the lying-in-state began.

Whitehall was open to the public at twelve o'clock,

24

but by six each morning a waiting crowd had
assembled. The entrance was by the Hall of the
Haleberdiers, and the people then passed through
three great halls, and came to one hung round
with coats of arms, and lit by numberless wax
candles in lustres. Much light must have been
required, for the hall was draped with black. So
was the balustrade which went across it, and in
front of this sat two maids-of-honour covered with
black veils. Behind the balustrade, the corpse lay
on a large four-post bed, with great candlesticks
draped with black at the corners. Over the bed
was a canopy decorated with four bouquets of
black feathers. The effect must have been extremely lugubrious, the only relief being the pieces
of silver cloth cut in the shape of flames, which
decorated the black draperies surrounding the
bed and balcony, and under the circumstances,
were certainly a strange form of ornamentation.

All the officers of the Queen's household, under
the direction of the Marquis of Winchester, were
present in the chamber of death, and the corpse
was guarded by four ladies-of-honour, who were
relieved every half-hour.

" Upon her head lyes the crown, and over it a
fine canopy ; at her feet lyes the sword of state,
the helmet and her arms upon a cushion, the
banners and scutcheons hanging round ; the state
is very great, and more magnificent then can be
exprest ; all persons are admitted, without distinction : she is to lye so every day from 12 till
5 o'clock till she is interr'd." [1]

The actual interment took place on March 5,
1695. All the shops were closed, and the procession, which started from Whitehall at twelve o'clock,
was very magnificent. First came the Knight
Marshal's men to clear the way. Then followed
three hundred poor women. The Lords, robed in

---

[1] Luttrell's " Relation of State Affairs," February 21, 1695.

scarlet and ermine, were the next to pass, and in
their wake walked the Commons in mourning.
This part of the procession was unique. Never
before or since have there been, theoretically at
least, two reigning Sovereigns in England, and
therefore never before had a sovereign been attended to the grave by a Parliament, for the
Parliament is always dissolved at the death of the
Monarch.

The body lay on an open chariot drawn by eight
horses, with two of the Queen's bedchamber women
in attendance. These ladies, it is carefully noted
in the directions for the printed funeral, were not
to be forgotten by the Gentleman Ushers at the
Abbey door, but were to be helped out, and conducted to their places ! [1]

The spot in Henry VII.'s Chapel where William
and Mary are buried side by side, is now only known
by the fact that their names are engraved on two
of the paving-stones. The magnificent mausoleum
erected by Sir Christopher Wren for the occasion,
has disappeared, and, looking at the crowd of
statues in Westminster Abbey, it seems as though
William and Mary receive scant honour.

The scene must have been impressive on that
snowy, cheerless day in March, when the procession,
more of them really sorrowful than is often the
case at a State funeral, filed in to Henry VII.'s
Chapel. The Duchess of Somerset, as chief
mourner, was led by two noblemen, her train being
carried by two Duchesses. She took her place
at the head of the body, inside a railing erected
round the mausoleum. The Ladies of the Bedchamber were also placed inside the railing, the
maids-of-honour and the dressers being, to their
indignation, obliged to stay outside.

So they listened to the Archbishop's sermon
and there was hardly a dry eye in the Abbey. It

[1] "Form of Proceeding for the Funeral of Queen Mary," 1695.

was a sermon which provoked controversy. In the course of it, after much praise of the Queen's many virtues, Tenison stated that she was

" a good Queen, an incomparable Wife, and one who I'm well assur'd had all the duty in the world for other relations, which after long and laborious consideration, she judged consistent with her obligations to her God and her country." [1]

Ken read Tenison's sermon, which contained an account of his ministrations to the Queen on her deathbed, with the utmost distress and indignation.

" Sir " [he says in a letter to the Archbishop],— " When I heard of the sickness of the late illustrious Princess, whom I had never failed to recommend to God in my daily prayers, and that yourself was her Confessor, I could not but hope that, at least on her Deathbed, you would have dealt faithfully with her. But when I had read the sermon you preached at her Funerall, I was heartily grieved to find myself disappointed, and God knows how bitterly I bewail'd in secret the manner of her Death ; and reflecting again and again on your conduct to her Soul, methought a Spirit of Slumber seem'd to have possess'd you ; otherwise it was impossible for one who so well understood the duty of a Spiritual Guide as yourself, who had such happy opportunities, and such signal encouragements to practise it in her case, should so grossly fail in your performance, as either to overlook or wilfully to omit that which all the world said besides yourself, and was expected from you and was of great importance to her salvation. You are a person of noted abilities, and had a full knowledge of your Duty ; you had been many years a Parish Priest and exercised your function with good repute ; none could be better versed in ye office for ye Visitation of ye Sick than yourself,

[1] "Tenison's Sermon in Westminster Abbey, March 5, 1695."

and the sick person was no stranger to you, and you very well knew her whole story.

" As you had a full knowledge of ye Person and of your Duty, so you had happy opportunities to put that Duty in practice. You had free and frequent access to her, and on Monday, when the flattering disease occasioned some hopes, but especially on ye next day, the Festival of Christ's birth, when those hopes were rais'd to a kind of assurance and continued so till night, ye peculiar favour of Heaven seemed to have indulged you, all that inestimable day, on purpose that you might carefully employ it, in clearing her conscience with God and man, and in perfecting her preparations for Eternity ; which, had she recover'd were so necessary, to render her Life holy and happy as her death.

" Your Joy enduring but a Day, and that Day being clos'd with a dismal night, you gave her the warning of her approaching Death, which you say, she receiv'd with a courage agreeable to the strength of her faith. You were set a watchman over her, and if you did not give her due warning of her sin also, when you had so proper a time for doing it, and saw her so capable of receiving it, God will require her blood at your hands.

" You had this advantage also, which is often wanting to such persons, yt in the visits you made her, you did not find her delirious, and the orders she gave for Prayers ; her calling for Prayers a third time, when she feared she had slept the time before ; the many most Christian things she said ; her appointing Psalms, a Chapter concerning trust in God, and a Sermon more than once, to be read to her, are signs she was not, or, at least that she was not so in the intervals wherein you officiated by her. 'Tis true she was often drowsy, but she was so sensible of her drowsiness, that she call'd for prayers before the time, for fear that

she should not be long composed and whenever
you applied yourself to her, she was wakefull
enough. You said indeed, That at the receiving
of the Holy Eucharist she found herself in a dying
condition, and you add, that she presently stirred
up her attention, and from thenceforth, to the
end of the office, had a perfect command of her
Understanding, and was intent upon the great
work she was going about; and methinks, Sir,
if you had been jealous over her soul with a godly
jealousy, when you gave her the Viaticum, and
that she was intent, you had another fit season
offer'd you by Heaven to have minded her of any
but probable defects in her Repentance, and
to have exhorted her to a short supplemental
Confession. Nay, to her very last, she seem'd not
wholly incapable of any pious Intimations you
might have given her, for her Understanding continued to a degree that nothing of Impertinence,
scarce a number of disjointed words, were heard
from her, insomuch that she said a devout Amen
to that very prayer in which her pious soul was
recommended to that God who gave it. So that
your own sermon will testifie against you, that
you had many happy opportunities of directing
her conscience. I must add that you had as signal
encouragements also. You had to deal with a
Person whose knowledge and wisdom you justly
commend, and who might easily have been convinced of any one instance in which she had mistaken her duty. You had to deal with one, whose
pietie, Charity, and humilitie, you in many places
magnifie. I only wish you had added her Justice
also, to have made her character compleat. However, those three Virtues were powerful inducements
to have used a conscientious freedom with her.
You had, as appears by the Character you gave
her, a pious, charitable, humble soul under your
care; a subject most happily disposed to work

upon—who had always been very reverent and attentive at sermons, who had an averseness to flattery, and who would thankfully have received any Pious or charitable humble admonition you had given her. I now beseech you, Sir, to spend a few thoughtful minutes in comparing your Performance as yourself represent it in your own Sermon with your knowledge, with the opportunityes and encouragements you had, and with the rubric of the Church. You mention a very Religious saying that fell from her, that she had learnt from her youth, a true doctrine, that repentance was not to be put off to a deathbed. But it was your duty considering the deceitfulness of all hearts, and the usual Infirmities and Forgetfulness of sick persons, to have supplied her oversights and omissions, and to have examined the truth of her repentance. Whether she truly repented of her sins, and where you knew of anything of moment which had escaped her observation, you ought to have been her Remembrancer. I therefore challenge you to answer before God and the world. Did you know of no weighty matter which ought to have troubled the Princesses conscience, though at present she seemed not to feel it, and for which you ought to have moved her to a special Confession, in order to Absolution? Were you satisfied that she was in charity with all the world? Did you know of no enmity between her and her father, nor variance between her and her sister? Did you know of no Person who ever offended her whom she was to forgive? Did you know of no one Person whom she had offended, and of whom she was to ask forgiveness? Did you know of no one injury or wrong she had done to any man, to whom she was to make amends to the uttermost of her power? Was the whole Revolution manag'd with that purity of intention, that perfect innocence, that exact Justice, that tender

Charity, and that irreproachable veracity, that there
was nothing amiss in it ?   No remarkable failings ;
nothing that might deserve one penitent reflection ?

" You cannot, you dare not say it ;  and if you
should, out of your own mouth I can condemn you,
for you yourself, in your serious interval, have
pass'd as severe a Censure on the Revolution, as any
of those they call Jacobites could do ;  you have
said more than once, that it was all an unrighteous
Thing ;  why did you not then deal sincerely with
this dying Princess, and tell her so when, you must
needs be sensible that, steering her conscience wrong,
you shipwrecked your own ? "[1]

The letter is too long to quote *in extenso*, but
it is a warning, I think, to us not to judge where we
are so much out of sympathy, that it is impossible
for us to take in the point of view of the person
we criticise.   Burnet knew Mary better than did
Ken, and he wrote of her :

" She was convinced that the publick good of
Mankind, the Preservation of that Religion which
she was assured was the only true one, and those
real Extremities to which matters were driven,
ought to supersede all other considerations."[2]

The Queen therefore, Burnet says, made a sacrifice of her own reputation to her religion.   She
knew that she incurred blame,

"but the Saving of the whole nation seemed to
require it and she considered that a special providence had raised her and her husband to preserve
religion."

Nevertheless, according to Burnet, she still
suffered :

" Nature still felt itself loaded ;  she bore it with
the outward appearances of Satisfaction, because
she thought it became her not to discourage others,
so she put a great constraint on herself."

[1] Plumptre's " Life of Ken," vol. ii. p. 88.
[2] " Essay on the Memory of the late Queen."

To quote further from Burnet, she "carried that Air of Life and Joy about her, that animated all who saw her"; and he asks pathetically :

"Why were so many great Ideas and vast Designs formed by her ? Why was she furnished with such Skill and Softness in the management of them ?

"When she received praises, these seemed scarce to be heard. They were so little desired that they were presently past over ; without so much as an Answer, that might seem to entertain the Discourse, even when it checked it. She went off from it to other Subjects as one that could not bear it."

Her sincerity and genuineness, and at the same time her tact, calmness, gaiety, and good-humour were remarkable.

"Lesser matters were not much stood on, an easy compliance in some of these, how little soever they were liked, on their own account, was intended to give Her advantages, in order to the compassing of greater things."

Burnet adds that the Queen never let any one discover more of her thoughts and intentions than she thought expedient ; and we gather, that as well as being a good woman, she was also a very clever one.

Burnet has been criticised as lavishing indiscriminate eulogies on Queen Mary, and certainly a beautiful, gentle Queen, harshly treated by an apparently unappreciative husband, attracts many admirers, even without possessing the brilliant qualities with which Queen Mary was gifted. On the other hand, a consensus of contemporary opinion encourages the belief that the picture painted by Burnet, in words which express a true and deep emotion, is substantially correct.

William, who had good opportunity for judgment, concurred with Burnet. "If," he said, "I could believe that ever any mortal man could be born without the contamination of sin, I would believe it of the Queen "; [1] and he must have uttered the words with a pang of remorse.

Now at any rate he spared no pains or expense to do what Queen Mary would have wished, and the memorial he raised to her, the fulfilment of what she had ardently desired, though her desire had been hitherto disregarded, was characteristically beneficent.

The many naval battles which had taken place during the times when Queen Mary was at the helm, had roused in her a strong sense of the need for some refuge where wounded seamen could be cared for; and she had often longed to convert the Palace at Greenwich into a Naval Hospital. William decided that the fulfilment of her wish would be a fitting monument to her, and, from designs furnished by Sir Christopher Wren, what is now known as Greenwich Naval Hospital, was erected as a memorial of William's sorrow—possibly of his remorse—to the remembrance of good Queen Mary.

[1] "Royal Diary," 1705—"Character of Queen Mary."

# INDEX

*Printed by Hasell, Watson & Viney, Ld., London and Aylesbury.*